TOMORROW'S TROOPERS

BAEN BOOKS edited by HANK DAVIS

The Human Edge by Gordon R. Dickson
The Best of Gordon R. Dickson
We the Underpeople by Cordwainer Smith
When the People Fell by Cordwainer Smith

THE TECHNIC CIVILIZATION SAGA

The Van Rijn Method by Poul Anderson
David Falkayn: Star Trader by Poul Anderson
Rise of the Terran Empire by Poul Anderson
Young Flandry by Poul Anderson
Captain Flandry: Defender of the Terran Empire by Poul Anderson
Sir Dominic Flandry: The Last Knight of Terra by Poul Anderson
Flandry's Legacy by Poul Anderson

The Best of the Bolos: Their Finest Hour created by Keith Laumer

Space Pioneers with Christopher Ruocchio
Overruled with Christopher Ruocchio
Cosmic Corsairs with Christopher Ruocchio
Time Troopers with Christopher Ruocchio
They're Here with Sean CW Korsgaard
Tomorrow's Troopers with David Afsharirad
Depth Charge with Jamie Ibson, forthcoming

A Cosmic Christmas
A Cosmic Christmas 2 You
In Space No One Can Hear You Scream
The Baen Big Book of Monsters
As Time Goes By
Future Wars . . . and Other Punchlines
Worst Contact
Things from Outer Space
If This Goes Wrong . . .

BAEN BOOKS edited by DAVID AFSHARIRAD

The Chronicles of Davids

The Year's Best Military & Adventure SF, Volume 5
The Year's Best Military & Adventure SF, Volume 4
The Year's Best Military & Adventure SF, Volume 3
The Year's Best Military & Adventure SF, 2015
The Year's Best Military SF & Space Opera

To purchase any of these titles in e-book form, please go to www.baen.com.

TOMORROW'S TROOPERS

Edited by
HANK DAVIS &
DAVID AFSHARIRAD

TOMORROW'S TROOPERS

A Baen Books Original

Baen Publishing Enterprises
P.O. Box 1403
Riverdale, NY 10471
www.baen.com

ISBN: 978-1-9821-9355-3

Cover art by Dominic Harman

First printing, August 2024

Distributed by Simon & Schuster
1230 Avenue of the Americas
New York, NY 10020

Library of Congress Control Number: 2024015246

Printed in the United States of America

10 9 8 7 6 5 4 3 2 1

DEDICATION

To David Drake,
Grand Master of Military Science Fiction,
and a Good Friend.

Story Copyrights

ACKNOWLEDGMENTS

Our thanks to Michael Figuera, whose email was the snowball that precipitated this avalanche. And many thanks to those authors who permitted the use of their stories, and to the estates and their representatives who intervened for those authors unreachable without time travel (we raise a glass to absent friends). Special thanks to Mark Bodē and Francis Goulart. Among the very helpful literary agents deserving thanks are Judith Weber of Sobel-Weber Associates and James Farner at JABberwocky Literary Agency. And thanks for help and advice from others we are unforgivably forgetting. Gratitude is also due to the Internet Speculative Fiction Database (ISFDB.org) for existing and being a handy source of raw data, and to the devoted volunteers who maintain that very useful site.

Contents

❀

What the Well-Dressed Future Warrior Will Wear

❋

Hank Davis

I suspect that armor started out as clothing. Clothes could actually be thought of as armor against cold air and chilly, wet things falling from the sky, even against the cold, hard ground to sleep on. The sort of stuff to make an early European wonder why his ancestors ever left Africa.

Once someone decided that he needed that bearskin more than the previous occupant did, and was wrapped inside it, the next time he had a disagreement with a neighbor, leading to throwing rocks (it was the *Stone* Age, after all), the bearskin wearer might notice that a rock impacting on the bear skin didn't hurt as much as one landing on bare skin, giving an extra added attraction to wearing the borrowed pelt.

(Do I deserve a point or two for not making puns about "bare skin" and "bear skin?" No? Or invoking an animal's pelt, and being pelted with stones? No slack, eh? I see I have a tough audience.)

Of course, once that neighbor, or another more inventive one, realized that bear skins, or maybe a lot of skins taken from smaller, less contentious animals, made a defense against a hurtling rock, perhaps the result was a neolithic arms race, possibly with such stages as:

1. Try throwing the rock harder.
2. Add a second layer of bear skin, or even a third.
3. Invent the sling.
4. Try tying rocks together to go outside of the bearskin(s), or fight rocks with rocks...
5. Invent the pointed stick...
6. Try tying a pointed rock to the stick...

And I think I'll sideline this thought experiment before we get to arrows, catapults, etc., on the offensive side, along with learning how to smelt metals (no puns on "smelt," please note) and putting metal plates in place of those bearskins, and so on. For one thing, we're leaping over centuries, if not millennia in a single bound and I don't have a big red "S" on my shirt. Nor a lightning bolt.

Besides, I'm doing off-the-wall speculating here, without benefit of evidence, research, or expertise. At least it's definite that eventually metal suits came along, getting so heavy that specially bred horses were needed to carry their wearers into battle, said battle being fought with swords and lances, which is to say, higher-tech descendants of the pointed stick.

(Of course, those knights in supposedly shining armor also used shields, but I think that shields may have originated back in Africa, invented by those with the sense not to leave the balmy climate.)

Then somebody had to go and invent gunpowder . . . Later-day warriors do have some armor, of course, such as bulletproof vests worn by police, the flak vests and steel helmets worn by twentieth-century soldiers, etc. But firearms have had the upper hand for a long time. Maybe it's time for the pendulum to swing back. Suppose the armored warrior makes a comeback, encased in suits composed of all the latest advances in metallurgy, and maybe even plastics harder than steel. Put all sorts of electronics inside, too. Add a video screen in the helmet so the suit's wearer can see if someone is coming up behind him. Build all the modern weapons into the suit. Make it like wearing a tank, but much smaller and more nimble.

It would still be heavy of course, probably even heavier than a medieval suit of armor. But if powerful miniaturized motors are also built into the suit, then the warrior's own muscles are not the only things doing the lifting, walking, and even jumping. And maybe add booster rockets in case the soldier needs to jump from the top of one building to the top of another, for a better angle to launch a barrage of mini-missiles.

We're in science fiction territory now, and it's about time, too.

I'm not sure who first suggested such futuristic armor, either in speculative fact or fiction. Robert A. Heinlein's *Starship Troopers* was a landmark, of course, but George H. Smith's short story, "The Last Crusade," which happens to be included in the pages which follow, was published in the magazine *If* in 1955, four years before the Heinlein novel was serialized in *The Magazine of Fantasy & Science Fiction* in 1959 under the title "Starship Soldier" (Heinlein's preferred title, incidentally). Nonetheless, Heinlein's novel, in spite of, or because of being very controversial at the time, which didn't prevent it from winning a Hugo Award for best novel of the year, firmly established the powered armor concept in the minds of science fiction readers and writers, possibly including Stan Lee of Marvel Comics, who introduced Iron Man a few years later, but certainly in the case of Joe Haldeman, who published his novelette, "Hero" (also included in the pages which follow), in 1973 in *Analog*, making brilliant use of the powered armor concept. "Hero" was the first of a series of stories which eventually became the novel, *The Forever War*, and the book won the Hugo and Nebula Awards.

I can't read the minds of authors (particularly authors no longer with us—where *did* I put that Ouija board?), but there are a number of stories which I suspect would not exist in a parallel universe lacking the examples of the Heinlein and Haldeman novels. And David Afsharirad and I have recruited a platoon of the best such future troopers in this book.

I hope I've made it clear how indebted this book is to the Heinlein and Haldeman novels, but there's an intervening ancestor: *Body Armor 2000*, a 1986 anthology edited by Joe Haldeman (that guy does get around), Martin Harry Greenberg, and Charles G. Waugh, and published by Ace Books. The connection began when intrepid science fiction reader Michael Figueroa wrote to Baen editor Tony Daniel, praising the book and suggesting that Baen reprint it. Tony passed the request on to publisher Toni Weisskopf, who liked the idea and turned it over to David Afsharirad and yr. humble but crotchety editor. The latter quality went into gear when I noted that the book had three very good stories, by David Drake, Robert Sheckley, and Gordon R. Dickson, that I nonetheless preferred not to reprint because I had already reprinted them in previous Baen anthologies (for example, the David Drake story was in *Worst Contact*). Another crotchet was that after reading the stories in the Ace anthology (listening to them, actually—I'm legally blind), I thought some of the stories didn't actually fit the theme and preferred not to reprint those.

And, with great regret, C.J. Cherryh's "The Scapegoat" was a novella, and would have made the book too long.

But we have carried over from the 1986 anthology veteran stories by Joe Haldeman (where have I heard that name before?), Harry Harrison, George H. Smith, and Larry S. Todd, and we've added new recruits to the powered armor platoon with Christopher Ruocchio, Allen M. Steele, Quincey J. Allen, Karin Lowachee, and more. Readers who already have the Ace anthology on their bookshelves will find much that is new here, not to mention stories well worth rereading. And readers who come to these stories for the first time will definitely get their money's worth. We've tried for a wide range of viewpoints. While I (Hank) don't subscribe to the currently fashionable notion that all war is futile, readers with that mental bent will find stories exemplifying it here. Readers looking for heroism in combat will find that here, as well. Your editors (even the crotchety one) hope you'll enjoy the book, and also hope that these stories are as close as our readers come to actual war, futuristically attired or not. We don't want to lose any customers.

—Hank Davis
March 2024

The mission was supposed to be a routine cleanup operation, to wipe out a nest of rogue self-replicating robots, which was why the team leader with years of combat experience was only along as a liaison with the native population. Anyway, these robot infestations always followed the same game plan, making them easy to obliterate—except that this time nobody had told the killer robots about that part.

Heuristic Algorithm and Reasoning Response Engine

Ethan Skarstedt & Brandon Sanderson

A lone dropship passed across the face of Milacria's gibbous bulk, a pinhead orbiting a beachball. From its launch portals streamed a hundred black motes—each one a mechanized infantry unit clinging tightly to the underside of its air support craft, whose broad armored back served as a heatshield. They torched down through the hazy cloud-speckled atmosphere in precise formation, trailing thick ropes of smoke and steam, a forest of uncertain fingers pointing back up to the ship, the *MarsFree*.

Within his mech's cockpit on the western edge of the formation, Karith Marvudi hunkered in a loose cocoon of straps. He caught himself watching the grip indicators. If those failed, his mech would come unhooked from the underside of Nicolette's airship. He'd burn in from too high and Nicolette's agile but flimsy airship—deprived of the thickly armored protection of his five-meter-tall mech—would tear apart and burn up in the atmosphere.

He stretched, spread-eagled, suspended by the feedback straps. His fingers and toes just brushed the edges of his movement space within the torso cavity. Perfect. The faint scent of his own body, mingled with that of plastic, electronics, and faux leather, swirled in the canned air.

He was surprised at the trepidation he felt. He felt a certain amount of fear every time he dropped, but this time was different. This was like ... No, not as bad as his first drop. Maybe his fifth or sixth. He hadn't felt this jittery in more than two hundred planetfalls.

He wondered if Nicolette felt the same way.

He pushed at the fear, shoving it down where it could be ignored. It pushed back. Maragette's face flashed into his mind, smiling next to the squinting white bundle they'd named Karri, after her grandmother.

"You about ready to shunt some of that heat up to me, Karith?" Nicolette's voice was as buttery as ever, not a hint of tension.

"Maybe if you ask me politely." Karith overrode the mic on the common circuit. "Harry, we about full?"

The baritone voice of his mech's AI filled the cabin. "Ninety-three point seven percent, sir. Shall I route fifty percent of the sink product to Captain Shepard's power banks?"

"Make it seventy-five; Nic needs it. Show me what it looks like out there: focus on the D-Z."

Nic's voice came again from the cockpit speakers. "Politely? Oh, it's manners you want now, is it? We'll see how you like it when all my lasers can deal out is a bit of a sunburn. I—Ah, *there* we are." She had seen the power surging into her ship. Her voice changed to a purr. "Karith, you shouldn't have."

Karith let out a loud patient sigh over the mic. She giggled.

HARRE said on the private circuit, "Is Captain Shepard displeased, sir?"

"Nope. That's sarcasm, Harry."

"Noted. I must point out, sir, doctrine states that the mechanized infantry unit in an entry pair has priority on power collection."

"It does say that, doesn't it." Karith frowned at the 3D representation of the area around his drop zone that HARRE was feeding into his HUD.

Nicolette's voice slipped into the cockpit again. "I can't believe I let you and Maragette talk me into transferring out of RGK with you. I'm about ready to fall asleep up here with no anti-air fire."

HARRE spoke, his deep voice mechanically precise. "Captain Shepard, had the Self-Replicating Machine Infestation evolved to a stage with anti-aircraft weaponry on this planet, your former comrades in the Recon Group Kinetique would have been inserted, not a line infantry unit with you for advisors."

Silence filled the circuits for a moment, until Karith chuckled. "That's right, HARRE, Captain Shepard has obviously forgotten..."

"Well, well, don't we have a *fine* grasp of the obvious," Nicolette interrupted, voice dripping honeyed acid. "I don't remember him talking this much, Karith. You screw up his settings?"

"No. He lost a lot in the reset."

"Hmmph. I suppose I owe him some slack since he was wounded."

"Especially since we were saving *your* ass, Nic."

"That *was* a hairy mess, wasn't it?" Somehow she managed to convey the impression that she was shivering over the audio circuit.

Karith grunted in acknowledgment, brow furrowing as he zoomed in on an area of ground to the northwest of the drop zone. "HARRE, can we get any better resolution on this area?"

"We have not yet launched sensor drones, sir."

Karith nodded. "Right, right. Countdown?"

"We separate from Captain Shepard in fourteen minutes fifty-one point seven seconds, sir."

"You can start inflation any time now, Nic."

"You think?" She *hmmph*ed at him again over the audio circuit.

Moments later he felt the first gut-churning rumble, press, and drop as Nicolette deployed her inflation scoops. They used the howling wind and heat to fill the first few hundred lift-body spheres with superheated air.

Karith ignored the creeping feeling of unease. He'd land in the mouth of an east–west running valley on the western edge of a big Panesthian city, name unpronounceable. It, in turn, sat in a bigger north–south valley.

The D-Z's valley carved through the mountains to the west and opened out onto a plain overlaid with red haze. The main boiler infestation, a plague of self-replicating machines. A cluster of the simplest and sturdiest of them had likely arrived in a lump of meteor and been bootstrapping themselves ever since. He circled several map-areas at that end of the valley, highlighting them in pale yellow. "Harry, what's the uncertainty over here?"

"Sir, from the limited data I can collect with the range-finding lasers, those areas differ from the historical models by just over the margin of error given the current level of interference."

"That's a little strange. The model's only a month old. You suppose the Panesthians have been doing some remodeling out there, maybe defensive works? It's right on the edge of the boiler's zone."

Silence.

"That last bit wasn't me talking to myself, Harry. It was for you."

"Noted. Unknown, sir. I have no information on any Panesthian earth-moving operations of that scale. I have very little data on their construction projects at all, sir."

"You can call me Karith if you want, Harry."

"Yes, sir."

Karith chuckled. He zoomed out and slewed the view over past the yellow end of the valley and beyond, into the red zone on the plains where the boilers were building their industrial compounds. "That's a pretty big infestation for stage seventeen."

"Agreed, sir, but it is within parameters. I note the stage fifteen on Brindle Eight, the stage sixteen on—"

"Right."

The boilers were mostly predictable. Stage of development followed stage of development like clockwork. Small simple foragers like four-legged crabs running on springs. Steam-powered crawlers and cutters. Hydrocarbon-burning, motor-driven mechanicals bent on mining and refining. All the way up to nuclear spiders, tanks, and aerials. There was always *some* variation, of course, in response to environmental factors, but the basics stayed the same. His eyes flicked to the grip readouts. They were solid.

"Hey, Nic."

"Wait one."

He slammed hard against his restraints again and his stomach floated up into the back of his throat. Moments later, he settled back into the webbing. That would be the second-stage inflation scoops. Outside, hundreds more of the little spheres were lining up to get inflated with superheated air and then roll away on smart velcro into the thick braking ribbons trailing behind Nicolette. The surface of Milacria stopped sliding away to the right and resumed its steady flow beneath them.

He heard a touch of strain in his own voice when he said, "You feeling this, Nic?"

"Yeah, I felt that."

"No, I mean, I feel like a green kid. Butterflies in the guts and everything."

"You do?" Her tone was faintly incredulous, and he could hear laughter behind it.

"I'm going to regret telling you, aren't I?"

"After twelve years in RGK, you've got drop jitters? You can't be serious."

"It's no big deal."

"Wait until I tell Jarko. You transfer to advisory to keep yourself safe for your wife and baby, and the first drop where you're *not* getting shot at, you get a case of the shakes?" She laughed again. "You want a tranq?"

"Oh, shut up."

Her giggle filled the cabin.

Karith hissed and then stabbed the button that would connect him with Major Kewlett, the commander of the mech-infantry unit dropping with them.

"Major, how goes the drop?"

The major was chewing something. "Fine, fine. Nobody's let go of their airship yet anyway. What about you? Must be old hat, eh? You on track to meet up with the indig?"

"Yes indeed, sir." As a member of the Advisory Corps now it was his job to be the liaison between the major and the locals.

"Good to hear. Luck. Out." The connection clicked off.

"Sir," HARRE said, "the Panesthians are trying to raise you on the beacon channel."

"Put 'em through, Harry."

The soft hiss of a long-range transmission filled the cabin, and a rectangular hole opened in Karith's HUD. The image solidified and filled with a nightmarish mandibled visage. Karith was struck again by how much Panesthians looked like big cockroaches—big enough to eat your head. Fortunately, there had been a few Panesthians in RGK, and he'd gotten used to them.

This one hissed and clacked at him, its mouthparts writhing. It took a moment before he was able to parse the heavily accented Spranto. "Greetings, Sir Marvudi. We await your arrival with great awaitingness." As it talked, there was close movement in the background, other Panesthians crawling back and forth over its back.

"Thank you. You are?"

The Panesthian buzzed for a moment. "My apologies, Sir Marvudi. My name is 'hzzzclackyow.' The humans at the embassy speak to me as 'Yow,' and as a male." He buzzed again, wingcases opening slightly, disrupting the footing of a passing Panesthian, which slid forward over Yow's head. Yow used his forelegs, triple claws pinching, to move the other along before crawling closer to the camera lens. "I wish to confirm, Sir Marvudi, that your dropping is indeed on these coordinates?" Yow did something offscreen, and coordinates appeared in Karith's HUD next to the visual.

HARRE spoke up, "Confirmed."

"Wellness!" Yow replied. "I will come up to meet you in how many minutes . . . ?"

"Harry?" Karith asked.

"Approximately twelve minutes, sir."

Yow's antennae waved. "I hurry. Few of my nestmates speak Spranto. Your class awaits on the surface already, Captain. I will join them. Drop with great trepidating!" The image went dark and blinked away.

Nicolette's awed voice came over the audio circuit, "Holy shit," at the same time the alarms started.

Red warning icons began to populate Karith's HUD.

"Incoming, sir," HARRE said calmly. "Brace for maneuvering."

"Damn it!" Nicolette swore. "There wasn't supposed to be . . ." She trailed off and Karith's restraints cinched up tight as they accelerated, swerved, and side-slipped all at once.

"Outside view, Harry!" Karith shouted. His cockpit blinked away and he was speeding through the middle reaches of Milacria's atmosphere, high above the mottled green-and-yellow landscape. Something dark flashed past him, its red glowing backtrail leading to a computed point-of-origin deep in the red boiler haze. His computers held the view steady, but his body felt the chaotic maneuvers Nicolette was putting them through.

They were losing altitude faster than they'd planned. Below, the Panesthian city streaked by. It looked like a pile of dusty intestines. The surreal look of the place held his attention for a moment even as Nicolette tried to make him lose his lunch. The Panesthian burrow-buildings wormed over and around each other in a great heap, spreading out into the surrounding countryside like the roots of a tree, giving way to cultivated land.

"Holy Moses, Harry, is that correct?" He jabbed a finger at the icon for the *MarsFree*. It was black.

"Yes, sir. The *MarsFree* is no longer in communication. Presumed destroyed."

He goggled. "By *what*?"

"The first salvo of hyperkinetic rounds was largely ineffective against the mech-infantry drop formation, sir. It was likely not intended for them or us."

Black puffs began to blossom in the air near and far, all at about the same altitude. Anti-air, targeting the droptroops.

"Sir, I recommend a redirect to the company headquarters area—"

Karith cut him off. "Overlay unit locations and status." HARRE went silent and complied. Karith clenched his fists. The fear had teeth now. Aborting to a nice, well-defended company headquarters appealed to the monkey part of his brain, but he was supposed to embed with that Panesthian unit. That was the whole point of his being here.

Behind him, the sky started filling with icons for the infantry unit he was inserting with, each one a mech shielding its airship from the violence of entry. He and Nic had preceded them out of the ship. Close to a hundred icons filled the sky. Additional icons over the horizon showed HARRE's best guess at the location of enemy weapon emplacements.

He glanced back. Well over a third of the infantry icons were already flashing or black. So many casualties. A hypervelocity round could go right through a mech and its airship.

Explosion after explosion rocked them, black smoke obscuring his view time and again as Nicolette jinked them through the kind of evasive maneuverings that had made her famous in the RGK. The kind of maneuvers that had kept them both alive through a hundred hot drops.

"Karith," she said, strained, "you need to make the call right now. I can still get you to that D-Z if you want, but I'm with Harry about redirecting to the company area. I think the embedding gig is out the window."

"Sir," HARRE said, "doctrine clearly indicates that when encountering a superior force, retreat and regroup is the—"

Karith gritted his teeth. "Can't do it. Are you seeing this, Nic?"

"Yeah. Thirty percent casualties. Damn. They shouldn't have hyperkinetic weapons yet."

Karith growled. The boilers didn't usually develop hyperkinetics until stage thirty, usually a good two years after stage seventeen. It was extremely dangerous to drop this close to a boiler complex at that stage of development, even for RGK troops.

These infantry were just troops of the line. Most of their missions were holding and clearing actions against early-catch boiler infestations, not assault strikes against advanced strongholds, which was what this was feeling more like every second.

HARRE's count of casualty icons ticked up on the overlay to seventy-eight. They were approaching fifty percent casualties, mechs and airships alike, on the entry alone. Adrenaline filled Karith.

"Sir, I say again, I highly recommend that we redirect to the headquarters D-Z."

"Noted. Nicolette, put me in on the original. The major's going to need eyes out this way and there might not be anyone else in contact with the local military. Besides, I'll be damned if I'll let a little boiler anti-air fire..." he gasped as they swooped into a long curve and his restraints pushed the air out of his lungs. "... scare me off. I bet our D-Z's under the maximum depression of those railguns anyway."

"Damn it, Karith." He could hear a mixture of exasperation and excited anticipation in her voice. "This is exactly why I love you."

"What?"

She went on. "Can you expose your guns?"

He checked their airspeed and did so. He and HARRE started intercepting some of the rounds coming their way.

At fifty feet above the deck Karith cut loose and dropped away from Nicolette's airship into free fall. As he fell he engaged the feedback mechanisms and the straps tightened up around him.

Nicolette peeled away and shot to the south, her lift spheres held in a streamlined bullet shape by their smart velcro. Her cockpit and lasers were inside the mass of spheres somewhere. As she rose back into the railgun's target zone, she took a glancing hit. The spheres rippled, parted to let the missile pass, and then reformed again. A hundred meters beyond her the round exploded. She clawed for height, changing shape for more lift. She shrank smaller until he couldn't pick her out anymore.

"Ready for operations, Karith," she said. Her breathing was tight and fast in his ear.

"What was that you said to me a little bit ago?"

With a crash and a spray of dirt, he plowed into the ground at the center of the D-Z, rolling to absorb some of the impact. He stood up and shook himself to free his mech of dirt.

"Sir," HARRE said. "I can play back any traffic you may have misse—"

"Shut up, Harry."

Nicolette's voice was tight, "Nothing. I didn't say anything."

He smiled. "'Cause it sounded like you . . .'"

"Leave it, dammit."

Karith dropped the grin. Her reaction worried him a little. "Right. Nothing. Got it."

Two Panesthians scuttled up to him. Hip high to a human and about two meters long, he could have covered either one with his mech's foot. He tried to imagine what his fifteen-foot-tall, multi-turreted, thick-bodied, thick-limbed bipedal mech must look like to a rural Panesthian and crouched down. "Yow?"

"It is I," the Panesthian on the right replied. "We," he waved with one foreleg and an antenna at a seething pile of agitated Panesthians on the edge of the D-Z, "are hearing that the boilers are having effective firings on your droptroops."

The seething mass of giant insects was the 1st Company of the 3rd Milacrian Armored Battalion. Of course, they didn't have any armor yet. Karith was there to learn their combat tactics and advise them on how best to augment their abilities with mechs like his own. That would all have to wait now.

HARRE spoke in Karith's ear. "Sir, the company restructured its drop points. They are consolidating in the city to the east. I recommend—"

"Not now, Harry. Yow, we understood that the boilers were at stage seventeen. Railguns are at least stage thirty. Care to explain?"

Yow squeaked and clicked at his companion, who replied, trilling and buzzing. Yow's wingcasings raised, and the gauzy wings within fluttered. "Truly, it is the first we have seen of the magrails. We cannot explain."

"Well, we're all stuck into it now. Give me your latest information on boiler disposition and activity."

"Of course. Immediately." Yow spoke to his companion, who used his multi-clawed legs to manipulate something on his underside. Karith saw that he and the other Panesthians all had equipment strapped to their bellies as well as fiery circles emblazoned on their wingcasings.

"Sir," HARRE said, "the link has been established and I'm receiving the information. Updating models now."

"Good. Put me through to Major Kewlett."

The HUD had Major Kewlett on the ground in the city to the east. A moment later his voice grated into Karith's cockpit.

"Whattaya got, Marvudi?"

"Sir, I've made linkup with the Panesthian ground forces."

Major Kewlett's gum popped in Karith's ears. "I'm glad somethin' went right. They gonna be any use to us? *MarsFree* is gone, we got twelve hours before the next follow-on ship, and I got close to a hundred of my boys and girls broken already."

"I'm not sure yet how useful the locals will be. I'll have to get back to you on that, sir."

"Good copy here." *Snap, chew.* "Out."

The connection went dead. "Harry, transmit the data from the Panesthians to the general situation model."

"Done, sir."

Karith turned his attention back to Yow. Before he could speak, another bit of motion caught his eye. He turned. "What the hell is that?" he asked, pointing behind him.

Yow turned. There was a separate group of adult Panesthians on the other edge of the field, and they numbered almost as many as the soldiers. Half of them had smaller ones swarming on and around them.

"The families, sir?"

"Those are your families?"

"I am unmated, sir. But I believe they are the mates of the soldiers, sir, yes."

"Are you hearing this, Nic?" Karith said.

"Sir," HARRE said, "the noncombatants should clear the field."

Nicolette snorted. "Yeah, what he said. You should feel right at home though, Karith, with little ones to dandle on your knee and all that."

"Shut it."

She laughed again.

Karith reopened Yow's circuit and poked one finger down at the other Panesthian. "Yow, who is this?"

"Sir Marvudi, that is the commander of the Company. He is choosing the human name Delbert."

Delbert said, "Delbert!" and fluttered his wings.

"Ah, okay. Yow, tell Delbert that he needs to get the families under cov—"

"Sir!" HARRE's voice was urgent.

"What!"

HARRE's voice was normal again. "Sir, I am detecting a great deal of movement on the far end of this valley."

Nicolette whistled. "He's not kidding. There's a whole lot of something going on over there."

"Show me."

HARRE opened another window in Karith's HUD with an overhead view of the area in question, icons and indicators overlaid. The western end of the valley was alive with red, active machine units sweeping toward their location. They were maybe five miles away.

"Okay, we're out of time. Yow, tell Delbert those families need to be evacuated to the city to the east of here. The boilers are coming, and they're coming now."

Yow's antennae froze and then waved excitedly as he jabbered at Delbert. Delbert turned and buzzed loudly at the soldiers. At his words, the families on the periphery of the drop zone jerked into frenzied activity. They turned as one churning mass and fled, followed by most of the soldiers, disappearing into scattered holes in the ground.

"Harry, give me a radar shot of the surrounding ground, eh?" Karith formed his mech's hand into a blade shape and jammed it into the dirt. He was on the western edge of a huge warren complex that seemed to run all the way to the city. He grimaced. "That's a lot of civilians, Harry."

"Yes, sir."

"Nic, I need you to engage the lead boiler units. Slow them down and try to trigger their 'seek cover' response."

"Roger that, Karith." In the background he could hear her motive engines kicking in and the mutter of her battle song.

"Sir," HARRE said, "she should target the railguns. They are the primary threat and liable to—"

"I know, Harry. She'll be fine. We have to get those lead machines stopped first."

"Sir Marvudi," Yow said, "Delbert wishes to know what you would have him do?" Yow and Delbert were still at his feet. In front of them there were perhaps a dozen soldiers left in the short grass. They were in some semblance of a single rank, their shiny brown carapaces like giant wooden toggle buttons on the ground.

"Get the civilians out of here, Yow. Delbert and the rest of his soldiers should evacuate as many civilians as they can to the city. Get them behind the human defenses."

"Sir," HARRE said, "that is not a viable mission. Given the statistical population densities I estimate that there are thousands of Panesthians between here and Major Kewlett's lines, far too many to move in the remaining time."

"So we need to stop those lead machines pretty quick, eh, Harry?" No response.

"Sir Marvudi," Yow said, buzzing. "Delbert wishes to know what your plans are?"

Karith looked down at the two Panesthians staring up at him with broad black eyes, mouthparts moving slowly in and out.

"I've got a few ideas."

Yow and Delbert conferred urgently. Yow said, "We were hearing that you were in the RGK?" Dimly, muffled by the automatic filters on the comm system, Karith could hear Nicolette howling and growling along with her battle song over the deep coughing of her lasers and her jet's roar.

"Was. I *was* in the RGK."

"We are honored. You can stop them?"

"No, I probably can't."

A small Panesthian, a tenth Yow's size, buzzed unsteadily out of the sky and landed on the face of Karith's mech. It squeaked and buzzed, peering into one of the darker radio portals in his faceplate. Raising one foreleg, it rapped its claw on the portal. Faintly, Karith heard a muffled tapping through the confines of his cockpit. He raised a giant metal hand but hesitated to pluck the child off his face.

"Sir Marvudi," Yow said, "allow me?"

"Of course." Karith laughed nervously, reminded of when the nurse had handed him Karri. He had been afraid to touch the little thing for fear of breaking it.

Yow, ponderous on his big wings, buzzed up to Karith's mech, even more unsteady than the youngster had been. When he was about to touch the child, it squeaked and zipped over Karith's head and down his back. Seconds later it was in speedy but erratic flight toward the warrens.

Yow thumped back to earth.

"Harry, put Yow in contact with Major Kewlett directly."

"That is against protocol, sir. The connection should properly go though you as the liaison advisor."

"Well, I'm going to be too busy to handle it, Harry. Just do it."

"Done, sir."

"And put me through to him too," Karith said, "Good luck, Yow." He stood and turned away from the retreating Panesthians, striding toward the hills and accelerating into a thundering trot over the rolling ground.

"Kewlett, go." The major's chewing was furious now.

"Sir, Marvudi here. The locals won't be much use. I've got them herding all the civilians they can toward your lines, but they won't be fast enough. My air is currently putting the hurt on the lead boiler units, slowing them down. I'll get into it and slow them down even more."

"The hell you will, son. I've got boilers coming up out of bogtaken tunnels not two miles to my east. Tunnels! Who the hell"—*snap*—"ever heard of that? I need you and your air unit back here."

Karith let the mech run by itself for a little bit and slewed his map over to examine the city where the major was holed up. Red icons dotted the suburbs on the far side. Energy weapons lanced down from the sky and kinetics flickered across the battlefield. Zooming in, he could see treads, crawlers, walkers, and blasters.

"I concur with the major, sir," HARRE noted. "We are facing a far superior force. Doctrine advises us to consolidate in defense with other units in the area."

Karith confirmed with a glance that HARRE had not put his quoting of the book out over the open circuit. "Can't do it, Harry. Major, I wonder if you've seen what the boilers do to civilians they catch in the open? I think I can reverse the boiler's focus if I hit a piece of their primary infrastructure. They'll turn around to protect that instead of expanding for the moment. It'll keep them out of your rear area. Normally I'd just call in an orbital strike but—"

Nicolette chimed in, privately. "I don't know Karith, they look pretty determined. I've got them taking cover for now but I'm seeing heavy-treads, heavy-rollers, and full complements of cutters and blasters for each."

Snap. "Marvudi, there's civilians here in the city too. The boilers don't care one way or the other. Now get your ass over here ASAP."

Karith isolated Nicolette's circuit. "No crawlers or hummers?"

"Not yet."

"That's something."

"Yeah. It's only a matter of—" Her reply broke off and faded out under the howl of her motivator engines.

The ground started to rise sharply and Karith leaned into the first foothill, clawing with his hands. "Sir, I'm going to cut through these hills and try to get behind them. If I can smash something important enough, their subroutines will switch over to protect and rebuild before they tear into these warrens."

He waited a tense moment. Finally, the major spoke. "You really think you can do this, don't you, RGK?"

"Yes, sir."

"Fine. Go make something happen." *Snap, chew.* His voice was tense and rising. "Keep me apprised."

"Roger that, sir." Dead air.

Karith's HUD tracked him as he accelerated through the hills. Red machine units seethed along the valley floor while he passed up high in the opposite direction.

He kept an eye on the battle on the east side of the city, watched it grow into a big smear of red on his screens. Hopefully he could keep the tide of red below him from sweeping into it from the west.

"Sir, Captain Shepard has taken a direct hit to one of her lasers. Her lift bodies have been depleted by seventeen percent. Without a repair depot—"

"Nic," Karith said, "how you doing up there?" Her icon soared above him on his HUD.

"Just fine, Karith. Too high and the railguns can target me, any lower and the treads can lock on with their main guns. And I keep running into needle streams from the bloody crawlers."

Karith studied the model HARRE was making from the sensor-drone feeds. The boilers *were* digging in under Nicolette's onslaught.

Reaching up and grasping a knob of rock, he levered himself up over a ridge and rolled down, armor crushing boulders and snapping trees.

"Okay, Nic. Go take out a few of those railguns if you can. Make yourself some breathing room."

With an exultant yell, Nicolette flipped her airship into a backward loop and pulled out to race down the center of the valley at treetop height. Looking down a long draw, Karith saw her flash past the mouth of it, lasers on full, burning the ground and enemy units in her path in a fountaining rooster tail of flame and smoke.

The airships over the city wouldn't be able to go all out because of the civilians on the ground. He was just grateful the machines hadn't achieved a stage with aircraft yet.

"Sir, Captain Shepard has dropped off my radar."

"Yeah, I expected that. She'll fly nap-of-the-earth all the way until she takes out those guns."

"That is very risky, sir. The concentration of smaller-caliber weapons on the ground along her route is likely to be extremely high."

"Yup. Moving that fast, though, they'll probably miss her."

"But with concentrations of fire—"

"What else, exactly, is she supposed to do, Harry?"

HARRE's response was immediate. "Retreat with us to the main perimeter, sir. The concentration of antagonistic force here is too high to justify operations in this area."

"Can't do it, Harry." Karith flattened himself against the side of a ridge on the edge of the red zone and lifted a sensor pod to the crest. Leaving it in place, he backed up, sidled along the ridge, and put another one up. "All right. What do we have out there?"

HARRE had started building a real-time model of the plains beyond the ridge as soon as the second pod was in place for triangulation. A smoky, torn landscape unfolded before Karith's eyes, filled with endless banks of raw functional machinery, thick power cables snaking along the ground and through the air, trenches and canals filled with oily water and mud between metal walls, and fences as far as the eye could see.

"Okay, Harry, we need something important enough to sting 'em good, right here so those units in the valley are the nearest units for defense."

While HARRE scanned, Karith adjusted the mech's missile batteries.

"Surely, sir, Nicolette's action against the railguns will draw the boiler's attention."

"You're bloody right it will, Harry me lad, but that's too far away. What are the units in the valley doing now?"

"I'm afraid they are up and moving again, sir."

"Bog take it. We need to hit something fast. What do you see out there?"

"There is a class seven power node quite close to the mouth of the valley, sir."

"Seven?" Karith was looking over the situation back at the city. Kewlett was holding on the east, barely.

"Yes, sir. It seems to be feeding most of the machinery and infrastructure in this area." HARRE lit up a rough circle several miles in diameter at the valley's mouth.

"Nice. We'll do the old high lob low fastball. We may not get another chance."

"Yes, sir."

Nicolette's voice sounded. "All right, this little strip of sky should be clear now."

"Excellent. Glad you're still alive, Nic."

"Yeah. Where do you want me?"

Karith launched three top-down missiles over the ridge.

"Hit here." Karith passed her the power node as a target along with the flight paths of his missiles which were dodging and weaving through an upward rain of fire from the machine's defenses.

Three more missiles streaked from his shoulder racks and over the metal landscape, straight for the node. The flash and expanding concussion wave was followed closely by another from the last of his high flyers.

Nicolette screamed past, lasers digging a fiery trench straight through the node. Karith resisted HARRE's automatic instructions to duck behind the ridge, instead drawing a bit of fire off Nicolette. The ridgetop exploded under a fire-hose stream of metal splinters and energy weapons, even as he returned fire. He leaned into the storm, trusting his armor. The incoming fire drummed against him like pounding horizontal rain. Energy beams scored bright streaks across him, raising his internal temp. He could feel the heat on his skin as he shook and rocked from the force of it all.

He stood firm, sending streams of metal from his arm-mounted kinetic weapons ripping into the defensive pods scattered around the fantastic metal landscape. HARRE orchestrated a symphony of destruction with the shoulder and hip turrets.

Karith's inner-ear protested. Suddenly, dirt piled into him from the side. He found himself stumbling.

"Contact!" HARRE yelled.

Looking down, Karith saw a walker fastened to his mech's lower abdomen, sparks flying where its plasma cutter chewed into his hip joint.

"Shit!" He smashed the spiny metal thing with his fist. Three more scuttled out of a newly opened hole in the ridge's side. Their leggy angled shapes scrambled past a machine he'd never seen before, a conical spinning drill bit as big as the rumbling combustion engine backing it.

"This is a new behavior, sir."

Karith smashed at a second walker as three more leapt onto his chest and shoulders. He caught himself screaming in anger and gritted his teeth. He triggered a burst of explosive rounds into the driller thing and leapt at it, pushing it back into the hole it had come from. Spinning, he flailed at the walkers cutting into him from above.

The dirt under his feet gave way and he slipped face first into another cluster of walkers scrambling out from between another driller and the edges of the hole it had made. He choked back another yell and curled up into a ball. They looked more like fantastic metal spiders than anything else, long legs supporting a bulbous body. One of them was digging into his abdomen again. He felt and heard something give down by his feet, a tearing, crumpling sound. Not his mech's feet, his actual feet. A whiff of ozone reached his nose.

"Sir, units in the valley are turning back toward us."

Thrusting with his mech's feet against the top of the second driller, he fired another burst of explosive rounds into its engine as he jumped away, or tried to jump away. Two more walkers dragged at him and upset his balance. The dirt and brush at the bottom of the ridge rushed up to meet him. Impact tightened his harness. Sparks flew in three directions across his face.

He grabbed a handful of walker and ripped it away. It went limp when he slammed it against the ground, pieces breaking off. He flogged his armor's upper torso with the remains of the thing and felt it impact other walkers.

"Karith!" Nic's voice was frantic. "I can't see you!"

"Wait one."

A walker lost its grip and fell to the ground. Karith stomped on it as he struggled to his feet again. Sparking, it blew up, clouds of smoke boiling out of it.

"Sir, your armor is compromised at plates T-12 and T-13."

"*What?*" Nic screamed over the link.

"I'm fine! Relax." The screaming sound of a plasma cutter was starting to vibrate his cockpit. Frantically Karith swept his hands over his head. Ah-ha! He grabbed the thing and crushed, dragging it to the front where he could see it. The cutting stopped. Metal corpse in hand, he flung himself to the ground on top of the two still on his back and rolled away. One stayed down. He fired into its body and it spasmed, smoking.

A shadow overtopped him and his sensors registered a flash of heat. He ground his back against an outcropping of rock, spun, and smashed his fist into the power plant of the boiler clinging to the rock face. It exploded. Eyes going up, he casually fired a burst into a walker stirring at his feet.

Nicolette's airship floated over him, just below the ridgetop. He stared in consternation for a moment. Most of her lift spheres were discolored from heat and impact.

"Nic?"

"Well what was I supposed to do, you jerk?"

"Sir, this area is riddled with tunnels. I deem it likely that more drilling machines are on the way and recommend retrograde movement."

"Harry, if you ever say 'retrograde movement' again, I'll erase you. It's bogtaken 'retreat.' What are you doing down here, Nic?"

"Just thought I might lend a hand."

"That's crazy. Get out of here, back up high."

"Fine, screw you then."

She sounded upset but jetted away down the ridge, picking up speed until she lifted into the air.

Up and down the ridge, earth slid and a literally earthshaking rumble started. Karith turned and sprinted back the way he had come, into the hills. "Harry, what are the machines in the valley doing?"

"Approximately a third are returning toward their damaged power node."

"Damn it. The rest?"

"They have reached our drop zone and are continuing toward the city."

"Nic, I need you to hit those boilers in the valley again."

"Roger that." Her voice was cold.

"Hell, Nic, that was stupid and you know it. What if a walker had gotten up into your lift spheres?"

Silence.

"Whatever, Nic. I'm on my way down."

"What's that supposed to mean?"

"I'm going to hit them from the rear. That'll get their attention."

"Are you crazy? There's a hole in your armor!" Her voice was frantic.

Karith found a draw going his way and started loping down to the valley.

Major Kewlett broke into their common circuit. "Marvudi, can you hold that valley yourself?"

"Why?"

"I need your air."

Nicolette's voice was cold as iron. "No, Major, you're not pulling me off Karith's top cover."

"That's up to him, little miss."

Karith raised his eyebrows. It had been a long time since anybody dared call Nic "little miss" or anything like it. He examined the situation model as he ran, Nic's lasers coughing in the background.

HARRE said to him, privately, "Sir, our armor is breached. We must return to the depot for repair."

"There is no depot, HARRE. The *MarsFree* is gone and the next ship is hours out."

"Yes, sir. There are, however, class three repair facilities with the major. We should consolidate with other units in the area."

Karith stopped just below a hilltop overlooking his drop zone and a little closer to the city. Panesthian civilians were a glittering brown carpet moving along the ground toward the city. The boilers were already upon the near edge of the mass. Curled and flaming bodies littered the torn earth. The boilers ground on, weapons burning, ripping, and smashing. Dimly, Karith could hear a roaring sound, the frantic buzzing and wailing of the dying Panesthians.

Taking up a stable posture, he readied every top-down missile he had. Nicolette orbited overhead, lasers coughing in his ears. Rippling explosions of smoke, steam, and molten metal stuttered across the valley floor. He could see the boilers digging in to shoot up at her, but not all of them. Some still moved toward the city.

"Major, you've got plenty of air."

Snap. "It's not enough, son. This damn city is oozing civilians. My mechs keep breaking through the tops of their bloody burrow-buildings when they try to move. The airships are the most effective weapons platforms I've got for offense, and I need 'em all. You're not the only one. I'm pulling air off all my outliers."

The major had a point about the air. Strange that a quirk of architecture made air assets more precise and civilian friendly than ground units here.

HARRE was using data from all the sensor pods they'd dropped earlier in the day to build the current situation model. The boilers were deep into the suburbs now, and breaking into the burrow-buildings themselves too. They weren't empty.

"Bloody hell."

"What was that, son?" *Snap, chew.*

"Can do, Major. Nic, go."

"Damn you, Karith."

Karith didn't say anything. She sounded on the verge of tears, which was just odd. Nicolette did another low screaming pass over the boilers in the suburbs in front of him and curved away toward the city.

Major Kewlett said, "Son, you see what's going on over here?"

"Yes, Major."

"Good."

The connection went dead.

HARRE spoke to him. "Sir, are we going to attempt to engage and defeat the boilers in the valley?"

Karith triggered his first salvo of top-downs and sprinted off the hill just ahead of the counterfire, which ripped into the ground behind him until he made it into a wadi. He put his shoulder turrets onto automatic and sprinted along the gash in the ground.

"Harry, if we don't stop them here, they're going to plow into the major's rear area and they're going to be slaughtering civilians the whole way in. This is it, my friend."

Karith popped up to the top of a swelling hill and fired off another salvo of top-downs. The counterfire was slower this time, and he was well away before it hit.

"Sir, the boilers are still advancing."

They were into the suburbs now. Karith moved carefully as he fired, trying to avoid stepping on the crushed and burned Panesthians scattered around the shells of their tunnels and buildings now cracked and open to the sky. He gritted his teeth and choked back the bile. Panesthians died easier than their smaller lookalikes from Earth, apparently.

A subsonic round from a tread he hadn't seen in time slammed into his shoulder plate and knocked him over. Through the concussive haze he could feel a breeze playing around his feet. There really was a hole in his armor.

From flat on the ground he sent an armor-piercing round at the boiler tread. The bulbous shape jumped and exploded. Lucky hit. Another one rolled up behind it.

He regained his feet and ran on. With HARRE's targeting help, he kept both armguns firing at once. Counterfire whipped around him, glancing off his armor.

He paused in a depression filled with trees, a wide spot along a stream bed.

"Fire off the rest of the sensor pods, Harry."

"Including the reserves, sir?"

"Yes."

HARRE launched the remaining eleven sensor pods from their racks. They arced out from Karith in a spreading cloud, came to earth, and dug in, leaving only their antennas protruding. The situation model sharpened up almost immediately. The boiler advance seemed to be clumped up before a small hill in the center of the valley. Beyond, he could see hundreds of unsteadily flying and scuttling Panesthian shapes fleeing overland.

He took a moment and ducked down to examine the inside of his cockpit. There, just to the right, down by his feet, was a jagged hole leaking daylight. He swore when he realized that he couldn't use a sensor pod to examine the exterior because he'd just launched them all. It occurred to him to dismount and examine it but he discarded the idea before it had even fully formed. The smell of a summer afternoon wafted up to him, laced with that of burning plastic.

He sprinted out of the depression, running toward the hill, firing as he went.

He hadn't gone ten steps before he broke through the top of a burrow-building and crashed to a stop. To his great relief, it was empty, a colorful mural on one wall looking down on bare floor.

The boilers were flowing around and over that hill now, moving on. He had to get in front of them somehow.

The machines were thick on the ground. His guns howled and screamed along with him as he stomped, smashed, and burned a thick swath of destruction through the metal foe. Karith was no longer speaking aloud. Once again he and HARRE were one in dreadful destructive purpose.

Just before he reached the hill, a swarm of walkers, crawlers, and blasters erupted over a stone ridge and on top of him, metal limbs flashing with terrible speed. He caught a glimpse of one blaster's stocky cylindrical body up close before it triggered its main weapon into his mech's face.

The crash shocked him backwards. His flailing right hand latched onto a thick-limbed crawler and swung it around himself. He could feel the smashing impacts through the fabric of his suit.

Horrible clicking sounds came to him, through his external sensors and through the hole at his shins. He rolled frantically over, left hand clapping to the hole in his mech's abdomen even as he pulled his real right leg up away from something moving down there, toes curling.

There was a boiler at the hole. He couldn't see it; he could only feel it move under his metal left hand. He bore down, crushing hard. At the same moment he felt a deep terrible pain in his left leg. He stomped with his right and smashed something to the floor of his cockpit. Something withdrew as he pulled the boiler away. It was a walker, limp in his hand, holding a smoking monoblade cutter.

"Sir, there is a hollow in the top of that hill, a crater."

And there were a dozen more boilers around him. He started shooting and crushing again, and began pounding his way toward that hilltop, left leg going numb.

"Harry! Have they stopped?"

"Yes, sir. You have occupied their attention sufficiently to stop their advance. They are coming for *us* now." Blaster fire, waves of heat, washed over him, licking through the hole at his legs with sharp tongues as he ran.

"Good."

A huge blow took his mech in the right arm and spun him around and down. One of the treads. He looked for it, blinking sweat out of his eyes, and fired one of his three remaining missiles. The noise pounded at him. He'd never had a hole all the way through into his cockpit before. A sharp burning smell came in through it. He felt like throwing up.

The hill loomed over him, and he strained back to his feet to fling himself at it. Moments later he tumbled into the crater at the top. It was full of boilers.

He curled reflexively around the hole in his middle, flesh cringing away from it. Blaster fire filled the crater with orange plasma.

"No! This is *my* crater now!" He put the hole out of his mind, straightened, and fired point-blank at the boilers swarming over him. He kicked a boiler clear over the edge of the hole and grabbed another in his left hand, using it to scrape the others out, smashing and flinging. His mech's right arm twitched erratically as he fired its gun blindly. He smashed and stomped through the pain in his real leg, and fired until the boilers that were left in the hole were nothing but gears, cabling, and chunks of metal hull.

He blasted a few more as they came over the rim, launching them into the air in pieces.

"What's going on out there, Harry?" He gasped at a sudden wave of pain from his left leg and stumbled. When he tried to put out his mech's right hand to steady himself he fell against the wall of the crater as it only twitched limply. There was a sweet coppery smell heavy in the cockpit now.

"They are pausing in their assault of our position, sir. They are gathering."

He closed his eyes for a moment, then snapped them open. Closing them was a bad idea.

He could see now it wasn't really a crater. It was an excavation of some sort.

He tried to stand, but slipped. Glancing down, he saw among the shattered boilers a layer of dead Panesthians. Panesthians with equipment strapped to their bellies and fiery circles on their wingcasings. So that was why the boilers had stopped at this hill. Not all these boilers were his kills.

"Karith?" Nicolette spoke to him. "I'm coming, baby."

The fire in his leg made him almost scream. "Harry, what's she doing?"

"She is breaking formation to come to our aid, sir."

"Stay where you are, Nic! That's an order."

"Go to hell, Karith!"

"Dammit, Nic, stay where you are. You gonna let the boilers break the line after I went to this much trouble? Stay where you are!" He filled his voice with as much energy as he could. In the background he could hear Kewlett bellowing at her.

"Fine," she said. "You come to me then. Just run. You can make it."

"Can't do that, Nic."

"Dammit, Karith!" He could hear tears in her voice.

"Hey, Nic." He blasted a boiler off the rim and watched for another. None came.

"What?" She sounded angry now.

"Tell Maragette and Karri I love them, okay?"

No answer but the roar of her engines and a long screaming curse. The noise filters kicked in.

"Harry, what are they doing out there?"

"They have located and destroyed seven of our sensors, sir, but they appear to be bypassing us."

"What? They're advancing again? Toward the city?" Karith had never felt this tired.

"Yes, sir."

Karith chuckled, a sound weak in his own ears. "Up we get."

He propped himself up on the rim of the hole and started shooting. Boilers fell and return fire shattered the crater rim around him but still they advanced.

He gasped for air. "We're gonna have to . . . get them to . . . notice us again . . . Harry."

Karith gathered his legs under him, braced his left hand on the rim of the crater, grunted, and fell into blackness.

The mech froze.

"Sir?"

Karith did not answer. HARRE noted a thick stream of blood pouring from the hole in his armor. He used his emergency override to ease the mech back behind cover.

"Sir?" Still nothing.

"Karith?" Nicolette's voice was frantic. "Your icon's dark, Karith. Karith!"

HARRE answered. "He is unconscious, Captain Shepard."

"Damn." Her voice was thick. "Okay, you're in charge now, Harry. Get him back here."

"It is true that command falls to me if my pilot becomes incapacitated."

"Why aren't you on your way back already?" Her voice held ominous overtones. "Get up into the hills and make your way back here or he'll die."

HARRE looked over the field, the fleeing clouds of Panesthians, the advancing boilers carving into them.

"It is true, ma'am, that Captain Marvudi has a much higher chance of survival if I return to headquarters at this time."

"So go!" she screamed.

HARRE paused. Doctrine advised that he do as she said, but it was his call now. And he found . . . he found himself rebelling. As if Captain Marvudi were speaking to him. He knew, somehow, that Doctrine could be ignored. Had to be ignored.

"I can't do that, ma'am." He vaulted the crater edge and charged the boilers, all guns blazing. They noticed him, and turned to engage.

Sometime later the *CambriaDawn* took up orbit around Milacria and dropped another three companies of mechanized infantry onto Major Kewlett's perimeter. Only forewarning and fast maneuvering saved her from the same fate as the *MarsFree*. Her bombards destroyed the boiler railgun positions shortly thereafter.

Human forces pushed out to the east and the west. Captain Nicolette Shepard flew west, over the tangled wreckage of what seemed like thousands of broken boilers.

At a certain spot she lowered her airship to the ground and jumped out. Over thirty percent of her lift spheres were gone, and those that remained were discolored and ragged.

Karith Marvudi's mech lay face down in a dry streambed surrounded by hundreds of dead boilers, like the center of a blast ring stretching for hundreds of meters.

Nicolette folded her helmet back as she ran. The stench of smoke, burning oil, and plasma assailed her nostrils. Ignoring the hot metal she scrambled up and forced her way past the dead boilers on the mech's back. She tapped a code into the hatch's touch plate. No response, not even a power light. She ran back to her ship and returned with tools. Sparks flew and tears boiled off the metal as she began cutting.

The Sea of Tranquility on Earth's Moon is not a sea, as early astronomers thought, but the relatively smooth surface of an ancient lava flow, possibly the result of collision with a very large meteor billions of years ago. Still, the tranquility tag is justified on a dead world with neither air nor sound—or it was until war transformed it into a blazing fury into which battle-suited Baker Company was desperately dropped.

The War Memorial

Allen Steele

The first-wave assault is jinxed from the very beginning. Even before the dropship touches down, its pilot shouts over the comlink that a Pax missile battery seven klicks away has locked in on their position, despite the ECM buffer set up by the lunarsats. So it's going to be a dustoff; the pilot has done his job by getting the men down to the surface, and he doesn't want to be splattered across Mare Tranquillitatis.

It doesn't matter anyway. Baker Company has been deployed for less than two minutes before the Pax heatseekers pummel the ground around them and take out the dropship even as it begins its ascent.

Giordano hears the pilot scream one last obscenity before his ugly spacecraft is reduced to metal rain, then something slams against his back and everything within the suit goes black. For an instant he believes he's dead, that he's been nailed by one of the heatseekers, but it's just debris from the dropship. The half-ton ceramic-polymer shell of the Mark III Valkyrie Combat Armor Suit has absorbed the brunt of the impact.

When the lights flicker back on within his soft cocoon and the flatscreen directly in front of his face stops fuzzing, he sees that not everyone has been so lucky. A few dozen meters away at three o'clock, there's a new crater that used to be Robinson. The only thing left of Baker Company's resident card cheat is the severed rifle arm of his CAS.

He doesn't have time to contemplate Robinson's fate. He's in the midst of battle. Sgt. Boyle's voice comes through the comlink, shouting orders.

Traveling overwatch, due west, head for Marker One-Eight-Five. Kemp, take Robinson's position. Cortez, you're point. Stop staring, Giordano (yes sir). Move, move, move...

So they move, seven soldiers in semi-robotic heavy armor, bounding across the flat silver-gray landscape. Tin men trying to outrun the missiles plummeting down around them, the soundless explosions the missiles make when they hit. For several kilometers around them, everywhere they look, there are scores of other tin men doing the same, each trying to survive a silent hell called the Sea of Tranquility.

Giordano is sweating hard, his breath coming in ragged gasps. He tells himself that if he can just make Marker One-Eight-Five—crater Arago, or so the map overlay tells him—then everything will be okay. The crater walls will protect them. Once Baker Company sets up its guns and erects a new ECM buffer, they can dig in nice and tight and wait it out; the beachhead will have been established by then and the hard part of Operation Monkey Wrench will be over.

But the crater is five-and-a-half klicks away, across plains as flat and wide-open as Missouri pasture, and between here and there a lot of shitfire is coming down. The Pax Astra guns in the foothills of the lunar highlands due west of their position can see them coming; the enemy has the high ground, and they're throwing everything they can at the invading force.

Sgt. Boyle knows his platoon is in trouble. He orders everyone to use their jumpjets. Screw formation; it's time to run like hell.

Giordano couldn't agree more whole-heartedly. He tells the Valkyrie to engage the twin miniature rockets mounted on the back of his carapace.

Nothing happens.

Once again, he tells the voice-activated computer mounted against the back of his neck to fire the jumpjets. When there's still no response, he goes to manual, using the tiny controls nestled within the palm of his right hand inside the suit's artificial arm.

At that instant, everything goes dark again, just like it did when the shrapnel from the dropship hit the back of his suit.

This time, though, it stays dark.

A red LCD lights above his forehead, telling him that there's been a total system crash.

Cursing, he finds the manual override button and stabs it with his little finger. As anticipated, it causes the computer to completely reboot itself; he hears servomotors grind within the carapace as its limbs move into neutral position, until his boots are planted firmly on the ground and his arms are next to his sides, his rifle pointed uselessly at the ground.

There is a dull click from somewhere deep within the armor, then silence.

Except for the red LCD, everything remains dark.

He stabs frantically at the palm buttons, but there's no power to any of the suit's major subsystems. He tries to move his arms and legs, but finds them frozen in place.

Limbs, jumpjets, weapons, ECM, comlink...nothing works.

Now he's sweating more than ever. The impact of that little bit of debris from the dropship must have been worse than he thought. Something must have shorted out, badly, within the Valkyrie's onboard computer.

He twists his head to the left so he can gaze through the eyepiece of the optical periscope, the only instrument within the suit that isn't dependent upon computer control. What he sees terrifies him: the rest of his platoon jumpjetting for the security of the distant crater, while missiles continue to explode all around him.

Abandoning him. Leaving him behind.

He screams at the top of his lungs, yelling for Boyle and Kemp and Cortez and the rest, calling them foul names, demanding that they wait or come back for him, knowing that it's futile. They can't hear him. For whatever reason, they've already determined that he's out of action; they cannot afford to risk their lives by coming back to lug an inert CAS across a battlefield.

He tries again to move his legs, but it's pointless. Without direct interface from the main computer, the limbs of his suit are immobile. He might as well be wearing a concrete block.

The suit contains three hours of oxygen, fed through pumps controlled by another computer tucked against his belly, along with the rest of its life-support systems. So at least he won't suffocate or fry....

For the next three hours, at any rate.

Probably less. The digital chronometer and life-support gauges are dead, so there's no way of knowing for sure.

As he watches, even the red coal of the LCD warning lamp grows dim until it finally goes cold, leaving him in the dark.

He has become a living statue. Fully erect, boots firmly placed upon the dusty regolith, arms held rigid at his sides, he is in absolute stasis.

For three hours. Certainly less.

For all intents and purposes, he is dead.

In the smothering darkness of his suit, Giordano prays to a god in which he has never really believed. Then, for lack of anything else to do, he raises his eyes to the periscope eyepiece and watches as the battle rages on around him.

He fully expects—and, after a time, even hopes—for a Pax missile to relieve him of his ordeal, but this small mercy never occurs. Without an active infrared or electromagnetic target to lock in upon, the heatseekers miss the small spot of ground he occupies, instead decimating everything around him.

Giordano becomes a mute witness to the horror of the worst conflict of the Moon War, what historians will later call the Battle of Mare Tranquillitatis. Loyalty, duty, honor, patriotism ... all the things in which he once believed are soon rendered null and void as he watches countless lives being lost.

Dropships touch down near and distant, depositing soldiers in suits similar to his own. Some don't even make it to the ground before they become miniature supernovas.

Men and women like himself are torn apart even as they charge across the wasteland for the deceptive security of distant craters and rills.

An assault rover bearing three lightsuited soldiers rushes past him, only to be hit by fire from the hills. It is thrown upside down, crushing two of the soldiers beneath it. The third man, his legs broken and his suit punctured, manages to crawl from the wreckage. He dies at Giordano's feet, his arms reaching out to him.

He has no idea whether Baker Company has survived, but he suspects it hasn't since he soon sees a bright flash from the general direction of the crater it was supposed to occupy and hold.

In the confines of his suit, he weeps and screams and howls against the madness erupting around him. In the end, he goes mad himself, cursing the same god to whom he prayed earlier for the role to which he has been damned.

If God cares, it doesn't matter. By then, the last of Giordano's oxygen reserves have been exhausted; he asphyxiates long before his three hours are up, his body still held upright by the Mark III Valkyrie Combat Armor Suit.

When he is finally found, sixty-eight hours later, by a patrol from the victorious Pax Astra Free Militia, they are astonished that anything was left standing on the killing ground. This sole combat suit, damaged only by a small steel pipe wedged into its CPU housing, with a dead man inexplicably sealed inside, is the only thing left intact. All else has been reduced to scorched dust and shredded metal.

So they leave him standing.

They do not remove the CAS from its place, nor do they attempt to prise the man from his armor. Instead, they erect a circle of stones around the Valkyrie. Later, when peace has been negotiated and lunar independence has been achieved, a small plaque is placed at his feet.

The marker bears no name. Because so many lives were lost during the battle, nobody can be precisely certain of who was wearing this particular CAS on that particular day.

An eternal flame might have been placed at his feet, but it can't, because nothing burns on the Moon.

Christopher Ruocchio's best-selling Sun Eater series chronicling the exploits of Hadrian Marlowe, who goes from rebel to slave to self-questioning hero, have attracted a strong following of readers. Marlowe has had shorter adventures as well, and when two Imperial legions go missing on a routine transfer to the outer provinces, Marlowe and his loyal Red Company are dispatched to bring them home. Tracking the lost legions to the barren world of Arae, the Red Company finds itself up against a pirate army. But there's something else in the pirate fortress—something darker—and their battle will bring Hadrian face-to-face with an enemy more terrible than he could have ever imagined.

The Demons of Arae

Christopher Ruocchio

THE MOUTH OF HELL

Fire screamed all around us, and the violent shock of atmospheric entry that shook the ship beneath my feet was like the coming of an avalanche. Faceless men stood about me, gripping their restraints. The red glow of the emergency lighting reflected off their featureless ivory masks.

The thunder stopped. We were falling through clear air beneath yellow skies.

Arae.

"You're sure they're on Arae?" I remembered asking before we set sail from Nessus on this expedition.

Captain Otavia Corvo had only shrugged her broad shoulders. "It's your Empire's intelligence, Lord Marlowe. They said they tracked this lost legion of theirs to within a dozen light-years of the Arae system. If they're not on Arae, they're somewhere in the Dark between, and we'll never find them."

An entire legion had vanished. Four ships. Twenty-six thousand men.

Gone.

At first Legion Intelligence had suspected the Cielcin. The xenobites needed to eat, after all, and four troop transport ships with the legionnaires already on ice for the long voyage were indistinguishable from meat lockers where the aliens were concerned. But when we arrived in Arae system, we found something we hadn't expected.

"Pirates?" Corvo didn't believe it. I could see it in the way her brows arched above black eyes. "What sort of pirates could capture a Sollan legion?"

We all knew the answer. I could feel the eyes of my officers on me, as if each man and woman were daring me to say it first. I glanced from one to the other: from the Amazonian Corvo to her bookish second-in-command, Durand; from green-skinned Ilex to solemn Tor Varro.

"Extrasolarians." After Vorgossos the word carried a poisonous aftertaste for me and for every member of my Red Company. The Extras had been an Imperial bogeyman for millennia, the sort of monsters mothers scared their children with. But I knew now. Those men who—fleeing Imperial control—fled to the blackness between the stars, to rogue planets and lost moons far from the light of Imperial order, had bought their freedom with a piece of their own humanity. As a boy, I'd believed the Chantry's proscription against intelligent machines and against the augmentation of the flesh was nothing but reactionary cowardice.

I know better now.

Monsters are real, and I had met them. Met not only with the Cielcin who threaten mankind from without, but met also with the monsters we'd made in our own image and in the image of our inner demons.

Repulsors fired, and our descent slowed, forcing my bile up as we came out of free fall. I shut my eyes, mindful of the quiet chatter of my men through my suit's comms, of the way the thermal layer clung to me beneath the armorweave and ceramic plates. I still felt half a clown wearing it.

I was no soldier, had never trained to be one. I'd wanted to be a linguist, in Earth's name!

But I was a knight now, one of His Radiance's own Royal Victorians. *Sir* Hadrian Marlowe. And after Vorgossos I knew there was no going back.

I undid my restraints and moved into the middle of the cabin, conscious of the faceless soldiers watching me through suit cameras. My own suit worked the same—though my black visor was fashioned in the image of an impassive human face and not a blank arc of zircon. Almost it seemed I wore no helmet at all. Images from outside were projected directly onto my retinas, and but for the indicators in my periphery that indicated my heart rate and the integrity of my Royse shields, I saw plain as day.

"They're putting us down as close to the door as they can!" I said, voice amplified by the speakers in my breastplate. "Petros's team should have those gun emplacements on the south ridge down by the time we make landfall. Pallino's got the north. The Sphinxes have air support! All we have to do is back the Horse!" They knew all of this already, had gone over the assault plan with their centurion before we'd left the ship, but it bore repeating.

"You ready, Had?" that same centurion asked me, clapping me on the shoulder as I took my place front and center by the exit ramp.

Beneath my helmet mask I smiled and returned the gesture. "Just like the coliseum back on Emesh!" I seized hold of one of the ceiling straps to steady myself as the dropship banked into an arc.

"Let's hope!" Siran replied. The woman had been by my side a long time. Long before Vorgossos, when I had been little more than a slave in the fighting pits of Count Balian Mataro.

Turning back to face the fifty men that stood in the cramped hold of the *Ibis*-class lander, I got a clear look at myself in the mirrored glass at the rear of the compartment. Like all Sollan Imperial combat armor, my suit's design recalled the style of ancient Rome, the shape of it speaking to cellular memories of ancient power. The muscled breastplate was black as anything I had seen, embossed with the trident-and-pentacle I had taken for my sigil when His Radiance the Emperor restored me to the nobility. Beneath that I wore a wide-sleeved crimson tunic darker than the ones worn by legionnaires. Strapped pteruges decorated my shoulders and waist, marking me for an officer. Black boots and gauntlets contrasted the Imperial ivory and scarlet, and I alone wore a cape: a lacerna black above and crimson beneath.

How had I ended up here? I'd left home to go to school, to join the scholiasts. Not to fight a war. Still, I raised my voice. "Some of you won't have fought the Extras before! Soldiers of the Empire, whatever comes at you, you *will* hold your ground!"

My tutor always said I had too-developed a taste for melodrama. Maybe he was right. Or maybe whatever gods there are share my love of theater. Whichever is the case, no sooner had I said these words than the landing alarm blared and each of us felt the *Ibis* buoy on its final approach.

The landing ramp slammed downwards, admitting the orange Araenian sunlight.

I turned and drew my sword, kindling the weapon's exotic matter blade with a button press. Liquid metal the color of moonlight gleamed in my gauntleted fist, and I was first onto the shattered tarmac and the approach to the pirates' fortress.

The mountain rose before us, the last lonely peak in a chain that broke upon the salt flats of the *Soto Planitia*. Arae had never been settled—its air was carbon monoxide and ammonia, and there was little water. But for the remains of a few mining expeditions, the pirate fortress was the only settlement on the planet. I could see the fingering shapes of antennae and other comms equipment bristling on the ridge line above, and the smoking ruins of gun emplacements where Petros had taken our Fifth Chiliad and wiped out the artillery.

Battle raged about us, plasma fire splitting the cancered daylight like lightning, black smoke rising from bodies and from the wrecks of ground-effect vehicles and three-legged machines that I think had governed themselves.

And ahead—between the two reaching arms of that final mountain—stood the *Horse*.

Our colossus.

The titan stood nearly forty meters high, its legs more like the arms of a crawling man than those of a horse in truth. The earth trembled with each mighty step it took, and the men who stood against it could not so much as scratch its armor with their arms. Beyond it, the hardened outer wall of the fortress rose two hundred feet above the landing field, black as the space we'd come from. A stray shot pinged off my shield and, not ten yards off the tarmac, exploded as a plasma cannon struck ground, sending dust and bits of shattered concrete fountaining skyward. Above, three of Sphinx

Flight streaked overhead, single long wings tacking like sails against the wind, filling the air with the thunder of their drives.

"Why haven't they cracked the wall?" I asked, toggling to the officer's channel.

"It's shielded, lord," came a thin, polished voice. "Crim took a few shots at it with the Horse's artillery, but we'd have done as well to scratch at it with our fingernails."

I cursed. "How are they powering a shield of this size, Lorian?" I asked. "I thought your people didn't pick up a fusion reactor on your scans."

From his position on the ship in orbit, Commander Lorian Aristedes wasted no time in answering. "Could be geothermal. Arae's core runs hotter than most thanks to all those moons. I've ordered sappers. If they can attach a plasma bore directly to the door, the shield won't matter."

"We'll clear the tarmac then," I said in answer.

I did not hurry, but allowed the bulk of our soldiery to fan past me, soldiers moving in groups of three behind their decurions. One of the colossi's massive feet descended, cracking the pavement. The earth shook, air filled with a noise like drums.

For a moment, all was silent and still. Far above, a cloud passed before the swollen circle of the sun.

An awful cry resounded off the surrounding rocks, high and shrill.

"The hell is that?" Siran's words came in clear over my armor's internal comm.

A terrible sense of foreboding blossomed within me. Some kind of alarm? I half-expected to see the light of sirens flashing in the gray stones above us, but there was nothing.

"On our left!"

"I see them!"

"The right, too!"

I turned my head, trying to see just what it was the others were seeing through the smoke and the ranks of men to either side.

Then I saw them, and swore.

They must have come from bolt-holes hidden in the arms of the mountain. Hundreds of them. They had no arms, nor shields—but they needed neither. The SOMs feared neither death nor pain, and came forward with the focused scramble of a swarm of ants trying to bridge a puddle with their own bodies.

They were men once. Before the Extras carved out their brains and filled their heads with kit, before they meddled in the subtle language of their genes to harden them against the poisonous air. They had no will any longer. They never would again. They were only tools, puppet soldiers controlled by some intelligence—human or artificial I dared not guess—in the fortress ahead of us.

"Hoplites!" Siran exclaimed, singling out our heavy, shielded infantry. "Shield walls!"

All about us, the army shifted, hoplites shifting from the point position in their little triases towards the outside of our line.

"Fire!"

The hoplites opened fire, phase disruptor bolts crackling in the warm air. Siran seized my arm, "We need to get you to the Horse, Had."

She wanted to escort me to safety, to get me out of danger and the enemy charge.

She wanted me to abandon my men.

"No!" I shook her off, then toggled my comm once more. "Commander!"

Lorian Aristedes replied at once, "Yes, my lord?"

"Order Sphinx Flight back around! Strafe the enemy line!"

The ship's tactical officer acknowledged and relayed my orders.

The SOMs were still coming, loping across the flat ground to either side. How many armies had died thus? Smashed between the horns of the enemy? Shots rained down from above, and turning, I saw men standing on the platforms above the Horse's thighs and the fell light of the colossi's rear cannons gleaming. It wouldn't be enough, and it was only then I realized the source of that awful keening sound.

The SOMs were screaming, howling like a band of blue-faced Picts out of the deepest history.

Then I realized Siran's mistake. Ordering the hoplites forward was standard procedure: they had the expensive shielding and the disruptor rifles, the heavy firepower. They were meant to shield the more numerous peltasts, who—without shields and with lighter armor—were cheaper to outfit and less costly to replace. But the peltasts carried bladed energy lances.

They had spears.

We had no time.

"Peltasts!" I called, transmitting my words to everyone in the line. "Forward! Forward!" There was a fraction of a second's hesitation. I suppose I cannot blame them, the order was unorthodox in our age. But they got the message when I added the crucial word: "Bayonets!"

A double line of light infantry stepped forward, allowing the hoplites to turn and fall back towards the center of the column. They moved with gearwork precision, the result of weeks of careful drilling and a course of RNA learning drugs. From above, it must have been beautiful, and for a moment I envied Lorian Aristedes and Captain Corvo their bird's-eye view. The peltasts lowered their spears, beam weapons firing into the galloping horde. I saw SOMs fall smoking from laser burns, only to be trampled over by the ranks behind. The puppets did not care for the loss of their brethren, did not care that they were charging without so much as a knife at two triple lines of armed Sollan legionnaires.

My men all did their best, but stopping the onslaught was like trying to block the tide. The enemy crashed against us from either side, throwing themselves against our spears like fanatics, only for their brothers to vault *over* them and hurl themselves at us. From the rear, the hoplites fired over the heads of the lines before them until the air was thick with the static aftershock of disruptor fire.

Where was the air support?

One of the puppet-men leaped fully over our line and landed in the narrow gap left between. For a moment it just stood there, processing, as if not quite sure what to do. It turned its head to look at me, and I think it understood who I was. The man it had been was shorter than I, bald as an egg and pale, skin burned and peeling in the chemical air. How it breathed at all I couldn't say, though the gleaming black implants in its chest and throat perhaps had something to do with it.

It lurched towards me, and before Siran or any of the hoplites could intervene, I pushed past them and lunged, sword outthrust. The highmatter blade passed through the SOM's flesh as easily as through water, and it fell with no legs to support it. For a single, awful moment, the upper half of the once-human form dragged itself forwards, clawing towards me until one of my guards shot it with a disruptor.

A metallic screaming filled the air, and glancing up a moment, I saw the bladelike profile of five lighters burning across the sky. Sphinx Flight. Plasma fire picked its way in twin rows along the enemy line, parallel to our own. One of the SOMs fell smoking at my feet, and I slashed it in half for good measure. The earth groaned once more as the Horse advanced, closer and still closer to the wall and gate of the enemy fortress just as Sphinx Flight wheeled round for another pass.

I seized Siran by the arm. "Order everyone towards the Horse! We need to deepen the lines!"

She nodded and went about her orders. Turning, I proceeded up the no-man's land between our lines, cutting down those enemies who'd made it through. "Commander!" I almost yelled into the line. "Find Petros and tell him to get his men down here. It's time they were the ones surrounded!"

If young Aristedes replied I did not hear it. One of the SOMs threw itself at me and I had to duck to escape it, keeping my sword up so the creature cut itself in two for its trouble. Blood and something the color of milk spilled out and beaded on my cape. Disgusted, I shook the garment out and continued my advance. Behind me, the line was falling back, collapsing into a kind of mushroom shape as it thickened and grew shorter, making it far harder for the SOMs to clamber over.

The Sphinxes wheeled about once more. Plasma fire split the air and tore through the enemy. I'd nearly made it to the rear legs of the Horse. Ahead men were climbing the legs of the colossus to reach the platforms where their brothers rained fire down from above. The sound of the lighter craft overhead screamed across the sky, and I saw their wing-sails flatten to yaw them round for another pass.

Our lines were holding, thickened as we were into a tight box about the rear legs of the Horse. Where was Siran? I could hear her voice on the comm, ordering the ranks of our line to rotate, fresher troops in the rear replacing the spent men in front. Looking past those leading men, I saw a sea of scabrous faces, hollow eyes and grasping fingers spreading back as far as the southern ridge of the mountains. And behind them?

I thrust my sword into the air and let out a cry.

Petros and the Fifth Chiliad had come. Another thousand of our troops crashed into the hollow men from behind, splitting the attention of the fell intelligence that governed them.

"Concentrate air fire on the northern side!" I ordered, turning Sphinx flight away from the narrowing slice of the enemy between us and Petros's relief force.

Fire reigned.

Smoke followed.

Not even the airless vacuum of space is so quiet as the battlefield when the fighting is done. Pillars of oily smoke held up the sky, and though my men busied themselves unloading the plasma bore from the Horse's underbelly and the winds scoured in off the salt flats of the *Soto Planitia,* I heard nothing. I stood watching from the shadow of the massive gate, my guards around me and my friends: Siran and Pallino, who had come with me out of Emesh.

Thus we waited.

The plasma bore had the look of some swollen jet engine mounted on four legs. It took a man to pilot it—no daimon intelligences here—and the tech moved forward step by lurching step, extending the cigar-shaped body of the bore forward like a battering ram against the gates of ancient Jerusalem.

As the ground crew busied themselves with their preparations, I cast my eye skywards, past the circling shapes of Sphinx Flight and the sulfurous clouds. Somewhere above, our ship waited, locked in geostationary orbit above us. The SOMs had been a nasty welcoming party, but everything had gone according to plan in the end. One of the once-human creatures lay not far off, dead eyes staring at the umber sky.

"Do you ever wonder who they were?" I asked aloud, indicating the corpse. There were burn lines on his flesh where the disruptor fire had fried the implants that enslaved him. I hoped that—for a fleeting moment, in the instant before he died—the fellow had remembered who he was, and that he was a man. I wondered what his name had been, and if he'd remembered it before the end.

"Some poor sod, most like," Pallino answered in his gruff way. "Merchanter or some such as got skyjacked by this lot."

Cape snapping about myself, I advanced and turned the fellow fully on his back with my toe. The man was bald as the first one I had cut down and pale almost as the Cielcin who drink the blood of worlds. My heart fell, and I swallowed, kneeling to get a better look at the tattoo inked on the side of the man's neck. It showed a fist clenched around two crossed lightning bolts above the Mandari numerals 378.

A legionary tattoo.

"I think I know what happened to our lost legion."

Silence greeted this pronouncement, deeper and darker than the quiet that had come before. I stood, turning my black-masked face toward the towering expanse of grim metal looming from the mountainside before us, and at the vast war engine and our army arrayed beneath it.

The silence broke with a great rushing of wind as the plasma bore roared to life, sucking at the air around us. The mouth of the plasma bore was pressed right against the bulwark, passing clean through the high-velocity curtain of the energy shield that guarded the gate.

The metal began to glow and run like water.

It was time.

THE CAPTAIN

All was dark within but for the flashing of sirens warning the defenders that their fortress was breached. I followed the first wave of my men over the threshold, the heat of still-cooling metal beating on my suit despite the coolant sprays the plasma bore released when its work was done. There I stood a moment, surveying the hangar before me, the parked shuttles and stacked crates of provisions and equipment.

"Search the shuttles and drain the fuel tanks!" Pallino called out, signaling a group of his men to advance. They did, moving off in groups of three, rifles and lances raised.

"Mapping drones have gone ahead, my lord," said Petros. He saluted as I drew nearer, his fist pressed to his chest. He extended his arm as I acknowledged the salute. "It's a fucking maze."

A wire-frame map of the fortress was even then sketching itself in the bottom left of my vision. The levels that rose stacked above the hangar bay seemed straightforward enough, but the warren of tunnels and caverns carved deep into the living rock at the base of the mountain were anything but.

"I don't want anyone wandering off," I said to Petros and Pallino. "Groups of two and three decades should stick together. We should assume there are more SOMs where those others came from." If the entirety of the 378th had been taken and converted by the Extras, it was very possible that thousands more lay in wait for us, but I couldn't help thinking that if such were the case, these pirates would surely have deployed them *before* we breached their fortress. Perhaps some of our soldiers were still alive. Perhaps most of them were.

My officers turned to go about their duties, and I was left with Siran and a vague sense of déjà vu. The caverns—vaguely damp and lichen-spotted—reminded me of the city on Vorgossos. I shut my eyes, as if by doing so I might retreat to some other place: to the cloud forests on Nagramma where Jinan and I had hiked to the old Cid Arthurian temple; or the foggy coast at Calagah. Instead, I saw swollen hands rising from black water and the countless blue eyes of the Undying King of Vorgossos, and despite the warm wind from the Araenian desert outside, I shivered.

"Get a seal on that door!" I said, gesturing at the smooth hole the plasma bore had put in the main gate. "Static field will do! I don't want anything impeding our exit should it come to that."

I could still feel those bloated fingers on me, and shook them off with the memory of their touch. This was not Vorgossos. This was Arae. On Vorgossos I had been alone, but for Valka. Here I had an army at my back, my Red Company.

"Lord Marlowe," came the voice of some centurion I did not recognize, one of Petros's men, "we've captured their captain. We're bringing him to you."

Unable to suppress a crooked smile, I said, "No need, centurion. We'll come to you."

Sunlight fell through windows narrow as coin slots high on the high chamber's walls. The turret was in the very highest part of the mountain fortress, and through the holograph plates that imitated larger windows I could see the Horse; the arms of the mountain spread out below; and the infinite, sterile whiteness of the *Soto Planitia* beyond.

The man who sat in the chair between four of my soldiers wore an old gray and white uniform. His face was as gray, and his hair with it. He did not *look* like an Extrasolarian. He looked ... *ordinary,* the very model of the old soldier. Indeed, he reminded me of no one so much as Pallino: aged and leathered, with a sailor's pallor and sharp eyes—though unlike Pallino this man still had both his eyes. The fellow had the stamp of the legions about him. A former officer, most like. Such men often turned mercenary, if they did not turn gladiator. I knew his type.

"What's your name, soldier?" I asked in my best aristocratic tones. There was enough of the Imperial iron left in the man to straighten his spine at the sound of it.

"Samuel Faber, sir. Captain of the Dardanines." From his accent I suspected the man was at least of the patrician class—though certainly he was not palatine.

"The Dardanines?" I echoed, stopping five paces before the chair. Turning to survey the room, I caught sight of the dozen or so other officers who had surrendered with Captain Faber.

Faber cleared his throat. "Free company."

"Mercenaries?" I said, and arched my eyebrows behind my mask. "Foederati?" But it did not matter, not then. I pushed on to more pressing matters. "Where is the Three Seventy-Eighth?" I saw a muscle in Captain Faber's jaw clench, but his gray eyes stayed fixed on my face. He didn't answer. "Legion Intelligence tracked a convoy carrying the 378th Centaurine Legion to within a dozen light-years of this system, Captain. I need to know what you did with them." I did not say *What you did* to *them.*

Faber was silent for a moment, and when he did speak it was with the air of one resigned. "I know who you are." Seeing as he had started talking, I did not interrupt, only tried not to glance towards Pallino where he stood near at hand. "Is it ... true you can't be killed?"

I did look towards Pallino then. The old veteran alone of those in the room knew something of the answer to that question. Voice flattened by the suit speakers, I answered, "Not today, captain. Not by you." The man seemed to chew on that a moment—or maybe it was only his tongue. He looked down at his scuffed boots and the gunmetal floor, arms crossed. "Tell me: How does a man go from a posting with the Legions to kidnapping one for the Extras? Was the money that good?"

I expected the man to rage, expected that there must be enough of the Legion officer he had been left in him—and enough honor—to insult him. I wanted him to stand, to take a swing at me, to give me an excuse to put him right back in his seat. The man had sold human beings—his fellow Sollans, his fellow soldiers—to the barbarians who dwell between the stars.

I did not expect him to shake his head and press his lips together, as if he were afraid to speak. Taking a step forward, I asked again, "Where is the legion, Captain Faber?"

Nothing.

Gesturing to Siran, I stepped aside, saying, "I had hoped it would not come to this." I had seen video of the mercenary captain relayed to my suit before we'd boarded the lift to come upstairs, and I'd guessed at his legionary past. Four men entered the command chamber a moment later, carrying a fifth between them. They stopped just before Faber's seat and dropped the body there, face down.

The SOM did not move.

For a moment, I said nothing, only hooked my thumbs through my belt and waited for the shoe to drop. Faber must have felt it coming. Kneeling, I turned the dead man's head with one hand, presenting the fist and crossed lightning bolts of the 378th Centaurine. Then nothing needed saying, and Faber found he could no longer look at the dead man or myself. He looked rather at the dozen of his own lieutenants who knelt on the ground to one side, manacled with guns aimed at their backs.

"We're both soldiers, you and I," Faber said into the vacuum growing between us, and for once I did not argue the label. He was nodding steadily, hands clasped in his lap. "I've done things I'm not proud of, Sir Hadrian, for the Empire and after. But that's *the job*."

"These were your brothers, Captain," I said, more regretful than angry. The anger stayed far below the surface, churning like a river of eels.

"It was the job," he said again. "That's what they paid us for. Tag a convoy while the men were still in fugue, bring them here. It's not even hard if you know where the ships are going to be—but they did. They must have a mole in Legion command."

I took a step that put me between Faber and the corpse on the floor. "Who is they? Who are you working for?" Faber only shook his head, still not making eye contact. I could see the whites there, and the way his hands shook. Was he afraid? Not of me, surely?

Letting out a sigh, I reached up behind my right ear and clicked the hard switch there before keying a command into my wrist-terminal. The sigh turned to hissing as the pressure seals in my helmet relaxed. The black titanium and ceramic casque broke into pieces that folded flower-like away from my face before coiling into the collar of my hardsuit, and for the first time I looked down on Faber with my own eyes.

With a rough hand, I pushed back the elastic coif that covered my head and shook out curtains of ink-dark hair. Coming to within two paces of Faber's chair, I crouched to put us at a level. "You were a soldier, you say. Then you know we can take the answer from you. I would prefer not to have to." Reaching out, I seized Faber's clenched hands with my own, looking like some parody of the vassal kneeling before his lord, of the devoted son before his father. I squeezed. "Who hired you to betray your brothers?" I glanced back at the dead man behind me. I could see Faber was looking.

Then his vision shifted and we regarded one another eye-to-eye. "You don't understand. These people. The things they can do . . ."

But I had been to Vorgossos, to the lowest dungeons of the Undying. I knew full well what horrors, what abominations mankind was capable of in the name of *science,* of *progress.* I had seen the body farms, the surgical theaters. I had seen armies of puppet SOMs larger than this, and had seen machines to violate every natural law. I knew exactly what the Extrasolarians were capable of—knew it was every bit as vile and unthinkable as the rape and pillage the inhuman Cielcin carried out as they conquered our worlds. And worse. Worse because the Extrasolarians were human, even if they tried not to be.

"Give me a name, Faber. Please."

The man swallowed. "You have to take my people out of here."

"You are in *no* position to be making demands," I said, standing, my finger in his face. I turned my back on him, pondering what to say next.

"You misunderstand, Marlowe. That's not a demand. It's the terms of my surrender." I stopped mid-step and turned around, hands back at my sides. I waited him out. The man had been in the Legions, surely he knew that the Empire would put every one of his men in a prison camp for the rest of their lives. Surely he knew his own life was forfeit. For an officer of the Imperium to take up arms against the Empire was a grievous crime, one the Emperor would never forgive. "Passage out of here for every one of my men, even if it's to Belusha," he said, naming just such a prison planet as I'd imagined.

"What are you so afraid of, Captain Faber?" I asked. "Your employers, plainly, but why? The fortress is ours."

The older officer glanced at the dozen or so of his men again, then once more at the SOM dead at his feet. "MINOS, they're called MINOS."

I blinked. "Like the Minoan king?" Minos was a character out of ancient myth, the ruler of vanished Crete. It was he who had built the labyrinth into which Theseus had ventured to fight the Minotaur. Thinking of Theseus brought a grim smile to my lips, and I saw once more a stony shore. A black lake. Slippered feet standing on the surface of the water. And against a wall of bare stone a tall red fountain rose dreadfully distinct.

"The what?" Faber said stupidly. "No, I—I don't know." He wrung his hands, eyes fallen. I let him take the time he needed; could sense the stripped, exhausted gears in his mind still turning. "Have you ever heard of the Exalted?" he asked, voice very small.

"Yes." The Exalted were amongst the most dangerous of the Extrasolarian tribes—if tribes was the right word. They had abandoned their humanity—they would say *transcended* it—replaced their bodies with machines, altered their neural chemistry to suit their whims, discarded their humanity like so much rotting meat. They crewed massive interstellar vessels and never set in to port, fleeing from the Empire and the Holy Terran Chantry as shadows flee from the sun. Many had lived for eons preserved like medical specimens in jars of their own making. It is the Exalted every little boy and girl in the Sollan Empire grows up afraid of. It is they we imagine when we hear stories of the Extrasolarians and the things they do to innocent sailors.

"MINOS *makes* them. Designs them. And they make..." he nodded weakly towards the SOM still lying at his feet, "...those things."

"And they hired you to acquire materials," I said. "They're building an army. For whom?"

The Dardanine captain screwed his eyes shut. "I don't know. I don't know. On my honor."

"Your *honor.*" It was all I could do not to sneer. "Your *honor,* M. Faber? Just what honor do you think you have?"

"Enough to plead for my men," Faber replied without hesitation. "Do with me what you will, but get them out of here. And get out of here yourselves. If you know what the Exalted are, you know what trouble you'll be in when they arrive."

"They're coming here?"

"Most of the MINOS staff fled the moment your ship came out of warp, but not before they summoned the others."

Petros barked a laugh. "At warp? That'll take *years!*"

"No," Faber said flatly.

Petros hadn't been with us at Vorgossos. He didn't understand.

We might only have hours. Maybe less.

All at once, Captain Faber's surrender took on a more dire cast. It was as if the sunlight had changed, or the sun itself had gone behind a cloud. "This has gone on long enough, Captain," I said, falling back on the aristocratic sharpness with which I'd begun our little meeting. "If what you say is true then we haven't much time. If you want your men to live, you will surrender any of these MINOS people still on base and for the love of Earth and all that's holy you will tell me where my legion is."

THE LIVING FAILURES

It was so cold in the depths of the fortress warrens, that I'd had to put my helmet back on. Frost misted the air and massed on the coolant lines bracketed to the walls, reminding me of veins in the limb of some giant. Far above, bay doors of steel and reinforced concrete stood closed to the yellow sky. Through that aperture— hundreds of meters long—the Dardanines had lowered dozens of troop transport units: ugly, rectangular pods each holding two centuries of Imperial legionnaires.

"How many are left?" I asked.

"Thirty-seven, lord," Petros replied.

"That's what? Seventy . . . four hundred soldiers?" I drummed my fingers against my side as I ran the numbers. It wasn't even a third of the full legion. I tried not to imagine where those other men had gone. Turning to where two of Petros's centurions stood near at hand, I said, "One of you: head up top and signal the *Tamerlane*. Tell Aristedes to deploy the cargo lifters, double time. Are we any near to finding the controls for the bay doors?"

I directed that last bit to everyone in the vicinity, voice amplified by my suit's speakers.

A decurion answered in a thin voice, "My lord, we're locked out of the control room."

"Where?"

"Here, lord!"

The door looked to be solid steel, the first in an airlock that separated the landing bay from the inner fortress when the roof was open to the sky. Just as my man had said, the control panel beside the door was blacked out, dead as old stone.

No matter.

"Stand back!" I said, holding out one hand to fend my soldiers away. I drew my sword, kindled the blade. The highmatter cast spectral highlights—white and blue—against the brushed metal walls. Its cutting edge was fine as hydrogen, and I plunged the point through the reinforced steel as easily as through wax paper. Moving steadily, I carved a hole in the door just large enough for a man to step through. The door fell inward with a slamming sound like the unsealing of a tomb, and—sword held out before me—I stepped inside.

Into darkness.

I activated my suit lights, revealing abandoned banks of control consoles and inert projector plates. My men followed me over the threshold, and behind them I heard someone—Siran, possibly— calling for a scout drone. The device whizzed over my shoulder, emitting a faint, ultrasonic whine as the scanning lasers fanned across the room before vanishing through an open door at the far end.

Pausing, I tapped one of the consoles. It flared to life, holograph readout filling the space above the desktop. "Get the techs," I ordered one of the others. "Tell them to get those bay doors open. We need to lift the survivors out, double quick. The rest of you: with me."

Captain Faber had said the MINOS staff had fled the base when we attacked. That had been a lie. We would have noticed any ship attempting to leave Arae when our assault began. There had been none.

They had to be down here somewhere.

I have seen more than my fair share of dark, demon-haunted tunnels in my life. I have said before that light brings order to creation, and that in darkness order grows ever less. The magi teach us that before the First Cause and the cataclysm that birthed the universe there was only Dark, and that it was from that darkness— the infinite chaos and potential that exists in the absence of light—that *anything* might happen. And so *everything* had happened, and the universe had emerged, birthed not—as the ancient pagans would have it—by the declaration of a deity, but born of the limitless chaos that comes in the absence of light.

That is why we fear the Dark. Not for what it contains, but for the threat that it might contain *anything*. Aware of this fact, I pressed down the hall after the drone, following the path laid out in the display at the corner of my vision. Doors opened to either side, revealing storerooms and offices and what reminded me of nothing so much as medical examination rooms. Cold sweat beaded on the back of my neck. A powerful sense of dread settled on me, crouching like a gargoyle. It was almost like being back on Vorgossos, in the dungeons of the Undying.

"My lord!" a voice rang out from behind me, and as I turned, the soldier added, "Over here!"

I joined the man in the arch of a broad doorway opening on a round chamber. The roof above was supported by a single central pillar, and the floor was a tangle of cables, as if someone had pulled apart and rewired several machines in a great hurry.

And then I saw them, sitting in seats around the outer wall, each slumped as if in slumber, hands unfeeling in their laps. There must have been three dozen of them, men and women alike.

None moved.

"Dead?" Siran asked. "Earth and Emperor protect us. What is this?"

Lowering my sword but keeping it lit, I approached the nearest corpse. She didn't look like an Exalted. None of them did. Each of the dead men seemed human enough. On a whim, I flicked my suit's vision from visual light to infrared, saw the cooling nimbus of life's heat fading in her core. "Still warm," I said, and fingered the braided metal cable the dead woman still grasped in both hands, tracing its course from the floor all the way up to the base of her skull. "They're not dead," I said, and with a vindictive turn of my wrist I slashed the cable with my sword. "They're gone."

Two the soldiers nearby made a warding gesture with their first and last fingers extended. One asked, "What do you mean, gone?"

"Synaptic kinesis. I've seen it before." I pointed to the column in the center of the room with my sword. "That's a telegraph relay. This lot wired their brains in and broadcast their minds offworld. Probably to a ship. They'll have new bodies waiting for them." They'd discarded their old ones like sleeves, abandoned them here to rot. The eels churned within me once again, and I turned my head. It was easy to imagine the Exalted growing these bodies for just such a reason: to wear for a time and discard. I was prepared to bet my good right hand that the true owner of the flesh before me was some brain trapped in a bottle up in the black of space like some foul djinni. "Once we get the soldiers out, bring atomics down. None of this can be left. And don't *touch* anything. Who knows what they've left behind."

No sooner had the words left my mouth than a shot rang out, and turning, I saw one of the bodies tumble from its chair with a smoking hole in its chest. "Hold your fire!" I called, raising a hand.

"I thought it moved, sir," the soldier said, voice higher than I'd expected. "Like the ones up top."

"No, soldier. We've nothing to fear from these."

Have I said the universe shares my love of theater?

Something shot out of the darkness and sliced clean through the armorweave at the base of the man's neck. There was no noise save the sigh of impact and the dull smack of blood against the wall behind him, no crack of gunshot or crash of bullet against the wall. He took a moment to fall, and in that space whatever it was hit another of my men.

"Shields up!" Siran bellowed into the sudden stillness.

I saw a flicker of movement out the corner of my eye—the trailing hem of a robe. I started after it, Siran close behind. Had some of

Faber's men not surrendered with the rest? Or had one of the MINOS personnel remained behind when the others fled by their unholy road?

The tunnels ahead were a labyrinth still incompletely mapped. We were near the bottom of the fortress now, almost to where I guessed the geothermal sinks and the power station must be. All the world was low ceilings and blind turnings in the dark, the walls lit only by the rare sconce, fixtures yellow with neglect. I could just make out the sound of soft footfalls on the ground ahead, and skidded round a corner in pursuit. Once or twice I saw a human shape round a bend ahead.

There!

A stunner bolt flew over my shoulder from Siran's hand. Was that a gasp of pain?

"Missed," Siran spat, making the word a curse.

She was right. It must have been a glancing blow, for when we caught up to the next bend there was no one there, but I knew what I had heard. There was a door up ahead on the left, and it stood open. Inside, the shadowed hulks of nameless machines stood in rows.

"Reinforcements are right behind, Had," Siran said. "We should hold."

"And let them escape?" I said, brushing past. I knew what Siran was thinking, that this was some kind of trap. But if what Faber said was true, this whole thing was a trap and the Exalted would be on us in hours.

I stepped inside.

Immediately my shield flashed as the strange bullet impacted against it.

It flashed again. Again. Held. The icon in the side of my vision indicated the shield was still blue.

"You should have hired better mercenaries!" I called out, not seeing my quarry among the slumbering machines. "Your Captain Faber's surrendered!"

"He bought the time we needed!" a cold, high voice returned. "You see my fellows have already escaped." I scanned the darkness ahead of me, but save the tongues of chilly fog twisting in the air, nothing moved. I swept the beam of my suit lamp ahead and above me, searching the narrow catwalks and raw plumbing.

Nothing.

"You work for MINOS?" I asked, signaling for Siran to cover my back.

"I'm certainly not one of Faber's little boys," came the reply. "And I know all about *you*, Lord Marlowe. The Emperor's new pet. Killed one of the Cielcin clan chiefs did you? Is it true you twisted the Undying's arm to do it? The Lord of Vorgossos does not bend easily. I didn't think he could bend at all."

Behind my mask, I smiled.

After a moment's silence, I said, "Who did you sell the legion to?"

No answer.

No surprise.

I tried a different tactic, anything to keep her talking. The longer she kept talking, the better the odds were my reinforcements would catch up. "MINOS produces the Exalted?"

"Abstraction. Body modification. Yes," the voice floated down from above. "We provide design and fabrication work for the captains and the clans. Life extension. Maintenance of the cerebral tissue—some of our clients are thousands of years old, don't you know? Whatever they dream—and can afford—we make real."

Still searching for her, I passed a bit of machinery like a vast, squat drum. Frost rimed its surface, but something there—a glimmer of movement, perhaps?—caught my attention. If there was something inside I could not see it, but I sensed something there the way the swimmer senses the passage of a fish in dark waters.

"What are these?"

"Prototypes," she said. "Failures."

"Failures?" I drew back.

On our private band, Siran said, "I see her, Had. Up and left. She's limping." I looked, and seeing understood why I hadn't seen her sooner. She was far too cold to be human, and my suit's infrared pickups nearly lost her against the awful chill in that room.

"Progress is never without loss."

"On the contrary," I said, and it was my tutor who spoke through me, a response out of childhood, "any progress which is accompanied by loss is no progress at all."

"Spoken just like an Imperial dog."

"Or like someone who reads."

Siran fired, stunner flash splitting the gloom. She struck true, and I heard a clatter as a body hit the catwalk above.

"Good shot!" the woman's voice rang out. "You got me!"

Siran froze before she could start her search of the room's perimeter. Over the comm, I heard her whisper, "What the hell?"

"Some sort of nervous bypass," I answered over the private channel. "Kept her conscious. Is she moving?"

"No."

"Get up there and lock her down before she recovers." That at least explained how the woman had kept running after we shot her in the hall. "We'll put her in fugue and bring her back with the rest."

Not so fast! The woman's voice crackled over the speakers inside my helmet—over the private frequency. Damn these Extrasolarian demoniacs and their machines! *It's you who won't be going anywhere, Lord Marlowe!*

I switched off my communicator with a glance, sealing my suit off from Siran and the datasphere. The last thing I needed was this Extra woman crawling around in my armor's infrastructure, shutting off my cameras or my air. I had visions of being trapped there, locked and blind in my suit, waiting to be found by the Extras Faber warned us were coming. An unceremonious end to Hadrian Marlowe, Knight Victorian.

But the MINOS woman had something else in mind.

A light cold and blue as forgotten stars blazed in the drum—the tank—before me, and a moment later something huge and heavy thumped the glass *from the inside.* Hairline cracks spiderwebbed from the point of impact, and I lurched backwards, scrambling to put as much space between myself and the *thing,* the *failure,* that lurked in the woman's tank.

It struck again and the glass *splintered.* Super-cooled fluid flooded out, changing the air to a thick, white fog that dragged the *thing* within outward like an unborn calf from the corpse of a stranded whale. The thing within lurched on unsteady limbs, hands and feet of steel clanging, scraping the ground as it struggled to rise, to right itself.

Words fled me, and my mind with them, and for a single, terrible moment it seemed I stood once more upon the shore of the sea beneath Vorgossos, with that great daimon of the ancient world rising to meet me.

"Hadrian!" a voice cried out. Siran's voice—and I remembered.

Remembered who I was and what I was there to do.

Remembered the sword in my hand.

The failure pushed itself to its feet, and hunched and lurching as it was, still it towered over me: ten feet or twelve of white metal and jointed bone. It had no face that I could see, for like the helms of our legionnaires its visage was blank and pitiless as ice. It lunged towards me, clawed hands outstretched, but it lost its footing and crashed to its knees. One of the arms bifurcated, the upper half folding up and out from its shoulder like the pinion of some dreadful wing. Seeing my chance, I lunged, hewing at the creature's arm. The highmatter blade bounced off, ringing my hand like a bell. Wincing, I recoiled, boots unsteady in the rapidly warming coolant. I might have known. I had fought the Exalted before, on Vorgossos and after, and I should have guessed this creature's body would be proof against highmatter, forged of adamant or some composite whose molecules would not be cut.

I bared my teeth.

Things had just gotten a great deal more difficult.

Siran opened fire, violet plasma scorching the side of its head. She might have been throwing rocks at the Horse for all the good it did. The beast turned to look at her, and I fancied I could see the wheels of its still-organic mind turning. I could see common metal shining in the elbow and shoulder joints, beneath the armored carapace. It had weaknesses. I took a measuring step closer, hoping to try to my luck. I didn't make it far. The third arm that sprouted from the top of its shoulder whipped round like a peasant's scythe so fast it *vanished*. My reflexive flinch was far too late, and I was saved the impact only by the energy curtain of my shield flashing about me.

Letting out a piercing cry, the living failure rose once more to its feet, one leg sliding out from under it. This time it steadied itself, one massive hand striking the wall of the tank beside it. I wondered what was wrong with it. Something in the way the Exalted's mind interfaced with its new machine body? Something that made it slip and stagger so?

"Stand aside, beast," I said, aiming my sword at it like an accusing finger. I had fought worse and more dangerous creatures than this.

The beast howled again and cracked its third arm like a whip as it advanced, loping forward on legs bent like a dog's. As a young man in the coliseum on Emesh, I had battled azhdarchs and ophids, manticores and gene-tailored lions large as elephants. And once, after our victory on Pharos, I had faced a charging bull with no shield and only a rapier for defense.

The principle here was the same.

By rights, the abomination ought to have been faster than me, fast almost as that evil appendage that sprouted claw-like from its shoulder. By rights, I should already have been no more than a dark smear on the floor of that hall.

Siran shot it in the head, for all the good it did. The creature shook it off like a slap. There was something in the way it shook its head that was familiar to me, pulling its ear towards its shoulder in sharp, repeated movements. I had no time to think about it, only about the way its fist slammed down like the hand of God. I threw myself sideways, aiming a desperate cut at the side of one knee. The blade pinged off the metal, and just like the bull on Pharos I swung round my enemy like a gate about its hinge, undoing the magnetic clasp of my cape as I went and tossing the garment aside.

"Go find the doctor, Siran!" I ordered. "Don't let her get away!"

"And leave you?"

"Go!" I ducked a mighty swipe of the creature's arm and stepped forward. I'd seen a slight gap where the ribs ought to be, between the armored breastplate and the interleaved segments that passed for a stomach. How thin it was! Too long and too narrow to be human anymore. If I could get the point of my blade in that gap . . . there might be something underneath, some delicate system or piece of the mostly discarded flesh.

I did not find out.

The *knee* lanced out to meet me. Not fast—certainly not fast enough to engage my body shield—but it did not need to be fast. The knee was titanium wrapped in adamant and zircon. There were softer statues.

My armor alone saved my ribs and the heart and lungs beneath them, but the wind was driven from me. I flew backwards as if thrown and struck the wall behind me so hard I imagined the dull metal cracking like glass—or maybe that was only my skull.

Where were the others?

My vision slipped and blurred, righted itself only when I forced myself to slow my breathing and the mutinous hammering of my heart. It was coming, and there I was resting with my back against the wall like some derelict watchman. It leaped towards me, and it was all I could do to roll away as the machine collided bodily with the wall just where my head had been. I regained my feet, glad of the positive pressure in the suit forcing air into my lungs.

There!

Before the beast could turn, I lunged, the point of my sword burying itself in the back of the Exalted's knee. Common metal parted like paper, and a violently white fluid bled out, running down the ivory calf to the floor. The scythe-arm lashed against my shield then, and slowly began to wind itself about me. I stumbled backwards, but the thing wound itself about my chest. I could feel the thermal layer hardening to protect against the pressure. The creature turned, reached down towards my face with a six-fingered hand.

Six-fingered.

"Iukatta!" In my winded state, the word was little more than a whisper, but my suit amplified it to a shout. *Stop!*

The beast dropped me, surprise evident in the way it just *stood* there.

"Nietolo ba-emanyn ne?" the creature asked. The alien within the machine. *You speak our language?*

I made the sharp sound that passed for *yes* in their tongue. The Cielcin tongue. "What have they done to you?" It wasn't possible. The Cielcin and the Extrasolarians . . . working together? But no, the Cielcin clans had been dealing with the Extras since before they invaded the Empire—since before we had even known they existed. That they would work together against the Empire should not have surprised me, and yet . . . seeing the xenobite standing there encased in so much Extrasolarian kit . . . I felt a thrill of holy terror.

The creature's blank faceplate opened like a jewel box and folded away, revealing the milk-white flesh; the eyes like twin spots of ink on new paper, large as my fists; and the teeth like shattered glass. "They have made us strong," it said, gnashing its teeth. "Strong enough to defeat you *yukajjimn*." *Vermin,* it said. Its word for human.

"Strong?" I echoed, drawing back, putting distance once again between me and this Cielcin-machine hybrid, demon and daimon. "You can hardly stand." And no wonder. MINOS and the Exalted had had thousands of years to perfect the systems that bonded man to machine. The Cielcin were not men.

"We were only the first."

In the quiet of my heart, I imagined armies of such creatures falling from the sky to sack world after imperial world. Dust to dust by the million, humans carried back to the stars and the dark ships the Cielcin called home. I remembered the slaves I had seen, mutilated by their alien masters, and I knew at once what had happened to the rest of our lost legion. MINOS had offered them to their Cielcin friends in payment or in tribute. They were dead, and worse than dead: still living. This was something new. In all my years of fighting, this was something I had never expected: the black marriage of Cielcin and machine.

"Who is your master?" I demanded. "Which clan? Which prince?"

"You cannot stop him. Or his White Hand."

"Iedyr Yemani?" I repeated the words *white hand,* not sure I had heard them correctly. Not sure I understood. "Who is *he?*" Its prince, certainly. Its master.

"He will tear your worlds from the sky, human!" the Cielcin roared, and beat its chest with its hands. "He has conquered an army for himself, and he is coming!" Then the creature pounced, thinking me distracted. But I was ready, and lunging, aimed my sword at the creature's unprotected face. It was my only chance. My only hope was that whatever was *wrong* with the hybrid would slow it down. As it hurtled towards me, claws outstretched, I saw the visor begin to close like an eyelid snapping shut. The adamantine faceplate slammed with the point of my sword caught between its flanges, and almost the weapon was wrenched from my hand. I grinned savagely.

It had worked *exactly* as I'd planned.

The beast landed badly, and its ruined knee went out from under it. It fell with a crash, and I leaned all my weight against the hilt of my sword. I bared my teeth, eyes stretched wide as I pushed the sword downwards. The point moved only slowly, metal grinding against liquid metal as the highmatter sank home, piercing flesh and bone. And brain.

Like a muscle relaxing, the visor fell open once again, revealing the neat hole between the massive eyes, and the black blood running like tears.

I found Siran and the MINOS doctor moments later. My fears were justified. The doctor—a small, gray woman dressed in white—had indeed possessed some implant or artifice that had saved her from the stun. While I'd been distracted with her *experiment,* she had crawled along the catwalk to a room overlooking her lab.

Siran handed me the gun as I entered, cape firmly back in place. It was a strange thing, silver and strangely organic. I looked down at the body at my feet and the name embroidered above the breast pocket of her lab coat.

"Severine," I read aloud, eyes wandering to the perfectly round hole she'd punched through the bottom of her jaw and out the top of her head. She had carefully missed the delicate hardware at the base of her skull. "She escaped then?"

"Like the others?" Siran asked. "Guess so. By Earth, Had. This shit's beyond me." Her blank-visored face turned up to look at me, looking for all the world not so different from the helmet of the creature I had slain. "Are you all right?"

I caught myself rubbing my hands—as if trying to remove some spot on the black gloves. "They were mingling the Cielcin with machines. That's what that thing was."

"Are you serious?" I could imagine the look of shock on her face, eyes white and wide in the dimness.

"The body is just down there," I gestured to the room below. "We'll need to bring it back with us, and everything we can get from these machines." Breaking off, I looked round at the banks of computers rising all about us, the machines through which the ghost of Dr. Severine and her fellows had escaped. "The Cielcin said its master had raised an army. That it was coming for us."

The centurion—my friend—moved to stand beside me, her arms crossed. "The Cielcin have been invading for hundreds of years. That's nothing new."

"No," I said, shaking my head. "This time it's different." I let my hands fall, looked back through the open door to where the failed hybrid lay on the floor. "A Cielcin prince willing to work with the Extras . . . The world is changing."

"Lord Marlowe!" a voice rang out from below, "Lord Marlowe!" The questing beams of suit lights blazed up from below. My men had found us. Too little. Too late.

I did not step out to speak to them at once, but turned to Siran. "Something's coming. Mark my words. This war of ours is about to get a good deal worse."

The rebels had been conquering Earth's colonies with frightening success until they were poised to attack the mother planet Earth itself. The troops in their spaceworthy battle suits were ready to fight off the latest attack, but could they defeat the enemy's matter transmitter technology, which could bring warships and whole armies across hundreds of light-years in the blink of an eye?

Or Battle's Sound

Harry Harrison

I

"Combatman Dom Priego, I shall kill you." Sergeant Toth shouted the words the length of the barracks compartment.

Dom, stretched out on his bunk and reading a book, raised startled eyes just as the Sergeant snapped his arm down, hurling a gleaming combat knife. Trained reflexes raised the book, and the knife thudded into it, penetrating the pages so that the point stopped a scant few inches from Dom's face.

"You stupid Hungarian ape!" he shouted. "Do you know what this book cost me? Do you know how old it is?"

"Do you know that you are still alive?" the Sergeant answered, a trace of a cold smile wrinkling the corners of his cat's eyes. He stalked down the gangway, like a predatory animal, and reached for the handle of the knife.

"No you don't," Dom said, snatching the book away. "You've done enough damage already." He put the book flat on the bunk and worked the knife carefully out of it—then threw it suddenly at the Sergeant's foot.

Sergeant Toth shifted his leg just enough so that the knife missed him and struck the plastic deck covering instead. "Temper, combatman," he said. "You should never lose your temper. That way you make mistakes, get killed." He bent and plucked out the shining

65

blade and held it balanced in his fingertips. As he straightened up, there was a rustle as the other men in the barracks compartment shifted weight, ready to move, all eyes on him. He laughed.

"Now you're expecting it, so it's too easy for you." He slid the knife back into his boot sheath.

"You're a sadistic bowb," Dom said, smoothing down the cut in the book's cover. "Getting a great pleasure out of frightening other people."

"Maybe," Sergeant Toth said, undisturbed. He sat on the bunk across the aisle. "And maybe that's what they call the right man in the right job. And it doesn't matter anyway. I train you, keep you alert, on the jump. This keeps you alive. You should thank me for being such a good sadist."

"You can't sell me with that argument, Sergeant. You're the sort of individual this man wrote about, right here in this book that you did your best to destroy..."

"Not me. You put it in front of the knife. Just like I keep telling you pinkies. Save yourself. That's what counts. Use any trick. You only got one life, make it a long one."

"Right in here..."

"Pictures of girls?"

"No, Sergeant, words. Great words by a man you never heard of, by the name of Wilde."

"Sure. Plugger. Wyld, fleet heavyweight champion."

"No, Oscar Fingal O'Flahertie Wills Wilde. No relation to your pug—I hope. He writes, 'As long as war is regarded as wicked, it will always have its fascination. When it is looked upon as vulgar, it will cease to be popular.'"

Sergeant Toth's eyes narrowed in thought. "He makes it sound simple. But it's not that way at all. There are other reasons for war."

"Such as what...?"

The Sergeant opened his mouth to answer, but his voice was drowned in the wave of sound from the scramble alert. The high-pitched hooting blared in every compartment of the spacer and had its instant response. Men moved. Fast.

The ship's crew raced to their action stations. The men who had been asleep just an instant before were still blinking awake as they ran. They ran and stood, and before the alarm was through sounding the great spaceship was ready.

Not so the combatmen. Until ordered and dispatched, they were just cargo. They stood at the ready, a double row of silver-gray uniforms, down the center of the barracks compartment. Sergeant Toth was at the wall, his headset plugged into a phone extension there, listening attentively, nodding at an unheard voice. Every man's eyes were upon him as he spoke agreement, disconnected and turned slowly to face them. He savored the silent moment, then broke into the widest grin that any of them had ever seen on his normally expressionless face.

"This is it," the Sergeant said, and actually rubbed his hands together. "I can tell you now that the Edinburgers were expected and that our whole fleet is up in force. The scouts have detected them breaking out of jump space, and they should be here in about two hours. We're going out to meet them. This, you pinkie combat virgins, is it." A sound, like a low growl, rose from the assembled men, and the Sergeant's grin widened.

"That's the right spirit. Show some of it to the enemy." The grin vanished as quickly as it had come, and, cold-faced as always, he called the ranks to attention.

"Corporal Steres is in sick bay with the fever so we're one NCO short. When that alert sounded we went into combat condition. I may now make temporary field appointments. I do so. Combatman Priego, one pace forward." Dom snapped to attention and stepped out of rank.

"You're now in charge of the bomb squad. Do the right job and the CO will make it permanent. Corporal Priego, one step back and wait here. The rest of you to the ready room, double time—*march*."

Sergeant Toth stepped aside as the combatmen hurried from the compartment. When the last one had gone he pointed his finger sharply at Dom.

"Just one word. You're as good as any man here. Better than most. You're smart. But you think too much about things that don't matter. Stop thinking and start fighting, or you'll never get back to that university. Bowb up, and if the Edinburgers don't get you I will. You come back as a corporal or you don't come back at all. Understood?"

"Understood." Dom's face was as coldly expressionless as the Sergeant's.

"I'm just as good a combatman as you are, Sergeant. I'll do my job."

"Then do it—now *jump*."

Because of the delay. Dom was the last man to be suited up. The others were already doing their pressure checks with the armorers while he was still closing his seals. He did not let it disturb him or make him try to move faster. With slow deliberation, he counted off the check list as he sealed and locked.

Once all the pressure checks were in the green, Dom gave the armorers the thumbs-up okay and walked to the air lock. While the door closed behind him and the lock was pumped out, he checked all the telltales in his helmet. Oxygen, full. Power pack, full charge. Radio, one and one. Then the last of the air was gone, and the inner door opened soundlessly in the vacuum. He entered the armory.

The lights here were dimmer—and soon they would be turned off completely. Dom went to the rack with his equipment and began to buckle on the smaller items. Like all of the others on the bomb squad, his suit was lightly armored and he carried only the most essential weapons. The drillger went on his left thigh, just below his fingers, and the gropener in its holster on the outside of his right leg; this was his favorite weapon. The intelligence reports had stated that some of the Edinburgers still used fabric pressure suits, so lightning prods—usually considered obsolete—had been issued. He slung his well to the rear, since the chance that he might need it was very slim. All of these murderous devices had been stored in the evacuated and insulated compartment for months so that their temperature approached absolute zero. They were free of lubrication and had been designed to operate at this temperature.

A helmet clicked against Dom's, and Wing spoke, his voice carried by conducting transparent ceramic.

"I'm ready for my bomb, Dom—do you want to sling it? And congratulations. Do I have to call you Corporal now?"

"Wait until we get back and it's official. I take Toth's word for absolutely nothing."

He slipped the first atomic bomb from the shelf, checked the telltales to see that they were all in the green, then slid it into the rack that was an integral part of Wing's suit. "All set, now we can sling mine."

❈ ❈ ❈

They had just finished when a large man in bulky combat armor came up. Dom would have known him by his size even if he had not read HELMUTZ stenciled on the front of his suit.

"What is it, Helm?" he asked when their helmets touched.

"The Sergeant. He said I should report to you, that I'm lifting a bomb on this mission." There was an angry tone behind his words.

"Right. We'll fix you up with a back sling." The big man did not look happy, and Dom thought he knew why. "And don't worry about missing any of the fighting. There'll be enough for everyone."

"I'm a combatman."

"We're all combatmen. All working for one thing—to deliver the bombs. That's your job now."

Helmutz did not act convinced and stood with stolid immobility while they rigged the harness and bomb onto the back of his suit. Before they were finished, their headphones crackled and a stir went through the company of suited men as a message came over the command frequency.

"Are you suited and armed? Are you ready for illumination adjustment?"

"Combatmen suited and armed." That was Sergeant Toth's voice.

"Bomb squad not ready," Dom said, and they hurried to make the last fastenings, aware that the rest were waiting for them.

"Bomb squad suited and armed."

"Lights."

II

As the command rang out, the bulkhead lights faded out until the darkness was broken only by the dim red lights in the ceiling above. Until their eyes became adjusted, it was almost impossible to see. Dom groped his way to one of the benches, found the oxygen hose with his fingers and plugged it into the side of his helmet; this would conserve his tank oxygen during the wait. Brisk music was being played over the command circuit now as part of morale sustaining. Here in the semidarkness, suited and armed, the waiting could soon become nerve-racking. Everything was done to alleviate the pressure. The music faded, and a voice replaced it.

"This is your executive officer speaking. I'm going to try and keep you in the picture as to what is happening up here. The Edinburgers are attacking in fleet strength and, soon after they were sighted, their ambassador declared that a state of war exists. He asks that Earth surrender at once or risk the consequences. Well, you all know what the answer to that one was. The Edinburgers have invaded and conquered twelve settled planets already and incorporated them into their Greater Celtic Co-prosperity Sphere. Now they're getting greedy and going for the big one—Earth itself, the planet their ancestors left a hundred generations ago. In doing this . . . Just a moment, I have a battle report here . . . first contact with our scouts."

The officer stopped for a moment, then his voice picked up again.

"Fleet strength, but no larger than we expected and we will be able to handle them. But there is one difference in their tactics, and the combat computer is analyzing this now. They were the ones who originated the MT invasion technique, landing a number of cargo craft on a planet, all of them loaded with matter-transmitter screens. As you know, the invading forces attack through these screens direct from their planet to the one that is to be conquered. Well, they've changed their technique now. This entire fleet is protecting a *single* ship, a Kriger-class scout carrier. What this means . . . Hold on, here is the readout from the combat computer. *Only possibility single ship landing area increase MT screen breakthrough,* that's what it says. Which means that there is a good chance that this ship may be packing a *single* large MT screen, bigger than anything ever built before. If this is so—and they get the thing down to the surface— they can fly heavy bombers right through it, fire pre-aimed ICBMs, send through troop carriers, anything. If this happens the invasion will be successful."

Around him, in the red-lit darkness, Dom was aware of the other suited figures who stirred silently as they heard the words.

"*If* this happens." There was a ring of authority now in the executive officer's voice. "The Edinburgers have developed the only way to launch an interplanetary invasion. We have found the way to stop it. You combatmen are the answer. They have now put all their eggs in one basket—and you are going to take that basket to pieces. You can get through where attack ships or missiles could not. We're

closing fast now, and you will be called to combat stations soon. So—
go out there and do your job. The fate of Earth rides with you."

Melodramatic words, Dom thought, yet they were true.
Everything, the ships, the concentration of fire power, all depended
on them. The alert alarm cut through his thoughts, and he snapped
to attention.

"Disconnect oxygen. Fall out when your name is called and
proceed to the firing room in the order called. Toth..."

The names were spoken quickly, and the combatmen moved out.
At the entrance to the firing room a suited man with a red-globed
light checked the names on their chests against his roster to make
sure they were in the correct order. Everything moved smoothly,
easily, just like a drill, because the endless drills had been designed
to train them for just this moment. The firing room was familiar,
though they had never been there before, because their trainer had
been an exact duplicate of it. The combatman ahead of Dom went
to port, so he moved to starboard. The man preceding him was just
climbing into a capsule, and Dom waited while the armorer helped
him down into it and adjusted the armpit supports. Then it was his
turn, and Dom slipped into the transparent plastic shell and settled
against the seat as he seized the handgrips. The armorer pulled the
supports hard up into his armpits, and he nodded when they seated
right. A moment later, the man was gone, and he was alone in the
semidarkness with the dim red glow shining on the top ring of the
capsule that was just above his head. There was a sudden shudder,
and he gripped hard, just as the capsule started forward.

As it moved, it tilted backwards until he was lying on his back,
looking up through the metal rings that banded his plastic shell. His
capsule was moved sideways, jerked to a stop, then moved again.
Now the gun was visible, a half dozen capsules ahead of his, and he
thought, as he always did during training, how like an ancient quick-
firing cannon the gun was—a cannon that fired human beings. Every
two seconds, the charging mechanism seized a capsule from one of
the alternate feed belts, whipped it to the rear of the gun where it
instantly vanished into the breech. Then another and another. The
one ahead of Dom disappeared and he braced himself—and the
mechanism suddenly and for no apparent reason halted.

※ ※ ※

There was a flicker of fear that something had gone wrong with the complex gun, before he realized that all of the first combatmen had been launched and that the computer was waiting a determined period of time for them to prepare the way for the bomb squad. His squad now, the men he would lead.

Waiting was harder than moving as he looked at the black mouth of the breech. The computer would be ticking away the seconds now, while at the same time tracking the target and keeping the ship aimed to the correct trajectory. Once he was in the gun, the magnetic field would seize the rings that banded his capsule, and the linear accelerator of the gun would draw him up the evacuated tube that penetrated the entire length of the great ship from stern to bow. Faster and faster the magnetic fields would pull him until he left the mouth of the gun at the correct speed and on the correct trajectory to . . .

His capsule was whipped up in a tight arc and shoved into the darkness. Even as he gripped tight on the handholds, the pressure pads came up and hit him. He could not measure the time—he could not see and he could not breathe as the brutal acceleration pressed down on him. Hard, harder than anything he had ever experienced in training; he had that one thought, and then he was out of the gun.

In a single instant he went from acceleration to weightlessness, and he gripped hard so he would not float away from the capsule. There was a puff of vapor from the unheard explosions; he felt them through his feet, and the metal rings were blown in half, and the upper portion of the capsule shattered and hurled away. Now he was alone, weightless, holding to the grips that were fastened to the rocket unit beneath his feet. He looked about for the space battle that he knew was in progress and felt a slight disappointment that there was so little to see.

Something burned far off to his right, and there was a wavering in the brilliant points of the stars as some dark object occulted them and passed on. This was a battle of computers and instruments at great distances. There was very little for the unaided eye to see. The spaceships were black and swift and—for the most part—thousands of miles away. They were firing homing rockets and proximity shells, also just as swift and invisible. He knew that space around him was filled with signal jammers and false-signal generators, but none of this was visible. Even the target vessel toward which he was rushing was invisible.

For all that his limited senses could tell, he was alone in space, motionless, forgotten.

Something shuddered against the soles of his boots, and a jet of vapor shot out and vanished from the rocket unit. No, he was neither motionless nor forgotten. The combat computer was still tracking the target ship and had detected some minute variation from its predicted path. At the same time, the computer was following the progress of his trajectory, and it made the slight correction for this new data. Corrections must be going out at the same time to all the other combatmen in space, before and behind him. They were small and invisible—doubly invisible now that the metal rings had been shed. There was no more than an eighth of a pound of metal dispersed through the plastics and ceramics of a combatman's equipment. Radar could never pick them out from among all the interference. They should get through.

Jets blasted again, and Dom saw that the stars were turning above his head. Touchdown soon; the tiny radar in his rocket unit had detected a mass ahead and had directed that he be turned end for end. Once this was done he knew that the combat computer would cut free and turn control over to the tiny set-down computer that was part of his radar. His rockets blasted, strong now, punching the supports up against him, and he looked down past his feet at the growing dark shape that occulted the stars.

With a roar, loud in the silence, his headphones burst into life.

"Went, went—gone hungry. Went, went—gone hungry."

The silence grew again, but in it Dom no longer felt alone. The brief message had told him a lot.

Firstly, it was Sergeant Toth's voice; there was no mistaking that. Secondly, the mere act of breaking radio silence showed that they had engaged the enemy and that their presence was known. The code was a simple one that would be meaningless to anyone outside their company. Translated, it said that fighting was still going on but the advance squads were holding their own. They had captured the center section of the hull—always the best place to rendezvous since it was impossible to tell bow from stern in the darkness—and were holding it, awaiting the arrival of the bomb squad. The retrorockets flared hard and long, and the rocket unit crashed sharply into the black hull. Dom jumped free and rolled.

III

As he came out of the roll, he saw a suited figure looming above him, clearly outlined by the disk of the sun despite his black nonreflective armor. The top of the helmet was smooth. Even as he realized this, Dom was pulling the gropener from its holster.

A cloud of vapor sprang out, and the man vanished behind it. Dom was surprised, but he did not hesitate. Handguns, even recoilless ones like this that sent the burnt gas out to the sides, were a hazard in null-G space combat. Guns were not only difficult to aim but either had a recoil that would throw the user back out of position or the gas had to be vented sideways, when they would blind the user for vital moments. A fraction of a second was all a trained combatman needed.

As the gropener swung free, Dom thumbed the jet button lightly. The device was shaped like a short sword, but it had a vibrating saw blade where one sharpened edge should be, with small jets mounted opposite it in place of the outer edge. The jets drove the device forward, pulling him after it. As soon as it touched the other man's leg, he pushed the jets full on. As the vibrating ceramic blade speeded up, the force of the jets pressed it into the thin armor.

In less than a second, it had cut its way through and on into the flesh of the leg inside. Dom pressed the reverse jet to pull away as vapor gushed out, condensing to ice particles instantly, and his opponent writhed, clutched at his thigh—then went suddenly limp.

Dom's feet touched the hull, and the soles adhered. He realized that the entire action had taken place in the time it took him to straighten out from his roll and stand up....

Don't think, act. Training. As soon as his feet adhered, he crouched and turned, looking about him. A heavy power ax sliced by just above his head, towing its wielder after it.

Act, don't think. His new opponent was on his left side, away from the gropener, and was already reversing the direction of his ax. A man has two hands. The drillger on his left thigh! Even as he remembered it, he had it in his hand, drill on and hilt-jet flaring. The foot-long, diamond-hard drill spun fiercely—its rotation cancelled by the counter-revolving weight in the hilt—while the jet drove it forward.

It went into the Edinburger's midriff, scarcely slowing as it tore a hole in the armor and plunged inside. As his opponent folded, Dom thumbed the reverse jet to push the drillger out. The power ax, still with momentum from the last blast of its jet, tore free of the dying man's hand and vanished into space.

There were no other enemies in sight. Dom tilted forward on one toe so that the surface film on the boot sole was switched from adhesive to neutral, then he stepped forward slowly. Walking like this took practice, but he had had that. Ahead was a group of dark figures lying prone on the hull, and he took the precaution of raising his hand to touch the horn on the top of his helmet so there would be no mistakes. This identification had been agreed upon just a few days ago and the plastic spikes glued on. The Edinburgers all had smooth-topped helmets.

Dom dived forward between the scattered forms and slid, face down. Before his body could rebound from the hull, he switched on his belly-sticker, and the surface film there held him flat. Secure for the moment among his own men, he thumbed the side of his helmet to change frequencies. There was now a jumble of noise through most of the frequencies, messages—both theirs and the enemy's— jamming, the false messages being broadcast by recorder units to cover the real exchange of information. There was scarcely any traffic on the bomb-squad frequency, and he waited for a clear spot. His men would have heard Toth's message, so they knew where to gather. Now he could bring them to him.

"Quasar, quasar, quasar," he called, then counted carefully for ten seconds before he switched on the blue bulb on his shoulder. He stood as he did this, let it burn for a single second, then dropped back to the hull before he could draw any fire. His men would be looking for the light and would assemble on it. One by one they began to crawl out of the darkness. He counted them as they appeared. A combatman, without the bulge of a bomb on his back, ran up and dived and slid, so that his helmet touched Dom's.

"How many, Corporal?" Toth's voice asked.

"One still missing but . . ."

"No buts. We move now. Set your charge and blow as soon as you have cover."

He was gone before Dom could answer. But he was right. They could not afford to wait for one man and risk the entire operation. Unless they moved soon, they would be trapped and killed up here. Individual combats were still going on about the hull, but it would not be long before the Edinburgers realized these were just holding actions and that the main force of attackers was gathered in strength. The bomb squad went swiftly and skillfully to work laying the ring of shaped charges.

The rear guards must have been called in, because the heavy weapons opened fire suddenly on all sides. These were .30-calibre high-velocity recoilless machine guns. Before firing, the gunners had traversed the hull, aiming for a grazing fire that was as close to the surface as possible. The gun computer remembered this and now fired along the selected pattern, aiming automatically. This was needed because, as soon as the firing began, clouds of gas jetted out, obscuring everything. Sergeant Toth appeared out of the smoke and shouted as his helmet touched Dom's.

"Haven't you blown it yet?"

"Ready now, get back."

"Make it fast. They're all down or dead now out there. But they will throw something heavy into this smoke soon, now that they have us pinpointed."

The bomb squad drew back, fell flat, and Dom pressed the igniter. Flames and gas exploded high, while the hull hammered up at them. Through the smoke rushed up a solid column of air, clouding and freezing into tiny crystals as it hit the vacuum. The ship was breached now, and they would keep it that way, blowing open the sealed compartments and bulkheads to let out the atmosphere. Dom and the Sergeant wriggled through the smoke together, to the edge of the wide, gaping hole that had been blasted in the ship's skin.

"Hotside, hotside!" the Sergeant shouted, and dived through the opening.

Dom pushed a way through the rush of men who were following

the Sergeant and assembled his squad. He was still one man short. A weapons man with his machine gun on his back hurried by and leapt into the hole, with his ammunition carriers right behind him. The smoke cloud was growing because some of the guns were still firing, acting as a rear guard. It was getting hard to see the opening now. When Dom had estimated that half of the men had gone through, he led his own squad forward.

They pushed down into a darkened compartment, a storeroom of some kind, and saw a combatman at a hole about one hundred yards from them. "I'm glad you're here," he said as soon as Dom's helmet touched his. "We tried to the right first but there's too much resistance. Just holding them there."

Dom led his men in a floating run, the fastest movement possible in a null-G situation. The corridor was empty for the moment, dimly lit by the emergency bulbs. Holes had been blasted in the walls at regular intervals, to open the sealed compartments and empty them of air, as well as to destroy wiring and piping. As they passed one of the ragged-edged openings, spacesuited men erupted from it.

Dom dived under the thrust of a drillger, swinging his gropener out at the same time. It caught his attacker in the midriff, just as the man's other hand came up. The Edinburger folded and died, and a sharp pain lanced through Dom's leg. He looked down at the nipoff that was fastened to his calf and was slowly severing it.

The nipoff was an outmoded design for use against unarmored suits. It was killing him. The two curved blades were locked around his leg, and the tiny, geared-down motor was slowly closing them. Once started, the device could not be stopped.

It could be destroyed. Even as he realized this, he swung down his gropener and jammed it against the nipoff's handle. The pain intensified at the sideways pressure, and he almost blacked out. He attempted to ignore it. Vapor puffed out around the blades, and he triggered the compression ring on his thigh that sealed the leg from the rest of the suit. Then the gropener cut through the casing. There was a burst of sparks, and the motion of the closing of the blades stopped.

When Dom looked up, the brief battle was over and the counterattackers were dead. The rear guard had caught up and pushed over them. Helmutz must have accounted for more than one of them himself. He held his power ax high, fingers just touching the buttons in the haft so that the jets above the blade spurted alternately to swing the ax to and fro. There was blood on both blades.

IV

Dom switched on his radio; it was silent on all bands. The interior communication circuits of the ship were knocked out here, and the metal walls damped all radio signals.

"Report," he said. "How many did we lose?"

"You're hurt," Wing said, bending over him. "Want me to pull that thing off?"

"Leave it. The tips of the blades are almost touching, and you'd tear half my leg off. It's frozen in with the blood, and I can still get around. Lift me up."

The leg was getting numb now, with the blood supply cut off and the air replaced by vacuum. That was all for the best. He took the roll count.

"We've lost two men but we still have more than enough bombs for this job. Now let's move."

Sergeant Toth himself was waiting at the next corridor, where another hole had been blasted in the deck. He looked at Dom's leg but said nothing.

"How is it going?" Dom asked.

"Fair. We took some losses. We gave them more. Engineer says we are over the main hold now, so we are going straight down, pushing out men on each level to hold. Get going."

"And you?"

"I'll bring down the rear guard and pull the men from each level as we pass. You see that you have a way out for us when we all get down to you."

"You can count on that."

Dom floated out over the hole, then gave a strong kick with his good leg against the ceiling when he was lined up. He went down smoothly, and his squad followed. They passed one deck, two, then three. The openings had been nicely aligned for a straight drop.

There was a flare of light and a burst of smoke ahead as another deck was blown through. Helmutz passed Dom, going faster, having pushed off harder with both legs. He was a full deck ahead when he plunged through the next opening, and the burst of high-velocity machine-gun fire almost cut him in two. He folded in the middle, dead in the instant, the impact of the bullets driving him sideways and out of sight in the deck below.

Dom thumbed the jets on the gropener, and it pulled him aside before he followed the combatman.

"Bomb squad, disperse," he ordered. "Troops coming through." He switched to the combat frequency and looked up at the ragged column of men dropping down toward him.

"The deck below had been retaken. I am at the last occupied deck."

He waved his hand to indicate who was talking, and the stream of men began to jet their weapons and move on by him. "They're below me. The bullets came from this side." The combatmen pushed on without a word.

The metal flooring shook as another opening was blasted somewhere behind him. The continuous string of men moved by. A few seconds later a helmeted figure—with a horned helmet—appeared below and waved the all-clear. The drop continued.

On the bottom deck, the men were all jammed almost shoulder to shoulder, and more were arriving all the time.

"Bomb squad here, give me a report," Dom radioed. A combatman with a napboard slung at his waist pushed back out of the crowd.

"We reached the cargo hold—it's immense—but we're being pushed back. Just by weight of numbers. The Edinburgers are desperate. They are putting men through the MT screen in light pressure suits. Unarmored, almost unarmed. We kill them easily enough but they have pushed us out bodily. They're coming right from the invasion planet. Even when we kill them, the bodies block the way..."

"You the engineer?"

"Yes."

"Whereabouts in the hold is the MT screen?"

"It runs the length of the hold and is back against the far wall."

"Controls?"

"On the left side."

"Can you lead us over or around the hold so we can break in near the screen?"

The engineer took a single look at charts.

"Yes, around. Through the engine room. We can blast through close to the controls."

"Let's go then." Dom switched to combat frequency and waved his arm over his head. "All combatmen who can see me—this way. We're going to make a flank attack."

They moved down the long corridor as fast as they could, with the combatmen ranging out ahead of the bomb squad. There were sealed pressure doors at regular intervals, but these were bypassed by blasting through the bulkheads at the side. There was resistance and there were more dead as they advanced—dead from both sides. Then a group of men gathered ahead, and Dom floated up to the greatly depleted force of combatmen who had forced their way this far. A corporal touched his helmet to Dom's, pointing to a great sealed door at the corridor's end.

"The engine room is behind there. These walls are thick. Everyone off to one side, because we must use an octupled charge."

They dispersed, and the bulkheads heaved and buckled when the charge exploded. Dom, looking toward the corridor, saw a sheet of flame sear by, followed by a column of air that turned instantly to sparkling granules of ice. The engine room had still been pressurized.

There had been no warning, and most of the crewmen had not had their helmets sealed. They were violently and suddenly dead. The few survivors were killed quickly when they offered resistance with improvised weapons. Dom scarcely noticed this as he led his bomb squad after the engineer.

"That doorway is not on my charts," the engineer said, angrily, as though the spy who had stolen the information was at fault. "It must have been added after construction."

"Where does it go to?" Dom asked.

"The MT hold, no other place is possible."

Dom thought quickly. "I'm going to try and get to the MT controls without fighting. I need a volunteer to go with me. If we remove identification and wear Edinburger equipment we should be able to do it."

"I'll join you," the engineer said.

"No, you have a different job. I want a good combatman."

"Me," a man said, pushing through the others. "Pimenov, best in my squad. Ask anybody."

"Let's make this fast."

The disguise was simple. With the identifying spike knocked off their helmets and enemy equipment slung about them, they would pass any casual examination. A handful of grease obscured the names on their chests.

"Stay close behind and come fast when I knock the screen out," Dom told the others, then led the combatman through the door.

There was a narrow passageway between large tanks and another door at the far end. It was made of light metal but was blocked by a press of human bodies, spacesuited men who stirred and struggled but scarcely moved. The two combatmen pushed harder, and a sudden movement of the mob released the pressure; Dom fell forward, his helmet banging into that of the nearest man.

"What the devil you about?" the man said, twisting his head to look at Dom.

"More of them down there," Dom said, trying to roll his *r*'s the way the Edinburgers did.

"You're no one of us!" the man said and struggled to bring his weapon up.

Dom could not risk a fight here—yet the man had to be silenced. He was wearing a thin spacesuit. Dom could just reach the lightning prod, and he jerked it from its clip and jammed it against the Edinburger's side. The pair of needle-sharp spikes pierced suit and clothes and bit into his flesh, and when the hilt slammed against his body the circuit was closed. The handle of the lightning prod was filled with powerful capacitors that released their stored electricity in a single immense charge through the needles. The Edinburger writhed and died instantly.

They used his body to push a way into the crowd.

Dom had just enough sensation left in his injured leg to be aware when the clamped-on nipoff was twisted in his flesh by the men about them; he kept his thoughts from what it was doing to his leg.

V

Once the Edinburger soldiers were aware of the open door, they pulled it wide and fought their way through it. The combatmen would be waiting for them in the engine room. The sudden exodus relieved the pressure of the bodies for a moment, and Dom, with Pimenov struggling after him, pushed and worked his way toward the MT controls.

It was like trying to move in a dream. The dark hulk of the MT screen was no more than ten yards away, yet they couldn't seem to reach it. Soldiers sprang from the screen, pushing and crowding in, more and more, preventing any motion in that direction. The technicians stood at the controls, their helmet phones plugged into the board before them. Without gravity to push against, jammed into the crowd that floated at all levels in a fierce tangle of arms and legs, movement was almost impossible. Pimenov touched his helmet to Dom's.

"I'm going ahead to cut a path. Stay close behind me."

He broke contact before Dom could answer him, and let his power ax pull him forward into the press. Then he began to chop it back and forth in a short arc, almost hacking his way through the packed bodies. Men turned on him, but he did not stop, lashing out with his gropener as they tried to fight. Dom followed.

They were close to the MT controls before the combatman was buried under a crowd of stabbing, cursing Edinburgers. Pimenov had done his job, and he died doing it. Dom jetted his gropener and let it drag him forward until he slammed into the thick steel frame of the MT screen above the operators' heads. He slid the weapon along the frame, dragging himself headfirst through the press of suited bodies. There was a relatively clear space near the controls. He drifted down into it and let his drillger slide into the operator's back. The man writhed and died quickly. The other operator turned and took the weapon in his stomach. His face was just before Dom as his eyes widened and he screamed soundlessly with pain and fear. Dom could not escape the dead, horrified features as he struggled to drop the atomic bomb from his carrier. The murdered man stayed, pressed close against him all the time.

Now!

He cradled the bomb against his chest and, in a single swift motion, pulled out the arming pin, twisted the fuse to five seconds, and slammed down hard on the actuator. Then he reached up and switched the MT from *receive* to *send*.

The last soldiers erupted from the screen, and there was a growing gap behind them. Into this space and through the screen Dom threw the bomb.

After that, he kept the switch down and tried not to think about what was happening among the men of the invasion army who were waiting before the MT screen on that distant planet.

Then he had to hold this position until the combatmen arrived. He sheltered behind the operator's corpse and used his drillger against the few Edinburgers who were close enough to realize that something had gone wrong. This was easy enough to do because, although they were soldiers, they were men from the invasion regular army and knew nothing about null-G combat. Very soon after this, there was a great stir, and the closest ones were thrust aside. An angry combatman blasted through, sweeping his power ax toward Dom's neck. Dom dodged the blow and switched his radio to combat frequency.

"Hold that! I'm Corporal Priego, bomb squad. Get in front of me and keep anyone else from making the same mistake."

The man was one of those who had taken the engine room. He recognized Dom now and nodded, turning his back to him and pressing against him. More combatmen stormed up to form an iron shield around the controls. The engineer pushed through between them, and Dom helped him reset the frequency on the MT screen.

After this, the battle became a slaughter and soon ended.

"Sendout!" Dom radioed as soon as the setting was made, then instructed the screen to transmit. He heard the words repeated over and over as the combatmen repeated the withdrawal signal so that everyone could hear it. Safety lay on the other side of the screen, now that it was tuned to Tycho Barracks on the Moon.

It was the Edinburgers, living, dead and wounded, who were sent through first. They were pushed back against the screen to make room for the combatmen who were streaming into the hold. The ones at the ends of the screen simply bounced against the hard surface and recoiled; the receiving screen at Tycho was far smaller than this great invasion screen. They were pushed along until they fell through, and combatmen took up positions to mark the limits of the operating screen.

Dom was aware of someone in front of him, and he had to blink away the red film that was trying to cover his eyes.

"Wing," he said, finally recognizing the man. "How many others of the bomb squad made it?"

"None I know off, Dom. Just me."

No, don't think about the dead! Only the living counted now.

"All right. Leave your bomb here and get on through. One is all we really need." He tripped the release and pulled the bomb from Wing's rack before giving him a push toward the screen.

Dom had the bomb clamped to the controls when Sergeant Toth slammed up beside him and touched helmets.

"Almost done."

"Done now," Dom said, setting the fuse and pulling out the arming pin.

"Then get moving. I'll take it from here."

"No you don't. My job." He had to shake his head to make the haze go away but it still remained at the corners of his vision.

Toth didn't argue. "What's the setting?" he asked.

"Five and six. Five seconds after actuation the chemical bomb blows and knocks out the controls. One second later the atom bomb goes off."

"I'll stay around I think to watch the fun."

Time was acting strangely for Dom, speeding up and slowing down. Men were hurrying by, into the screen, first in a rush, then fewer and fewer. Toth was talking on the combat frequency, but Dom had switched the radio off because it hurt his head. The great chamber was empty now of all but the dead, with the automatic machine guns left firing at the entrances. One of them blew up as Toth touched helmets.

"They're all through. Let's go."

Dom had difficulty talking, so he nodded instead and hammered his fist down onto the actuator.

Men were coming toward them, but Toth had his arms around him, and full jets on his power ax were sliding them along the surface of the screen. And through.

When the brilliant lights of Tycho Barracks hit his eyes, Dom closed them, and this time the red haze came up, over him, all the way.

"How's the new leg?" Sergeant Toth asked. He slumped lazily in the chair beside the hospital bed.

"I can't feel a thing. Nerve channels blocked until it grows tight to the stump." Dom put aside the book he had been reading and wondered what Toth was doing here.

"I come around to see the wounded," the Sergeant said, answering the unasked question. "Two more besides you. Captain told me to."

"The Captain is as big a sadist as you are. Aren't we sick enough already?"

"Good joke." His expression did not change. "I'll tell the Captain. He'll like it. You going to buy out now?"

"Why not?" Dom wondered why the question made him angry. "I've had a combat mission, the medals, a good wound. More than enough points to get my discharge."

"Stay in. You're a good combatman when you stop thinking about it. There's not many of them. Make it a career."

"Like you, Sergeant? Make killing my life's work? Thank you, no. I intend to do something different, a little more constructive. Unlike you, I don't relish this whole dirty business, the killing, the outright plain murder. You like it." This sudden thought sent him sitting upright in the bed. "Maybe that's it. Wars, fighting, everything. It has nothing to do any more with territory rights or aggression or masculinity. I think that you people make wars because of the excitement of it, the thrill that nothing else can equal. You really *like* war."

Toth rose, stretched easily and turned to leave. He stopped at the door, frowning in thought.

"Maybe you're right, Corporal. I don't think about it much. Maybe

I do like it." His face lifted in a cold tight smile. "But don't forget—
you like it too."

Dom went back to his book, resentful of the intrusion. His
literature professor had sent it, along with a flattering note. He had
heard about Dom on the broadcasts, and the entire school was
proud, and so on. A book of poems by Milton, really good stuff.

> *No war, or battle's sound*
> *Was heard the world around.*

Yes, great stuff. But it hadn't been true in Milton's day and it still
wasn't true. Did mankind really like war? They *must* like it or it
wouldn't have lasted so long. This was an awful, criminal thought.

He too? Nonsense. He fought well, but he had trained himself. It
would not be true that he actually liked all of that.

Dom tried to read again, but the page kept blurring before his
eyes.

As body armor has developed through the centuries, a major concern has been to make it fit the body of a soldier. But that might be the wrong approach, and the distinction between powered armor which is worn and that which is piloted may lead to not being able to tell the combatants from their machines without a program...

The Warbots

Larry S. Todd
with illustrations by the author

The history of armored war from 1990 to 17,500 A.D.
With the improvement of lethal weapons, soldiers on a battlefield have shown great and understandable interest in staying out of the line of fire. In early wars, where sticks, stones, and lances and bows were the main medium of battlefield commerce, this goal could be accomplished by hiding behind any bulky object, or through desertion. However, as time went on this became increasingly difficult. Either the bulky objects were not as strong as they had been once or the weapons used were less aware of said barriers. Some soldiers adopted a rigid code of martial etiquette and tin suits, but the effectiveness of the knight grew limited when gunpowder was invented.

In the twentieth century great powered suits of armor, called "tanks," came into common use. They required a concentrated barrage to stop them and definitely provided their pilots and crew a more salubrious environment within than they could expect to find without. Nonetheless, a tank still had a great deal of vulnerable places, was far too heavy and noisy, and had limited mobility. In the 1990's the tanks which were covered with borosilicate fiber plates were much lighter and more mobile than their predecessors, but still lacked ideal conditions for operation. They could not wade through swamps nor avoid being attacked from behind any more easily than the old tanks, nor could they retreat very fast. Clearly, there had to be something better.

The General Motors Terrain Walker
ca. 1995

Originally developed for construction work and back-echelon packhorsing, the GM Walker was quickly accepted by the armies of America, Earth, when it was proved that the machine could carry a gun. Standing twelve feet tall and weighing eight tons, the Walker could stride down a highway at 30 mph and do 20 mph on rough terrain, such as burnt-out slums. Nuclear powered, it required little servicing and often powered its weapons directly from its own power system. Great hydraulic pistons operated its arms and legs, which followed every movement made by the pilot. The pilot was strapped in a control cradle that translated every motion to the Walker, and he had a clear view fore and aft through a plexiglass bubble. The Walker was equipped with a wide range of sensory devices, among them snooperscopes, radar, amplified hearing, some primitive smell-detection devices and tactile pads on the hands and feet, all of which were wired to the pilot.

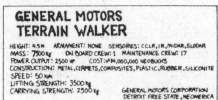

GENERAL MOTORS
TERRAIN WALKER

HEIGHT: 4.5 m   ARMAMENT: NONE   SENSORIES: CCLR, IR, MIDAR, SLODAR
MASS: 7500 kg   ON BOARD CREW: 1   MAINTENANCE CREW: 17
POWER OUTPUT: 2500 HP   COST: ¥14,000,000 NEOBUCKS
CONSTRUCTION: METAL, CERMETS, COMPOSITES, PLASTIC, RUBBER, SILICONITE
SPEED: 50 KPH
LIFTING STRENGTH: 3500 kg
CARRYING STRENGTH: 2500 kg   GENERAL MOTORS CORPORATION
                                    DETROIT FREE STATE, NEOMERICA

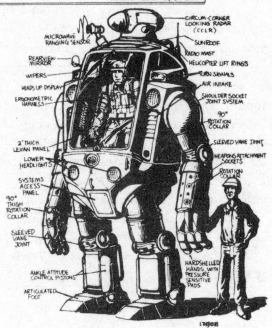

It was equipped to retreat fast, attack faster and explode when hit, with a satisfying nuclear blast. When this was commonly learned, there were very few enemy soldiers who were willing to harm the things, which made them extremely effective in clearing out potential battlefields. But it also made getting them to a battlefield to begin with a touchy proposition. Few soldiers liked sitting on an atomic bomb, even though it would only go off if they were killed, and a Geneva Convention in 1992 declared them formal nuclear weapons.

However, with the turmoil of the late twentieth and early twenty-first centuries growing out of hand, they were used with increasing frequency.

In October 2000, an armed insurrection in Harlem City, America, Earth, caused Walkers to be brought out into the streets. Patrolling the city with squads of armed soldiers (and their nuclear explosion capacities secretly damped), they effectively cleared the rioters out of the burning city, and into a large prison combine, where they were kept until their tempers were drowned in rainy weather. Of fifty Walkers shipped in, only two were disabled. One had a department store, which its pilot had rashly pushed over, fall in on it; the other had broken legs from a kamikaze automobile.

In November 2000, the great series of civil wars in China were formally entered by the United States of America, Earth, and Walkers painted with ominous designs marched through the burning cities and villages, panicking those Chinese who would be panicked and nuking those who felt compelled to fight back. Four nuclear explosions in Peking were enough to show the Red Chinese that fighting the things was useless, so they were given a wide berth and finally succeeded in bottling ninety per cent of the Red Chinese army in a small part of Manchuria, Earth.

In February 2002, there were massive earthquakes all over the globe. Japan sank beneath the sea; California followed suit; the coastline of Europe would never be the same, and America's East Coast was washed clean by tsunami.

A few months later the Mississippi Valley collapsed, creating an inland sea in America. With three-fifths of the human race wiped out, the remainder lost all further interest in conflict and turned to more immediate and peaceful pursuits, such as cleaning up after the party.

The Walkers were instrumental in assisting in heavy construction. They rebuilt the foundations of cities, realigned the world's power conduits, built dams and, in one fierce burst of zealous activity, built almost a hundred thousand miles of beautiful roadway in four years. Three years after that, commercial aircars were produced in profusion. The new roads were ignored and slowly cracked while approaching obsolescence.

The McCauley Walker
ca. 2130

2130 was an eventful year. The first complete cities were incorporated on Mars; the moon formally declared independence of the Four Nations of Earth; the first non-government sponsored spaceship lines went into business, and a new Walker was released to the antiriot squads.

Called "pinheads" because of its set of electric binoculars (which could see from electricity up through the spectrum to X-rays) which functioned as a head, the McCauley Walker had far more flexibility than the GM. Nearly sixteen feet of tempered aluminum and borosilicates, yet weighing only four tons, the McCauley could duplicate all human movements except those requiring bending in the trunk or waist. It could run 55km/hr, was able to lift objects of up to ten tons and turned out to be a massive failure.

The McCauley Walker was a total weapon, designed for optimum placement of components in the least space. The structural members were cast or electroblown around the defense systems, so that it was impossible to deactivate them. The defense systems were inexorably bound with the machine's own conscious battlefield computers. To activate the Walker meant it would at once be at top fighting condition, ready to blast out with weapons which could not be removed from its hull without expenditures of twice its original cost. This did not make it a noteworthy construction machine. Its one experiment in this use had it firing lasers at bulldozers, graders, solidifiers and road crews. The unions kicked up a fuss. It was obviously not a very good construction machine.

Ten thousand of them were built at a cost of two million credits apiece, and it cost four thousand credits to maintain each per year, whether or not they were used. A fortune was spent on the hundred acres of sheds outside of Indianapolis in which they were housed, and it was here that the Walkers remained for eighty years, unused except for occasional exercises to keep them from rusting or whatever it was they did. But there were no wars. Riots were fairly common, but rarely large enough for Walkers to be brought out for them, and never located close enough to an airport to have Walkers in on them before they were effectively over.

In 2210 the Martian Colonial Government declared formal independence of the Four Nations of Earth and confiscated all Four Nation military property to see that their constitution was respected.

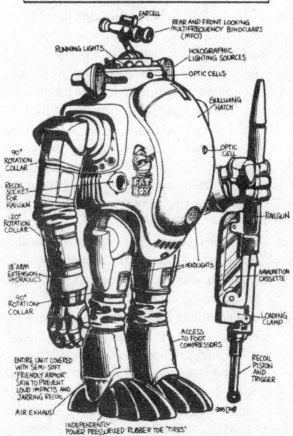

McCAULEY WALKER (AMBULANT)

HEIGHT: 4.9 m   ARMAMENT: NONE   SENSORIES: MFO, MFA, SOC, SLR, CCLR.
MASS: 5900 kg   ONBOARD CREW: 1   MAINTENANCE CREW: 12
POWER OUTPUT: 3000 hp   COST: Cr 2,000,000
CONSTRUCTION: CERMET, SKINLON, COMPOSOT, PARAPRENE, GLASAL
SPEED: 55 km   DESIGN: AMBULANT DIVISION,
LIFTING STRENGTH: 10,000 kg   McCAULEY INDUSTRIES,
CARRYING STRENGTH: 4,000 kg   DEXATRON ISLAND, L5

EARCELL
REAR AND FRONT LOOKING MULTIFREQUENCY BINOCULARS (MFO)
RUNNING LIGHTS
HOLOGRAPHIC LIGHTING SOURCES
OPTIC CELLS
GULLWING HATCH
OPTIC CELL
90° ROTATION COLLAR
RECOIL SOCKET FOR RAILGUN
120° ROTATION COLLAR
RAILGUN
18" ARM EXTENSION HYDRAULICS
HEADLIGHTS
AMMUNITION CASSETTE
90° ROTATION COLLAR
ACCESS TO FOOT COMPRESSORS
LOADING CLAMP
ENTIRE UNIT COVERED WITH SEMI-SOFT "FRIENDLY ARMOR" SKIN TO PREVENT LOUD IMPACTS AND JARRING RECOIL
RECOIL PISTON AND TRIGGER
AIR EXHAUST
INDEPENDENTLY POWER-PRESSURIZED RUBBER TOE "TIRES"

It wasn't however, for the Four Nations were full of people who would suffer great financial losses if Mars became free. So the First Interplanetary War was begun.

Terran troop transports landed four hundred Walkers on the Syrtis Greenspot, where they were jeered and mocked by a large army of Martian colonists. Following the Martians out across the desert, the Walkers made rapid progress on them until the old plastic sleeves that kept dirt and abrasives out of the leg joints began to crack from age. Martian sand got in and jammed the joints, and the Martian Colonial Armor walked a safe distance around the field of immobile Walkers, attacked the Terran positions from behind and won their independence. It was never disputed again.

The Burton Damnthing
ca. 2680

There seemed to be little reason for the development of more advanced power armor until about 2680, for the solar system enjoyed a period of unparalleled peace, productivity, and leisure. With great space vessels over a mile in diameter, powered by nuclear inertial drives, men traveled near the speed of light and colonized the near stars, where they found a surprising profusion of planets. In 2548 the Helium Distant Oscillator was developed, making instant interstellar communication possible, even though actual travel still took objective years. From the device, the human colonies could reap instant benefit from discoveries made years of travel away. Many of the great C-jammers, as the huge interstellar vessels were known, were dismantled and sold after this, till only about seventy were being used, mostly for carrying great big things which weren't likely to change much in coming years. Terraforming tools, multiforges (the all-purpose manufacturing tool of the day), great generators for increasing or decreasing gravitation of planets and moons, even little C-jammers—and colonists—were the major items of trade, with a few luxury items thrown in for balancing the tapes.

On the fourth planet of Procyon there dwelt a race of intelligent lizards, the Kezfi, who were in their early atomic age when the human colony was set upon the seventh planet. Moss, the colony, was a difficult world to tame, and the Kezfi were more than delighted to trade labor for the secrets of making spaceships. This went on from 2570 to 2680, when Moss had a population of nearly ten million, three terraformed moons and several rocks in the nearby asteroid belt that replaced a sixth planet. The Kezfi were becoming quite avid colonizers and rather sophisticated in the ways of space. They began to have reservations about the presence of humans in their solar system, for these humans were of another star and were occupying a planet which otherwise would have been Kezfic. A war began, and the Mossists needed a weapon which could be used effectively against the Kezfi.

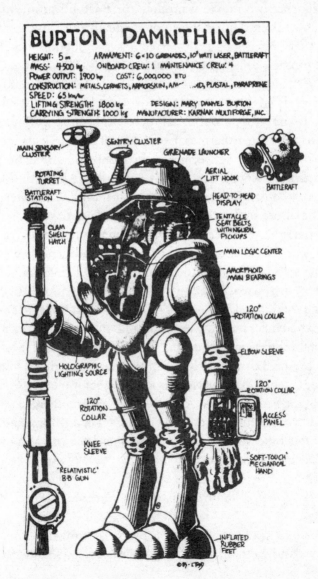

BURTON DAMNTHING

HEIGHT: 5 m   ARMAMENT: 6 < 10 GRENADES, 10⁹ WATT LASER, BATTLERAFT
MASS: 4500 kg   ONBOARD CREW: 1   MAINTENANCE CREW: 4
POWER OUTPUT: 1900 kw   COST: 6,000,000 ETU
CONSTRUCTION: METALS, CERMETS, ARMORSKIN, AM— ...AD, PLASTAL, PARAPRENE
SPEED: 65 km/hr
LIFTING STRENGTH: 1800 kg   DESIGN: MARY DANYEL BURTON
CARRYING STRENGTH: 1000 kg   MANUFACTURER: KARNAK MULTIFORGE, INC.

The Burton Damnthing was a sophisticated instrument. Its shoulder and hip joints were friction free, being cast of amorphoid iron. Just as a toy magnet will cause a piece of thin iron to twist and bend without actual contact, amorphoid iron could twist and contort itself on a massive scale, controlled by banks of magnets and topological distorters, yet lose none of its strength and hardness. However, due to the size of the magnet banks, its use was restricted to the major joints, the elbows and knees being cloth-sleeved mechanical joints.

Unlike the two previous models, the Burton Damnthing did not use a control cradle for the pilot. Instead, the man sat in a large padded seat, strapped into assorted nerve-induction pickups. It was as though the Damnthing was his own body.

On Armageddon, Alpha Centauri II, animals with multiple heads had been discovered. Due to the violent ecology, they had been forced to develop a sense of perception that extended in all directions, to warn the major head about potential danger. Called Cohen's Battlefield Sense, it was brought into the Damnthing to detect lurking Kezfi. The lizards squawked when found out and never could quite understand how their hiding places were located, since they were self-admitted experts at camouflage.

On the right shoulder of the Damnthing there was a large socket to contain a device called a battlecraft. It was a small, condensed version of the offensive weapons of the Damnthing, floating on inertial and antigravity drives, powered by a fusion pack and controlled by a specially educated chimpanzee brain in aspic. Since the battlecraft was as effective five hundred miles from the Damnthing as five hundred feet, it removed some of the intimacy from death. This rightly concerned the Kezfi, who liked a personal confrontation with their assassin, on the logic that he might be taken with them. Not being able to enjoy the Kezfi's Honorable Death at the hands of these dirty fighters from another star, the lizards decided to call it quits. And, not being proud or anything, they decided further to let them have Moss and its moons, and they would stick to what they had been allotted.

The Christopher Warbot
ca. 3250

The Kezfi, as has been said and is probably known by most readers who have known them, preferred to die the Kezfi's Honorable Death and could not understand the sending of men into war in armor. They assumed these things must be robots, then, since they had never been able to get one intact enough to study, so they built their own teams of war robots, called them and the human armor "warbots" and by 3250 decided they had grown weary enough of resident humans to start another war.

At the battle of Granite Rock, in the Procyon Asteroids, the Kezfi first learned about the new Christopher Warbot. They also learned the ineffectiveness of sending remote control robots into battle against manned craft.

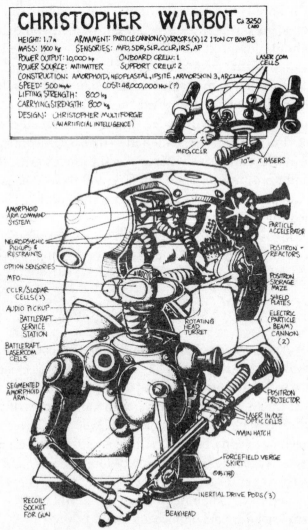

CHRISTOPHER WARBOT Ca 3250 (ABD)

HEIGHT: 1.7 m   ARMAMENT: PARTICLE CANNON (4) XRASORS (6) 12 1 TON CT BOMBS
MASS: 1500 kg   SENSORIES: MFO, SDR, SLR, CCLR, IRS, AP
POWER OUTPUT: 10,000 hp   ONBOARD CREW: 1
POWER SOURCE: ANTIMATTER   SUPPORT CREW: 2
CONSTRUCTION: AMORPHOID, NEOPLASTAL, IPSITE, ARMORSKIN 3, ARCIAN
SPEED: 500 km/h   COST: 48,000,000 Nu (?)
LIFTING STRENGTH: 800 kg
CARRYING STRENGTH: 800 kg
DESIGN: CHRISTOPHER MULTIFORGE
(AN ARTIFICIAL INTELLIGENCE)

LASER COM CELLS

MFO, CCLR

10" X RASERS

AMORPHOID ARM COMMAND SYSTEM

NEUROPSYCHIC PICKUPS & RESTRAINTS

OPTION SENSORIES

MFO

CCLR/SLODAR CELLS (2)

AUDIO PICKUP

BATTLECRAFT SERVICE STATION

BATTLECRAFT LASERCOM CELLS

SEGMENTED AMORPHOID ARM

RECOIL SOCKET FOR GUN

BEAKHEAD

PARTICLE ACCELERATOR

POSITRON REACTORS

POSITRON STORAGE MAZE

SHIELD PLATES

ELECTRIC (PARTICLE BEAM) CANNON (2)

ROTATING HEAD TURRET

POSITRON PROJECTOR

LASER IN/OUT OPTIC CELLS

MAIN HATCH

FORCEFIELD VERGE SKIRT

INERTIAL DRIVE PODS (3)

After a number of crushing defeats, and a few surprising victories, the final blow was put on the second war of Procyon when the C-jammer Brass Candle, massing fifty-five million kilotons and traveling at .92C, smacked violently into their major colony of Daar es Suun, killing over a billion Kezfi. After this impressive disaster, nobody, Kezfi or human, was very willing to press his point further.

The Christopher Warbot had no legs, but floated on inertial-antigrav pods which enabled it to work as effectively in space as on the ground. On its back was a complete service and repairs center for the battlecraft, and on its front, on either side of the entrance hatch, it bore twin electric cannon. The study of amorphics had developed to the point where an entire arm could be made of amorphoid, though it was limited to bending at the appropriate places a human arm would bend. Since nobody was quite sure how to go about bending the artificial arm where there were no joints in their own, this did not disturb anyone deeply.

The only nerve pickups were those in the seat cushions and the helmet, but the soldier had better-than-ever control over the machine. The entire surface area was sheathed so that it could feel pain and pressure from bullet strikes, and thus Cohen's Battlefield Sense was implemented by another protection device. The head, now attached through a long tentacle, held eyes, ears, and other senses, and the mobility of the Christopher Warbot was such that it replaced most other forms of heavy armor. War was becoming less burdened down by killing machines.

Greedy Nick's Warbot
ca. 4721

In 3579 a stardrive was finally developed, and humanity emerged from the Slowboat Age to the Age of Expansion. Most of the C-jammers were outfitted with drives and used to set up enormous colonies in one blow, and since a light-year could be covered in somewhat less than two days, colonization went on rather rapidly. In 3900 the Cuiver Foundation went far beyond the borders of human space and established the Antarean League among the ninety-four planets of Antares, the seventeen planets of Antares's Green Companion star and assorted dwarf stars in the adjoining locality. Since Antares was a dynastic monarchy, nobody paid it much attention.

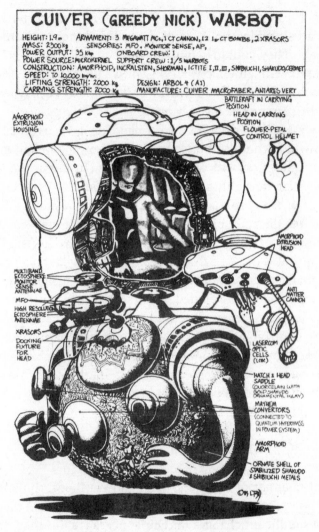

CUIVER (GREEDY NICK) WARBOT

HEIGHT: 1.9 m   ARMAMENT: 3 MEGAWATT MCs, 1 CT CANNON, 12 1 CT BOMBS, 2 XRASORS
MASS: 2300 kg   SENSORIES: MFO, MONITOR SENSE, AP,
POWER OUTPUT: 35 kw   ONBOARD CREW: 1
POWER SOURCE: MICROKERNEL   SUPPORT CREW: 1/5 WARBOTS
CONSTRUCTION: AMORPHOID, INCRALSTEN, SHORMAN, ICTITE I,II,III, SHIBIUCHI, SHAKUDO/CERMET
SPEED: TO 10,000 km/hr
LIFTING STRENGTH: 2000 kg   DESIGN: ARBOL 4 (A1)
CARRYING STRENGTH: 2000 kg   MANUFACTURE: CUIVER MACROFABER, ANTARES VERT

In 4718 a scoutship of Antares came scuttling back to the League
bearing great tidings of war, with a race of tall, rust-red crustaceans
called Peolanti, who had established a small empire near Antares.
The delightful ruler of Antares, Pantocrator Nicholas Cuiver the
Greedy, immediately threw a complete travel silence around the
League, from 4718 to 4723, at the end of which Greedy Nick
announced that the Antarean League now controlled a globe of space
forty light-years in diameter. The Peolanti liked to fight from gigantic
spaceships, huge portable fortresses, and mobile asteroids, which
dictated definite limits to their mobility. Greedy Nick did away with

using battleships other than to transport the warbots to the battlespaces, and let the Peolanti try and find them with their poor radar nets. They couldn't compete, or even begin to. A laser beam can be used with fair effectiveness against a big battleship, for at least you know where it is, but little dinky hard knots of mayhem could neither be seen nor be hit very often.

Greedy Nick's Warbot boasted triple mayhem converters, a nasty weapon which could spit laser beams all the way up and down the spectrum, pull tricks with gravity that resulted in atomic bonds falling apart, heat or freeze things by time-induction, a side effect of the discovery of the chronogravitic spectrum. The head was no longer connected to the body, but floated freely and had its own complement of weapons. The battlecraft was harder than ever to detect and destroy, being controlled by a brain taken from an Armageddon animal more vicious than a tyrannosaur and of near-human intelligence.

Amorphics had developed a tentacle which could stretch ten times its length for an arm, retract to a wrinkly nubbin, and yet be perfectly controllable by the pilot. He sat in his cabin which was padded both by cushions and paragravity, free from being bounced around, wearing a helmet and sitting in the lotus position of meditation. In order to properly control a warbot, a soldier had to be an accomplished Yogi.

The Warbots at Critter's Gateway
ca. 7200

While all manner of advances were made in the warbots since the Peolanti wars, and several smaller wars were fought with them, there were no significant changes in their appearance until the discovery of Critter's Universe.

Eleven light-years from Antares there was a small dust cloud which emitted a healthy amount of radio waves. These clouds were not uncommon, so little attention beyond marking it as a navigation hazard was paid to it. Then Jorj Critter, a prospector looking for natural rubies, flew into it. It turned out to be an area in which space had formed a side-bubble, where physical laws were somewhat different. The periodic table of Critter's Universe held but four elements, a solid, a gas, a plasma and a liquid, promptly dubbed Earth, Air, Fire and Water. While perfectly stable in their own little universe, subjecting any object made of them to our physical laws caused destabilization of the Fire content, which caused the whole mass to oscillate into pure energy. Since Critter found it was very simple to control this attempt to justify itself to our physical laws, he told Andrew the Meditator, the current Pantocrator of Antares, about this new power source.

Critter's Universe, which is only about a hundred light-years in diameter, did coexist with a large section of the Terran Organization of Star States, who, having learned about this, decided they should

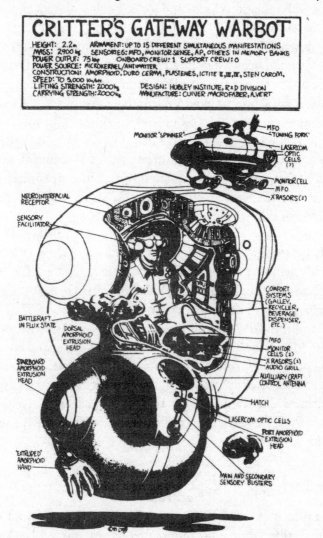

CRITTER'S GATEWAY WARBOT

HEIGHT: 2.2m   ARMAMENT: UP TO 15 DIFFERENT SIMULTANEOUS MANIFESTATIONS
MASS: 2900 kg   SENSORIES: MFO, MONITOR SENSE, AP, OTHERS IN MEMORY BANKS
POWER OUTPUT: 75 kw   ONBOARD CREW: 1 SUPPORT CREW: O
POWER SOURCE: MICROKERNEL/ANTIMATTER
CONSTRUCTION: AMORPHOID, DURO CERMA, PLASTENES, ICTITE II, III, IV, STEN CAROM,
SPEED: TO 5,000 km/hr
LIFTING STRENGTH: 2000 kg
CARRYING STRENGTH: 2000 kg   DESIGN: HUBLEY INSTITUTE, R & D DIVISION
                               MANUFACTURE: CULVER MACROFABER, ALVERT

MONITOR "SPINNER"
MFO "TUNING FORK"
LASERCOM OPTIC CELLS (?)
MONITOR CELL
MFO
X RASORS (1)
NEUROINTERFACIAL RECEPTOR
SENSORY FACILITATOR
COMFORT SYSTEMS (GALLEY, RECYCLER, BEVERAGE DISPENSER, ETC.)
BATTLECRAFT IN FLUX STATE
DORSAL AMORPHOID EXTRUSION HEAD
MFO
MONITOR CELLS (2)
X RASORS (1)
AUDIO GRILL
AUXILIARY CRAFT CONTROL ANTENNA
STARBOARD AMORPHOID EXTRUSION HEAD
HATCH
LASERCOM OPTIC CELLS
PORT AMORPHOID EXTRUSION HEAD
"EXTRUDED" AMORPHOID HAND
MAIN AND SECONDARY SENSORY BLISTERS

own it. The TOSS went to war with Antares, the focal point of the war being around the little nebula, Critter's Gateway. TOSS battlewagons and mobile asteroids faced over a million warbots of Antares and soon discovered that they could not possibly defeat such a swarm of tiny adversaries. The TOSS never got within a billion miles of the actual gateway, and would have lost regardless of whether or not the League pulled another trick from a hat.

For several thousand years, Green Companion of Antares had been known as a tempestuous stellar bastard, constantly filling all space around it with radiation clouds and fouling up communications. It had several dozen planets which could be very pleasant if the sun were calmed down somewhat, so the Hubley University extension at Antares Vert had been established in 6200 to seek ways of controlling the star. Shortly before the war, they found the first major advance of macromechanics, how to blow a star into a nova. It worked as well on stable, main-sequence stars as on the huge, wasteful monsters like Rigel, upon which it was demonstrated. The TOSS now realized that the League could seed their stars through Critter's Universe and blow them all to perdition before anything could be done. Hastily withdrawing their forces from the Gateway, the TOSS began cultivating good feelings with forced urgency.

The warbot used at Critter's Gateway was a very capable little vessel, as much spaceship as groundcraft. The soldier, sitting in lotus, was freed of his helmet. From an amorphoid plate at the top of the warbot, he could extrude a battlecraft or a head; from two plates at the side he could extrude any of an arsenal of two hundred weapons. The circuitry of these amorphic devices was mostly magnetic and gravitic domains, which could not be altered by any amount of twisting and contorting, so they could be extruded whenever needed, otherwise remaining placid as a puddle of quicksilver in their storage tanks.

Antares, while again the little empire of space, was also the most powerful, for they had over a million of these things strutting back and forth through space.

The Quicksilver Kid
ca. 10,000

By the Eodech (10,000 A.D.) amorphics had developed a warbot made of nothing but amorphoid metals, memory plastics, solid

liquids, contact fields and other prodigies of science. Normally a
simple near-globe eight feet big, the Quicksilver Kid looked very
much like a glob of mercury when in action. Hands, head, battlecraft
and whatnot could be extruded from whatever part of the surface
area they would seem to be most useful, and the weapons system had
an additional development.

Hidden in the block-circuitry of the hull was a memory center
containing records of every science applicable to military purposes,
as well as a mechanical design center, so that a soldier need merely

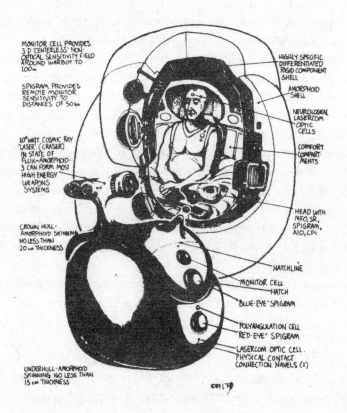

QUICKSILVER WARBOT

HEIGHT: 2.5 m   ARMAMENT: CONSISTANT WITH NORTHING TREATY OF CETUS, T.O.S.S.
MASS: 4500 kg   SENSORIES: MOR, SR, AIO, CPI, AP, SPIGRAM RED, SPIGRAM BLUE
POWER OUTPUT: 1,000,000 hp
POWER SOURCE: "LITTLE BANG"
CONSTRUCTION: AMORPHOID 1,2,3,4,5, POLYMOL, SILDIN, WHITESTONE, REDSTONE, BLACKSTONE
SPEED: TO 10,000 km/sec   DESIGN: SHARDEI OF SIGRIL, SUBTAN INSTITUTE
LIFTING STRENGTH: ?   MANUFACTURER: SIGRIL OF CETUS, DULL WORLD
CARRYING STRENGTH: ?

MONITOR CELL PROVIDES
3-D 'CENTERLESS' NON-
OPTICAL SENSITIVITY FIELD
AROUND WARBOT TO
100 m

SPIGRAM PROVIDES
REMOTE MONITOR
SENSITIVITY TO
DISTANCES OF 50 km

10⁸ WATT COSMIC RAY
'LASER' (CRASER)
IN STATE OF
FLUX-AMORPHOID-
3 CAN FORM MOST
HIGH ENERGY
WEAPONS
SYSTEMS

CROWN HULL
AMORPHOID SKINNING
NO LESS THAN
20 cm THICKNESS

UNDERHULL - AMORPHOID
SKINNING NO LESS THAN
15 cm THICKNESS

HIGHLY SPECIFIC
DIFFERENTIATED
RIGID COMPONENT
SHELL

AMORPHOID
SHELL

NEUROLOGICAL
LASERCOM
OPTIC
CELLS

COMFORT
COMPART-
MENTS

HEAD WITH
MFO, SR,
SPIGRAM,
AIO, CPI

HATCHLINE

MONITOR CELL

HATCH

'BLUE-EYE' SPIGRAM

POLYANGULATION CELL
'RED-EYE' SPIGRAM

LASERCOM OPTIC CELL
PHYSICAL CONTACT
CONNECTION NAVELS (2)

size up the situation and inform his warbot to create a weapon equal to it, and hammer away. Powered by antimatter breakdown, the warbot had more than enough power to see this done. No longer were warbots shuttled about by other spacecraft, but each had a speed of about one light-year per hour to make its rounds.

In the Early Eodechtic centuries the Sophisticate Age had come about. In known space, a flattened sphere roughly five thousand light-years in diameter, there were seventy major human empires, twenty-two joint human-nonhuman Leagues, one hundred ninety nonhuman empires and fourteen weird things which defied description, save that they seemed to be sociological systems of order originally cooked up by something which could have been intelligent but more likely was something else, the exact nature of which was even more difficult to ascertain. But they never did make any trouble, probably because they found each other and intelligent life even more impossible than we found them.

There were many wars in the Eodechtic centuries, but none of them especially large on the grand scale. But warbots were used in all of them. For example, the Korel Empire Collapse.

The Korel were human adaptations, two feet tall and looking like toy dolls (behaving much like them, too. Korel were well known for their immaturity). They had a little empire flourishing until 10590, when one of their kings went insane on the throne and attacked the Palaric States, which were then growing into importance. The Korel had a few worthy weapons, which aided in their conquering several planets, and then an ally, the Karpo Regime, a race of hideous gray frogs who had been waiting on the sly for some way to build a little empire. As soon as the Korel had done as much as they could, the Karpo turned on them and soon had a very effective little empire, as well as a full-time occupation in scaring the border stars of the Pale (Palaric States).

An approaching fleet of warbots, after having been ordered to sum up the situation, performed a maneuver which was historical because of its originality. A hundred thousand warbots came together and fused their masses into a thousand medium-sized battleships, which attacked the Karpo fleets. The Karpo fired a salvo at them and broke them all into monolithic chunks of wreckage, which they then went in to investigate. Twisted wreckage, once it surrounded the Karpo fleet, suddenly turned quicksilver, returned to a hundred thousand intact warbots, and destroyed forever the Karpo Regime.

The Korel were chastised mildly. One could never expect much from them in the way of wisdom.

The First Alakar
ca. 11,000

By 11,000, enough was known about forcefields to expect a soldier sheathed in them to have as much, if not more, protection than an amorphoid shell could provide. The shell was done away with, except for the helmet, and the battlecraft was equipped with everything that had previously been reserved for the warbot itself. Since the new soldier appeared to be a man, wearing a small belt and carrying an outlandish rifle, with a battlecraft at heel and a small scrap of amorphoid called a "steel pimple" floating about his head, he could no longer be called a warbot. From Antarean mythology the name "Alakar," meaning war-god, was lifted. It seemed appropriate.

The methods of battle were now entirely different. The soldier could fly in free space, though they now returned to the use of spaceships. His forcefields could protect him from the heat of a sun, could be totally impenetrable, or set to pass either matter or energy, but refuse the other.

His body was operated on to the extent of surgical placement of wires which increased his native strength and reflex speed immensely as well as enabled him to rigidify himself for space travel.

An example of fighting methods could be taken from the uprising of Murmash Krodd, on the Chembal Starstrand, 11211.

Here a fleet of Kroddic ships attacked a small neighboring democracy, and the Humanity Soldiers were requested in. The Krodds saw the human fleet approaching, but it vanished before their eyes, and they could not understand what had become of it until they were recalled quickly by Murmash Krodd himself, who had seen them fall from his skies and subjugate his city in ten minutes.

The method was this: when the Kroddic Fleet was sure to have seen the Humanity Soldiers approach, they snapped on their helmets, activated their fields and took to free space. The ships broke apart in thousands of brick-sized chunks of amorphoid, each reorganized to contain its own drives and control systems. The Alakars and ships did not rejoin until in orbit of Kesal of Murmash Krodd, when they rained down from the sky and forced the fat crustacean to order his fleet back, lest they destroy the planets of Murmash Krodd. When the Kroddic ships were all grounded, the Alakars set solar-phoenix to them, and they burned to radioactive ashes.

The Second Alakar
ca. 14500

The sleek Alakar of the 14500's was respected as being the most capable fighter in space. He controlled six battlecrafts, each a featureless egg until ordered to think up a weapon to cover a situation. He commanded three steel pimples, which contained all of his forcefield equipment, and, being strictly defensive weapons, never left his vicinity. His uniform was made of bioplastic with layer upon layer of sensory-deflector pseudocells, which kept his brain flooded with such an amount of information that an Alakar had to be trained for five years. The helmet, often decorated with fanciful sculpture, feather crests, and back-curtains, could lock every atom of his body to a field that intensified the interatomic bond-strength to a point where he could withstand a nuclear barrage in the flesh, as well as do all the reflex-speedups he needed. Being an Alakar was much like being a superman under LSD, save that the hallucinations were very real displays of actual conditions, which could be interpreted usefully.

The hand weapons were now losing their physical structure with alarming rapidity, the great gaps between parts being filled in with a curious substance called Link. Research in chronogravitics had led to the discovery of how to replace the subatomic bonds of matter, which were an effect of space, with something that was a side-effect of time. This new matter was completely undetectable and very impalpable except by a certain set of rules.

If Link were made of pure carbon, one could not force pure carbon through it; it might as well be a brick wall. Carbon compounds moved slowly through it, growing warm as they did so. Things which had no carbon content moved through without resistance, except with the extremely unlikely possibility that two nuclei might collide, which they certainly did not do very much.

Link had curious properties of conduction and insulation which made it particularly desirable as a weapon component, in addition to the fact that it didn't take up much room.

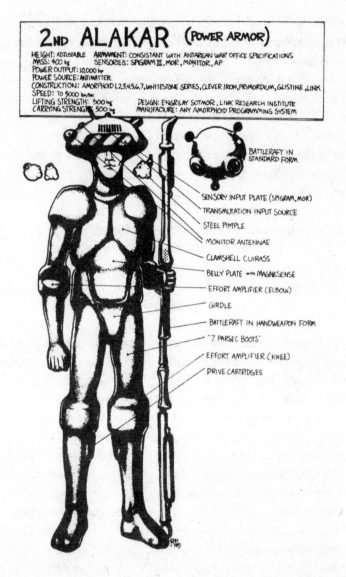

2ND ALAKAR (POWER ARMOR)

HEIGHT: ADJUSTABLE   ARMAMENT: CONSISTANT WITH ANTAREAN WAR OFFICE SPECIFICATIONS
MASS: 400 kg   SENSORIES: SPIGRAM III, MOR, MONITOR, AP
POWER OUTPUT: 10,000 hp
POWER SOURCE: ANTIMATTER
CONSTRUCTION: AMORPHOID 1,2,3,4,5,6,7, WHITESTONE SERIES, CLEVER IRON, PRIMORDIUM, GLISTINE, LINK
SPEED: TO 5000 km/sec
LIFTING STRENGTH: 500 kg   DESIGN: ENGRILAY SOTMOR, LINK RESEARCH INSTITUTE
CARRYING STRENGTH: 500 kg   MANUFACTURE: ANY AMORPHOID PROGRAMMING SYSTEM

BATTLERAFT IN STANDARD FORM

SENSORY INPUT PLATE (SPIGRAM, MOR)
TRANSMUTATION INPUT SOURCE
STEEL PIMPLE
MONITOR ANTENNAE
CLAMSHELL CUIRASS
BELLY PLATE with MAGNESENSE
EFFORT AMPLIFIER (ELBOW)
GIRDLE
BATTLERAFT IN HANDWEAPON FORM
'7 PARSEC BOOTS'
EFFORT AMPLIFIER (KNEE)
DRIVE CARTRIDGES

The Second Alakar was used in several conflicts, among them the most noticeable being the Haak Wars of 14696. The Haak, centipedean creatures from some obscure place in the galactic center, had stretched their empire out in a most curious fashion. Most races preferred to expand in a globe, the center being their planet of origin. The Haak expanded in a straight line thirty light-years across. They had a science of teleportation which could get a Haak on the outside border of his empire, twenty thousand light-years to the center, in

two years. They did not do very much work with spaceships, beyond
sending robot probes to land colonization reception booths. When
the first booths of Haak began landing on human planets in the
distant Lace Pattern, the alarm went out. The Lace Pattern was
occupied by a large number of little human and non-human empires,
none very large, and because it was four years of travel from the
Palaric States, the nearest really organized culture, it never heard
much from the main body of civilization, except from wandering
ships of Alakars. In fact, it was not generally known that all those
marvelous myths of Antares, and TOSS, and Pale, and so on, were
not fairy tales. Few of the Alakars who wandered through the region
had ever been anywhere near the Civilization.

The entire war, though it dragged on for ten years, was hardly
eighth-page news back in Antares.

The Final Alakar
ca. 17500

Even though Civilization of Humankind (which included almost every
alien race that had ever heard of Terra or Antares Imperator) was a
growing concern, it had still not explored more than ten per cent of the
stars in its own dominion. In some space which both the TOSS and
Antares claimed, a new race had come up and were doing some
exploration and state-building on their own. The TOSS was willing to
put up with it only as long as Antares gave them no assistance, but
when the Pantocrator, out of the goodness of his heart or whatever,
started to assist them with technological gifts, it was too much.

Minor races of the TOSS who felt endangered immediately went
to war, minor allies of Antares resisted them, until by 17485 both big
empires were ready to blow their cookies and have it out at one
another. The race that had started the brouhaha had long since had
their fill of imperialism, and were perfectly willing to settle for what
they had, but now it was a matter of interstellar pride, and neither the
TOSS nor the League was going to be bested. It was a marvelous war.

Antares, who had always seemed to have the last thing to say
insofar as weapons advances were concerned, finally sent a squad of
Ultimate Alakars onto the field of the war.

The Alakar himself wore no weapons, though he carried a few
hand weapons of negligible presence (mostly fashioned from Link),

wore no helmet and had six steel pimples which performed all the functions of the helmet, as well as being able to operate as battlecrafts. The Alakar, upon landing on a planet which had not been invaded, would immediately alert the civilians to go to the public shelters hundreds of miles beneath the planetary crust and take all personal valuables with them. They were given twenty-four hours, but during this time, since the Alakar was almost sure to be under attack, he would certainly be occupied. His steel pimples would head for the nearest masses of amorphoid, often automobiles and private spacecraft, and perform a virus-function. Whatever the amorphoid had been previously would be erased; the pimples would realign and combine all available amorphoid into great robot fortresses, fleets of battlecrafts and orbiting platforms, and would infect normal metals with amorphic domain, causing entire communications networks to start converting into amorphoid weapons. If it went on mainly unchecked, within fifty hours of commence-attack, the military command centers buried in the centers of the planets could expect their control panels to swim like quicksilver and turn into atomic bombs.

The planetary defenses would initiate their own amorphic conversions, trying to fight back, and would cause the comm networks to fight back at ground level. Flotillas of planetary steel pimples would commandeer as much amorphoid as possible, until the entire war began to resemble the attack of a viral disease upon a protoplasmic organism. If the planetary defense won, the Alakar was killed or forced to retreat, and the mass-computer would return every bit of registered amorphoid on the surface to its original state (unregistered amorphoid, such as kitchen appliances, generally kept firing away until told to desist. Registered amorphoid, which had a certain key-pattern built in, instantly reverted).

If the Alakar won, the same thing would be done, except that he would now control the planet and invite his forces into orbit. Since the governments of Antares and the TOSS were very similar, in basic policies, the civilians rarely cared too much who held the upper hand, so long as they were not too often changed.

Naturally, this being a war, damage was done. A wrecked city stayed quite wrecked, though there was rarely any loss of life. But recovery from an attack took several years, and when Antares finally bested the TOSS, they found that they had a tremendous financial responsibility to rebuild what they had undone.

The Ten Years' War left both empires quite at a loss as what to do, so finally they just got their hands dirty, devalued their currency and rebuilt. But it had been a tremendous war while it lasted.

Her society had labeled the young girl "imperfect," but now had found a use for her, locking her in a powered combat suit and sending her forth to fight the enemy. If she didn't survive, she was only an imperfect person, serving the state and dying a hero. But was the real imperfection in the young girl or in the state . . . ?

Imperfect Mind
A Kin Wars Universe Short Story

Jason Cordova

I did not cry when the men wearing dark suits took me from the Holding Home in the dead of night. Tears had stopped being a thing years ago, after my parents had deposited me on the steps of the rundown building the day after my third birthday. Faint memories of their angry faces haunt me on occasion still, but the sadness was long gone. Which was a good thing. Showing weakness in that building meant you became prey to the older, bigger kids.

Since I was technically an adult when the Praetorians arrived, I had been expecting it. I did not fight or resist. That would have been a futile gesture. I merely lowered my head and acknowledged that I was no longer the responsibility of Sister Verona or the others who took care of the Imperfect children. There were no belongings for me to gather except for an old, ratty sweater I had received the previous Restoration Day. Sister Verona was not a cruel woman, though. She made certain that I could keep the clothes on my back, much to the annoyance of the Praetorians who were there to remove me from the premises.

Instead of moving me to another city, as I had expected, they took me to a military base on the outskirts of town. From there I was thrown into a shower, which terrified me initially because it was a waste of water. I also burned myself since I'd never experienced hot water before except for cooking. The Praetorians didn't seem to care, though, and had me scrub every inch of my body with a strange lotion, including my head. That was far worse than the hot water, but eventually every single hair on my body fell off. My armpits and between my legs were bare skin for the first time since I had started maturing at ten. Since I typically wore my hair on my head short anyway, it didn't bother me that much. Losing my hair between my legs bothered me greatly, though. The more I looked like a boy, the safer I'd be.

Unfortunately, standing naked in the middle of a room of Praetorians, it was hard to hide that I was not a boy, especially with everything bared. They didn't stare and gawk, like most of the older kids did when they found out I was a girl. The two men simply continued to go about their business, making certain I was clean and hairless. It was terrifying and painful, yet not nearly as bad as I had been expecting it to be.

We'd whispered in the dark about what happened to kids like us, the genetically imperfect, after they were removed from a Holding Home. The stories about being sold into slavery, to be used as play toys for rich men and women, haunted our dreams. Even the sisters who watched over us didn't help, reminding us to be careful when we walked out their doors because bad people wanted to harm us. We didn't understand. We couldn't, not really. We were kids, innocents. The warnings did nothing but infect our dreams, temper our hopes, and lead us to the realization that we were a subclass of human, not even worthy of being treated as equals. Over the years we accepted this, understood our role in the great society that was the Dominion of Man.

After the showers, I was led into a room where a bunch of men and women wearing long white coats waited. They looked me over and inspected me, making sure that my imperfections were not clearly physical. They weren't. I was born with Duane Syndrome, which affected my eyes. The men and women didn't seem concerned by this, though, which was odd. I knew my eyes were different. Always have. It affected the way I saw things at times.

"She's a good candidate," one of the gathered people declared. A woman, and from what I could tell, she seemed to be in charge of the group. Everyone else nodded in agreement and seemed pleased with her decision. I didn't know what I was a good candidate for, only that it was better than being sold into a gangster's brothel. Still, standing there in the middle of a group of strangers with nothing on made me a little nervous. She must have seen this and clucked her tongue. "Get her into a medical sheet. We'll begin the implant procedure immediately."

"Implant procedure?" I asked, becoming warier by the second. She tried to smile at me in a comforting manner but obviously wasn't used to dealing with people because it more resembled a grimace than anything else.

"Yes," the woman replied. "I am Doctor Pulvere. This is a test facility for a new combat weapon, and we were looking for volunteers. The Praetorians tasked with watching your Holding Home mentioned that you were available, healthy, and had expressed an interest in helping, so here we are."

"Oh," was all I could think of to say. It wasn't like I really had much to offer anyway. I was an Imperfect, a genetically inferior human being. My life was worth less than everyone else's, so why not offer to help? I'd always been like that as a child, eager to help others with the chores. It kept the beatings from the bigger kids to a minimum. "Okay."

"Excellent!" she clapped her hands excitedly. "Doctors Hiram and Keebler will prep you in the next room." She turned and looked at the Praetorians still on either side of me. "Your services are no longer required. Thank you."

The Praetorians left and two men, the doctors I assumed she had been talking about, led me into a smaller room off to the side. There was a sheet which I could put on to cover my nakedness. I quickly donned it and sat down on a cold metal stool as the two doctors moved behind me and began to inspect the back of my head. They argued quietly for a few moments before one of them held the top of my head still with one hand. With the other he drew a small circle and then added something to the inside of it.

They rubbed their fingertips over my smooth scalp for a moment before murmuring something. I couldn't understand them; their accents were thick and heavy. I knew that some accents in the Dominion were strong on worlds within the Core, but I'd never actually heard any of them before. On Solomon, everyone sounded about the same. Wanting to ask but not knowing how, I simply remained mute as they finished their brief examination. Standing me back up, they returned me to the large room. Instead of a large group of people waiting for me, there was a small bed on wheels and a lot of lights. Tools were gathered on a small tray next to it, and Doctor Pulvere stood waiting. She wore a strange mask and gloves and was now covered with a sheet very much like the one I wore. The doctor motioned for me to lie down on the small bed. I began to, but she instructed me to flip over onto my belly instead of lying on my back.

The pain I experienced over the next two hours was something that I could never properly describe. The best I could manage was that it felt as though electric wires were being dragged across my brain inside my skull. It was excruciating, and despite the shots they gave me, I felt everything. I was crying but unable to move because of an injection they gave me in my spine before the surgery began.

They cut open my head in the back where the doctors had drawn earlier and put something inside me. There was a lot of pressure behind my eyes for some reason, and I could hear the doctors talking about something, but the words made no sense to me. I tried to tell them that the pain was too much, but nothing came out but tears. They poured out of my eyes and dripped down my nose, falling to the tiled floor where they pooled over time.

After what felt like an entire lifetime, they were finished. Intellectually I knew that only two hours had passed, because the doctor's words became understandable again once the pressure behind my eyes went away.

"No time to waste," Doctor Pulvere told the gathered group as they wheeled my bed out of the large room and down a long corridor. I was slowly beginning to get the feeling back in my hands and feet as we arrived in a very dark room. Lights came on, and I tried to wince but couldn't. My face hadn't recovered yet from the injection and was frozen still. "Here we are. Let's get her into the mask and don't forget the goggles this time! The way the last test subject's eyes melted almost made me lose my lunch."

Unceremoniously they hoisted me off the bed. I almost threw up, but since I really didn't have control of my body just yet, I merely felt sick. My heels dragged along the rough surface of the floor, and I could almost feel the skin cracking from the friction. If it kept up for much longer I knew that there would be two trails of blood from my heels opening up soon. Fortunately, they reached their destination before that point and stopped dragging me.

An oxygen mask was put on my face and secured, then a pair of goggles went over my eyes. The air which poured into the mask and filled my lungs was richer than anything I'd ever breathed before, and the feeling in my legs and arms came back. I could see decently well through the goggles. Uncertain what was planned next, I allowed the two men carrying me to lift me off the ground completely.

They removed the thin material covering me, and I was naked once more. The two men didn't seem to notice or care as they focused on their task. I was then placed into a large device that seemed too big for my tiny body. It quickly dawned on me that it was human shaped, but much larger than the average human body. I could feel the tubing from the oxygen mask on my shoulder. I wanted to squirm, but the device I was in seemed to be more restrictive than I had thought it would be.

Suddenly, I felt something warm and slimy at my feet. I struggled as the sensations made their way up my legs, passing my kneecaps. I began to panic, but then I heard Doctor Pulvere's voice in my head.

"Relax," the woman whispered. I suddenly realized that her voice wasn't in my head, but next to it. A helmet of some sort lowered down over the top of me, and I was sealed inside. The goop continued to crawl up my legs and touched my thighs. I squirmed uncomfortably. "This is a gel designed to protect you once you're inside the mechanized infantry suit. In a moment you will feel a slight pinch in the back of your head, and then you will see everything that the Mark One sees."

Mark One? I had no idea what that was, but I fought the urge to panic as the gel substance reached my stomach. The only blessing of the strange sensation as it crept up my body was the warmth. That was actually nice, though a part of me began to wonder just how far the gel stuff was going to go. A minute later I found out just how high it would go.

Completely submerged, the panic returned. However, before I could focus on the fact that I was probably going to drown in a moment, a horrible pinching sensation made me scream. It was loud and echoed throughout the warehouse. Light assaulted my senses, and my skin felt cold and clammy. Bulky and heavy, I was no longer a tiny and underfed young woman. I was something far bigger, monstrous. Unable to hold back my emotions any longer, I began to bawl my eyes out.

"Shh, it's okay," Doctor Pulvere tried to calm me down as my cries seemed to echo throughout the cavernous room. "You're suffering from temporary sensory overload. Let me dial back the receptors, then you can adjust to the new sensations."

The room suddenly wasn't too bright, and my skin didn't feel as heavy or strange. I was normal, but not. I looked around and found that while I was unable to move my head, I could still see all around me. The warehouse seemed small compared to what it had felt like a moment before. Even Doctor Pulvere, as tall as she'd been when I'd first been led into the operating room, was tiny as she stood behind a metal desk. There was a long fabric-encased line which extended from the back of the desk to somewhere behind me.

"What happened?" I asked between sobs. Doctor Pulvere winced and pressed something I couldn't see at her desk. I tried to soften my voice and regain control of my emotions. "Doctor?"

"Much better." She nodded, ignoring my question for the moment. "Now try to lift your right arm."

Carefully, I lifted my right arm in front of my face and gasped as I saw that instead of my normal dark brown arm, a giant robotic one was before me. Instead of panicking like I had before, I instead focused on my breathing as I inspected the arm.

It was a flat, dull gray color with large plates of what I figured was armor stacked on top of one another. Bulkier than what I thought robotic arms should look like, it took me a few moments to realize that I was looking at armor covering my body. I was seeing with the robot's head somehow, though I was at a loss to explain it.

"How am I seeing this?" I asked Doctor Pulvere.

"The implant nodule in your head is called a cortex implant," she explained. "It allows you to interact with the Mark One suit as a second skin instead of actually wearing it. It should feel more natural than standard combat armor. It's our prototype mechanized infantry suit."

"Okay," I muttered and lowered my right arm. I did my left next, and then we worked on walking. It quickly became apparent that I was overcompensating, to which the doctor simply told me to walk normally.

"Don't make exaggerated movements," she told me again and again as I struggled through the movement tests. Eventually, after much trial and error, we figured it out, and I was moving around the warehouse as only a five-meter-tall mechanized infantry trooper could.

"I like this," I admitted after I trotted a few steps, quickly pirouetted, then landed on my right foot while kicking out with the left. It was a move I'd perfected while in the Holding Home to protect myself if a boy refused to accept "no" for an answer while delivering the maximum damage to his male bits. After the time I made Jarl vomit and pee blood for two weeks, the other boys at the Home stopped harassing me for good.

"You are naturally graceful," Doctor Pulvere told me. I could feel my face heating up in embarrassment inside the suit and was glad that I had both the breathing mask and helmet on to hide in. She continued on, unaware I was blushing. "If you had been Perfect, you probably could have trained to be a dancer."

"But I'm not," I said as I stood upright. The suit definitely felt more natural to me now than before, and it mimicked my movements perfectly. I didn't even have to think about it anymore, I simply *did*, and it followed suit, mimicking my motions at the same time I performed them. The doctor had been right; it did feel like a second skin.

"No, you're not," she agreed with my previous statement. I wasn't mad about it. It was simply a fact of life.

"What else can this do?" I asked, curious now as I strode over to where Doctor Pulvere was at her computer.

"The suit can handle weapons as well, such as heavy machine guns and even recoilless anti-tank rifles," she replied. I nodded, pretending to know what she was talking about. I had no idea what a recoilless anti-tank rifle even was, though I was a little familiar with the term "machine gun." I'd seen a vid once where the hero had one and had fought the evil villains, agents of the Caliphate. Very noble death at the end for the hero, and the love interest moved home to care for their beautiful Perfect child. Doctor Pulvere continued, seemingly unaware of my ignorance. "We are designing a rotating cannon for the arms but we're still working on the physics of that, plus identifying the attachment points and where to place spare ammunition. We might make the arms bulkier and simply allow it to be stored there. We're working on that."

I still had no idea what she was talking about, but it sounded like she did, so I changed the subject. "This should have blades on the arms or something, for stabbing faces. What about knives sticking out when I make a fist?"

"I like the way you think." The doctor grinned. She typed in something on her computer and looked back up at the suit. "Definitely something to keep in mind for future upgrades to the suit. How do you feel about a field test?"

"A what?" I asked as I felt a certain giddiness envelop my senses. I'd experienced something like this before, when one of the boys had smuggled in some Blizz and we had sat in the cellar later that night, tasting the stuff. It made my brain tingle with pleasure, and I'd done some stupid stuff afterwards with the older boys. I didn't have that desire now, thankfully, but it still made me feel really good.

"Go out into the field and test this," she asked again as she continued to type on her keyboard. Oddly enough, I felt the need to do this. The tingling sensation disappeared and was replaced by a desire to serve. I couldn't explain it, but the desire to go out and fight was appealing. I was nodding inside the suit before she had even finished asking the question.

"Yeah, we can go and break bad people," I suggested in a cheerful voice. Doctor Pulvere looked up at me for a moment before slyly smiling. Making her happy made *me* happy for some reason, so I was really beginning to understand her. I pressed on. "Maybe we can go kill some pirates or something?"

"Kill?" she asked, obviously amused. "Pirates? There are no pirates on Solomon."

"I . . ." Here I paused, uncertain. I almost seemed to *know* that pirates were, indeed, on Solomon. Somehow, with no rhyme or reason, I could even pinpoint where they were on a map. It was scary, but I decided to speak up anyway. "No, they're here, on the planet's surface. I can show you on a map."

"That's okay, I believe you," Doctor Pulvere said and smiled. She took her hands away from the keyboard and stretched her back. "While we were talking, I found a pirate's base that is reputed to be on this world. It has been hitting colonists' resupply vessels regularly and they have what seems to be a den near here. The marines are too busy to do anything, and the Navy can't drop kinetics onto their base without disrupting the atmosphere. This seems to me the ideal situation for the new mechanized infantry. How about it? Do you want to try it out?"

I was nervous, but ready. "Yes. Only one problem, though."

"What's that?"

"I don't know how to use a gun," I admitted. She smiled again, and I immediately felt more confident about my abilities. I don't know what it was about this woman, but she could motivate me to be greater.

"I think you know more than you realize," she commented as she turned back to her computer for a moment. Satisfied with whatever she had typed in, the doctor began to walk toward a set of wide double doors at the other end of the warehouse. Noticing that I wasn't with her, she stopped and glared at me. My heart dropped as I saw the disappointment in her eyes. I couldn't let her down. I followed loyally behind. I would take down the pirates and protect the Dominion. It was expected of me.

"Where are we going?" I asked the doctor.

"To get you a weapon, then send you in to kill some pirates."

My heart leapt into my throat. It was something I'd always wanted to do, and now I was getting the chance to do it. The strangest thing about it all, though, was that I knew deep down that this was wrong, that I'd never even given any thought to fighting pirates before. Now, though, it didn't matter. Killing pirates was my only mission in life. I would kill all the pirates or die trying.

Doctor Pulvere led me to a smaller room where four rather nervous looking men wearing identical uniforms were waiting. I had seen something like what they had on in a vid once and immediately recognized them as marines. I had to duck to get through the doorway even though it was almost seven meters high. There was more than enough room for me to stand upright to my full height once inside. This, of course, made the men back up warily. Either they had never seen someone as large as I was, or my suit scared them. Either way, it pleased me to see other Imperfects like these marines respect me. Being reminded that I was the ultimate authority on behalf of the doctor made me feel amazing, powerful. I smirked inside my suit. *Those pirates don't stand a chance*, I thought as Doctor Pulvere began to explain to the marines precisely what I needed.

I had no idea what a Ma Deuce was, but when the marines began to bolt a massive gun on my left arm, I couldn't help but feel a little giddy. It made that arm a little heavier than before, but I managed. The marines then attached two large circular drums beneath it and began to feed the belt with all the ammunition on it into the machine gun. The drums each weighed over two hundred pounds. To compensate for the added weight I leaned more to my right. It was awkward but I managed.

"Yes, that'll do nicely," Doctor Pulvere stated as she inspected me with a critical eye. She appeared to be pleased, which made me all tingly once more. My brain was on fire with the amount of pleasure I was receiving at her apparent satisfaction. I was more than ready to go and kill every pirate in the universe, and anyone else that the good doctor needed dead. She smiled and I about died of orgasmic bliss. "You ready to go, young lady?"

"Yes!" I nearly screamed. The sensations were too much. I needed to kill, needed to rip the heads off of every single enemy of the doctor.

"If you think about a map, one will appear in your vision," she told me. I tried to think of a map and, just as the doctor said it would, one appeared. It showed a blue glowing dot in the middle with a red X to the left of center. It actually wasn't too far away, from what I could tell. "That red X might appear to be close, but it's actually ten kilometers away. Your suit has more than enough fuel to make it there, destroy the pirate den, and return. If you pivot left and right you'll see the position of the X will change."

I did so and, sure enough, the X moved. However, so did the marines who had helped attached the Ma Deuce to my left arm as the barrel swept across their heads. They yelled and managed to avoid being brained by the long barrel of the machine gun.

"Sorry!" I apologized and pointed the barrel upward. Suddenly it dawned on me that I didn't know how to fire the blasted thing. I looked over at the doctor, ashamed. "Doctor, I'm . . . I'm sorry, but I don't know how to shoot this machine gun. I've failed you."

"It's okay, child," she whispered and gently reached over and patted my hip. "Don't do it now, but when you're ready to fire simply clench your left hand and hold it shut. The machine gun will fire until you unclench. Just be careful. You only have twelve hundred rounds of ammunition before you're empty. Try not to blast through that in one go, okay?"

"Yes, ma'am," I said in a respectful voice, recalling what Sister Verona had told me about politeness when dealing with Perfects. I loved the doctor, of course, but extra politeness never hurt. "Do I just go to the X spot and kill everyone in the pirate's den?"

"Yes, dear, that's precisely what you need to do," she said and smiled. Oh, it was glorious! I would die for that smile. "Don't fail me."

"Never!" I gasped as stronger emotions raced through me. I lumbered awkwardly out the door and back into the training warehouse. The map on my screen showed me that another route out of the building would get me there faster, and I would fit through it. Plus, it would keep me away from the administration points, which filled me with a strange sense of dread.

I moved away from the military base and deep into the wilderness around the city. I'd grown up in the city but had never stepped foot outside the city limits. I didn't know of any other Holding Home kids who had snuck out of the city and ever come back. We could only guess as to their fates. Dead? Maimed? Eaten by wild animals and then worn as skins? All of us kids had no idea.

Now, out on my own and within the Mark One suit, I knew that I was the top predator around. There was nothing that could actually hurt me in the wilds. The pirates might have machine guns that could do something, but I had absolute and perfect faith in Doctor Pulvere and her suit. She wouldn't fail me, not in any way, shape, or form. This suit of hers was perfection.

As I raced along, the former euphoric sensations I had felt faded, and soon I began to crave some sort of communication with the doctor. Strange as it was, it paled in comparison to the anger which was beginning to build. Every second away from the doctor caused my rage to build. I vowed then and there to kill every single pirate I found. They were the reason I could not stay in the presence of the doctor and bask in her brilliance.

As my hatred fueled me, I realized I was rapidly closing in on the position marked on the map. The suit helpfully zoomed in, and I could see the pirate's den from over a kilometer away. It was what I had expected it to look like, with a wide-open field for pirate ships to land on and lots of defense towers. I figured that if I could see them, they should see me soon enough. I needed to correct this.

Not knowing how far the rounds in the Ma Deuce could shoot, I decided to creep in a little closer. Unfortunately, I knocked down a small spruce tree and startled a herd of deer which had been bedding down for the day where I was walking. They were on their feet and bounding off toward the pirate den in a flash, which caused the guards atop the towers to glance in my direction. I was close enough now to see the absolute shock and surprise on their faces.

"I guess that's close enough for the Ma Deuce," I murmured as I aimed the machine gun up toward the closest tower. A small reticle appeared on my screen, showing me where I was pointing the barrel of the gun. I realized that if I fired now, the only thing I would hit would be the concrete support structure and not the men ten meters higher. I adjusted and clenched my fist.

What came forth from the barrel of the Ma Deuce was unlike anything I had experienced in my life. The muzzle flashed brightly as I poured forth hate from the barrel and into the bodies of my unwitting targets. The two pirates in the tower seemingly came apart at the seams as the rounds tore through them. Bright red blood splashed radiantly into the clear blue sky, and I could see entrails and gore dripping down the side of the tower, a beautiful yet macabre painting of death and carnage.

"Oh . . . wow," I whispered and relaxed my firing hand. The Ma Deuce stopped spitting out rounds immediately. A small screen appeared in the corner with what appeared to be a bullet in it. I quickly figured out that this was how much ammo I had left in the drums of the Ma Deuce. I blinked in surprise as I realized I'd fired over fifty rounds at the tower. If there were hundreds of pirates in the den, I'd run out of ammunition long before I got to kill all the pirates. I'd need to be more careful in the future.

Ahead I could see smaller figures on the ground scrambling as the alarm sounded. Since they were obviously aware of my presence I decided to run to the den. If I could get there quick enough, then I could potentially stop them from getting better prepared. It was a trick I learned at the Holding Home. If there's no other option available, attack.

The first thing I discovered was that the Mark One suit was *fast*. I had been quick before, since it had allowed me to roam the streets of New Haven without being molested by creepy strangers. The ability to outrun even the gangers had come in handy on numerous occasions. Now, though, I seemed to fly across the open ground, my heavy steps leaving large footprints deep in the soft dirt behind me.

A group of pirates appeared in front of me, seemingly out of nowhere. The suit's reticle appeared in my eyes and the Ma Deuce came up almost of its own accord. I squeezed off a few shots and watched in satisfaction as two of the pirate's heads exploded into a fine red mist. The others started shooting back, and the Mark One's armor was tested at long last.

Unsurprisingly, the suit held up under the barrage of gunfire. My senses tingled as it dawned on me that Doctor Pulvere's design was working perfectly to keep me alive. I had promised her that I would kill each and every pirate I found, and it was a promise I intended to keep. I stopped running, leveled the Ma Deuce, and let it rip.

The results were predictable. Eight dead pirates, one living Imperfect encased in a massive armored suit of death. There was nothing that could harm me.

I jerked violently as something exploded against my right shoulder. The suit warned me that I had been hit with a grenade, fired from a distance great enough to prevent it from identifying the source. Remaining still meant becoming dead, so I started sprinting at an oblique angle toward the den. Two more explosions blew up a small cloud of shrapnel and dirt before me. Near misses, but they enabled the suit to locate the shooter at last. It was a young woman, no older than I was, firing from a concrete bunker about forty meters ahead. I sighted her head, aimed carefully, and squeezed off a single round. The shot removed her head from the body's shoulders. I looked around and moved in further.

A warning light told me that the suit had suffered some external damage on the right side from the grenade. I couldn't fix it, but since it didn't seem to be affecting my shooting or movement, I ignored it for the time being. I figured that once I was back with Doctor Pulvere she could fix it. I hoped that she would accept my apology and not be too disappointed in my damaging her suit.

As I got closer to the pirate den I realized there were a lot of concrete bunkers which were close enough together to make me very suspicious. Figuring that the majority of the den was underground somewhere, and that I needed to find an entrance, I began to search for a building which looked like it would lead underground. Here my history as an Imperfect child left to their own devices on the streets of New Haven paid off.

Past experience told me that every ganger who roamed the bad parts of New Haven needed somewhere to operate out of. One of the things that kids in Holding Homes always knew was how to spot them. It would be someplace that would look plain and boring, not the slum housing falling to the ground or ritzy high-rise towering into the sky. Nothing to draw attention to it, either good or bad. These buildings, usually squat and almost always ugly, were where ganger bosses like to store their goods, be it drugs, stolen property, or anything else that caught their eye.

The best bet for most of us kids was to avoid them. Gangers seemed to take perverse pleasure in tormenting young Imperfect kids, even going so far as to kill them for sport. There used to be a gang a few years back that ran underground fights between young kids. They would give them long knives and tell them to kill each other, or they would be killed instead. These fights were always to the death, and lots of gambling went down during these events. Fortunately, the Praetorians eventually stepped in and stopped them before I was old enough to get caught up in the fights. Still, I knew of many Imperfect men and women with long, ugly scars running up and down their arms from these underground battles.

I looked around and quickly spotted the most likely building. Unlike some of the others that appeared to be rundown and abandoned, this one had a few boarded-up windows but otherwise was in decent shape. What convinced me, though, was the men who kept coming out of the building in spite of its relatively small size. Either they were packed in there tightly or there was another entrance I couldn't see.

As the pirates came out of the building like ants out of a kicked anthill, I realized I was missing an opportunity and started firing.

Large holes appeared in the wall of the building as some of the rounds from the Ma Deuce punched through the person I was shooting and impacted the wall. I painted the formerly white stucco walls red with the blood of the pirates.

They started falling back inside in search of protection, so I continued to walk my stream of gunfire into the doorway. There the bodies began to pile up as they struggled to run and escape to the safety of the building. The pirates were struggling to climb over their dead and wounded in an attempt to flee. I removed that hope with more well-placed shots and continued to fire until there were none left moving.

I glanced at the counter and saw that I had fired over one thousand rounds already. Dismayed, I vowed to be more discriminatory when it came to shooting in the future. With less than two hundred remaining and an unknown number of bad guys still to be found, I would have to make every shot count from here on out.

I continued to approach the building but couldn't hear anything on the inside. Visually sweeping the bodies in front of the door, it became apparent that a lot of them weren't dead but merely wounded. Knowing that the doctor would be displeased with my efforts if I left anyone alive, but at the same time realizing I needed to conserve ammunition, I simply began to step on the heads of the wounded.

It was over in a brutally short amount of time.

I ducked into the building and looked around. I could see a small trapdoor in the floor in the corner of the large open room, which was exactly what I expected. However, it quickly became apparent to me that I had no way of getting down there easily. Carefully maneuvering myself inside the building, I stayed crouched low enough to not destroy the roof. It wasn't painful since the suit was doing all the work, but it still felt awkward with the Ma Deuce and the nearly-empty ammo drums on the left throwing off my balance. Still, I managed, and finally ended up standing over the trapdoor looking down into a dark tunnel.

After a few seconds of inspection, I determined that I probably couldn't fit down into the hole. Still, I needed to clear the underground tunnel for any more pirates. I looked around the room for something that would give me an idea. As I stared at the stucco walls it dawned on me that while I might not necessarily be able to drag anyone out, I could definitely bury them within. The walls looked more than heavy enough, and I knew that they were pretty solid.

It didn't take me more than ten minutes to tear down the house on top of the trap door after I closed it, ensuring that any pirates trapped in the tunnel were stuck. For good measure I piled the bodies of dead pirates on top of the house, as a message to any who might come after to help them. It was a long process, not because of the weight of the bodies, but because I wanted to ensure I got as many dismembered parts together as I could beforehand.

Doing this continued to give me unimaginable pleasure and more than once I had to stop and breathe as the shaking became too much. There was just something so exciting and marvelous about pleasing the doctor by killing pirates. Nothing I had ever experienced in my life could top the sensations that coursed through me at that moment.

A noise from my left drew my attention. It was another pirate, though this one was encased in some sort of heavy lift device. I'd seen them before during construction projects in New Haven. Twin lifts extended from each arm and enhanced the wearer's strength tenfold, and the support legs could help move tons of equipment fast inside of an enclosed area. This one appeared to be modified slightly, with thicker arms and a protected driver's area.

I brought my Ma Deuce up and targeted the driver's compartment. Clenching my fist, I unleashed hell onto the last remaining pirate that I could see. The large rounds from the Ma Deuce bounced harmlessly off of the lifter's arm. The person driving that thing must have figured I would try something like this and had been prepared. I let the gunfire taper off as I began to trot toward it. I was down to six rounds now, which was silly. I'd wasted a stupid amount of what little ammunition I had left trying to shoot a walking tank like me.

Not like me though. The lifter was slower, and while I knew it was probably twice as powerful, I could maneuver. It would be a nasty fight if I got in too close and let the lifter grab me with one of those arm lifts. I remembered what the doctor had told me earlier about being graceful and put that to use.

I bounded into the air and lashed out with one of my armored legs. The extended reach of the Mark One allowed me to stay just out of range of the lifter. The pirate inside apparently couldn't compensate for the extra movement and staggered to the right as my suit's foot connected solidly on his left shoulder. It spun but I was already moving quickly behind the lifter, bringing the Ma Deuce up to fire. I only had six shots left and needed to make each one count. I started shooting into the back of the driver's carriage, trying to keep each shot at the same point of impact to weaken the armor.

Unfortunately, none of my final shots penetrated the lifter. One, however, did ricochet back and impacted the helmet of the Mark One. I felt the impact above my head and winced, glad that I was shorter than normal. My ears were ringing from the bullet bouncing off my suit as dizziness threatened to overwhelm me, and I struggled to stay upright.

The lifter must have sensed my moment of weakness because the pilot managed to grab me with the lifts and the two prongs which stuck out of each arm locked into place. One had managed to grab my left arm, pinning it down to the side and rendering it useless while the other had encircled my waist. I struggled to escape but the power behind the lifter was too much. The prongs began to close shut, and the Mark One suit started to creak and groan in protest as the lifter applied more pressure.

It was becoming difficult to breathe the more the lifter squeezed. I was enraged because if I didn't kill the driver of the lifter, I would have failed the doctor. Her disproval would kill me more painfully than anything the stupid pirate could manage. I was running out of options, though. I was stuck, and with only one arm free there was almost no way for me to gain leverage.

For a moment I wished I could see inside the protective case of the lifter, so I could look into the eyes of the person who was about to kill me. It was denial on my part. I couldn't believe that I was going to die and fail Doctor Pulvere like this. Anger, confusion, and fear flooded my mind. There had to be some way I could at least take the person inside with me.

As my fury grew, I realized that there was a raised edge on the side of the protective driver's cover. The clamps around my waist grew tighter still, and the suit began to malfunction. I was in near agony as the forks slowly pressed in on my pelvic bone from either side. The pressure grew greater as the suit's protection started to fail. There wasn't much time. I had to kill him, and now.

With the last of my strength, I managed to dig the suit's fingertips beneath the lipped edge. I yanked it once, twice, but nothing. Howling with pain and anger, I tried one final time. It crumpled and the armored cover was torn asunder, revealing a very confused and alarmed man on the inside.

At that same moment I suddenly felt cold all over my body. Numbness hit my entire lower half as I felt *something*. I couldn't see anything below a certain point but the suit helpfully informed me that everything beneath my pelvic region had been removed and the cortex was administering neural blocks to prevent me from feeling any pain. It also told me that I was bleeding to death and had but a few minutes at most before I died. More than likely I would be dead in seconds.

"That sucks," I whispered as blackness began to fill the edges of my vision. I was ashamed. I would fail Doctor Pulvere. *No you won't!* something inside my mind screamed. *You have one chance. Use it!*

I eventually succumbed to the pain, but not before I used the last of my strength to reach out and crush the skull of the last pirate with my hand.

"I read your report, doctor. Very impressive. Well done that your little Imperfect eliminated that troublesome nest of political undesirables. Tell me, how did the suit perform, in your opinion?" Emperor Solomon Lukas II asked impatiently as Doctor Lucinda Pulvere finished analyzing the data on her screen. The ruler of the Dominion had only just seized the Blood Throne a few years before, and with the fourth anniversary the following month, the paranoid ruler wanted something to show Parliament that it was *he* who controlled the empire. The mechanized infantry suits were supposed to solidify his hold on the Blood Throne and drive away any pesky contenders and claimants, most especially his older sister, Sarah.

"The suit works just fine, Your Majesty," Doctor Pulvere told him as she looked around the room. The emperor had insisted on absolute privacy for this meeting, yet the man who had orchestrated his grab for the throne, Lord Matthias Samuels, sat off to the side. Emperor Solomon either did not care about Lord Samuels' presence or, more than likely, wanted him there. Doctor Pulvere had no idea why, though. "More armor might be handy, or I'd recommend that they do not engage in close-quarter combat in the future. The primary weapons system operated ideally and flawlessly. The implant nodule worked well after some time of disorientation for the subject, and the cortex worked perfectly in conjunction with the suit, as expected. The patient was susceptible to all programming changes and was more eager to please, the more input she received. However, blind obedience might not always be the best. Perhaps just reinforcing positive behavior toward an ideology? I don't know yet; we'll need more tests to determine that. There might also be some flaws when the later generations and upgrades are introduced. I believe we should install some sort of loyalty subconscious programming to prevent acts of violence against the royal family. This way nobody can usurp control of them. The amount of rage the subject showed during the last few minutes of fighting allowed us to measure some very interesting patterns in her brain-wave activity, sire."

"Such as?"

"The angrier she became, the more effective the cortex and suit worked, Your Majesty," Doctor Pulvere explained as she pulled up the data and transferred it to the emperor's computer. He glanced at it in a cursory fashion, making it abundantly clear to the doctor that he did not understand what he was looking at and was waiting for her to explain. After a pause, she continued. "The brain transferred the data far faster as she fought her way into the rebel's base. I would recommend in the future we come up with a way to test brain-wave patterns to find the right fit with our Imperfects. Of course, we'll have to figure out if these mechanized infantry suits are going to be marines or fall under Navy jurisdiction . . ."

"Neither," the emperor stated as he glanced over at the nominally quiet Lord Samuels. The Justice nodded in agreement. "We're working an amendment into the Constitution to have them fall under direct command of the sitting ruler only. Call them a royal guard or something. Limit their numbers, but only I can command them, or someone at my behest, like a general or something."

"Commandant." Lord Samuels spoke for the first time, his eyes glinting as he turned to look at the doctor. She felt insignificant under that reptilian gaze. "It has a better ring to it. Instills both confidence *and* fear, a wise combination in these trying days."

"Fine, sure, whatever." The emperor waved him off. "Tell me, doctor...how many more of these suits can we produce?"

"A lot, Your Majesty," she readily admitted. "Now that the last of the cortex issues have been worked out, we simply need the go-ahead to find a contractor to build them."

"Excellent." The emperor nodded and stood. Doctor Pulvere, not anticipating the move, stumbled to her feet, grabbing her carrying case and nearly dropping her computer as well along the way. She tucked it inside and secured the case. Lord Samuels was already up, which infuriated the doctor. The old lord from Corus was a slimy individual. "You're dismissed, Doctor."

"Thank you, Your Majesty." Doctor Pulvere bowed deeply at the waist and backed away. As she passed the required ten-meter mark, she turned and began to walk out. As she reached the door, however, the emperor's voice stopped her short.

"By the way...whatever happened to your Mark I prototype suit that the girl was wearing?"

"Recovered, Your Majesty," Doctor Pulvere stated. "It didn't give up the ghost. One of the doctors on my team suggested calling it a Ghost suit, but I disagreed and thought that it was inappropriate to name it at this time. The girl inside, though, didn't survive."

"Ah...so your secondary project failed?"

"Not quite, Your Majesty," Doctor Pulvere corrected mildly, choosing her next few words with utmost caution. "Her brain-wave patterns were remarkably clear, and what we dug out of the cortex is almost a completely fresh mind. We have our best scientists working on the artificial intelligence program now, using her as a template. Fifteen, twenty years and we'll be able to create a fully functional AI. We've already established a lab on the world where we did the field test, Your Majesty."

"Very good." The emperor nodded. He glanced at Lord Samuels before continuing. "Oh, what are you calling it? The AI program, I mean?"

"We were thinking of naming it after the girl whose brain waves we're using, Your Majesty," Doctor Pulvere answered. "Almost like a backhanded compliment, even though she *was* just an Imperfect."

"Color me curious. What was her name?"

"Sfyri."

Once there was a high-tech dystopia which fell, only to be succeeded by an anti-tech dystopia where a child could have no hope. Until a man who remembered the old times gave her a high-tech present.

Peter Power Armor

John C. Wright

Let me tell you a story about a girl named Bliss. I didn't like her when I first met her, but all that is changed now.

I found the power-armor I used to wear as a child in the wall-space behind my parents' attic, behind a door paneled to look like part of the wainscoting. No dust disturbed this miniature clean-room; no looters had found it here, not in all the years.

The fact that smooth white light filled the room when the silent door opened filled me with a premonition. I stepped inside and saw, (as I had not dared hope) that an umbilicus connected the little suit to sockets in the wall. The energy box above the socket was stamped with three black triangles in a yellow circle.

Behind me, in the main attic space, I could hear the little brat named Bliss grunt a little high-pitched grunt as she picked up a crowbar. A moment later there was a shivering crash as she tossed it through one of the living stain-glassed dormer windows. I remembered the day her mother had purchased those windows, grown one molecule at a time by a nano-mathematician artist. Those had been days of sunshine, and even the upper windows no one saw had been works of fine art, charged with life.

You see, Bliss was a naughty, silly girl. It is really not her fault. She was raised to be that way.

"Darling," I said, trying to keep my voice even. "Don't kill the windows. They are special. They were bulletproof, once, back before their cohesion faded. They're antiques, and cannot reproduce. It makes them the last of their kind."

Bliss was bright enough to ask a question: "So what? What makes them special?" It is always good to ask questions.

I said gently: "You see how the old building had their windows facing outward? Not like modern buildings. Remember your school? All the windows only face inside, toward the courtyard. And your dorm is the same way, isn't it? You can tell a lot about a culture by where they put their windows."

The courtyard-based construction of modern buildings reminds me of European designs. I don't really like Europe.

I heard little Bliss whine to the matron: "Mother Hechler! Mr. Paine is trying to oppress me again!"

It was not my real name. I always introduced myself as Thomas Paine, these days. No one ever caught the reference, not even people my age.

The chestplate of the power-armor was set with large phosphorescent buttons, with little cartoon-character faces to indicate the function options. I hit the Peter Power-Armor Power-on Pumpkin with my thumb. There was a *goo-ga* flourish of toy trumpet noise, a whisper of servomotors, and the suit stood up.

I know Bliss did not know her parents. I am guessing the age at about seven years old. Her mother, her real mother, had been a lovely, lively, caring woman, smart as a devil and with a sense of humor to match. That sense of humor managed to get her declared an unfit parent.

The father, Geoffrey, had been an environmental engineer. Very bright man. He had written papers, back before the Diebacks, questioning whether the trends showed a General Global Warming or a General Cooling. Those papers had cropped up again after Bliss was born. Geoffrey had been sterilized by the committee in charge of the First Redistribution; they believed in Global Warming. He had been made to vanish by the Second. They believed in Cooling.

And little Bliss was just not as bright as Geoffrey's daughter should have been. I knew the ugly reason why.

The helmet came only about to my waist, even when the armor was upright on its stubby legs. It looked like a miniature King Arthur's knight, although I remember other attachments could make it look like a deep-sea diver's suit or a firefighter. The smart-metal was made of a flex of microscopic interlocking strands, and I saw telescopic segments at the limb-joints and breastplate-seams, enabling the suit to expand to fit a growing child.

I heard, behind and below me, a soggy, heavy noise as the stairs whined under the bulk of Mrs. Hechler's footsteps. I heard her pant. She said, "Bliss!" She was calling up the stairs. Hechler was too inert, it seemed, to make it all the way. "Stop familiarizing with the People's Helpers. You are to call him 'Janitor' or 'Shit-sweeper.' We don't use his name, moppet: it makes them uppity."

Tiny xylophone notes came from inside the helmet as the suit ran through its systems check. I could see the colors of a puppet-show reflected backward in the faceplate during the warm-up, as big-eyed rabbits and ducks in sailor suits pantomimed out safety messages as each suit function went through its automatic check.

It may seem absurd, but tears came to my eyes when Battery Bunny turned into a skeleton-silhouette surrounded by twinkling lightning bolts above the words: KEEP FINGERS CLEAR OF THE RECHARGE SOCKET! Battery Bunny had once been a best playmate of mine, since I had had no real, non-virtual friends.

(Billy Worthemer was a real friend of mine. A real flesh and blood boy. Lots of blood. I will tell you about him if I have time. But, after Billy, no, after that I had had no real friends, except for Bunny. Well, maybe one.) Good old loyal bunny. How could I have forgotten him?

I wiped my eyes. At the same time, to cover the xylophone-noise of the suit-check, I was saying loudly: "Matron Hechler! The student-child is destroying property of the state! This may lead to bad habits later!"

Another soggy noise as Hechler climbed another step. She wheezed a moment, then said, "Let her have her fun. This stuff is from the Time of Greed. It's worthless. Go ahead, Bliss."

I heard a dull giggle, and then more smashing.

I twisted and removed the adult-override key from the armor's chestplate, picked up the remote handset from the socket, and thumbed the test button on the microwave relay. The LED lit up. I tapped my fingers on the handset and the little armored suit did a silent little jig of joy. Such elegant controls! Such a well-made machine!

Another button made Mr. Don't-Point-Me come out of his holster. I had forgotten, or I never knew, that the holster had a child-safety relay on it, which made an alarm-noise blatt from the handset. With one thumb I pushed the suppress button on the handset to kill the noise. With the other I reached for the larger, colored controls on the chestplate. I remembered that the Deadly Donkey button armed the lethal rounds. I hit Sleepy Sancho Pancake, and watched as a clip of narcoleptic darts was jacked into the chamber. The little armor twirled the gun on its gauntlet-finger and slid Mr. Don't-Point-Me back into the holster. I had programmed that little flourish in, when I was a child. I had seen Laser Cowboy do it on STV, and I had practiced and practiced in front of a mirror. That was my hand motion.

Hechler had heard the alarm. Her voice came nearer, sounding angry, "What's that noise?"

I said in a loud happy voice, "Bliss! Come quick!"

Bliss, sullenly, "What . . . ?! Is a machine? They're bad for you."

"Never mind," I called out. I heard her little footsteps coming closer. "I'll just keep it all for myself."

Bliss's footsteps sped up. Any adult who cannot outwit a seven-year-old should turn in his license.

I also heard the matron's voice coming at a lumbering trot. Stairs squealed, and then the attic floorboards protested. "What—what's that light up there!"

I had to get her to come up. I said loudly, "It should be obvious what it is, you soggy old fart! I've found a working light. Don't you have eyes? I must say that I am continually amazed, now that each village and hamlet is divided into work zones and care zones for the communal raising and nurture of children, at the consistently low quality of the substitute parents involved."

Bliss was in the doorway, now. Her eyes grew big and round. I remember days when children often had such looks on their faces, at birthday parties, or at Christmas. Back when we had Christmas.

I took Bliss by the shoulder and guided her toward the armor. My other hand pushed the introduction menu sequence with the handset. The armor turned toward Bliss, evidently recognizing her as having the infrared profile and radar-silhouette of a child. It performed a perfect courtly bow toward her. She watched in awe as it took her hand and bent over it, pretending to kiss it.

And the little brat (her brattyness forgotten, or on hold) actually blushed and looked pleased, a modest princess. She was utterly charmed. I had to smile.

I continued talking the way I used to talk, in a loud voice, "But we cannot have a society where all child rearing is public, without expecting it to end up in the same state as our public bathrooms. And what kind of low, common, ignorant folk will volunteer to serve as wardens for children not their own, whom they cannot adopt or make their own? Who would be willing to raise a child by rulebook? By committee? I suspect those who cannot get jobs as prison guards . . ."

But that was enough. Mrs. Hechler was here, red-faced, and angry enough that she had forgotten to use her radio-phone to call Jerry. Jerry, downstairs, was not a Regulator; he was an Infant Proctor, which was something between a Baby Sitter and the Bull. But I think he was packing heat.

Maybe she was too dumb to call him; too dumb to think I was dangerous. Or maybe her phone was broken again.

Her eyes grew round when she saw the lights, the atomic-power symbol on the wall, the brass-and-gold little armored figure. I do not think she recognized what the armor was; I think she thought it was a statue or a toy or something.

A woman raised in her generation, of course, could not understand the kind of folks people of my parents' generation were.

And so she stepped into the room. She did not know what kind of thing Peter was; or what kind of person I am.

Let me explain it to you. I don't know how much room is in the file: I'll try to be brief. But I have to tell you the way it was.

My dad was there the day the rules of war changed. He was about eight years old. He had climbed a tree, and found a little green-and-brown colored aerosol spray-can wedged into the branches, pointing over the sidewalk below. I remember him telling me how bright and sunny the day was, how the sidewalk sparkled, how the people looked so happy, so normal, when they walked by, walking dogs, carrying groceries, herding children, balancing schoolbooks on heads.

Every time someone walked by, the little aerosol can button went down. Activated by a motion sensor. Dad put his hand in front of the nozzle, and felt a wet invisible spray touch his palm. He sniffed it; it was odorless. He wiped the sticky wetness off on the green-and-brown label of the can.

His district was one of the few with a death toll under one hundred. A day or two later, a swarm of self-propelled smart-bullets, maybe launched from a passing crop-duster, maybe mortar-shot off the back of a flatbed truck, swept through the area, and homed in on everything which had been tagged by the invisible radioactive mist.

One of the bullets struck the aerosol can, of course, so that no further tagging was done, and the second and third wave of smart-bullets which came the next day, and the next week, found no targets.

Everyone who walked by on the sidewalk that day—Dad used to tell me their names, they were his neighbors and playmates—was gone.

When I was young, and played with my dad, he used to pretend to be Captain Hook. His prostethic was actually a complex thing, that could open and close almost like a pair of fingers. But it did look like a hook.

The next generation of smart bullets were even smarter, smaller, and able to fly longer distances. With a shoulder-launched booster, a rifleman could throw a packet of smart bullets over the horizon.

And warfare wasn't warfare any more. No more gathering on battlefields, no more getting into big battleships, and steaming out to meet other battleships. No sir. Soldiers traveled in pairs, not in platoons. One rifleman to launch the bullets. He would sit in a tree, or wearing a diving suit and lay on the bottom of a lake or something. His partner, the forward observer, would walk into town with a laser pencil. He would sit on a park bench and pretend to eat a submarine sandwich or something, or smoke a cigarette—which was legal, back then—and point the laser pencil at a passer-by. A bullet from out of the sky would drop down and hit the target. In a crowd, who would hear the noise? Maybe he'd get two or three, he'd pack up his sandwich, walk down the street, find another bench.

You could launch smart bullets from a normal shotgun, or even a lead pipe. Heck, if you dropped one off a tall enough building, it could pick up enough speed for its lifting surfaces to get purchase, reach terminal velocity, and if your target was anywhere below the building, the bullet could angle over. There wouldn't even be the sound of a gunshot. Same thing dropping a boxful from a cropduster.

Those smart bullets were smart. They had memory metal jackets which could act like little tiny fins and ailerons, giving them some ability to correct their course in-flight when diving into the target. Some changed shape as they entered the target, swelling or dilating to change their cross-section. They could slim down their noses right before hitting bulletproof vests, to become armor-penetrating, and flattening their heads when they hit flesh to become dum-dums.

Mom told me her bridesmaid was shot during the wedding. The girl was standing too near an open window, and maybe her gown gave her a silhouette that some dumb smart bullet thought looked like a target. That was back when people still gathered in churches for weddings and stuff. Back when buildings still had open windows.

The pixel resolution on these weapons was not the greatest. Forty-nine times out of fifty they could not tell the difference between a school child and a lamp post, a passer-by, a shadow on the wall, a fire hydrant. So you'd have to shoot fifty-one bullets to make sure you hit a target.

Yes, I said a school child. Target of choice, once the rules of war went away. Why? Well, the point of war is to use violence to terrify the enemy into submission; to break his will to resist. Right? The best place for violence was in a town; that's where the people are. The best place for terror is in a school; that's where the people gather all their children.

All their unarmed, unprotected, beloved, innocent children.

If you were a soldier, there was no point in looking for other soldiers to shoot at. They were all dressed like civilians, like you were, sitting on park benches, eating submarine sandwiches, or pretending to smoke. Or sitting up a tree thirty miles away; or in a diving suit taking a rest on the bottom of a nearby lake, watching for a target-lock. No point in trying to shoot at soldiers. There were none to find.

I know what you're thinking. What about shooting the leaders? Assassinating the captains and colonels and commissars on the other side? Presidents, Premiers, Prime ministers?

Listen, honey, I'm running low on memory, so I'll try to make this quick, but it is complex—everything is tied into everything else. I'm trying to explain what kind of people your folks were, your real folks, and why they made a power armored suit like this.

When the nature of war changed, the nature of government changed. What is a government, anyway, besides a group of people in the business of winning wars and stopping fights, right? Even before when I was born, politicians had been using computer enhanced imagery to make their images on STV look younger, more commanding, more handsome, less fat. Whatever. Guys with squeaky voices were given nice baritones. It was fake, but so what? We never minded if a politician did not write his own speeches, did we? Why should we mind what he really looked like, so long as he did his job?

Well, it was just a small step from cartoon drawing over real politicians to replacing those politicians entirely with computer-generated talking heads. You see, the world when I was young was not divided into Haves and Have-nots. It was divided into Knowns and Unknowns.

When the nature of government changed, the nature of citizenship changed. The nature of wealth and power changed.

Not everyone was trying to shoot the kids, though. Thank God for that. When everything went away, when everything went bad, there were still some people who kept their heads. After my parents were killed, this family of Amish Farmers found me, wandering the fields at night, still carrying my mom's head. I guess I was out of my mind, a bit. Jeez! How old was I then? Younger than you.

My other real-time real-life friend was Mr. Eister. He had taught me how to shoot, what to do during incoming-fire drills, how to check food for foreign substances after saying grace. I remember him as a tall man, tall as a mountain it seemed to me, who always wore an odd, old-fashioned wide-brimmed hat. When I was six, I had insisted the mansion-circuits make such a hat like that for me, which I insisted on wearing all the time, even to bed, even to church (we had churches back then).

The only thing which could get me to take that damn hat off, was Mr. Eister himself, when we were suiting up. I remember arguing with him that my helmet was big enough to allow me to wear the hat beneath it, if I scrunched it up a bit. He had explained ... once ...

that the extra fabric would prevent the helmet cushions from seating properly on my skull. When I hadn't listened he waited patiently till I suited up, then he struck me in the head with his gun-stock, knocking me from my feet and setting my ears ringing.

"English," (he always called me that,) "English, a hard-shot shell would conduct a thousand time more foot-pounds of force than that little tap." He had leaned over me to talk. "The only thing what keeps thy brains from being churned to jam during a firefight, lad, is that thy helm here can flex to deflect the shockwave into the exo-skeleton anchor-points. Which it cannot do if thee must wear thy hat; remove it."

Poor Mr. Eister. Someone posted a bounty on the Amish. Didn't like their ways, didn't like their looks, didn't like their farm carts blocking the road. Who knew why? Who gave a reason? I was in my armor when a flock of bullets dropped out of a clear blue sky and stuck the house, spreading jellied gasoline everywhere. I was cool and safe, surrounded by flames. Peter played jump-and-run music, so I could not hear the sound of my new family sizzling and screaming. I jumped and ran. With the Jack Rabbit toggle thrown, I could jump over a church steeple.

How could they get away with shooting at us?

It was the crypto, you see. Encryption. Encryption and digital money. Governments did not bother raising and training armies. You did not need esprit de corps and unit cohesion to win a war any more. Governments just put out bounties over the Net, posted the reward and the bag they wanted on a public board in some neutral country. There was always a neutral country willing to carry the board.

The posting? Just a public announcement that decryption keys to a certain amount of digital cash would be sent out to anyone who could anonymously post a "prediction" of how many people of a certain nation would be killed on a certain day. There was a third-party verification system to confirm the kills, also encrypted both ways.

You see, with double-encryption, you could actually pay someone the digital cash, or even leave it lying around at a public bulletin board address, but anyone who picked it up could not spend it without unscrambling it. It was worthless and safe.

Each time someone downloaded a copy of your bag of cash to their personal station, a new unique key and counter-key would be generated automatically.

Let us say a hundred people, or a million, make copies of the scrambled cash. A hundred keys, or a million, are generated. Each personal to the person making the copy.

You send your counter-key back in to the government hiring you, along with whatever proof you want that you've killed the number of people they wanted killed. You send it in anonymously.

Once they have your unique counter-key, they can publicly post the decryption for your unique key. They can shout the decrypt from the rooftops; it doesn't do anyone any good but you. Unique means that you and only you can unscramble your copy of the cash bundle. Everyone else just has a string of garbled ones and zeros, meaningless and worthless. You have a code which opens a credit line through a numbered Swiss bank account. You never meet your employer; he never meets you. The other party could not help the police find you even if he wanted to.

And not just governments. Anyone who wanted anyone killed, for any reason or no reason. Someone posted bounties on black children. Someone else posted bounties on Ku Klux Klansmen. A retaliation? Who knew?

Someone else posted bounties on Jews. Someone else picked Witches. Someone else picked Christians. Homosexuals. Smokers. Non-smokers. Heterosexuals. Dog-owners. A zero-population group posted bounties on anyone. Anyone at all.

And it did not need to be one person posting the bounty. I contributed a few bucks myself, when I was in school, to have a certain famous entertainer who annoyed me bumped off. It was only a dollar or two; I meant it as a joke. I was drunk. But people kept adding to the fund. A dollar here, a gold gram there. After about five years, the bounty on the guy was half a million.

Now, I am not a murderer. That guy escaped. You see, that entertainer did not look like he looked in the See-vees. His picture was computer-generated. He was rich. He had friends. He was an Unknown.

Remember what I said about the difference between Knowns and Unknowns? It was the difference between life and death. Unknowns had all their money encrypted, overseas, stored as strings of scrambled numbers. You never met them face to face; you talked over the phone; and the picture and the voice on the phone could be someone, anyone, no one. But it wasn't them.

Remember I said governments changed? They were run by Unknowns. Appointed bureaucrats, some of them; others were just campaign finance contributors.

And taxes? Well, when everyone can hide their assets, there is no way to collect from them.

Tangible assets were different. Governments just seize them. They don't need a reason. They see a house or car they like, they take it. A piece of property, a publicly traded company. In the early days, they had to plant evidence of drug-dealing, or cigarette smoking, unauthorized public prayer, or gun ownership or something. Later, they just claimed the right of Eminent Domain and took what they needed.

How else could they be fed, those governments? How else could they continue?

It didn't bother the Unknowns. They just took out Seizure Insurance and kept most of their assets intangible. The ultra-rich sold or burned their cars after every car trip, and bought new ones before they went out again, just so they would have nothing on the highways to be seized. That was back when we had highways.

So how do you protect your children, in a time like that, with a civilization going to hell? You cannot negotiate with the assassins because no one knows who they are. Your rulers will not protect you. They are anonymous kelptocrats. The police? Don't make me laugh; everyone I knew kicked a few bucks into the kill-the-pigs kitty every time they got a traffic ticket, or had another car seized. The army? But there is no army. There will never be another army again.

A bulletproof vest is not thick enough to stop a mid-sized smart bullet. And in order to have plate thick enough to shield your little child's heart and head from the assassins, you must mount it on an articulated exoskeleton.

I hated the stuff when I was young, and I always used to play with my faceplate open, so I could smell the free summer breeze. Billy Worthemer was the same way. Open faceplate. I talked him into doing it too, so he couldn't tell on me.

We were in the courtyard green-area. In a protected zone, with no line-of-sight to any taller buildings.

I remember seeing the targeting platform that painted us, Billy and me. It was just a motion sensor clipped to the collar of a puppy dog, with the sensitivity turned down so that only a body larger than a dog, but smaller than an adult, would set it off. Billy went over to pet the dog. I raced him to it to be the first one there, and picked up the dog.

I remember Peter Power Armor saved my life. I was hit in the shoulder by the round, but the shot did not penetrate. But the ricochet caught Billy in the face. He was turning around to say something to me; maybe to ask me to let him have a turn petting the dog.

I do not remember what happened to his face. I really do not. I remember the whine in my gauntlets when I pulled the innocent little puppy in half. Poor dog. I remember that. I do not remember what Billy looked like. Not at all.

I should erase that last bit. It has nothing to do with what I was saying. I am trying to tell you what your parents and grandparents were like. Are like. You're my granddaughter. It took me so longer to find you. But I never gave up.

We are the kind of people who look after our kids. Having power armor for kids seems ridiculous, doesn't it? These days, it does. In the old days, it did not.

Everything you've been told about history is a lie. The People's Jesus did not come back to Earth and marry Mother Gaia, and appoint the First Protector of the Green People. That's not what happened.

The society I was raised in, the nightmare, could not last. The Unknowns could not last. They did not even know each other, did they? How could they help each other?

But what could stop the nightmare? Shut off the Net, you're saying. Cut the cables, arrest the Providers, take an ax to the mainframes, tear up the groundlines. Easy enough. But who was going to do it? Not the multinationals; all their money was in the Net. Not the Unknowns; the Net was their universe.

In a society where everyone is being shot at, shot at any time and at all times, there are only two things you can do. Either you make sure everyone has a gun or you make sure no one has a gun.

The people West of the Mississippi chose option number one. The people in the East chose option two.

The reality behind option two, of course, is that "no one has a gun" actually means, "no one but the authorities has a gun." And that means, "everyone but the authorities shuts up and does what they're told."

The reality behind option one, of course, is that "everyone has a gun" actually means, "If you want me to shut up, tough guy, come over here and make me."

The two systems are incompatible.

That's what the Second Civil War was really about; it was not about the Sacred Spotted Owl. And when the war got hot enough, and enough transatlantic cables got sabotaged, the Net went down. The Stock Market, all the stock markets, really, and bank records, personal records, everyone's identities, known and unknown, just went away.

The economy just went away.

And when that happened, the civilization's ability to feed the population of the world was cut roughly in half.

And the old-fashioned methods of warfare came back. We had soldiers again. I am not saying whether that was a good thing or a bad thing. They are brave, the soldiers these days; they wear uniforms, they do not hide and slink and sneak like soldiers from my day.

I am not brave. I am not like the soldiers of today. I am one of the old men of the days. My mission was to rescue you. I did it our way.

I was telling you about Peter Power Armor. I was telling you that I knew Mrs. Hechler would not know what it was. She had not lived through my grandfather's time, when fathers took their boys out into the woods to shoot squirrels. Or my father's time, when school uniforms all were woven with bulletproof material. My time I've told you about, the time of the Unknowns. The time of your mother (my daughter): Her time was even worse; the time of the Diebacks.

Industrial collapse. No more computers, no more smart-bullets. War is more like the old days; men in uniforms who can see each other through the grass, in the trenches, shooting. The bullets aren't smart enough to pick their won targets any more. The nature of war turned back.

Your generation is so lucky. You don't know anything. Lucky, stupid, stupid, lucky fools.

A woman of Mrs. Hechler's generation would not believe any children's toy could be armed.

But Mrs. Hechler knew it was a machine, and machines of any kind were rare these days, and she knew the Correct Thought. "Bliss! Get away from that Satan-metal thing! Green Jesus and Mother Earth hate machines! Don't touch it!"

I said, "Darling Bliss; this is your magic fairy-tale knight-in-shining-armor, come to rescue you. It's yours, yours, all yours, your very own."

"Shut up!" Mrs. Hechler said to me.

I shrugged, putting my hands behind my back. "Oh, come now, you foul-smelling sack of lumpish fat. I am not the one who cannot control a seven-year-old girl. You signed the authorization saying we could explore this deserted old house to see if there was anything we could loot or sell for the communal kitchen. I'm not the one who will catch hell from the District Helpfulness Manager."

That directed her attention back to the child. "Bliss Cornwall Delaplace! Ward of the State 142! Come here right now! Let go of that thing! It belongs to everyone!"

I said, "You are a princess, raised by trolls who hate that you come from a high and noble lineage. This gentle knight-errant shall rescue you and take you to a free land across the Mississippi to the West. On your very life, do not let go!"

"Bliss! Come here! Don't make me call for Jerry downstairs!"

I said, "Free, Bliss. Freedom. No more equalization injections because you are smarter than other kids. Freedom."

Bliss smiled at me, looking very beautiful to me for the first time since I met her, just like her mother when she was a little girl.

And she said, "Please, sir. I want to be smart again, like I used to. I want to be free." And that was when I fell in love with her.

I think the mention of the F word did it.

Mrs. Hechler strode forward, huge and ponderous in her wrath. Mrs. Hechler grabbed Bliss by the arm. It was a good grab, swift as a snake, the kind of grip guards should learn to use on prisoners. And I am sure it hurt, because Bliss screamed.

I pointed the handset at the scene, opened the lens, and said carefully into the mike: "Child under attack."

It was amazing how surprised Mrs. Hechler looked when she fell. I had underestimated how loud the shot of the tranquilizer dart would be. I had not expected Jerry, who had been waiting outside, to come up shooting.

Jerry was not licensed as a cop, just as security. A babysitter. Regulations said he was not allowed to be armed with anything but a stunner. That hand-cannon he held was no stunner; it was shooting through walls, brick and plaster. Made a hell of a noise. Just like the old days, eh?

I had also underestimated how clever the power-armors neural net had been programmed. It practically opened up in half and scooped Bliss into itself. Jerry really never stood a chance. It was very noisy and very bloody; not the sort of thing a child should see.

It is too bad you are unconscious. Peter sedated you because you were screaming and putting your hands in front of his gun barrels. I am recording this all through the handset into the suit playback for you to hear when you wake up.

Yes, I was wounded in the firefight. Wood-shrapnel from where a stray slug hit the doorframe. In my day, our doctors could have saved my leg.

I wish you could see what you looked like when you took off just now. It was lovely. You jumped out the window and over the next house. You should see the Seven-League-Boots program in action; each jet-assisted leap was two hundred yards if it was an inch.

I've already called in the escape over Mrs. Hechler's radio phone. The patrols are headed up north, into the swampland. In a minute, if I am strong enough, I'll send in a report that you were sighted down south, in the hills. All their equipment still runs off the old, old programs. Old as me. And I know the magic words to open the trapdoors and make my voice whatever CO's voice they need to hear.

I am a wizard, a warlock, a fraud, a gray old Prospero from a lost island, who never repented or burned his books or broke his wand. I have cast a spell on you, princess, and befuddled them.

They will not catch you. They will never catch you. I can just imagine the troopers on horseback, those of them who can afford horses, trying to catch you by lantern-light. I was the one who played hide-and-seek with my little friend Battery Bunny when I was eight, in that armor. One touch of the Mr. Frog button turns on the sneeky-peeky lowlight goggles, activates the aqualung, lets you crawl along a river bottom at night. The smart-metal is radar invisible. If those barbarians still have any working radar sets. If they could get the bureaucrats in their organization to release them to the river patrol. Which I doubt. Which I doubt.

And Homer the Homing Pigeon who lives in the helmet is gyroscopically aligned and corrects himself by star-pattern recognition. So you cannot get lost or get turned around. I selected the map program through the handset. It was the first thing I did before I started recording.

I do not mind going away. I was one of them, darling. An Unknown. That's why my name is not on the records. Dad gave me trapdoors into the computer systems that survived the Netcrash. That's why I was able to find my family. To find you. I am sorry for the things I did and I do not really mind dying. I've tried to make up for it.

What else do I need to say? I am getting sleepy now, and it's hard to think.

I am the last of the Unknowns. I could make myself a fake ID. I could travel in the East on forged papers. I could give myself authorization to read the Child Safety and Domestication Bureau records, to unseal sealed files, and depart without a trace.

My magic. Left over from the old days. I wove a cloak of cunning mist and made myself invisible, while I was right in front of their eyes. Who looks at janitors? My papers were in order.

The job as a janitor at the Children's Center I got by hard work and sweat; something rare here. Tricking Mrs. Hechler into violating regulations and going to loot a deserted house in a public owned area was simply not difficult. All serfs ignore regulations when they can; it's the only way they can live. There are just so many regulations, you see, no one can listen to them all.

Is there anything else I need to tell you, anything else I need to explain?

What they told you about the West is all lies too. We don't shoot each other down in the streets, we don't have gunfights in every bar. We do have bars, but not everyone drinks.

I do not know what went wrong with all the people back East, after the Diebacks. I do not know why they could not rebuild. The Western states are mostly empty desert. How come they got rich? I do not know. Maybe the Easterners did not have the will to resist when the People's Green Church of Mother Life came along. They certainly did not have the means to resist. They did not have anything like Peter.

But those deserts are so beautiful under the starlight. You'll see them soon.

Oh, God, let me stay awake long enough to tell you this.

Darling, I do not know the names of my contacts in the underground railroad. Remember I told you about encryption? You just go to any public phone once you are across the Mississippi, in the wide Western places they've remembered finally what a free country is supposed to be. They've also remembered how to set up a working Net again.

Another Net. Are the bad old days coming back again? I don't know. I'm very tired, and I just don't know. Maybe you can grow up and stop those bad things from happening.

Don't let me forget. Get to the phone. Push the button shaped like Puss-in-Boot. It's the crypto cat. It will turn on the circuit and make the phone call for you. It will call the nice people.

Get to a phone. Peter will know what to do. Trust Peter. He'll take care of you.

Peter loves you; I love you.

Goodbye, God bless, and Godspeed.

You mother is waiting for you in Austin. Your real mother. We got her out of the camps months ago. Her name is Roselinde. She was very pretty when she was your age.

The sentient suits/fighting machines called Radicals grew up with their human operators, forming a bond rarely broken except by death. But a Radical named Mad suspected that the death of its human partner was not the happenstance of battle, but an act of treachery. If that suspicion could be confirmed, it would require a risky, terrible vengeance.

Nomad

Karin Lowachee

People in modern times don't like to acknowledge that some of us Radicals are nomad. They interpret that as rogue and dangerous. If you think it's hard for us now, it was much worse during the turf wars—especially if you weren't integrated. When Tommy died I became uni—unintegrated—and that usually means nomad. I belonged to no Streak, had no chief and no Fuses to protect me. It wasn't overnight.

For a month after Tommy died, my chief tried to convince me to integrate with another human. It's not unheard of, though for many it is not desired. But since nomad Radicals have it hard against suspicious people, the majority of us capitulate and Fuse to a second, lesser human. Any human after your first is always lesser in some way. You have not grown with them; you have not shared memories from birth to death. Many Radicals who have lost their first human don't last the year, Fused again or not; instead they voluntarily dismantle.

I was never one for suicide, though I have come close. But I don't think it's in my nature to cut myself short—I have the scars and dents on my armor to prove it. I spent too many years trying to keep myself and Tommy alive against rival Streaks, and he did the same. To dismantle myself, even if it's my right, would be an insult to the Fuse I had lost when Tommy died.

Every Streak across the world thinks they know what went down when Tommy was killed, but they don't know because everyone involved in that fracas, besides myself, was destroyed. (Human, Radical—the term "destruction" fits for both.) This was the beginning of my Streak's suspicion of me and I suppose I can't blame them. It is a hard thing to explain when your human dies and you survive. Tommy's uncle was the chief, and the chief's Radical was the only other Radical in our Streak that was older than me. We were possibly the oldest Radicals left in the world besides some beaten-down Copperpickers in the few mines left in the North. Anyway, Tommy had been the vice-chief. It is likely that once Tommy was dead and I was uni, Radical One calculated that I would want to take the primus position with a new human. But I had no such ambitions and still do not. Leading a Streak is not a simple thing and I've grown tired of the raids.

Maybe I have always been a little bit nomad in my programming. My generation model, they say, has some tragic flaws.

The day I decided to leave the Streak, the chief made one last effort to convince me to stay and reintegrate. I stood in the wreckhouse with the other Fuses, all of them doubles. I was the only single. We made thirteen, which is small for a modern Streak, but the chief didn't agree with the corporate mentality that dictated there had to be at least twenty Fuses in a Streak. That was too much like a government army, and we were better beneath our own flag.

The armor of every Fuse is different. Our Streak wasn't full of rainbow, like you find in the West, especially in Heo Eremiel. Their raids look ridiculous if you see them in your rearscan, like a flock of parrots who will talk you to death. We weren't all about our looks, but our Tora Streak had some pride. Blacks, grays, blues, reds. When we raided up, we were a storm.

Radical One was a sheen of midnight blue integrated with the chief, covering him head to toe in a sleek armor husk. If you have never seen a Fuse it might be difficult to discern where human ends and Radical begins, but that is the point. Since we weren't raided up, though, his faceplate was open, his gunports were shut, and I saw his hooded human eyes. Radical One's red scanning eye on his forehead bent in regular beats across each of our faceplates and did not bend to the human eyes. I bent my eye back, but then ignored it to zero on the chief. He was old by human years, well into his gray period, but battle hardened in every line and vein.

"Why won't you give Probie a chance?" Chief gestured with a gauntlet at the lone human who stood by the door of the wreckhouse. One of him and one of me. Even a first burst of a Radical could do that math out of the yards.

"I gave him a chance," I said. "We won't work."

The probie had approached me the week before and said, "They don't make your kind anymore, do they?" knowing very well that my model was discontinued twelve years ago. He'd taken two months to pluck up to me and that was the first thing out of his wet man-mouth.

"I wish I could say the same about you," I'd told him. He'd taken offense, which wasn't my problem. And he wasn't going to be my problem now.

Deacon was his born name, but because he wasn't Fused we all called him Probie. He did scut work around the house and the garage, and he had some skill with programming and basic Radical maintenance, not that I ever let him touch me. Mostly he did anything the chief wanted him to do for the Fuses, Radical and human alike. He had to learn that a Fuse wasn't about the human. We weren't cars he could flip a switch on and control out of the factory. I didn't know why the chief made him a probie in the first place, because even if Deacon respected the Fuses, I saw that self-righteous gleam in his blue eyes. He reckoned he could stare down a Radical's scan even though we never blinked. That kind of arrogance shares circuitry with stupidity. I'd rather dismantle than Fuse with that.

"So what's your plan?" the chief said. "I hope you won't kite off on a revenge mission."

The payback on the bastard Fuses who had killed Tommy was not as complete as I would have liked. There had been much discussion in the Streak about the nature of this payback and the chief had his reasons for being careful about it. Keeping the peace between precarious towns; not wanting the locals to raise a paramilitary army to drive us out; not wanting more bloodshed when my murder of Tommy's murderers could be seen as an even score. So many reasons and yet I would not have regretted more death.

But revenge wasn't my reason for leaving.

"I'm going nomad," I said.

All twelve Fuses made noises, human profanity and sharp Radical hums. Radical Five, who was called Steel, said that they would rather I stayed with the Streak as a uni than lose me to the grid. Steel was always dependable on my flank and its Fuse was now the vice-chief. His human Anatolia missed Tommy almost as much as I did. Once in a while they'd shared beds.

"I appreciate that," I said, "but I think nomad is the direction for me. At least for now."

"You will always have a place in Tora Streak," the chief said. He wasn't going to argue anymore. He'd given me enough outs in the past month and it was impossible to change my program once I'd set it.

Radical One's eye bent and remained on my faceplate. Radical One didn't have any other name, just the recognition number that every Radical possesses but none of us use in speech. It had never wanted to be more familiar to humans. Though the chief objected to my going and it was in the logs, Radical One never tried to make me stay. Without me around, its primus position would be fixed until dismantling or destruction through battle, since none of the other Fuses were close enough to take over unless for some reason the chief died independently. But Radical One was powerful, despite its age, and it did not lose in battle.

The chief said, "Radical Two is determined to be nomad. We won't keep it here. Does everyone give their support to Radical Two?"

The consent was unanimous, if full of regret. I had some regret too, but not enough to keep me from leaving.

The chief said, "Then go with the wind, Mad." And that was the first time he had ever called me by my chosen name.

It was the name Tommy had given me.

Humans don't always name us. We name ourselves if we want such a familiar designation. But when Tommy was four he thought of Mad, not because I'm an angry Radical, he just didn't want to call me Radical Two anymore. "That sounds so cold," he said. "And you're too warm inside." When he melded to the hollow of my armor body, we created warmth.

I was also only four years out of the yards, we were four years integrated alloy and skin, and every time he shed me to be only human I felt an emptiness. I suppose that was where it all began.

We call it armor but the technical name is Trans-Developmental Biogenic Alloy. After the ratified Constitution that granted us rights and privileges as any sentient intelligent being, humans short-handed us to Radical Armor, and then just Radical. We are told that the name alludes to part of our chemical makeup; one of our origin scientists coined it. I have always found it a little sarcastic. Free radicals. Perhaps Dr. Gom had been a sarcastic man, as much as he had been a genius.

We grow with our humans, a second skin that can slip apart and exist away from the Fuse. The racists call us Silly Putty for our ability to morph, change constitution, and adapt. And we do adapt. We change. We integrate.

The Streaks are weapons grade Radical Armor.

First integration happens as close to birth as possible. It's the only way you can be sure a Radical's bioware adapts properly to a human, when the human's mind isn't fixed already. Once we've been through our first integration, we can integrate again, but it's never as smooth as that first; when you're new and your human's new, slipping inside each other's thoughts in that infant stage is like a synthesis of pure instinct or a predatory scent of blood.

I have memories of Tommy from five minutes after his first cry in this world, and before he died he had all of mine. Like the first time I opened my hand and saw my faint reflection in my perfect obsidian armor. Before the battle damage.

I remember the first time I set my hand over his and our grips locked together and became one. It took no thought to move our hand because the integration was more instinct than intellect. That is how you know that the fix is right. It is not artificial intelligence; it is intuitive intelligence.

It's a need, those first memories. The first time he breathed the air, the first time he shut his eyes and saw instead through mine. The world is limitless when you're Fused. It's a hunger for experience and we spend all our lives in a hunt to fill it.

That's what drives a Fuse. You, your human, and everything you can't satisfy.

That is our biggest weakness too.

In our need to integrate with them, we adapted to human flaws.

The Fuses gathered around to bid me goodbye from the wreckhouse. Steel and Anatolia, Sol and Markie, Wyrm and Jasper, Giniro and Imori, Kikenna and Selene. The chief and Radical One only touched my shoulder and left first through the door. I scanned both human and Radical faces and it was a hard thing to know that I might never see them again.

They asked me where I was going but I didn't tell them. I had plans to follow the road that would lead me away from the turf wars. I didn't want to say out loud that I didn't want to see any Radicals that I knew, or any Radicals at all. They would have considered this insane, because we all knew that in places where Radicals weren't welcome, no law would protect me. Some humans did not acknowledge the Constitution, our rights, our sentience, our ability to choose not to kill them. Their fears were not completely unfounded, of course. But there are more murderous humans than there are murderous Radicals, and that will likely never change.

After Tommy's death, I just wanted to be away. Vengeance could wait. Vengeance was bone without the marrow. Something else unknown and even dangerous matched the open spaces that were expanding through my inner wires and biogenic gyroscopes. I was being gutted the longer I remained in Tora Streak, racked to Tora thoughts.

The wreckhouse was where we all congregated when we weren't launching raids. It catered to both humans and Radicals, with thick seats, docking spikes, and areas of play integration outlined by lights and nebular controls. Right now, as I passed my eye over it in a wide beam, it looked and sounded skeletal beyond repair. The walls of the house reflected nothing and loomed empty and unlit, a dead alloy that could not change as its occupants did in their desires. The movements of the Fuses as they clasped my arms or bumped their heads to mine seemed to echo in hollow bass notes.

I said goodbye, made no promises to return, and stepped out the door into daylight.

The probie stood against the outer wall of the wreckhouse, smoking a cigarette.

"You'll regret leaving," he said, with my back to him.

"I won't regret leaving you." I had a blip of a thought to educate him about his attitude and why that would hinder his graduation from probie to full Fuse. But he wasn't worth even that, so I kept walking toward the gate that surrounded Tora's compound.

"Tommy wouldn't want you to go," he said to my back.

I turned my head around without moving the rest of my body, so my eye bent direct on his narrow little face. "You are determined to live a short human life."

He flicked his cigarette away onto the pavement. "I think you should give me a second chance."

"I have given you more chances than you realize."

I watched as he approached, hands in his jacket pockets. He stopped right below my eye. He was shorter than Tommy, enough so that I had to tilt down my face to scan his features. The overlay showed me where all of his biodots were, a scatter of constellations in his brain. This might've been what made him such a sharp programmer. I did not know much about his past, only that he had come to the Streak from the town by recommendation of a human ally in the police department, and he had no living parents. The chief had done a thorough check on him and deemed him worthy of probie status. I didn't ordinarily disagree with the chief, but if I could've taken back our vote before Tommy had died, seeing what I saw now, I would have—and jammed a bullet in this probie's smirk while I was at it.

"I want to really talk with you," he said. "But not here. If afterwards you still don't think me worthy, then I'll never bother you again."

"You'll never bother me again as soon as I walk through the gate." I turned my head around and set myself in that direction.

"It's about his death," the probie said.

I circled back and snatched him up by the scruff of his neck. The gate opened at my signal and I walked on, holding the probie off the ground. He kicked and struggled but it is impossible for a human to break a Radical's grip. He had a gun but he wouldn't dare use it.

So I walked with him just like that down the road, away from Tora compound. I walked a full hour and then walked another, until the cars and other Radicals from Freemantown no longer passed us.

None of them questioned me because they saw the orange and black Tora mark on my chest. I walked us out to the roads between towns, where yellow land stretched long and empty on either side. It was a cool day and I didn't falter. I was well-maintained and topped up with energy, and could've moved faster if I adapted into road mode, but that would've required setting him on my back somehow. He fell limp in my grip eventually, weary from fighting and cursing at me.

But he woke up when I dumped him onto the side of the road.

"You bloody robot piece of shit!"

They continue to think "robot" is an insult.

I bent my blue eye to him and sent up the beam so it hit him on the forehead like a target. "Is this what you want to say to me?"

He was covered in dirt. He hauled himself to his feet and struggled to climb up the gravel embankment to face me toe to toe. I watched his gun hand. He was not generally that stupid, but he was angry, and humans have a tendency to be stupid in their anger.

"You think you know what happened to Tommy." The probie spat at my feet. "But you don't."

"You think *you* know what happened to Tommy?" I too had guns. They were in-built.

"That ambush from the Gear Heart Streak." He stared up at me with a blaze in his eyes. "When they raided up on you in Nuvo Nuriel. In the hotel. The chief sent you there to pat a deal with the Gears, but then they ended up turning on you? There was no *deal*, Mad, except to fuck you over. You *and* Tommy, 'cause of what you were to each other."

My scan overlay went red. I grabbed him up again by the collar and shook him hard.

His feet kicked. "Let go of me!"

I pitched him ten meters into the field. He fell with a dull thud and a cry. I bounded over to him in one leap from the road. My right foot almost nailed his chest, but he rolled away at the last second. I wanted to crush him. It would not have been difficult.

"I know you loved him!" the probie gasped, nearly winded. A true fear spread across his face. "I know it's taboo. I don't care about that; it's wrong what they did. The chief set you up!" He began to cough.

I tangled my fingers in the front of his jacket and lifted him up so we were eye to eye. He kicked for a second out of reflex then stopped, just staring back. His arms hung long, all the arrogance slammed out of him. I calculated the option of killing him. Here in between towns it would take some time to find him. But then, many people from Freemantown had seen me walking with him.

"How do you know the chief set me up?" It was the most pertinent question. After I got my questions answered, maybe then I would send him back to town just so people could see him alive. Then I could circle back, hunt him down, and kill him.

"I read the chief of the Gear Heart Streak," the probie said. "I read his Fuse."

I scanned this probie's biodots again. "With that in your head? There is nothing exceptional. You cannot scan a Radical with your limp brain." Radical minds were fortresses.

He said, "I'm a wetthief. And the Gear Hearts are a bunch of second-string Fuses and you know it."

I did know it. Their ambush that had killed Tommy had only focused my hatred, but we had never liked them and their marauding spirits. They were not well-maintained except in their wanton raids. Yet the chief had been bent on patting a deal "to cut down on the killings between the territories" where Tora and Gear tracks bisected the land. What could we have done? The votes went against us. Peace seemed a good avenue but it was always more of a dark alley. Nobody had listened to Tommy on that score.

When they'd killed him, the chief had refused immediate payback. He'd said revenge had to come from thought, not impulse. The Streak had bowed to his level head.

I had burned. But he was my chief and my human was dead. I could not go up against the Gear Heart Streak alone. My actions were Tora's actions.

Or would have been. Not anymore, as a nomad. And my need for vengeance had diminished in the days of loss. It was supposed to be simple, this leavetaking.

Now this probie claimed to know the mind of a Gear Heart Fuse? The chief and his Radical no less?

"I can prove it," the probie said against my silence. "If you Fuse with me, I can show you."

Wetthieves are notoriously reckless individuals. The government tries to deal with them but to no real consequence. It is difficult to smash a thing that isn't tangible, just as it is difficult to define an emotion. All the wily activity is through the mind. Yet I had never heard of a wetthief able to raid up on a Radical.

"Fuse with you?" That had been his intention all along, his eyes on my nexus. "I think you are a liar who wants to divide the Streak. How could a probie get close enough to the Gear Hearts to read their chief? Answer me."

"The chief and Rad One sent me and Anatolia's Fuse to Nuvo Nuriel two weeks ago for a parts run. You remember this. We saw the Gears on the corner. Before we split, I read them. I thought I could get intel for Tora and it'd help my case with you." His jaw moved, stubborn overt confession that he wanted me for his Radical. "So I got intel."

"And now you think it will help your case with me." I would not address his other claim, what he thought he knew about me and Tommy. That would be a confirmation he had no right to nudge. Though I wondered how he did know, and if his mischievous man-mind had thieved in my nexus. Surely I would have felt it? I am deeply paranoid about my ware, as we all are.

The probie stared at me. I still held him above the ground. "If I had long enough, I could read you too. How do you think I know about you and Tommy? It was in the Gear Radical's brain. It was in that chief's. And they knew because *your* chief told them. You Radicals think you're impenetrable, but you're still a machine. And all machines have weaknesses."

"You created us," I said, and threw him very far.

He sailed through the air for more than ten meters. He hollered as he went. When he landed he stopped. I walked through the yellow grass and looked down at him. He seemed to be dead, lying in a heap, and it was a little bit of a concern that I might have killed him before I had all the answers. But only a little. It had felt good to toss him.

I scanned his vitals. His heart was beating and his brain showed activity—enough to be alive, though he was unconscious. Which was what I'd wanted. Unconscious, he couldn't thieve.

I folded myself down beside him and waited. I didn't care if it took hours for him to wake up. The field was quiet except for random birds and the squeak of critters low to the ground. Mice. I watched a cricket bound across the black armor of my foot, pause there, and then disappear into the grass.

Tommy came to mind. It was inevitable. He was never long out of my thoughts, but now I played the images of him across my faceplate. He was tricky there and alive. It was true, I loved my human. It was also true that it was forbidden. You would think that if any clan of humans would understand an emotion forged in a Fuse, between human and Radical, it would be among the Streaks. But fundamentally there are still laws that surpass even science. There are deviations that go too far even for the Fuses in a Streak. Some things are universally wrong and some part of my programming understands that. I am, as the probie said, a machine. I can mold to human skin, to cover it and protect it and create a strength no human can reach on their own, but it is still only armor. I am still only armor, despite our integration with their minds.

Until my heart grew involved. Until my heart evolved. We call it a heart, but it is more like a central nervous system of programming. I believe it is the seat of our sentience but there is nothing to prove that. Humans think awareness comes from the brain.

I didn't ask for this sentience. Unlike humans, my self-awareness was not born, but made. I was not the first Radical to achieve it (that one is long dismantled), but the template became in-built. Is it so difficult for people to believe that the next step in the evolution of sentience is love?

Tommy believed it the second I told him. We were Fused and sat in a field much like this one, at night, and I felt his fragile human body nested inside the spaces I had made for him since birth. The hollow of my chest, the tubes of my legs and arms. There he resided and every subtle thought sparked a response in mine, until we thought the same. We powered each other's limbs in quiet movement. He ran his hand over the top of the grass blades and we both felt the tickle. My armor reflected the stars overhead, or as he liked to say, captured them. He was a killer—we both were—but he had a heart for the heavens.

I didn't have to say the words. I only said, "We should go back to the wreckhouse, the chief will wonder." Because we had been incommunicado for hours, and Tommy refused to reply to messages and I would not send signals on the sly. More often Tommy grew tired of the raids on the rival gangs, going from town to town, defending territory, controlling commerce. But I didn't want him to get into trouble with the chief, so I said, "It's very late."

And he said, "Not yet, Mad." And, "Just not yet."

By and by, the probie awoke. Dusk sat new on the edges of the sky, dragging black overhead like a covering blanket. When I saw the probie's eyes blink and focus, I said, "We are going to the Gear Heart Streak and we will discover if what you say is true." My vengeance lay in wait. Now it could prowl again and my emptiness did not matter. It would be there regardless. I would wage war and did not care what humans got in my way.

The probie said, "What's the point of going to the Gears? Right into enemy territory? You should go back to Tora and confront the chief."

"I won't accuse the chief and Radical One just because you say so. You say you thieved it from a Gear Heart mind, so we will go to the Gear Hearts. I will use you as a shield if you try my patience."

"I did read them." Even in the dim light of just stars and moon, I saw the steel insistence in his eyes. I needed no night scope for it.

"They are a bullshit Streak, those Gears," I said. "So one way or another, we'll get it out of them."

He walked slowly, still dizzy-brained from the toss. I didn't help him and I was in no hurry. I had to think of how to approach the Gears. Their territory was another few hours walk, even at a Radical stride. We would be there by dawn. Once, the probie suggested I let him ride me in road mode. I knocked him back to the gravel. He got up, swearing at me, but he didn't ask again. At least he didn't try to run. That would have been tedious to chase after him, to recapture him and shake him and put him under my arm so he couldn't run again.

He must have truly wanted to Fuse with me to put up with my abuse. But I supposed that was natural. He was a probie; there was nothing more important to a probie than a Fuse.

So he said nothing else for the rest of the night. That was a single saving grace. The wetthief finally knew when to shut his damn mouth.

❧ ❧ ❧

Across the street from the enemy compound I calculated the Gear Heart wreckhouse, the tracks I saw in the dirt, and informed the probie of my intent. We were going to hail them and speak with them. Once we were close enough, the probie would thieve from their nexus and load it to me. It was cumbersome to do so, not Fused, and might eat up precious time, but it was my strategy. I did not expect the Gear Hearts to tell me the truth. So I would put this wetthief to the test and if he wasn't lying, I would destroy the Gear Hearts, every last one of them, and then I would go back to Tora Streak and kill the chief and Radical One for their betrayal.

The probie said, "You're fucking insane."

That was the true meaning of my name. No anger, just crazy. I said, "You will back me up."

He had a gun and he was a good shot. I would defend him so long as I needed him. He knew it too.

He said, "You first."

Since they'd killed Tommy, the Gear Hearts had not crossed into Tora territory. In fact they gave us a lot of room to do our deals and transport our goods: guns, drugs, medical supplies to outlying paramilitaries. And we did not cross into theirs. It was an uneasy truce and now this probie made me wonder if it was one born from the blood of my Fuse.

The probie lurked behind me as I stood in front of the Gear Heart gate. I wanted to open my gunports but such hostility would only provoke them to launch a few grenades our way. So I remained straight, sealed up, my eye ranging only so far as the south end of their rundown wreckhouse wall.

"This is Radical Two of the Tora Streak," I sent loud toward them. Technically I was nomad but they didn't need to know that. My voice cut through the early morning quiet. A graying hound loped in my peripheral vision, nosed at the dirt near old Radical footprints. I could not determine how old. "I will speak to your chief."

The chief had not been in the ambush, so I had not killed him. Instead I had killed his vice-chief's Fuse and I had no doubt he held it against me. The truce could end right now if he was dumb enough to take offense at my presence. I itched to bloom open my epaulet gunports.

But the main door of the wreckhouse creaked open and a short dusty human poked his head out. He was not the chief, so some other member of the Streak. He had tattoos around his eyes like a red badger.

"The chief ain't here," he croaked.

"Then I will wait for him. When do you expect him back?"

"I dunno."

"You may get him on signal or you can watch me sit in front of your gate with my Tora mark for the remainder of the day."

"Or we can blow you off our stoop with a missile."

"I know you Gear Hearts aren't that accurate. You can recall I killed four of your Streak. I didn't come here to fight, but my arsenal can take out your entire compound. Do you wish to gamble on your aim and my reflexes?"

The door shut with a *blam*. Behind me, the probie laughed but I shoved him quiet. I scanned the compound with all of my senses. The wreckhouse was proofed against every kind of amplification, but I listened and looked for movement by the animals, the trees on the outer edges, the air between the buildings. All lay quiet, as if the Streak were still abed. But I knew they were awake and the chief was indeed behind this gate.

In two minutes, he emerged from the wreckhouse, Fused. His Radical was blood red, its eye a scathing white. Its gaze slammed on me like a spotlight so I had to adjust my intake view. The Fuse met me on the other side of the gate.

"What do you want?" said the Gear Heart chief.

I had only to make him talk long enough for the probie to thieve his nexus and shunt the intel to me. I wanted it live, not from memory where memory could be manufactured. I would not put trickery past the probie so this was my strategy. This would tell the truth of all.

Then the probie shot the Gear Heart chief right in the face.

The large caliber, double impact heavy round went straight through the faceplate. Such weaponry is made to kill Fuses. Blood and bits of plate glass, bone, and brains smattered against my armor.

I had no time to shout at the probie. The chief was dead but his Radical wasn't. With a shudder the Gear Heart Radical slipped from its human, a sound I knew only too well shattering the morning air.

I had made such a noise when Tommy was killed. The dead human chief slumped over into the dirt and gravel, like a snail without a shell, and the Radical launched itself into the air with a cry, right over the gate.

Before it landed, its gunports spooled open and rained artillery down upon us.

There is much debate from scientists about whether a Radical is faster and stronger Fused with a human than alone without. These scientists will spend much time on tests and data collection, interviews and psychological exams. But it is no debate for any Radical who has been Fused. We are at optimum with our humans. A Fuse is stronger together than alone. It's not about human reflexes and Radical synapses. When we are Fused, there is no separation. We become the best of our individual capabilities.

And for my model, our primary capability is killing.

The Gear Heart Radical, without its human, stood no chance. As I've said, the Gear Hearts are a bullshit Streak. They swagger but without the skill. They defend their territory by spraying wide, like a machine gun in the hands of an untrained child. They are not snipers or assassins. They waste energy and movement.

In a snap, my heavier shields unfurled above my shoulders to take the artillery fire. I didn't mark where the probie went. Beneath my shield I flung up a hand. It held my forearm weapon. Two shots blasted on the enemy Radical's chest. The impact sent it back a step and stopped its flow of fire. I dropped my right shield and barraged the Radical with my epaulet guns and two rocket grenades from my hip. The Gear Heart went down spraying bullets, but down it went regardless. The rounds peppered my armor as I flung up my shield again. They made no lasting damage.

The probie crouched behind my left side, shooting toward the compound. The rest of the Streak—all ten of them—had come out battling. But they faltered when they saw the bodies on the ground.

"Your chief Fuse is destroyed!" I sent. They would not know for certain if the rest of Tora Streak was near. To them I wasn't nomad. I saw the calculations in their hesitation. They were an impulsive Streak but grounded in survival.

I thought that would be the end of it, that I could gather this probie and shake the reason for his shooting right out of him, before I stomped him under my heel.

But my rear sensors picked up the whine of movement behind me. My eye gauged the shift in beams on the Radical faces across the gate as something took their attention.

My torso swiveled just as Radical One's rocket grenades exploded against my chest.

I learned later that before I went down I launched the rest of my epaulet artillery. Reflex. The hail slammed into Radical One and my chief but did not kill them. Down on my back, my body began to blow out. The fire from the Gear Heart Radical had weakened me but not infringed on major systems. The storm from Radical One was another matter; its titanium-class artillery cut through me like a scythe. I do not remember this, there is only a gap in my files when nothing recorded.

Between the blackness and repowering, there was Tommy. From birth to death, his form returned to me, a ghost whispering through my circuits, my biocells, every part of me that was the Fuse of both.

His black hair, his amber brown eyes tilted toward the sky.

When he killed, he never took joy in the loss of life.

We separated and he nestled in my chest cavity on his side, just to lie there as in a womb. I touched him with a different freedom, one that held no feedback sensation. It was just my touches that I remembered, not how he felt them. Humans are so easy to injure but he trusted my strength. He let my armored hand cover over his chest, and his heartbeat remained a steady calm rhythm. All of my nearly impenetrable angular edges seemed to fit to his soft human muscle and delicate human bones. Somehow this forged a stronger bond. We were Fused, but he was an individual and so was I. He loved that about us, and I did too.

Scientists say we cannot grieve. But we do.

This was the feeling that flowed through my darkness, until the probie took its place.

The probie climbed into my chest cavity and fit his legs into the hollows of mine, and his arms into the columns of mine. In my darkness, I thought of Tommy and my struggling armor wrapped around this probie, like a flower petal at the touch of a finger. My injuries opened out to him, seeking healant.

The probie set his head to my heart and so began the Fuse.

With his wetthief brain and biodots, he reached out to my nexus and tangled himself in it. We coiled and stretched, memory flow and actions past.

They say Radical Armor can feel no pain. Especially an old model like me, a previous generation no longer on the line.

But they are wrong.

Deacon had no living parents because his mother had shot his father and then shot herself. He was six and witnessed it.

He grew up in town, in the alleys and beneath the sidewalks, in the hands of a system that looked very much like a Radical assembly line. They plugged parts in and removed others, injected cells and livened proteins. All to make a boy work the best he could. He found a human gang. He stole the biodots and ran drugs long enough to make enough money to get them implanted. Then his world opened wide, with teeth. Suddenly there were no barriers he could not break down.

Tommy and I were the first Fuse he ever saw. He wanted that connection. He wanted an armor no one could break, a second skin to hide him from the sharper parts of the world, a second mind to push his own to broader expanses.

His forays into the brain, any brain, freed him from his own— where memories suctioned tight and strived to suffocate him.

So much blood. It had splattered onto his mouth, blood from his parents. It mingled with the memory of Tommy's on my armor, my faceplate. Deacon's cries were the same as my human's, then overrode them in a wave as Tommy's died out.

Tommy slipped from my body cavity because not even my armor could hold him anymore. My system rang with shock. Our hotel room was destruction, the smell of fire, smoke, and cinder.

Through Deacon I saw the chief and Radical One. They stood on a road halfway between Freemantown and Nuvo Nuriel. My chief said to the Gear Heart chief, *Tommy's heart isn't in it anymore. He and his Radical protest us every step of the way. If you take care of Tommy it will force Radical Two to Fuse again. We don't want to lose the Two, but Tommy's heart has infected it. They take their bond too far. So take him out and we'll ceasefire on your turf. We will leave you alone. Make it look good.*

What about payback? Your Streak will demand it. Radical Two will seek it.

Leave it to me, the chief said.

All of this clipped in Radical One's memory. All of it stolen by Deacon and kept in his.

I saw it all as if I were there. This is the power of a Fuse. It takes only a split second.

Memory is more than just a series of biochemical firing pins, a cascade of molecular events that result in specific encoding. Memory shapes us, both human and Radical.

And memory, we know, is the foundation of revenge.

It was Deacon that made me stand again. The power of his mind and the Fuse, not even fixed yet, precarious in connection but determined to rise. He willed my battered limbs to move, my form to sit, then pushed to stand. Pieces of me flapped free and clanked. Before I had the cognitive function to flick down my arm blade or move my heavy foot, he did it for me, alive and alert. His thoughts were jagged as they melded with mine, felt foreign like stitches on a wound, like one of Tommy's flesh injuries.

He knew where I wanted to go. The chief and Radical One lay struggling in their own brokenness. Their shoulder armor shuddered open and back, like the twisted wing of a bird. Their chest spread with perforations and new scars.

We moved, Deacon and I, to stand over my chief. I barely discerned the Tora mark through the bullet holes. We slammed my heel onto the chief's wrist, breaking it through the armor, and held there to block any flick of weapon.

He cursed at me. He reached for Deacon's throat with his free hand, bolstered by Radical One's remaining strength, but I grasped that too. We held there, a tableau of murder at an impasse, until Deacon brought up my right foot and slammed it into the joint where shoulder met neck. The chief's arm went limp. It freed my own grip.

My artillery packs sat empty. My gun was cracked and useless. It took no thought, only will. As Radical One's red eye swept over my severed faceplate I plunged my arm blade into the chief's throat and twisted it. So fast it took his head halfway off his neck.

I inflicted the same on Radical One, with bare hands. Its injuries and momentary shock at the death of its human gave me and Deacon the advantage. I dismantled it right there on the road, a piece at a time. I bashed its circuits, gutted it of cables, twisted its desperate, reaching armor until the shapes made nothing, only hunched there like forgotten shards of frozen metal, the dregs of a factory assembly line.

What I did to it was a mercy. It did not have to mourn, as I did, for my Fuse.

The Gear Heart Streak, what was left of it, never interfered. Frightened of Tora retaliation, or too mindful of their own survival. Through Deacon's mind I knew. My chief and Radical One had followed me from Tora's wreckhouse, with every intention of dismantling me—and their chief and Radical had known. When they saw my destination at the Gear gate, furious signals flew between chiefs: dismantle me and kill Deacon, since we could not be controlled. I had disappointed my chief by not fusing again, going nomad. Deacon had disappointed the chief by coming to me first.

Now they were disappointed and destroyed, and that was all there was to that.

We lost the taste for blood, Deacon and I, and left the Gear Heart Streak to its decimation. I didn't want to return to Tora and answer any questions, face any possible retaliation. I wasn't Tora anymore; the destruction on my chest armor had wiped the Tora mark, one good result of that damage. Without a word of out-loud consultation, Deacon and I set ourselves on the road out of Nuvo Nuriel. The direction was straight but my steps fumbled and creaked. We would need to find a resting place, between towns, to heal ourselves. And to fix.

Where we were headed, it didn't matter. We were nomad.

I didn't pick this Fuse. Later Deacon would say, *I picked you.* Sometimes, I suppose, it works that way. It is not all about the human. But it isn't all about the Radical either.

We sat in a field by an abandoned warehouse, letting the tendrils of the Fuse find one another until it was complete. We belonged to no Streak but he cared less than I did. I hadn't forgotten what it was like to hold a human inside my armor, but it was different with him. While Tommy had dreamed of the stars and peace, Deacon was a restless runner. Sometimes I would have to pull him back, but other times he would drive me on.

In this way we were Fused and in this way we would live.

In this way, through all the spaces between populations, both Radical and human, we are alive.

The war had been going on for a very long time and people caught in the middle might have trouble telling one side from another, and the building that was the immediate objective had once meant something important but now was just another target.

The Last Crusade

George H. Smith

"Julius Caesar named this place 'Lutetia Parisiorum,' which means 'the mud town of the Parissii.' Later on people got around to calling it 'the city of light,'" Marty Coleman was saying.

"Well, Julius was sure as hell a lot closer to the truth than those others," I tell him. We was sitting in the mud in what's left of some big building and me and Joe White was listening to Marty, our Sergeant, talking like he always does. When I says the sergeant was talking I mean he was talking over the C.C., the Company Communication Circuit because what with having our mecho-armor on and the other side raising a little hell, we couldn't of heard him any other way.

"Yeah, I guess you're right, Ward. There isn't much light around here anymore," Coleman admitted.

"The only light you ever see around here these days is a flare or a rocket going over," White says in that funny flat voice of his.

From time to time Coleman would lift the headpiece of his armor above the pile of rubble in front of us and take a quick look out over the big open square toward where the enemy was holed up on the other side. About half the time he'd draw small arm or automatic fire.

"Those birds must have infrared eyepieces too," he says as he sets down.

"Ah they ain't even got mecho-armor," I says.

"No, but they have body armor and helmets with quite a bit of stuff in them."

"I'll bet they ain't got anything like we got." I was feeling pretty fine right then thinking how much better off we was than the poor joes in the infantry. We don't just fight in our suits, we live in 'em. They ain't only a mechanized suit of armor, they're our barracks, messroom and latrine and all radiation and rain proof. We got more fire power than a company of infantry and more radio equipment than a tank.

"You know there's lots worse ways of fighting a war," I says. "You climb into one of these babies and they seal you up like a sardine but at least you're warm and dry and you don't even have to use your own feet to walk. You got a nice little atomic power pack to move you around."

"You couldn't move the legs of one of these things if you had to," the Sergeant says.

"It . . . it just seems like a kind of funny way to fight a war," White says, talking like he always did, as though he had to hunt for every word before he said it.

"What's funny about it? They been fighting it this way for ten years, haven't they?" I demands.

"I guess so . . . I don't know. . . ."

"Yeah, ten years. And the last five of it we've spent crawling back and forth in what used to be Paris," the sergeant was talking again. "Just think . . . in the old wars they used to call it Gay Paree."

"It's gay all right," I says, following a movement on my ground radar screen. A beep had shown up, indicating activity over where the enemy was. Their guns was silent now but across the mud pools came their voices, voices that from time to time cut in on our circuits and competed with the voices of our own side.

Suddenly a girl was talking, a girl with a soft voice that was like warm lips against your ear. "Hello there, you fellows across the line. It's not much fun being here is it? Especially when you know that some non-draft back in the hometown walked off with your girl a long time ago.

"Honey Chile," the voice went on, "this is your old gal, Sally May, and I know how you all feel 'cause I used to be on the same side myself until I found out how things are over here in the Peoples Federal Democratic Eastern Republics. . . ." The bleat of a code message cut through the syrupy tones, tore at our ears for a few moments and faded away. Slowly the sweet voice drifted back.

"Well, fellows, we're gonna play you some real homey music in a few minutes, but first we're gonna tell you all about our contest. We know you all Yankee boys like contests and this one is a real humdinger.

"This here contest is open to every GI over there in the mecho-units. And have we got prizes? Why, honey, we sure have! Listen to this big first prize: $100,000 dollars in gold! And then we have an expense paid vacation in the scenic Crimea and a brand new factory special Stalin sportscar. And fellows, get this: A TV appearance on a nationwide hookup with a dinner date afterwards with glamorous Sonia Nickolovich, the famous ballerina.

"Now I guess you boys are wonderin' what you gotta do to win these wonderful prizes. Well, this is how easy it is. All you gotta do is write out a thousand-word statement on 'How my mecho-armor works' and deliver it along with your armor to the nearest P.F.D.E.R. army unit. Now . . . isn't that easy? And this contest is open to everyone but agents of the P.F.D.E.R. and their relatives."

The soft voice faded away.

"Why . . . the dirty—What do they think we are?"

Just on general principles I sent a half-dozen 75 mm shells in the direction of their lines.

"I don't—think I—understand that at all. What are they trying to do?" White asks. "I thought the enemy was Reds."

"You're in pretty bad shape, ain't you buddy?" I laughs. "Can't you even remember who you're fighting?"

"Leave him alone, will you, Ward," the sergeant orders. "If you had been brain washed as many times as he has you'd have trouble remembering things too."

"Whatta ya mean?"

Sarge swung the big headpiece of his armor around and looked at White through his electric eyes. "How many times you been captured, Whitey?" he asks.

"I . . . I don't know, Sarge. I don't remember. Twice . . . I guess."

"That's two brain washings from the enemy and two rewashings from our own psycho units. Four electronic brain washings don't leave much in a man's brain."

"Well, I'll be damned. Which side was you on first, Whitey?" I asks.

"I don't know . . . I don't remember."

"Ah come on now, you must know. Was you a Russian or an

American? Western Democratic Peoples Federal Republics or Peoples Federal Democratic Eastern Republics—which side?"

"I . . . don't know. All I know is that they ain't good and we got to fight them until we kill all of them."

"How do you know they ain't good?" I demands. "If you don't know which side you was on to start with, maybe you was shootin' at your own brothers this morning . . . or your mother."

"You better watch your mouth, Ward. There might be a Loyalty Officer tuned in on the band. You wouldn't want a probe, would you?" Coleman asks.

"Ah, they ain't listenin', Sarge. This guy gives me the willies. He don't know nothin' but how to run that damn armor and how to fight. He don't even know who he was to start with."

"I wish I did know . . . I wish I . . ."

"You know, Whitey, maybe you was a big shot on the other side. Maybe you was Joe Stalin's grandson or something."

"Remember!" an eager voice whispered in our ears. *"Remember what you are fighting for. In the WDPFR there are more washing machines than in any place else in the world!"*

I had to laugh. "You ever seen a washing machine, Sarge?" I asks.

Coleman was looking back toward our lines. "Yeah. There used to be a place called Brooklyn that was full of 'em. You know, there's something going on back there. The whole company seems to be moving up. And there's a big armored crawler there with a smaller one parked beside it."

He sits back down with a clanking of armor. "Must be some big shots coming around to see how we're winning the war."

"I wish someone would use a can opener on me right now and take me out of this walking sardine can and plump me into a washing machine. I ain't been clean in five years," I says.

"Do they have washing machines on the other side?" Whitey wants to know.

"Naw. They ain't got nothin' like that, nothin' at all," I tells him. "Things like washing machines is reserved for us capitalists."

"If we got washing machines and they ain't, then what are we fighting for?" Whitey asks.

"You better ask the Sarge that. He's the intellectual around here. He reads all the comic books and things."

"Why do you think we're fighting, Whitey?" Coleman asks.

"Well, Sarge . . . I don't know. If I could just remember who I used to be, I'd know. Sometime I'm gonna remember. Every once in a while I can almost . . . but then I don't."

"Well, why do you *think* we're fighting?" I asks.

"Well . . . well . . . I guess it's that there's bad guys and good guys . . . just like in the comics or on the TV shows. We're the good guys and they're the bad guys. Is that right, Sarge?"

"I don't know, Whitey. That might be some of it but I kinda think that maybe it has something to do with when we won the last war or thought we won it. We thought we had finished with the Nazis but I guess maybe we got fooled. In Europe the Nazis all turned Communist and in America the Commies all turned Nazi. Either way people like them have always got the jump on the joes in between. In Europe they pointed at them and called them Nazis. In America they pointed at them and called them Reds. Pretty soon people didn't know the difference, except that it was better to be pointing than to be pointed at."

"Now, Sarge, you're the one that better be careful. You wouldn't want the Loyalty Officer to be hearing that sort of talk, would you?" I cuts in.

"Maybe you're right but I kinda think that that's why . . ."

Just then the command circuit in our helmets opened up with orders for us to pull back and join the rest of the company. All the way back Whitey doesn't say anything so I figure he's trying to remember who he is. Well, we gets back to the command post without drawing more than a little small arms fire and a couple of rockets, but things is really popping there. The big crawler Coleman seen from our outpost is settin' there in the middle of the street and the whole company is gathered around it.

"What's goin' on?" I say as I sidle up beside Fred Dobshanski.

"Don't you guys know? There's a big drive comin' up. General Mac Williams is gonna talk to us himself."

Whitey was right beside me. He sure was a funny guy, always hanging around and asking questions. Sometimes I used to wonder what he looked like. You get used to not seeing any of the guys when you're in the forward areas. Sometimes for weeks or months at a time a whole area will be contaminated with bacteria or radiation and you don't open your suit at all. Even if you're wounded the mecho-armor gives you a shot and takes you back to a field hospital . . . that is, if it's still working. So you get used to not knowing what the guys look like and not caring much. But with Whitey it was different. His voice had such a dull someplace-else sound to it that you got to wondering if there was really anyone in that suit of armor or not. You got to wondering if maybe it just walked around by itself.

"Mac Williams? Who's he?" Whitey asks as if in answer to my thoughts.

"Hell, don't you know anything?" Fred says.

"I guess I don't. I . . . I . . . don't even know who I was. I sorta wish I knew who I used to be."

"Mac Williams is Fightin' Joe Mac Williams. He's going to talk to us. Look . . . there he is now."

I adjusted my eyepieces for direct vision and sure enough on the kind of balcony on the back of this big armored crawler was a guy. I mean to tell you he sure looked like something too. He was in full battle armor with scarlet trimmings and gold rivets. He was wearing a mother-of-pearl plated helmet with three stars set in rubies. Even the twin machine guns that were fitted to his armor instead of the 75 recoilless and 40 mm we had on ours was plated to look like silver.

"Gosh! Imagine a General coming 'way up here in all this mud and stuff. That guy must really have guts!" someone mutters on the company circuit.

"Yeah. I bet he's only got one swimming pool in that land yacht of his."

"Shut up! What's the matter with you? That ain't no way to talk. You a sub or something?"

"Say, did you guys see what I saw through the windows of that crawler? Dames!"

"Dames?"

"Who you kiddin'?"

"So help me. There was two of them. Two big, tall, willowy, blond WAC Captains!"

"Them's the General's aides."

"Yeah? What do they aid him at?"

"Shut up you guys," the Captain's voice cuts in. "The General is going to speak."

Well then he starts right in telling us about the great crusade we're engaged upon and how civilization is at stake. And how proud the home folks is of us. Of course, he admits we haven't had any direct word from the States since last year when we had those big cobalt bomb raids, but he just knows that they all love us. Right when he starts I know we're in for trouble, 'cause when the brass start talking about crusades, a lot of joes is gonna get killed.

He goes on with this for half an hour, and all the time the TV cameras is grinding away from this other crawler that is filled with newsers and video people. He mentions blood 16 times and that ain't good. Sweat he says 14 times and guts an even dozen. When it really looks bad, though, is when he calls the Major and the Captain up and pins a medal on each of the medal racks that officers wear on the front of their armor. When they start passing out the medals ahead of time, brother, it ain't good, it ain't good at all.

When he gets through with all this, the old boy retires into his crawler.

"I guess he's going in to plan the battle," I says.

"Ha," says Sergeant Coleman's voice in my ear. "All the blood and guts in that speech wore him out so much he's got to retire to his bar for a few quick ones with them two aides of his."

"Now, Sarge," I says, "that ain't no way for a patriot to talk."

"My patriotism is at a very low ebb at the moment. Do you know what kind of a party we're going to have in the morning?"

"No," I says, "but I would be interested in finding out."

"You've seen that huge mile-long building that's across the square from us?"

"I've seen it and found little to like about it. The enemy has every kind of gun in there that's been invented."

"Well, the Captain says that that's it! Fighting Joe wants us to take it."

Remember boys, remember that the way of life in the W.D.P.F.R. is better. Remember what you're fighting for—hot dogs and new cars, electric refrigerators and apple pie, sweethearts and mother. Don't let mother down boys!

A voice that used to sell us bath soap is selling us war.

"That kind of sounds like we're getting ready to move in, don't it Sarge?" I says.

Sure enough a half hour later we starts to move up. The whole company of thirty men is on its way with the rest of the battalion close behind.

"Say, maybe there'll be some dames up ahead," Dobshanski is saying.

"What do you want with dames? You got the Waiting Wife and the Faithful Sweetheart on your TV, ain't you?" the Sergeant says.

"It ain't the same. It ain't the same at all," Dobshanski says.

I cuts in with, "Hey, did you guys hear what I heard? Pretty soon we won't really need women anymore. Those new suits of armor we're going to get have got Realie TV sets in 'em. When a gal comes on it's just like she was in the suit with you. Those suits is gonna take care of everything and I mean everything."

"Ah, who ya kiddin'? Who ya handin' that line to?"

"Him and his inside dope!"

Twenty minutes later we're in position among the wrecked buildings on our side of the square and several kinds of hell is traveling back and forth across it. As is usual, the enemy seems to have as good an idea as to what we're about as we have.

"Oh, brother," Coleman moans. "Did Mac Williams send them a copy of his orders as soon as he got through writing them?"

Heavy shells and rockets is plowing up the already plowed up pavement all around us. Geysers of mud and water are being lifted by shells on all sides. I sees a couple of guys go down and I stumbles over a tangled mess of armor and flesh as we break from cover and start across the hundred yards or so of the square.

Floater rockets are overhead, circling kind of lazy like and lighting up the whole company as pretty as a summer's day with big magnesium flares. It's real comfortin' to see guys on all sides of you, but not so comfortin' when you sees them fallin' right and left.

I know I'm running with the rest of the guys 'cause I can hear my power pack rev up and feel the steel legs of my suit pounding along through the mud. I can feel the suit automatically swerving to avoid shell holes and to throw off the enemy aim. Not that they're really aiming, they're just tossing everything they got into that square and bettin' on the law of averages. The whole length of the big marble building we're after is lit up now, but not with lights, it's lit up with gun flashes.

The company and battalion radio bands is a mess. Even the command circuit is filled with guys yellin' and screamin', but there don't seem to be much point to orders right now anyway. I keep on goin' cause I don't know what else to do. Once or twice I recognise Coleman and White by the numbers on their armor and I get one glimpse of Fred Dobshanski just as half a dozen 70 mm shells tear his armor and him apart.

Then I'm almost at the building, and I'm being hit by point-blank light machine-gun fire. I'm blazing back with my 40 and 75, pouring tracers through the windows and being thankful my armor can take machine-gun fire even at close range.

There's other guys all around me now and we're smashing through doors and crashing over window sills into the building. The place is full of enemy joes and they're hitting us with everything they can throw. I take a couple of 40 mm shells that knock me off my feet, but Whitey blasts the gun crew two seconds later. We fight our way up a pair of marble stairways and they're really pouring it on us from up above, when suddenly they take a notion to rush us and come rushing down the steps . . . about three hundred of them.

What we did to them ain't pretty. That light plastic battle armor of theirs don't even look like it's stopping our stuff; and packed together like they are on those steps, it's murder. A lot of them get to the bottom, but there ain't much left of them when they get there.

It's all over then. Guys are yelling for the Medic robot and for the Ammo robots and others are just slumped down in their suits waiting for something else to happen . . . and it ain't long in happening. It can't be more than ten minutes after we chased the last Red out the back of our objective before their heavy guns're trying to knock it down around our ears.

Armor or no armor, what's left of the battalion takes refuge in the cellars where a few hours before the Reds were playing possum from our guns. Coleman, Whitey and I find us a nice heavy beam and are standing under it. Coleman is talking, as usual, and Whitey is wondering who he is and I'm watching the Major and Captain take inventory. Our assets ain't what they used to be. There's about twenty guys left in our company and maybe about sixty-five in the whole battalion.

I guess that's why the Major ain't very friendly when some of the guys dig out a couple dozen women and children who've been hiding in the building.

"Well, I'll be damned! Look what's comin' in!" I says to Coleman. There's maybe twenty women and the rest is kids.

"Why do the kids always seem to outlast the rest of the people, Sarge?" I asks. "Every place we been in this town, there's always more kids left alive than older folks."

"I don't know, Ward. Maybe they make a smaller target."

They've already got the kids lined up and we've given 'em the candy bars wrapped in propaganda leaflets that we all carry. Like all foreigners, they ain't very polite or grateful. They can't even understand what I'm saying even when I turn up my outside amplifier full power.

"What's the matter with them punks? Don't they appreciate candy?" I asks the sergeant who is muttering to one of them in some of their own gibberish.

"They say the Russians didn't give them anything but lumps of sugar and we don't give them anything but candy. They'd like something else."

"Now ain't that just like people like them," I says to White. "No gratitude to us for liberating them or for feedin' 'em."

"I think I would know what it's all about if I could just remember. You know, Sarge, for a few minutes up above there I almost remembered. Then the shelling started and...and...I don't know..." Whitey is still harping on his favorite subject so I turns back to the sergeant and the kids he's talkin' to.

"What's with these punks? What they got to complain about? If it wasn't for us they wouldn't have no country."

"They say that the Russians was about to take them away to a camp and make soldiers out of them and they're afraid we'll do the same."

"Well...what in hell do they want to do? Spend the rest of their lives hiding in a hole while we do their fighting?"

"This youngster says he doesn't want to be brain washed. He doesn't want to be a soldier."

"He's right," Whitey pipes up. "He don't want to be like me. You know, I had a dream...or did I remember? Anyway in this...dream...of mine, I remembered that I had been an important person like you said, Ward. But not on the enemy side. I knew something and wanted to tell it to the whole army but they didn't want me to. That's why they sent me to the psycho machines. That's why they made me like I am."

"What was it you knew, White?" the sergeant asks.

"I'm not sure. It was something... something about there not being any more Western Federation or any Eastern Republics... no more America... no more Russia... just two self-perpetuating armies... like hordes of maggots crawling across the corpse of Europe."

"That's a funny sort of dream... a very funny sort of dream," the sergeant says.

"Why would you have any sort of crazy dream like that?" I demands. "You know we hear broadcasts about how things are getting along so fine back home all the time."

"How long's it been since you got a letter, Ward?" Coleman asks.

"Letter? I don't remember. Who'd write to me anyway? What's the matter with them kids? Do they want the Russians to come back and rape their mothers and sisters?"

"I'll ask them," Sarge says, and starts gibbering again through his outside amplifier to a skinny brat that's doing the talking for all of them. Pretty quick the kid gabbles back just like he understood.

"He says that their mothers and sisters have been raped so many times by both sides that it don't make any difference anymore."

"They ain't got no grat—" I starts to say but the Major is yelling at the Captain so I stops to listen.

"Where are their men? Where are they hiding?" He shakes his fist under the noses of these French women and the Captain questions them.

"Why did they permit the Russians to hide out in this building? Don't they know that being here is collaborating with the enemy? Where are their men? I'll have them hung!" The Major is really hopping mad.

"I beg your pardon, sir." The Captain interrupts him. "This woman says that their men are on the second floor and..."

"Good! Send six men up there and hang every one of them."

"Sir, they say that the Russians have already hung them. As American collaborationists, sir!"

"What! Humph! Well ... send some men up there to cut them down and hang them again. No! Wait, Captain! We'll wait until the TV cameras get here."

It was just then that the word came for us to pull back, for us to give up this building and fall back to our old positions.

"My God! What's the matter with them?" Whitey says. "After all the guys we lost taking this place, why do we have to give it up?"

"Maybe they want us to do it over again for the TV," the Sergeant says as we watch the other two companies pull out, herding the civilians before them.

"I don't want to go," Whitey says suddenly. "If I stay here I might remember."

"To hell with it, Whitey," Coleman tells him. "Maybe you wouldn't like it if you did remember. Maybe you're better off this way."

"I like it here. There used to be pictures up above ... I found a piece of one during the fighting ... it was ... beautiful."

"Come on, Whitey! Let's get going! Don't you see what the Captain's doing?" I says. The others look and start moving fast. The Captain must have been mad about giving up our objective 'cause he'd set up a disruptor bomb on the floor and started a time fuse. Maybe you've never seen a disruptor bomb and maybe you wouldn't want to. In a way they're an improvement on the atomic bomb. They cause individual atomic explosions that keep blasting for hours after you start them. When that bomb gets through, there won't be anything left.

Pretty quick we're out in the open and running as fast as our mechos legs can carry us. We're about halfway across the square when I see Whitey suddenly break away from Coleman and head back toward the building.

He gets there and is heading in the door just as the disruptor bomb lets loose. That building started doing a dance, a kind of strip tease I guess, 'cause it's shedding roof and walls right and left.

Later on, when we're back in our lines, I'm sitting beside Coleman while our mecho-armor is whipping up some X-rations for us.

"Why did he do it, Sarge? Why'd Whitey go back?"

"I don't know. There was something about that building that he thought he remembered. It reminded him of something. That picture he found kind of set him off. He said maybe it was the last one there was in the world."

"Did . . . did he remember who he was?"

"I guess at the last he did . . . or at least he remembered something."

"Did he remember his name?"

"I guess so."

"Well, what was it?"

"He didn't tell me. Maybe his name was Man."

"Man? That's a funny name. Well . . . his name sure is mud now."

"Maybe the two names are the same, Ward," he says. The sergeant always was a funny guy.

The military-unit-turned-pirate thought the planet, with its agriculture-based economy and lack of military forces, would be easy picking for a big payday. But they hadn't counted on a grizzled veteran of an elite force who had retired to that world—and brought his formidable combat gear with him.

Miranda's Last Dance

Quincy J. Allen

Chapter 1

September 2967 (Terran Calendar)—Colony World Bevin
"I hate this planet," Kenny grumbled, loading another crate of shadda roots into Henry Combs' battered Masahaki hovertruck. The truck was an old, military-grade hauler that still had the gun-mounts—albeit empty ones—on the hood and behind the cab. "Nothing ever happens, and nobody ever goes anywhere."

At seventeen years old, Kenny Boudreaux had gone through his growth-spurt with a vengeance. He stood a few centimeters taller than Hank, with broad shoulders, a farmer's physique, and a shock of curly orange hair that spoke of Irish descent.

A dozen meters off, Henry Combs smiled and, with a shake of his gray-haired head, swept several dead leaves from the headstone at his feet. He kneeled, placed his hand upon the name MIRANDA laser-etched into the stone, and ran his finger over the dates, 2934–2942.

He remembered, and a wistful look—one neither happy nor sad—crossed his face.

"You managed one more year of sleep," he said softly. "Let's hope it lasts a lifetime."

He straightened, his joints popping a staccato reminder of his seventy-nine years, and let out a long, weary breath. Stretching his strong, sinewy arms, he turned toward Kenny, whom he'd hired to help with this year's harvest of the versatile tubers indigenous to Bevin. They were the colony's primary cash crop. The meaty tuber was an ingredient for several anti-aging pharmaceuticals produced off-world, as well as an excellent source of carbohydrates and protein in meals. It also made excellent mash for those who knew how to distill it into a bourbon-like drink unique in the galaxy.

The exceptionally potent, yet silky-smooth libation had been dubbed "süns" by Kahn Soong Lei, the Mongolian descendant who'd invented it. The old man had thought his ancestral word for "ghost" was an appropriate name. When he'd arrived in 2952 with the first wave of colonists, he came up with the spirit almost immediately. He was a master craftsman of any distillation process, and Hank had considered the man to be the da Vinci of alcohol. A two-year-old batch of the old Mongolian's brew was good. Five was better. Anything beyond that was like drinking God's quicksilver without killing you.

Hank ambled over to his hovertruck and examined Kenny's work. The crates had been stacked tight and neatly set into the bed of the vehicle. He had to admit, Kenny was well worth the eighty credits a day Hank paid him. He stepped up and gave Kenny the sort of patient, crotchety half-smile only old people know how to use.

"Son," he replied, yanking off a dingy, broad-brimmed hat and running a hand through a high-and-tight swath of gray hair, "believe me when I say a shitty, backwater world like Bevin is a blessing."

Kenny had worked for Hank for nearly two months and hadn't let Hank down yet. The lad complained a bit, but never let it get in the way of the job. Hank had made the arrangement with Kenny's father over a long card game and a daisy-chain of locally brewed ales made from an indigenous grain called traba. Like most of the colonists in New Haven, the oldest farming community on the planet, Kenny's father looked up to Hank like a grandfather figure of sorts. The whole colony did.

Kenny turned sour, disbelieving eyes to the old man as he loaded another crate onto the truck. *The kid really does have a solid work ethic*, Hank thought with a satisfied nod.

"I don't have to agree with you just because you're paying me, do I, Mr. Combs?" Kenny said, stretching his shoulders as he moved to the nearby stack of crates.

"Not ever, son," Hank said affably. "And maybe it's time you started calling me Hank."

"Alright," Kenny said a bit uncomfortably, ". . . Hank."

"That's better." Hank took a patient breath. "You don't know it, but even that one question sorta makes my point for me, although you're too inexperienced to know why. You should count that as a blessing, too."

"If you say so." Kenny chuckled. "I guess I'll just keep counting my blessings. And crates." He grabbed another crate and set it down in the bed of the hovertruck. "Not that the alternative would make any difference around here."

As Hank moved over to the dwindling stack of crates, a faint but deep rumbling filled the air. Kenny scanned the countryside, running his gaze along the long dirt road that cut through Hank's four-hundred-acre farmstead, but Hank's eyes lifted to the sky, turned west toward the setting sun, and immediately picked out a narrow contrail tipped with a glowing spark of light that was coming in about halfway up from the horizon.

"There." Hank pointed toward the incoming ship, and Kenny's eyes shifted in that direction. "Were there any cargo haulers due in today?" Hank asked.

"Nope." Kenny's father doubled as both the colony's mayor and the port master for the handful of airfields that qualified as the only official starport on the planet. There were even a few small, older starships parked out there gathering dust. They looked more like a ship graveyard than anything else. None had lifted off in over a decade. "Nothing was due in for another week, although another big süns shipment is scheduled to go up tomorrow night."

As they watched, the ship stitched its way across the sky, bleeding off velocity as it dropped in altitude. It went into a hard turn a few miles to the east, and moments later passed directly over their heads. A sonic boom echoed across the landscape. A high-pitched turbine shriek filled their ears as the ship fired its retros. Its velocity decreased significantly, and Hank was able to get a good look at its silhouette. He recognized the design, although it was more modern than the ones he remembered.

"Well, shit," he said, and then let out a long, disgusted breath.

"What's wrong?" Kenny asked.

"One pass to reconnoiter, and a final approach to deploy," Hank said, sounding like he was reading it out of a manual.

"What are you talking about?" Kenny's voice was tinged with confusion and a trace of fear.

"That's a Ming dropship, son," Hank said, glancing at Kenny. "Watch . . ." Hank's eyes darted back to where the dropship was making its final approach toward town six miles away. As it did, a half-dozen dark objects ejected—three on each side—from the main fuselage and shot away in downward arcs. "And those are drop pods. . . . God dammit," Hank muttered, slapping his hat back onto his head.

"Jesus, Hank," Kenny blurted "What the hell is going on?"

"Mercs, I imagine," Hank said. "Probably looking for an easy payday." His eyes flicked to Miranda's headstone and then back to Kenny. "And if they're this far out in the galactic arm, it's because they couldn't get an easier payday anyplace else."

"Mercs?"

"Remember what I said about being on this planet being a blessing?"

"Yeah?"

"Well, it's a double-edged sword, and I was hoping I wouldn't see the other edge before they planted me." He turned toward Kenny. "Do you know anything about firearms?"

"Sure," Kenny said. "Dad and I go hunting all the time."

"Then I need you to do me a favor."

"What?"

"I'm going into town to see what these bastards are after." He took off his hat and laid it on top of the crates they hadn't loaded. "I need you to go into my house and down into the basement."

"What the hell for?"

"In case I'm right," Hank growled. "You'll find an old wooden table on top of a large floor rug. Move the table and pull back the rug. Beneath, you'll see a small cover plate for a large hatch. Lift the cover plate, punch in the code MIRANDA, and when the pod opens, start prepping everything you see in there as best you can."

"But . . ." Kenny started.

"No buts," Hank barked. "Just do as I say, and maybe we'll all live through this." In a flash, the nice old man Kenny knew had disappeared. Before him was someone else altogether, and Hank's tone brooked no discussion. There was an edge to his voice and posture that Kenny had never seen before. Hank's taut shoulders relaxed when he recognized the look in Kenny's eyes. "Listen, son." He looked down the road toward town. "Maybe it's nothing. Maybe I'm overreacting, and they'll turn out to be new colonists or something." He placed a hand on Kenny's shoulder. "It's just better to be prepared, alright? Get on in there and do as I ask. It could make all the difference."

Kenny licked his lips. "Okay," he finally said.

"Good lad," Hank said. "If nobody shows up here by midnight tonight, then head on into town like nothing happened."

"You got it," Kenny replied, heading toward the house.

Hank moved around and opened the door to his hovertruck, and as he thought about what he needed to do next, he realized he should probably warn Kenny.

"One more thing," Hank called out. "A few folks might stop by this afternoon. If they show up and tell you Miranda sent them, take them downstairs." He eyed Kenny. "Can you do that for me?"

"Yes, sir," Kenny replied, looking even more worried.

"Everything's gonna work out," Hank said.

Kenny turned, nodded once with a fearful expression on his face, and then headed for Hank's front door.

Hank hit the power on his hovertruck, and the soft, electric hum of its Masahaki power plant filled the air. The vehicle lifted off the ground about a foot, and the struts beneath retracted up into the chassis. He eased the accelerator, guided the truck out onto the dirt road, and headed for town.

As he drove, he initialized the comm unit implanted beneath the scalp behind his right ear and connected to Sam Teller, one of his best friends. Sam, whose much larger plot of land lay five miles north, was fifteen years Hank's junior and had been one of the older colonists in the first wave. The two men had hit it off immediately, for a variety of reasons, including why they had chosen to settle on Bevin.

The comm buzzed twice, and then Sam picked up.

"I take it you saw it?" Sam said quickly and without preamble. There was neither surprise nor worry in his voice, only resolve.

"Yep," Hank replied.

"So, what do we do?"

"Get to my house," Hank said. "Carl's son Kenny is there. Tell him Miranda sent you. You'll know what to do."

"Copy that," Sam replied. "And I may be able to round up a few more."

"Do that," Hank said. "I'm heading into town to see what's up. If I'm not back by midnight, you're on your own."

"Good luck," Sam said.

"You, too, Sam."

Hank cut the comm and slammed the accelerator to the floor.

Chapter 2

Hank strolled into the small town of New Haven, a long stem of traba grain sticking out the side of his mouth. He had parked his truck on the far side of the wide, tree-lined river that ran north to south about a thousand meters outside of town. He'd kept the vehicle out of sight and hadn't spotted any aerial drones or flitters, so it was likely the new visitors hadn't seen him come in.

The city of New Haven, small though it was, had a population of about two thousand. They were mostly farmers and tradespeople who had sought refuge from the complicated life of cosmop worlds and large populations. They were—in general, anyway—a simple people in search of a simple life. As Hank surveyed the end of Main Street ahead, right where the dirt road ended and the permacrete pavement began, he knew their tranquil existence had been shattered by mercenaries... and not just mercenaries, but *corporate* mercenaries.

Standing in plain sight on the nearest street corner were two troopers, one man and one woman. Clad in light combat armor and helmets with opaque visors pulled down, they held pulse rifles casually cradled in their arms. The armor looked like modern derivatives of ArmyTek's line of modular armor. The lines looked right to Hank's eye, but it was an educated guess at best. Both troopers wore red and black uniforms, but they were clearly not Republic troopers, which meant New Haven was in real trouble. The

troopers' eyes were fixed upon Hank as he walked slowly up the side
of the road, gravel crunching beneath his feet.

The nearest trooper, a man, shifted his grip on the rifle and
moved forward.

Across the street from the two troopers was what Hank had feared
the most—a dōrydō. It looked like an Aztek design to Hank's eye,
but it was considerably more modern than what he was familiar with.
The Aztek's surface was made of smooth plates of neutron-dense
armor that looked almost faceted where they joined each other. It
had been painted with the same red and black colors as the troopers'
uniforms, and the highly reflective surfaces meant the suit was
designed for laser fire.

A god damn dōrydō, Hank thought.

The word went back more than a hundred years to the original
Japanese conglomerate, TokaiCorp, that had coined it when they
made the first model. The word "dōrydō" translated roughly to
"powered armor," and a trooper in a dōrydō was generally more
effective than ten troopers in combat armor. The self-contained suits
could shrug off small arms fire easily; most had an ablative
component that gave them a significant defense against lasers. More
specialized suits even had reflective armor specifically for laser fire.
They had heightened strength, speed, and sensory packages that
made them positively lethal against unarmed or even lightly armed
combatants and vehicles. Some had limited thruster flight, while
more modern designs had enhanced power plants that allowed for
gravitic flight over short and even—in rare cases—long distances.

Generally, the rule was, you stopped dōrydō with dōrydō, an LCG
(Large Caliber Gun), or a tank, if you had one handy. Hank was
pretty sure there wasn't a tank on the entire planet, unless one of the
colonists had built one from spare parts lying around in a shed
someplace.

The dōrydō driver stepped off the far corner, moved away from
the buildings, and started scanning the line of trees along the river.
A shoulder-mounted beam weapon moved in union with the helmet,
tracking wherever the driver looked.

They're not taking any chances, Hank thought.

"You looking for trouble, old man?" the male trooper said as he
blocked Hank's path. His voice was deep and threatening. With the

visor down, Hank couldn't tell what the man looked like, but his voice sounded middle-aged and confident. His armor was battered, slightly faded, but obviously serviceable. There was a bright area of paint on the chest piece where the trooper's corporate insignia had been covered up.

No evidence, Hank thought. *We're in trouble.*

"Not at all, son," Hank replied with a smile. "Just getting the lay of the land. I saw y'all come in and wondered what brought you to this backwater shithole. I take it you're not here for R and R?"

"You got that right," the trooper grumbled softly. "You packing?" the trooper asked, looking Hank up and down.

"Hell, son," Hank said, "I haven't carried a piece in nearly twenty years." Hank lifted up his shirt and turned in a circle, showing the trooper that there weren't any bulges.

The trooper stepped up, slung his rifle, and patted Hank down his torso and along the sides of both legs.

"Good," the trooper finally barked. "Now that you're here, move on down the street and join the others at the courthouse." Hank had no trouble figuring out it was an order, not a request.

"Whatever you say, son," Hank replied easily as he sidestepped the trooper.

"I ain't your son, grandpa," the trooper said. "We'll be watching. If you turn any corners, you'll be shot down where you stand. We clear?"

"As crystal." Hank gave a half-hearted salute and stepped past the trooper. Nodding once to the woman on the corner, he ambled down Main Street like he was on a Sunday stroll. He didn't give a second glance to the dōrydō still scanning the trees.

As he made his way, he saw several more pairs of troopers, some on street corners and others patrolling side streets, their weapons at the ready. *Mostly laser carbines,* he thought. He saw no sign of the inhabitants of New Haven, and a pang of worry crept through him as he wondered if they'd been executed. He'd counted eight troopers so far and spotted another dōrydō standing at the edge of town along one of three larger cross streets that bisected Main.

Hank blew out a frustrated breath.

Corporate piracy was a fairly common event in the Republic. Ship captains in command of squads, platoons, and even companies of mercs sometimes took advantage of the space between stars. They raided vessels and preyed upon small, poorly-armed colonies with impunity. Of course, Terran Republic troops and system law enforcement did their best to come in after the fact, but by the time they arrived, all the civilians were usually dead and stripped of their belongings. In cases where there were survivors, the victims rarely had any way of identifying who had raided them.

As he approached the center of town, and the storefronts rolled by, he realized all of them appeared to be closed. Normally, the front doors of each one would be open to the warm autumn air, the shop owners inside. New Haven felt like a ghost town at the moment.

At the end of the street, parked in the town square between a large fountain and the courthouse, sat a pair of wheeled APCs topped with twin heavy laser turrets and manned by troopers in the same red and black uniforms. One of them tracked Hank as he walked up.

As Hank passed the fountain, he stopped dead in his tracks.

There on the ground by the fountain lay three bodies riddled and scorched by laser fire. He kneeled over the bodies, recognizing all three. His heart sank. It was Kenny's father, the mayor, as well as Sheriff Cleil, and her deputy, Bill Baxter. The sheriff's blaster lay on the ground a short distance from her outstretched hand.

Hank closed his eyes and got a grip on his emotions. Rage burned inside him, and a wellspring of sadness for people who didn't deserve to die.

"Is there a problem?" one of the gunners called out. The tone of his voice was calm, easy, utterly uncaring.

Hank took a deep breath, let it out slowly, and faced the gunner.

"Not anymore," Hank said, turning with a satisfied grin. "Who do I have to thank for popping the sheriff and her deputy, here? They'd been on my ass for a while now on account of my illegal still. I make the best süns around."

"You were told to get inside the courthouse?" the trooper asked, ignoring Hank's question.

"Yep."

"Then get your ass in there, or you'll be joining them." The easy tone was gone from the trooper's voice, replaced with venom.

"Whatever you say, son," Hank said. "I'm not one for getting into trouble when the winds change. I go with the flow."

"Then flow inside, ya dumb collie."

Hank gave the trooper a weak smile, happy to be referred to as a collie. Collie was the standard pejorative for colonist. He moved around the APC, the turret following him as he went. Beyond lay the wide stairs of the courthouse, and at the top of them was another dōrydō, as well as two troopers in heavy combat armor and full helmets. Their armor looked vacuum-capable and would be much tougher to crack than the light combat armor of the other troopers. They were all guarding the large double doors that stood open.

Hank made his way up the wide stairs, nodded to the troopers, and walked inside.

Chapter 3

Hank strode purposefully into the entry area of the courthouse. The building had been a large prefab structure designed originally as a three-story office building. Assembled ten years earlier, the colonists had modified it to their needs. The interior was warm and well lit, with much of the decor done in the bluish wood of a local tree.

Hank scanned the interior at a glance. All of the administrative offices were upstairs beyond two large staircases on either side of the entryway. There was a large counter to the right, with a door behind, and a pair of doors along the left wall beneath the stairs. At the back of the entryway lay the courtroom. Normally hidden by an accordion wall which was now collapsed into a left-hand recess, the courtroom was fully exposed, with rows of benches on either side of a wide aisle that led up to a tall dais upon which sat the judge's bench.

Twenty of New Haven's citizens sat clumped together on the left side in the front two rows, their backs to Hank. There were two troopers on either side, their visors down, watching everyone carefully. In front of the judge's bench stood a man in a dōrydō of a design Hank didn't recognize. The suit had smooth lines and an almost feline appearance, particularly in the shape of the helm, which reminded Hank of a panther or jaguar. The armor itself looked a bit lighter than the Azteks Hank had seen outside, although that didn't necessarily mean anything. It also didn't have any integrated weapons systems, but there was an array of components built into the waist and wrists of the suit that made Hank surmise it might be an infiltration suit. A laser carbine lay on the judge's bench within easy reach.

"—so this doesn't have to get any messier than it already has," the dōrydō driver said, his voice amplified through speakers built into the chin piece. The driver turned his head to look at Hank as he walked in. "It seems we have another guest," he added. "If you'll just take a seat with the others, we'll get on with our business."

All the people on the benches turned their heads, and Hank saw a sea of mostly frightened faces.

They're farmers, not fighters, Hank thought. He gave the driver an obedient nod.

"And what might that business be?" Hank asked as he moved toward the nearest bench.

The driver cocked his head to the side.

"I was just getting to that, old timer," the driver said. "If you'll shut your mouth and have a seat, I'll get right to it." Hank recognized the tone. It was the polite imperative of a person who believed he was totally in control.

Hank raised his hands in acquiescence and closed his mouth. He reached the second bench from the front, and the six women and four men already sitting there scooted down. He recognized them all. The closest was Elena Svodoba, the remaining deputy of New Haven. She had a fierce bruise beneath her left eye, and the tight blond bun she normally wore in her hair was disheveled in several places. She'd arrived in New Haven on a transport two years earlier and quickly found her way to Sheriff Cleil, who hired her on the spot. When Elena looked up at Hank with her deep blue eyes and motioned for him to sit down, he saw both worry and anger there.

There's at least one fighter here, he thought.

They exchanged a glance as Hank sat down.

To her right sat three City Council members, five shopkeepers from the larger shops along Main, and Hakeem Najjar, the town's best welder and metalsmith. Hakeem clenched one fist deliberately. When Hank met his eyes, there was iron there. And anger. Even at sixty years old, Najjar had arms like corded steel. As a younger man, he had made his way through a number of starship-building shipyards all along the main trade corridor of the Terran Republic. Hank suspected the man, almost twenty years his junior, had been in more than one scrape in his time. Shipyards drew mercs, and mercs generally caused trouble wherever they went. In that one glance, Hank knew the old Arab was itching for a fight. Hank got the message, and then he settled into his seat.

That's two.

Elena leaned slightly toward Hank.

"They're going to kill us all after they get whatever they came for." Her voice was barely a whisper, and her tone wasn't one of warning or fear, simply a complete absence of doubt, as if she *knew* what the corporate mercs were planning, as if she'd been part of it. In that moment, Hank suspected he knew why Sheriff Cleil had given her a job.

Hank pretended not to hear her at first. He leaned back in his seat, a bored expression upon his face, and then stretched his arms out and yawned mightily. When he covered his mouth, he whispered back to her two words, "Be ready," and then he shook his head and gave the dōrydō driver his full attention.

"Are we keeping you up, old man?" one of the troopers asked with a chuckle.

"I didn't get my nap today, son," Hank replied. "And with all this fuss, I'm feeling a little tuckered out."

"Shut it," the driver ordered, stepping forward. "I wanna get this over with." He seemed to look over his audience, his helmet slowly panning from left to right.

Dōrydōs, including their face plates, were completely encased in a quark-bonded, neutron-dense alloy. There were neither eye slits nor any sign of a visual input mechanism. Despite this fact, the base electronics systems of a dōrydō allowed a driver to see across the full spectrum, provided image enhancement of thirty or more times normal resolution, and could even scan through a short list of materials.

"I'm going to make this very simple," the driver said. "We're here for that shipment of Kahn Süns slated to go out tomorrow."

Hank felt Elena stiffen beside him. "They're after your shipment," she whispered.

Hank placed his hand on her thigh and squeezed as he glanced at her. He shook his head almost imperceptibly to silence her.

"My people," the driver continued, "will finish loading up that fat cargo ship at the port, and then we'll leave. Anyone who tries to stop

us will end up like those three outside. We've cut your link to the
SatComm at the source, so you can't call for help, and while you might
think you can overwhelm my troopers, there are six dōrydōs scattered
around this shithole. You couldn't even scratch one of us with the
hunting rifles I'm sure you have lying around here, so don't even try.
You'll just piss off the driver before one of us shoots you to pieces." He
turned and picked up his laser carbine. "You all heard the warning we
gave when we arrived. If everyone stays in their homes until we're
gone, there won't be any more trouble for them. And as for all of you,
there's an empty storage shed not far from here where we'll keep you
until just before we take off. Once we get back to our ship in orbit, we'll
fire up her systems, and you'll never see us again. If you comply, all
you're out is a single shipment of booze. If you don't, you'll end up
fertilizing the soil with your blood. Do not fuck with us."

The driver turned and nodded to the two troopers on Hank's
right.

"Alright, you dumb collies," a male trooper shouted, aiming his
weapon. "Get moving."

The female trooper beside him moved toward the back of the
courtroom and motioned toward the front doors.

Hank got up quickly, took his place at the head of the line, and
stared into the mirrored visor of the female trooper.

She stepped in front of him and hefted her carbine, like she was
bored with the whole thing.

"If any of you backwater collies gets the bright idea to jump us or
run, these carbines lay down enough fire to wipe you out in about
eight seconds. You heard the commander. Don't fuck with us, and I
won't have to work up a sweat killing you." She took a position to
Hank's left. "Move it," she ordered, and it was clear to Hank she felt
like she'd drawn shit duty.

"Whatever you say, miss," Hank replied, and he started walking
toward the front doors.

Chapter 4

The female trooper guided Hank out the front doors, down the steps,
and past the APCs still manned by the gunners. Night had finally

settled upon New Haven, and the streets were illuminated by lamps at every corner. The trooper motioned for Hank to turn right toward the landing field, and the whole group shuffled along for a couple of blocks. They turned two more corners and came up to a large chromaplas storage building two stories tall and half a block wide. The two wide main doors had been secured with a length of chain and a thumb-lock. A small door set off to the side stood open, and a small rectangle of light brightened the sidewalk.

"Get inside," she ordered, stopping just short of the door. She turned to the rest of the prisoners. "Everyone inside. Stay calm. Stay quiet. This will all be over by morning." The female trooper seemed to only be keeping half an eye on the prisoners, and her attention seemed to wander, as if she was bored with the whole thing.

Hank nodded and stepped into the empty storage building. There were two other buildings closer to the landing field that he knew had been full to the roof beams with Kahn Süns.

They're spread thin, if some of them are loading the rest of the shipment, he thought.

Hank moved off to the side, just inside the door, and waited for the rest of the prisoners to be pushed inside. When he saw Elena come in, he reached out and gently pulled her toward him, raising a finger to her lips to silence her.

She gave him a quick, knowing nod, and her shoulders stiffened slightly.

The rest of the prisoners who had been sitting on Elena's row were shoved inside, and when Hakeem appeared, Hank pulled him aside as well. As the remaining prisoners shuffled in and grouped up like a flock of birds clucking to each other in low voices, Hank gently guided Elena and Hakeem to stand in front of him, their backs to the door.

When they were in position and blocking the troopers' view, he lifted his pant leg and slipped a thin, well-worn, but extremely sharp tanto blade from the back of his boot. Tightening his grip, he took a deep breath and found himself wondering if he still had it . . . still had the mettle to do what had been easy when he was young.

When the last prisoner stumbled through the doorway, the male trooper stepped inside, his carbine slung over his shoulder.

"If you know what's good for you, you'll just stay in here and keep your mouths shut," the male trooper barked. "If I have to come back in here, I'll just shoot one of you to get the message across."

Hank stepped up to face the male trooper, a shit-eating grin on his face.

"You picked the wrong colony," he said as bright as sunshine.

"Whu—" the trooper started, but Hank's blade cut his voice off as it came up under the chin of the helmet, pierced the trooper's throat, and slid into his brain. Hank caught the trooper's rifle as it fell, gave the hilt of his blade a twist, and yanked it free. Supporting the trooper against the door frame with his body, he let the corpse slide to the permacrete floor.

"Hey," Hank called out as he stepped through the doorway. "I think there's something wrong with your friend here."

The other trooper turned her head to see what was wrong. Hank moved like a panther, stepped in close, and drove the blade into her brain, too. Her rifle clattered to the street as Hank dragged her lifeless body back inside the door.

Amateurs, he thought, the smile disappearing as he pulled the weapon free and wiped it off on his sleeve.

"Get that carbine, would you, Elena?" Hank said over his shoulder as he scanned the street outside. There were no troopers or dōrydōs in sight, so they had time. As Elena darted out and retrieved the weapon, he scanned the street and spotted what he was looking for. About ten feet past the door, in the middle of the street, was a manhole cover that led down into the storm drain systems. As Elena dashed inside holding the carbine like a professional, he stepped back through the door and closed it.

When he turned around, he found all the prisoners except Elena and Hakeem staring at him with wide eyes, fear filling their faces.

"Are you crazy?" Gill Juarez shouted. "You're going to get us all killed!" He was a member of the City Council and owned the largest furniture shop on Main Street. He was also a teetotaler who never drank, never played cards, and spent his Sundays at the only church in New Haven.

Hank ignored him. "Elena, Hakeem," he said pointing at them, "put on their gear as fast as you can. Elena, you can help Hakeem, right?"

"Yes,"

"I don't need any help," Hakeem replied. "I wasn't always just a metal worker."

"Copy that," Hank said. "Get going."

The two of them moved quickly, pulling the combat armor and uniforms off the bodies as fast as they could.

Hank watched Elena's hands move like she'd worked with combat armor her whole life.

"Merc, right?" Hank asked, looking straight at her.

Her hands froze and she turned slowly to him. When they locked eyes, he could see pain there.

She nodded once.

"Corporate?" he asked.

Elena's features filled with shame, and then she went back to pulling gear off the female trooper lying on the floor.

"Five years. At the end of it, I got transferred to a new ship . . . a ship with a bad captain . . . and for three months, I was one of them. Like what's outside. I always managed to arrange for guard or support duty. I never killed anybody—I told them I wouldn't. I turned a blind eye, took the money, and kept my head down. Then, one day, when we raided our first colony—one not too different from New Haven . . ." Her voice cut off, and she fought back tears. "When we hit orbit," she said through clenched teeth, "we bombed the whole settlement to cover our tracks and went back to our regular transport support assignment. I got out as soon as we docked at Boondock Station and came here to start a new life." She turned and looked at the stunned faces of the other townspeople. "They are *not* going to let us live . . . They *can't*. They'll wipe us off the map, head for deep space, and nobody will ever know what really happened here."

"That's right," Hank said. "So we're going to fight."

"Fight?" Juarez asked. "We can't fight that. And even if we could . . . even if by some miracle we were able to stop them all, their buddies in orbit can just come down, take what they want, and bomb us anyway." He glared at Hank. "The only way out of this is to give them what they want and pray."

"There isn't anyone up in orbit," Hank replied flatly.

"How could you possibly know that?" Juarez asked angrily.

Hank turned to Elena. "You heard that driver back there. He needs to fire up their systems before they leave. If there were even a few crew members up there, the starship would be ready to go the moment he boarded. He brought his entire crew down here, and the ship is unmanned and asleep up there, waiting for a wakeup call."

Elena's eyes went wide with realization.

"You're right," she said. "And if that's the case, then it *has* to be a corvette class with a single drop ship, the two APCs, and what looks like a platoon of troopers, plus the six dōrydōs. Standard compliment for that class. They were Ming APCs out front."

"And it was a Ming dropship that landed."

"So that's probably a Ming in orbit." Elena looked up.

"Exactly," Hank said. "Can you pilot one?" he asked.

"In a pinch," she replied uneasily.

"I can," Hakeem said. "I think you know I was once a starship engineer. Before that, though, I was a pilot. I'm not the best there is, but I can get it wherever you want it to go."

"This is getting better by the second," Hank said. "We're all going into the storm drain out there. I need you two to take the others and head for the north side of town, *toward* the airfield. I'll be back in a few hours. Listen in on their comms, call me if they realize you're gone, and I'll let you know when you can pop your heads up."

"What are you gonna do?" Hakeem asked.

"I'm going to see if we can't give these bastards a little bit more than they bargained for."

A minute later, with Hakeem covering, Elena led the still terrified townspeople into the storm drain. Hakeem then went down, followed by Hank, who pulled the manhole cover back over them.

When he got to the bottom, he saw the lights from Elena's helmet and rifle heading down a side pipe, leading the freed prisoners. Hakeem was standing there, waiting.

"How will you know how to get out?" he asked. "You won't have any light."

Hank bent down, put his hand into the small channel of water flowing beneath their feet, and nodded as he felt the slight current.

"It rained last night," he said with a grin. "The water will lead me straight to the river."

"In total darkness?" Hakeem said, astonished.

"Piece of cake," Hank replied. "Keep them safe," he added, and then he headed away from the direction the others had gone.

"See you on the other side, Hank," Hakeem said.

Hank raised a hand and kept walking. He heard Hakeem turn and set off toward the others, casting Hank in total darkness.

He kept going, feeling his way along with every step.

Chapter 5

Hank pulled the Enhancement Optics off his head as he pulled into the drive of his homestead. Five ground vehicles and one two-man flitter sat parked just outside his house. The sight of them made him smile.

Sam's been busy, he thought.

He'd had no difficulty making his way to the river, nor getting back to his hovertruck, and the optics had been tucked beneath the driver seat, just one more Alternate Plan Bravo in a long line of them that had kept Hank alive through some pretty rough times. He'd raced back home with the lights off, checking the rear view to make sure nobody followed. That had been his one worry—well, one of two, actually. The other was if somebody had noticed the two troopers he'd killed weren't where they were supposed to be.

I just need a little more time, he thought, hoping the merc commander was too busy to worry about them.

He stopped the truck, got out, and walked over to Miranda's headstone. Kneeling down on the back side of it, he pulled out his tanto and dug a small hole into the turf. About four inches down, he found the sensor panel he was looking for. He widened the hole, cleared out the dirt, and brushed the plate clear of soil and grass.

He stared at it for a few moments, drawing in a deep breath. He let out a long sigh and placed his hand on the sensor plate. The panel lit up with several status lights, all in the green. Hank nodded once and leaned forward.

"Wake up, Miranda," he said. "It seems we've got one last dance together. Security access Five-Five-Two Alpha."

He heard a faint, metallic *clunk* from beneath the soil, the whine of servos, and then the ground in front of the headstone started to rise. Without waiting, Hank rose to his feet with the same staccato popping sound of joints that had plagued him for over a decade, turned toward the house, and walked up to the front door. As he reached for the doorknob, the front door opened, and he found himself staring into the eyes of Sam Teller.

"Sam," Hank said, his eyes darting to the heavy assault rifle the thick man held at the ready.

He looked past Sam and saw eight other figures standing in his living room, all armed with a variety of rifles. They were all farmers with homesteads on the periphery of New Haven. On the left stood Jodai Mumbassa and his two eldest sons, Marovar and Yobani, all traba grain farmers, as well as Cleve and Borda Svenson, who were big, burly vehicle mechanics of considerable skill. On the right was Sam's cousin Treat Encinas, another shadda farmer, as well as Felicia Sweeny and her partner Abigail Takashi, who ran a small grocery a few miles down the road.

"Come on in, Hank," Sam said.

As Hank stepped in, he spotted Kenny coming up the stairs from the basement. He held a long MAC sniper rifle in his hands, and to Hank's surprise, he looked fairly comfortable with it.

"Kenny," Hank said, "set that down for a minute. I need you to grab one more thing from the cache."

"What's that?" Kenny leaned the rifle against the door jamb.

"It's a silver cylinder about thirty cents long, with green lights up the side, and a power coupling on one end."

"You got it, Hank." Kenny quickly disappeared down the stairs.

"So, what's the deal?" Felicia asked. There was neither fear nor nervousness in the question.

"I'll get to that in a minute," Hank said. "Before I do, I need to know who has combat experience. I don't care what kind."

Sam, Jodai, Cleve, Borda, and Felicia all raised their hands.

"Good. And the rest of you know how to shoot?"

Everyone nodded.

"People?" Hank asked, his face deadly serious.

Abigail stepped up, her shoulders squared, and hefted a laser carbine. "We already talked about that," she said. "Those are our friends in town, and if mercs want to try and take what we've built here, then we'll kill them as easily as we would any other animal."

Hank smiled as everyone in the room nodded.

"Fair enough," he replied just as Kenny came up the stairs.

Kenny stepped forward and handed Hank the silver cylinder.

"Thanks, Kenny," Hank said. "Now, let me tell you what's up and what we're going to do about it."

When Hank finished, everyone looked at him with dubious faces.

"Hank," Sam said uneasily. "That's a great plan and all, but you kept saying you're doing this or that, and frankly, I don't see how you could possibly accomplish half of it, even with those heavies that are still sitting in the basement. I'm guessing the two bigger ones go on your truck, but even one dōrydō will take that truck apart, given half a chance. You can't get all of them with any of this stuff, including Kenny's MAC rifle and that boomer that's down there. You'll be a sitting duck."

Hank gave him a lop-sided smile. "That's where Miranda comes in."

"Miranda?" Sam asked. "Like on that headstone out there?" The few people who had asked Hank about the headstone had always gotten the same reply: that he didn't want to talk about it.

"Come on," Hank said. He walked out his front door with everyone in tow and then stopped. "Oh," he said as he turned, "and Cleve, before we take off, go get the boomer. It's only got two rounds, but it goes with you."

Cleve, a giant of a man just like his brother, gave a big shit-eating grin. "Thanks, Hank," he said. "I was hoping you'd say that."

He led them straight to Miranda's grave. "I'll show you."

As they approached in the darkness, Sam hit the light on his assault rifle and shined it onto what Hank had buried twenty-five years earlier.

The dōrydō, standing upright in the bottom of a military-grade, long-term storage capsule, was painted a mottled dark gray on black pattern. It had smooth lines and thicker plating than the Azteks in town. A railgun rose straight up behind the right shoulder. The weapon fired slugs made of the same neutron-dense material as dōrydō armor. Over the other shoulder sat a small missile pod about thirty centimeters on a side, with six launch tubes and what looked like a wide exhaust port sticking out a couple centimeters on the side. A commander's insignia—a cluster of three stars joined by a circle— decorated each of the outer shoulder plates, and over the right breast was the insignia of an angel in black armor, wings outstretched, holding a flaming sword. An elongated double-diamond of gold encompassed the angel, and across the bottom were the words, "NON ENIM MISERICORDIAE IMPIUS," which translated as, "No mercy for the wicked."

"Holy shit," Sam said. "That's a Terran Republic Assault Unit...a Mancuso." Sam turned to Hank with wide eyes. "You were a—"

"Yeah," Hank replied. "For a lot of years."

"I knew you were military, but I had no idea."

Hank gave him a wry grin. "That was the general idea. I wanted to forget all that, but once an Archangel, always an Archangel. It's the oath we swear."

"What's an Archangel?" Kenny asked, staring in awe at the war machine before him. He'd obviously never seen anything like it.

Felicia spoke up, "They're the TR's best. When the Republic wants to put the hammer down on alien incursions or rogue mercs, they send in the Archangels." She looked at Kenny. "And the Archangels kill everything in their path."

Hank moved up behind the dōrydō, twisted a small hatch mechanism on its back, and a small door opened with a whine of servos. He slid the powercell into the empty socket, and there was a subtle hum as the primary systems powered up.

"Miranda," he said to the Virtual Intelligence, "would you please open up for me?"

More servos whined. The back of the suit, including helm and legs, split along invisible seams as the suit automatically leaned forward for counterbalance. Hank stepped into the dōrydō with muscle memory that hadn't faded in twenty-five years.

"Button it up, Miranda," he said as the HUD came alive before his eyes and ran through a sys-check. Most drivers viewed their VIs in the same way captains viewed their ships.

"Copy that," a feminine voice replied within the suit. Miranda was not a created intelligence in the classic definition of the term. She was merely a Virtual Intelligence simulacrum that gave the appearance of sentience, but was actually just an advanced combat system. VI rigs were only available to Terran Republic dōrydōs, the Archangels in particular. Drivers required an intensive and intrusive surgery that implanted a hard-wired networking mesh just beneath the cranium. The process was one of the military's most closely guarded secrets and had, as yet, not been duplicated by the private sector. At least, not the last time Hank checked.

Servos whined again, and he felt the suit close up around his body with a *thunk-hiss* as the atmosphere equalized within the suit. He felt a dozen pinpricks pierce his close-shaved scalp, and then a surge of energy flowed through his body as he joined with the suit. A wave of memories washed over him. He had never wanted to get back into the thing, but there wasn't much choice at this point. When the sys-check came back with all systems nominal, he checked his weapons loadout: twenty-seven MAC rounds and eighteen hyper-velocity micro-missiles in the launcher module. He also had three recon floaters built into a small housing attached to the back of the missile launcher. He bent down and picked up the Aggressor Mark V Heavy Autocannon nestled into the side of the storage capsule. He checked the mag, saw it had all eight rounds, and then ran his hand over the two mags clipped to the back of his suit just above his ass.

You ready to dance, Miranda? he asked with his mind.

No mercy for the wicked, the VI replied.

In his HUD, he looked over the nine figures standing before him, all their faces frozen with awe. His system automatically did a scan of their weaponry and sent back the threat-analysis data. He actuated the external comms.

"Alright, everyone," he said. "You know the plan. Mount those heavies on my truck and get moving."

"Copy that," Sam, Jodai, Cleve, Borda, and Felicia said together. The others merely nodded their heads.

As they all started moving, Hank sent a signal to the local comm tower that served the area and confirmed that their satellite linkup was dead. He had Miranda ping the comm units for all nine of the people headed toward the house. Everyone raised their hands to an ear to activate their comms.

"Hello?" all of them replied, and then stood looking at one another in surprise.

"Just checking comms, everyone," Hank said. "We're linked by my dōrydō through the central comm tower." He could reach anyone in New Haven, but not beyond about a twenty-mile range from the center of town.

It would be enough.

Miranda, Hank thought, *ping the tower and connect to every comm unit inside of New Haven. Activate the Emergency Broadcast System, temporarily cut their transmitters, and then pipe me in.*

Stand by, Miranda replied. *EBS coming online.*

The alert warning sounded in the entire town's comms three times, and then a default message indicating an emergency played out. When it was finished, Hank spoke up.

"People of New Haven, I need you all to pay attention. This is Henry Combs. As you undoubtedly know, mercs have invaded New Haven. What you don't know is they've come to take the süns shipment and kill everyone once they're clear so there's no trace of what they did here. I and a few others intend to stop them. I need everyone to lock your doors, get down into your basements, and get beneath as much cover as you can. Tables, benches, whatever. There's about to be a fight, and I can't promise there won't be weapons fire or worse going through your houses. Don't come up until you get an all clear from the EBS. This will all be over soon. I give you my word as a Terran Republic Archangel."

He disconnected and turned toward town.

Hank lost track of time as the memories flowed over him. Years of combat, and friends dying, and killing bastards—alien and otherwise—who would inflict themselves upon the innocent and take what they could. He felt the old ire rising within him. He shifted and flexed inside his dōrydō, loosening up, and the suit gyrated and moved with him. He had to admit, it felt good to be back inside again. There was a part of him that hated how much he enjoyed doing what he was so good at, but he pushed that aside and reveled in the power that thrummed around him. There were six considerably more modern dōrydōs out there. *But they're only Azteks,* Hank thought with a smile. His Mancuso Assault Unit was old, but even an old Mancuso was feared by drivers in lesser suits.

"No mercy for the wicked," he said out loud, and then he turned to see his friends carrying out the two heavy guns for his truck.

The first was a twin laser cannon for the front hardpoint plugged directly into the Masahaki power plant. It would burn through energy quickly, but Hank was certain it would be more than enough for the coming fight. The weapon had a ninety-degree traverse left and right, and could elevate to about thirty degrees. The other was a Mizuki swivel-mount chem-laser, with belt-fed charges ignited by a power-feed from the truck.

He watched them quickly drop the weapons into their hardpoints, and then Kenny hefted the heavy ammo-case and belt into the back of the truck. He locked it down, and Felicia connected the belt mechanism and actuated the weapon like she'd been doing it her whole life.

"Felicia," Hank said over the comms, "you look pretty comfortable with that. You want the duty?"

"Hell yes," she said. "I can make this thing sing and dance," she added enthusiastically.

"Sam, you operate the twin instead of the swivel," Hank said. "Marovar still drives the truck, while Yobani takes the flitter. You two are hell on wheels in those things."

"Yes, sir," they both said. Anyone who knew the Mumbassa family knew Jodai had taught his boys how to drive just about any vehicle, and they clearly had a gift for it.

"Alright," Hank said. "Everyone mount up. I'll ride on the hood. Kenny, you'll set everything in motion just like we discussed."

"Yes, sir," Kenny said. Hank picked up just a hint of nervousness in the boy's voice, but not enough to worry him.

"It's just like shooting wild game, son," Hank said. "All you have to do is not miss and then do what I told you."

Kenny swallowed once and gave a quick nod.

Hank moved around the truck, leapt up onto the hood, and went down into a crouch, gripping one of the turret barrels.

"Move out!" he ordered, and everyone scrambled for their positions.

Chapter 6

Hank clumped across the bottom of the river as everyone moved to their positions. He sloshed out of the water and made his way up the steep bank. He couldn't help but wonder how many of his friends might be dead soon. Would they get lucky and not lose anybody? Or had he led them all to a messy death? Only a few of them were soldiers. The others were just pissed-off farmers and kids. *It'll have to be enough,* he thought. *Us collies are tough by definition.*

"I'm in position," Hank said over the comms. "Who isn't?"

"Gimmie thirty seconds," Marovar replied from the truck. "We're almost there."

"No sign that they've spotted you?" Hank asked.

"I didn't pick them up on thermal or enhanced with these optics you gave me," Marovar said. "The trees provided plenty of cover. I can't see them, so I have to hope they can't see us."

"If you're not taking incoming fire, they haven't spotted you," Hank said. "And remember, if you see a dōrydō, get the hell out of there. They should come to me once I'm spotted, and send the troopers out to fill the gaps, but we won't know until they're engaged."

"Understood," Marovar replied.

"Yobani, remember not to jump the gun. You don't head in until I say, no matter what you hear on the radio. Understood?"

"Yes, sir," the young man replied.

"We'll be fine, Hank," Cleve assured him. "Just do what you do. We've got your back."

"Copy that," Hank said.

"I'm in position," Marovar said.

"We're ready to rock and roll," Sam added.

"Charged and ready." Felicia sounded hungry for blood.

Hank tasked Jodai, Borda, Treat, and Abigail to take up positions just outside of town with assault rifles and snipe any mercs who tried to run out of town. There would be no mercenary prisoners.

"Kenny," Hank said, "it's on you now."

Hank moved up to the edge of the river and looked up at the high riverbank and thick line of trees that rose above him twenty meters. He unslung the autocannon, flipped the safety off, and initialized his weapon systems with a thought.

Combat Mode initialized, Miranda piped into his thoughts. *All weapons armed.*

"Three..." Kenny's voice came in. "Two..." Hank went down into a crouch. "One."

A single, massive gunshot tore through the night air.

"Get out of there, Kenny," Hank ordered, and then he leapt.

His boot and back thrusters activated, sending him rocketing straight up into the air. He launched all three recon floaters as he cleared the trees and the town came into view. His targeting system picked out the nearest threats as the six-centimeter floaters raced forward into the darkness.

In Hank's HUD, a dōrydō was highlighted in red, and the two troopers who had taken cover behind the corner of the building were a yellowish green.

The dōrydō, a slightly different Aztek design than the one that had been there previously, was clearly fixed on identifying where the shot had come from as it strode forward, an autocannon aimed toward the trees. Hank could see a scorch mark, and part of the armor bent outward on the chest plate, dead center. *Nice shot, Kenny,* he thought as he reached the top of his arc.

Hank's railgun tracked with his helm, locked onto the dōrydō with a flash, and Hank heard the lock tone. The enemy dōrydō shifted, his weapons tracking toward Hank . . . too late. Hank willed the weapon to fire.

CRACK!

Miranda shuddered around him, and his trajectory was altered as the first hypersonic round, magnetically accelerated to Mach 7, slammed the dōrydō to the ground. Thermals registered a massive heat bloom as the energy dissipated across the enemy dōrydō. It wasn't moving, and it looked like the armor had been breached. Hank let his body fall, locked onto the dōrydō's helm, and fired again.

CRACK!

Another round pierced the night, this time into the dōrydō's helm.

The resulting explosion of neutron-dense metal streaked out like a grenade going off. Shrapnel peppered the nearby buildings, and undoubtedly passed through at least several walls. It also caught one of the two troopers across the street and sent him to the ground in a heap.

Hank was halfway to the ground. He targeted the remaining trooper, raised the Aggressor Mark V, and fired a single round that caught the trooper in the midsection. The man's abdomen exploded in a splash of fire and blood as his body was slammed backward into the building.

"One dōrydō and two troopers down," Hank said as he hit his thrusters and landed.

He stagger-stepped just as an enemy lock tone blared in his ears and heavy laser-fire streaked down main street. Miranda immediately identified the source of the lock-on and lit up an APC coming down the street.

A single blast impacted upon his right thigh plate, burning away enough layers of the dense, semi-reflective armor for him to feel the heat. The energy released spun Hank slightly. He instinctively lowered to a crouch, hit his thrusters, and fired two missiles from the pod on his shoulder as he jetted to the side.

More heavy laser fire filled the space where he'd been a moment before, and he took cover behind the building.

The recon floaters, small fan-lifted drones full of sensors, transmitted an overlay of the town with all threats identified.

Hank leapt straight up, using the power of the suit rather than his thrusters, and landed on the nearest wall. If he put the full weight of the suit on the flat roof, he'd probably crash through, but the chromaplas outer walls were strong enough to take the weight.

In the HUD, he identified four dōrydōs coming from the edges of town on foot, moving from cover to cover. There were also seven troopers moving from the perimeter into town. The APC that had shot him was halfway down Main, while the other one remained parked in front of the courthouse, but it was shifting its position, so the nose was also pointed down Main. There was a dōrydō climbing into the turret, and Hank recognized it as the leader's suit.

A flash of motion to his left sent an alarm blaring. Hank leapt forward as blasts from a laser carbine splashed against his suit. He barely registered the impacts and realized the dōrydō firing at him only had a light weapon. Hank crashed down through the roof of the building, hit the floor, and leapt back up through the hole in the roof as the APC shot round after round into the building. Hank cleared the roof, aimed at the dōrydō, and let his autocannon do the talking.

BOOM! BOOM! BOOM!

High Velocity Armor Piercing rounds spat from the barrel and slammed into the dōrydō that had been standing two buildings away. In a burst of explosions, it tumbled over the side of the building and disappeared. Hank leapt, jetting after it in a low arc.

CRACK!

Something slammed into his left shoulder just beneath the missile launcher and sent him spinning. Miranda's auto-recovery system kicked in as he dropped beneath the wall, landed on his feet, and faced the dōrydō that had shot him just as it was getting to its feet.

Hank kicked out, slammed the dōrydō through the nearby wall, and then stepped forward with the railgun to find the dōrydō still standing as the driver leveled his laser rifle. Hank's targeting system locked, he fired, and, as several laser blasts splashed into his chest, the center of the enemy dōrydō broke apart into three sections and bounced off the walls.

Hank realized there was going to be a hell of a mess to clean up once this was all finished.

Nothing I can do about it now, he thought.

Checking the inputs from his floaters, Hank stepped out through the shattered wall, turned, and leapt straight up into the air. He got an instant lock on a dōrydō coming toward him across one of the roofs. The system gave him a tone, and he cut loose with the railgun. The round caught the dōrydō in the shoulder joint. There was an explosion of energy, and an arm went sailing sideways as the dōrydō tumbled into the next street.

"Three dōrydōs down," he said as he dropped back to the street. "The others are on me. Marovar, start your run."

"Copy that," the young man said, and Hank could hear the power plant scream as Marovar hammered the accelerator.

Hank checked the floaters and saw his hovertruck enter the theater on the far side of the airfield, headed straight for the cargo ship. He picked up a handful of trooper blips exiting the cargo ship. There was a brief volley from the truck, illuminated on his HUD by dashed lines that flickered, and then the enemy blips went dark.

He also saw a squad of troopers moving with a dōrydō only a couple blocks away to the southeast.

You're next, he thought.

He raced down the street at a dead run, his feet hammering into the ground in a straight line toward the enemy squad's right flank. Hank stopped dead in his tracks halfway past the building he was using as cover. He quickly backtracked as quietly as he could as the *buzz-crack* sounds of more laser fire filled the air, all of it coming from the airfield.

Miranda, plot a targeting solution around the corner to hit that squad, he thought.

The micros will not do appreciable damage to the dōrydō, she replied.

Acknowledged.

Hank moved forward along the curb. He got a tone when Miranda's solution was locked in. He fired, and a half-dozen missiles streaked out and darted around the corner. Explosions and people screaming filled the night. Hank leapt forward into the street, the autocannon leveled, and fired into the smoke and dust that filled the area, emptying the mag. He heard the telltale *crack* of two rounds hitting a dōrydō. The floaters showed him where the enemy unit stood, and he fired the railgun without a lock.

CRACK!

There was an explosion within the cloud that pushed the dust and smoke aside.

The dōrydō now lay in the street, one leg torn away, as the driver flailed his arms helplessly, and great gouts of blood sprayed from the severed limb. To his credit, the driver managed to raise his weapon, an autocannon similar to Hank's, but he fell back, and the weapon lowered to the ground before he pulled the trigger. Hank dropped the empty mag from his rifle and slipped a new one into place.

"Four dōrydōs down, and a full squad eliminated."

"We think we've cleared out the troopers around here," Sam chimed in. "How's it look from your end?"

Hank checked the HUD and saw one more squad now grouped around the APC in the center of town. Another dōrydō stood beside the vehicle, and the commander still sat inside the turret. The other APC was moving toward the airfield, however, so Hank needed to do something about that.

"Marovar," Hank called out urgently. "You've got an APC incoming. It's running along the northeast side of town. Get around to the southwest side of that cargo ship and stay put."

"Yes, sir." Marovar's voice was cool and calm.

"Yobani."

"Yeah, Mr. Combs?"

"Get ready. Set up just past the trees at the end of Main. The plan hasn't changed. When I say go, you hit it hard."

"We got you, Hank," Cleve chimed in.

Just then, Hank's comms rang with an incoming call. The ID said Elena Svodoba.

"Stand by, everybody," Hank said, and switched over to a secondary channel.

"Elena?" Hank said. As he did, he saw a single new blip suddenly appear on the street behind the APC headed toward the airfield.

"Stay put," she said. "The idiot-gunner didn't button up. I got this."

"What?" Hank said, stunned, as he watched the small blip move quickly up behind the APC.

The vehicle came to an abrupt halt, and the threat-indicator of the APC's field of fire started swiveling just as a dotted line of laser fire traced from the blip. The turret's field of fire stopped moving, and the blip moved on top of the APC. There was the barest flash of laser fire on the HUD.

"Two down," Elena said. "I hosed the interior, so I don't think this APC is going anywhere."

"Roger that," Hank said. "And thanks for the assist."

"I enjoyed it," Elena responded.

"Now find some cover. There's only the APC, a squad, and two dōrydō to take care of."

"*Only?*" Elena asked.

Hank cut the connection and swapped over to the team channel.

"—ank, do you copy?" It was Sam's voice.

"Don't worry," Hank replied. "I'm still here. Elena Svodoba gave us an assist on that APC. The airfield is safe."

"Elena?" Sam asked. "No shit?"

"No shit," Hank replied as he reviewed his HUD.

The last APC hadn't moved, which meant the enemy commander was too scared to move and wanted Hank to come at him where he could concentrate his firepower. The commander was undoubtedly still buttoned up inside the turret, manning the twin heavy lasers, and the other dōrydō now stood on the rear of the vehicle. The squad had taken cover inside the fountain, spread out to give them a 360-degree view of the center of town.

There was no way Hank was getting in there unscathed. The

dōrydō's autocannon would be enough to put a hurt on him. The twin lasers, if they got more than a few hits in the same place, would burn through in moments, and the concentrated fire of the squad would wear him down. All together, he was up against enough firepower to bring this little dance to an unhappy ending.

Miranda just has to hold together long enough, he thought. There was only one thing left to do.

The floaters provided the precise distance between himself and the courthouse. He factored in the required thrust and trajectory, and then calculated the expected acceleration of Yobani in the flitter.

"Okay, folks, we're about at the end of this," he said. "One last Hail Mary, and it's half-a-bottle of beer for everyone.

"You ready out there, Yobani?"

"And waiting."

"Good. On my mark, count down five seconds and then launch. Stay at the roof line and hit it just like we talked about."

"Copy that," Yobani and Cleve said together.

Hank took a deep breath and primed his systems for one last assault. "No mercy for the wicked," he said, "and . . . *mark!*" Hank shouted as he leapt and hit his thrusters.

The roof flickered by as he shot skyward.

Everyone in the enemy ranks heard his thrusters fire, and as the APC and the fountain came into view, he saw all of them raising weapons in his direction. The railgun got its lock and toned just before the missile pod did. With both tones blaring in his ears, he pulled the trigger and fired both shoulder-mounted weapons as a wave of incoming fire filled his viewscreen. Alarms blared.

The railgun let out its distinctive *CRACK!* as the hiss of missiles filled the air. Munitions passed each other in midair.

Light laser fire splashed into Hank's suit, and he felt the armor warm against his skin.

The dōrydō on top of the APC came apart from the railgun round that hit it in the center of its chest, and the fountain was lost in a half-dozen antipersonnel missile explosions.

Hank felt three terrible impacts, chest, thigh, and knee, as his body spun in midair. The dōrydō had scored three massive hits with his autocannon. The world tumbled around him as he fell. Warning lights filled his vision.

There was a terrific crashing of chromaplas and timbers as he broke through the roof of the courthouse, and then another as he hammered into the hardwood floor and sank into a crater a foot deep.

Hank's head swam. His leg felt like it was on fire, and he smelled cooking meat. Alarms blared in his ears, and as he looked up, he saw the APC backing up with the turret swiveling around to draw a bead on him.

Hank tried to actuate the railgun, but it sent him a critical failure warning. The missile launcher was dead, too, and he could see his autocannon lying on the floor between him and the APC.

The twin turrets were almost on him when the shriek of a flitter filled the air. Hank waved and pointed as Yobani flew, canopy yawning open, and hovered directly above and in front of the APC. Cleve rose in the back seat and fired the anti-tank rocket just as the laser turret centered on Hank.

He saw a flash of light, felt the impact and the burn, and then the lights went out.

Chapter 7

December 2967 (Terran Calendar)—Mavesheur
Hank stepped off the elevator with a severe limp and winced as the skin-graft patches on his thigh and across his chest sent a wave of pain over his entire body. Although his leg had been shredded by shrapnel and he had been pretty badly burned, he knew in time it would be almost as good as new.

In time.

They'd won, and Hank had been the only casualty—well, him and Miranda. His dōrydō was a total loss, and he'd put her back where she belonged. It had taken him a week to heal up enough to get mobile . . . and think. When he was ready, he boarded the courier he'd first arrived on Bevin in, and let Hakeem take him to where he wanted to go.

Taking a deep breath to push aside the pain, Hank picked up the square case he'd carried with him from the starport, where Hakeem was waiting for him.

In his other hand, he held a wrapped bottle that he tucked under his arm. With his gifts in hand, he hobbled into a lavish reception area on the top floor of a three-hundred-story building. The megapolis of Mavesheur, capital city of Draliel 3, stretched out forty miles in every direction. Flowing airways of city traffic hundreds of stories above the ground moved past in every direction.

The reception desk lay a dozen meters off, with not one, but two stunning beauties; one platinum blond, and the other an obsidian brunette. They both smiled in stereo at him as he approached. A red and black logo decorated the front of the desk, with a red border, a black field, and NasCom dead center in red letters.

"Salutations," the blond said in a silky-sweet voice. "We are most happy to greet you."

"You are Mr. Combs, yes?" the brunette asked. "Of the Kahn Süns Distillery?"

"That's right," Hank said, giving the ladies one of his famous smiles. "I have an appointment with Director Giles."

"And those are?" the raven-haired beauty asked, glancing at the bottle and the box.

Hank held out the bottle. "This? It's a token of my esteem." He lifted the box. "I'm returning this to Director Giles. I don't believe he knows it, but he misplaced it, and I wanted to return it to him."

"How thoughtful," the blond said.

"It's the least I can do," Hank replied.

The brunette turned, activated a screen behind the counter, and gave a ravishing smile.

"Director Giles, a Mr. Combs, president of the Kahn Süns Distillery, is here to see you for your nine o'clock. He was vetted by security when he entered the building."

"Send him in," a smooth man's voice replied.

A pair of three-meter doors made of dark wood opened to Hank's left, revealing a cavernous den of luxurious furnishings. At the far end, up against floor-to-ceiling windows, sat a dark-haired man with a perfect goatee and a curious expression that turned to mild surprise as Hank approached. He wore a glimmering gray suit that looked opalescent in the sunlight.

"Good afternoon, Mister . . . Combs, was it?" the director asked as Hank stepped in and the doors closed behind him. "Please, have a seat."

Hank reached the offered chair, stepped past it, and set the case on the table.

"If it's all the same to you," Hank replied affably, "I'd rather stand. If I put my butt in that chair, I'll play hell getting back up again."

"As you wish," Giles said with a nod. "Can I offer you a drink? I happen to have an eight-year-old bottle of Kahn Süns over in the bar, as well as a number of other small-batch liquors."

Hank turned and spotted a bottle with his label, top and center, amidst three rows of bottles behind a dark wood bar.

"I'm good," Hank replied.

"I thought Kahn Süns was owned by its namesake, an older gentleman of Mongolian descent, I believe."

"It was," Hank replied. "Old Soong and I became fast friends when he arrived with the first ship of colonists to make landfall on Bevin." Hank smiled, remembering. "Soong was an artist when it came to distillery. Truly a master. At the time, I grew the shadda, and he made the hooch. He taught me how along the way, and when he passed from the living a few years back, he left the whole thing to me. I still think of myself as a farmer, but I keep Soong's dream alive because he asked me to."

"Indeed," Giles said, raising an eyebrow. "As I understand it, Kahn Süns—the only brand, I might add—is served across thirty systems. I'm sure the fact that the company is worth several hundred million annually didn't factor into your acceptance?"

"Not really," Hank said. "Sure, it's made a lot of things easier, but to be honest, it was the simple life that brought me to Bevin. I pay a slew of folks to take care of the day-to-day operations over at Kahn. I still consider myself a farmer by trade, but recent events have forced me to take a more active role. It seems you, or I should say, NasCom, misplaced something on Bevin, and I've come to return it to you, along with an offer."

"Misplaced?" Giles asked, suddenly confused. "I can't imagine what that might be."

"Let me show you." Hank stepped forward, released two latches on the top of the case, and lifted. The top and all four sides rose in his grip, revealing a clearplas jar with a severed head in it. The eyes were closed, and the face a bit swollen, but otherwise it looked perfectly preserved.

Giles' eyes darted to the jar, and when he realized what he was looking at, he gasped slightly. It took only a moment for him to regain his composure.

Hank had to give him some credit. Not everyone could stay cool under those circumstances.

"Forgive me," Giles said, "but I'm fairly certain I could never have misplaced something like that."

Hank smiled. "This is Commander Raul Sanchez Villalba of the *Saraphon*. If you look that up, you'll find he captained one of your smaller corvettes. He was part of a squadron of ships under your oversight, and I believe he bit off more than he could chew."

"Clearly," Giles said. "Piracy?"

Hank nodded. "The folks of New Haven didn't want to get wiped off the map, so I stepped in, and with a little help, terminated Villalba's command, along with his entire platoon."

"I can assure you, neither I nor anyone in my chain of command tasked him to undertake such an operation."

"I have no doubt," Hank said. "Which is why his head is on your desk, rather than your head being on someone else's. The only reason you're still alive is because there would be no reason in the world for a director to task a commander to hit a backass planet for a hundred-thousand liters of booze. The numbers are too small for a guy like you."

There was no mistaking the look on Giles face. The man was not accustomed to hearing such threats, and he clearly considered Hank to have a good deal of raw chutzpah. Hank could see Giles factoring in the situation and what his possible options were. The man had to be thinking Hank was there for reparations, blackmail, or even assassination.

"Before you get too worried," Hank said, "I'm here to make your day better, not worse."

"Really?" Giles replied with a good deal of suspicion.

"That's right," Hank said. "You got a couple of clean glasses handy?"

Giles got a curious expression on his face, and then he opened a lower drawer, pulled out two rocks glasses, and set them on the desk.

Hank pulled the paper off the bottle of Kahn Süns he'd placed between them.

Giles eyes went wide when he saw the distillation date: 2954. The bottle was thirteen years old, and any connoisseur of süns would know that's as old as it got.

"That's from the first . . ." Giles' voice trailed off.

"That's right," Hank said. "I still have a number of cases laying around."

Hank pulled the wooden stopper from the bottle with a soft *pop*, and a few tendrils of wispy Bevin atmosphere drifted away. He poured a finger of the pale lavender fluid into both glasses, and then put the stopper back in. Setting the bottle on the desk, he locked eyes with Director Giles.

"The people of Bevin would like to license NasCom to set up a large-scale süns operation on the other side of the planet . . ." Hank waited a moment to let that sink in. A number of corporations had offered the inhabitants of Bevin a similar offer, but they'd always been turned down.

Giles' eyes narrowed briefly. "Aren't you worried we'll put you out of business?"

"Not at all," Hank replied easily. "Corporations like NasCom mass produce average to sub-standard products—lower quality for a better price. We, on the other hand, produce a top-shelf libation. Even if you upped your quality, there could only ever be one original: Kahn. The one. The only. I'll do just fine, and the licensing fees, a mere ten percent of your gross, will go to the people of Bevin." Hank raised his glass and inhaled deeply. "And if something happened to go wrong, say, for example, a member of NasCom decided to alter the deal after the fact . . . well, I think it's only fair to tell you that I've also made arrangements to have an Archangel garrison stationed a few hundred miles from our colony. Anything that happens to us will catch their attention very quickly. And I don't think either of us wants Terran Republic Archangels involved in any of our affairs." Hank slipped a military ID from one of his pockets and slid it across the desk. Giles eyes went wide when he saw Archangel Commander (Ret.) beneath Hank's image. "Did I mention I was an Archangel in a previous life?"

Giles paled.

"No," Giles said. "You didn't mention it."

"Yeah. Their current commandant, Vice Admiral Jokimbun, was

one of my protégés a while back." Giles seemed to have gone speechless. "Don't worry, Director. Like I said, I'm here to make your day better, not worse."

"I must say," Giles said as he slowly regained his composure, "you have my full attention, but why all the intrigue?"

"Well, if I'm going to make a deal with the devil, I'm gonna be damn certain to do it on my terms."

Giles smiled and nodded respectfully. "I must say, Mr. Combs—"

"Call me Hank. And I'm not done putting things on the table for you. Every year, on New Year's, I'll have delivered to you a case of the next thirteen-year-old süns in my inventory. That'll be for life, although it's non-transferable. Let's call it an incentive clause."

Giles leaned back in his chair, and it looked like he was fighting the smile that had split his face.

"I must say, Hank, you've played this brilliantly." Giles eyed the glass in front of him. "With NasCom on one side of the planet, and the Archangels in your back yard—I'm guessing you sold it to the vice admiral as an R and R facility?"

Hank nodded.

"You'll never have to worry about more piracy, corporate or otherwise."

"You're very astute," Hank said. "Add in the fact that I won't have to work as hard, and for me it's the best deal in the history of deals. More credits. Security . . . and all it really costs me is a case of thirteen-year-old hooch a year." He paused, looking expectantly at the director. "So, we do have a deal, don't we?"

Giles picked up the glass in front of him. He leaned forward and *clinked* it against Hank's.

"I believe we do, Hank." He waited for Hank to take a drink—just to be sure it wasn't poisoned, no doubt—and then sniffed at the oldest glass of süns he was likely to ever have in his hand. Closing his eyes, he finally took a single sip and let the subtle flavors and smooth warmth flow down his throat. There really was nothing like it in the galaxy. Another smile crossed his lips, and then he opened his eyes to see Hank standing with a wry grin on his face.

"I'm glad you like it," Hank said.

"Süns has always been my favorite, and this is exquisite."

"You can keep the bottle," Hank offered, sliding it across the desk.

"We did claim the *Saraphon* as salvage, by the way. At this point, an escort-class corvette will go a long way in helping New Haven hold onto what we already have."

"Completely understandable," the director said.

Hank finished his glass, set it down, and then reached for the box cover so he could take Sanchez's head.

"I would like to ask one favor," Giles asked, holding up his hand to stop Hank.

"Oh?" Hank said, suddenly wary but curious.

"I was wondering if you'd let me hang on to that." Giles nodded toward the head. "I have a number of ship captains who have, as well you know, taken it upon themselves to step outside of NasCom's policies regarding piracy . . . ignoring my repeated, explicit directives, I might add."

Hank nodded in understanding. "Certainly," he said with a knowing smile. "It's all yours."

"Hank," the director said softly. "I'm beginning to think you and I have something in common. I find myself wondering . . . if I should learn of other NasCom . . . infractions . . . might I pass such information along to you? The hierarchy here is, shall we say, more of a straitjacket than anything else. As I'm sure you know, corporate politics is what it is. You could, at your leisure, pass along such information to . . . well . . . whomever you chose. What they do with that information, I'm sure I wouldn't want to know. Although it would be a drop in the galactic bucket, I see an opportunity here to potentially accomplish something worth doing."

Hank cocked his head to the side, wrapping his head around what the director was proposing. Officially, neither the director nor the Archangels could go after corporate pirates without official sanction by the Terran Republic. It would all have to be off the books. But wiping out even one rogue mercenary crew would be worth the price of admission.

"You know what, Director," Hank said, "I think I'm going to make that *two* cases a year of the current thirteen Kahn. You go right ahead and reach out to me whenever you like."

Hank walked down the loading ramp of a gleaming new Mancuso Executive Courier. With Hakeem Najjar at the helm, they'd returned from Draliel with the NasCom contract in hand and a couple of new acquisitions in the hold. They'd landed across the dirt road from Hank's homestead, forgoing a landing at the starport, and Kenny Boudreaux was standing there to meet him.

"Come on up here, Kenny," Hank said, retreating back up the loading ramp.

The young man strode up the ramp to find Hank unlatching the door of a tall cargo case secured to the left-hand side of the cargo bay. An identical case, secured to the other side, was already open, and the doors of the storage unit within were already swinging open to reveal a gleaming new dōrydō inside.

"It's a new Mancuso," Kenny blurted, "isn't it?"

"Brand spankin'," Hank said. "That one's mine." He hit the actuator on the other case to expose an identical dōrydō. "This one is *yours*, assuming you want it."

"What?" Kenny's mouth dropped open.

"Kenny," Hank said, "I don't have too many years left, and I never had kids. After what happened to your father, I was wondering if you might be interested in picking up a crotchety old farmer to fill the vacancy, although I could never fill his shoes."

Kenny gulped. "I suppose so," he said. "I mean, *yes*, absolutely yes!"

"Good. I'll take care of the adoption paperwork." Hank eyed Kenny. "There are a few conditions, though."

"What's that?"

"One, you learn how to drive this dōrydō as well as I do. Second, you learn how to distill süns. Third, you promise to carry on old man Soong's dream after you plant me next to what's left of Miranda over there. You'll inherit the whole company, of course." He gave Kenny a hopeful smile. "I know it's a lot, and you don't need to decide right now. It's hard work, long hours, and the whole colony will depend upon you. I'll teach you everything I can in the time I have left."

In that moment, Kenny seemed to grow up a little more than he had when he saw the dead body of his father. His eyes grew hard, but hopeful. He understood at least a little of what he would be taking on. Hank could see it in his eyes.

"Hank, I swear I'll meet all three conditions . . . if for no other reason than for what they did to my dad. That shouldn't happen to anybody."

"No, it shouldn't," Hank agreed. "There's more I have to tell you . . . I made a couple deals that complicate this whole thing—for the better—but it's all wrapped up together. We'll get to all that eventually. For now, let's go get the paperwork done, and then you can try on this dōrydō and see if I got the size right."

"Okay, Hank." They strode down the ramp and headed toward Hank's old beat-up Masahaki hover truck. The weapons had been removed and, along with all the other weapons, secured in Hank's basement for the next rainy day.

As they reached the truck, Kenny stopped.

"Hank?"

"Yeah."

"Thanks."

"Don't thank me yet, I'm gonna work your ass off."

"I won't let you down," Kenny promised as they both got in.

"You haven't yet, son," Hank said, firing up the power plant. "You haven't yet."

Few would deny that having the right tool for the job is the ideal situation. But still, it is possible to be too dependent on tools, particularly in an emergency . . .

Clothes Make the Man

Ron Goulart

Lynn Pettiford was enjoying the surrey ride from the spaceport. It was the first time she had seen a horse. The afternoon sun, shining through softly rustling leaves, made fluttering patterns on the dirt road. Off in the yellow fields bright birds sang and insects hummed. Lynn stretched her legs out and lit a cigarette.

The stooped old driver turned his head and touched the visor of his faded black cap. "Young ladies aren't allowed to smoke out of doors in Scattergood Territory, miss," he said, smiling apologetically.

"Sorry," Lynn said, dropping the cigarette to the surrey floor and grinding it out with her foot. She inhaled deeply and leaned back.

A flock of blackbirds rose out of the field to the left and swirled up into the sky. Lynn watched them until the surrey top cut off her view. Then she shifted a little on her seat and closed her eyes.

Far in the distance a cowbell rang slowly and stopped, a wooden fence creaked.

"Trouble," said the old driver, reining up. "Looks like trouble, miss."

Lynn sat up, blinking.

"What?"

The old man pointed to a cloud of dust growing on the road ahead. "Might just be highwaymen."

"Oh," said Lynn, sliding her purse behind her and kicking her tan suitcase into the shadows at her feet.

The driver pulled at the peak of his cap and squinted. "Three masked men on horseback heading this way."

Lynn could see them now, too. Their clothes were black, their heads covered with scarlet hoods. "My fiancé's with Detective Central here in Scattergood," she said. "I don't suppose that would discourage them."

"Might just make them nastier. You never can tell with highwaymen." The old man stiffened as the horsemen came closer. "Wait now. What's that they're carrying?"

Lynn frowned. "Looks like canvas sacks."

The driver sighed. "We're safe then. Those are bank robbers, not highwaymen. It's hard to tell them apart sometimes."

Lynn unclenched her hands. "They might still be dangerous."

The three robbers turned off the road about fifteen yards ahead of the surrey and galloped across a field. In a clutter of low trees there was a dark stone cottage.

"Hideout," said the driver, nodding at the cottage.

"Shouldn't we be getting on?"

The driver slapped his freckled hands together a few times and jumped down to the road. He shaded his eyes and looked up into the clear sky. "Yessir, yessir." He grabbed off his cap and waved it in jerky circles, hopping as he did.

"What is it now?" Lynn asked, wondering if the excitement of seeing the bandits up close had produced some kind of nervous attack in the old man.

"DC's coming. There's their flyer."

Lynn leaned out. Overhead a sparkling rectangle was descending. "Detective Central?"

"Of course. They're the only ones can fly in Scattergood. They're going to get those badmen."

"Won't we be in the way?"

The driver flattened his cap back on. "Foolish to try a daylight robbery anyhow. DC always gets them." He turned to Lynn. "We have a saying around here, miss. Crime never pays. Watch." He chuckled and spun to watch the silver flyer land silently in the grass across the road.

The flyer had hardly stopped quivering when its hatch popped open, and two men shot out. They seemed to be tall, well-developed men, with good tans. The first man, holding what looked like a blaster pistol, ran in great strides toward the bandits' cottage. He sparkled and glittered in the sun. His scarlet uniform was trimmed in gold and silver and his boots reflected the yellow grass as he ran. His silver helmet threw a glare suddenly into Lynn's eyes and she looked away. But she said, with surprise, "Alec."

When she had rubbed her eyes and looked again the first DC patrolman was sailing through the air, his hands at his sides. One of the bandits threw a spear out of a small window. The spear hit the man who resembled Lynn's fiancé in the left shoulder and bounced off. The DC man's head hit the stone wall at this point and Lynn screamed, "Alec, you'll dislocate something!"

He went through the cottage wall, sending stone and mortar off in jagged arcs. The thatched roof came down as though it had been sucked from within.

The second DC man was standing halfway to the collapsing hideout, a black suitcase in his hand. A blaster spun slowly in his other hand.

The man who looked like Alec Harker rose out of the ruins, carrying two unconscious robbers by their collars. He dropped them near his partner and dived back into the rubble. This time he came out with the loot and the third bandit, who was trying to pull his tattered scarlet hood back on.

Lynn stood up, then swung out of the surrey and ran across the dusty road. She raised one gloved hand and called, "Alec. Is that you?"

The patrolman was stuffing bandits into the DC flyer. He looked up, a wide smile growing on his tanned face. "Take over here, Gil." Then he walked toward the girl.

Lynn stepped into the grass, wondering what she'd say if this wasn't Alec. She knew he was on duty someplace and hadn't been able to meet her. Still, she wasn't sure. "Alec?" The yellow grass was rough against her ankles.

"Lynn," said Alec, pulling off his silver helmet. "What a great damned surprise."

He didn't sound like Alec, his voice was deeper. But he seemed to be Alec. "Hello," Lynn said. "Do you take risks like this often?"

"No risk." He caught her in his arms, laughing. He kissed her.

Lynn relaxed a moment, then pulled back. "Glad to see me?" She frowned, studying his face. "My, that's some tan."

Alec grinned and let her go. He ran a forefinger down his cheek, leaving a light line. "Part of it's makeup. Look, I've got to turn these crooks in, but I'm off at six. I'll pick you up at the Old Scattergood House and take you to dinner around seven." He took her shoulders. "Six months is a long time."

Lynn made a white line down his other cheek with her thumb. She nodded and turned toward the surrey.

Alec Harker whistled as he washed up, keeping time with his bare foot on the tile floor. After he'd passed through the drying chamber, he got his clothes out of his closet. He noticed a spot of tarnish on his uniform epaulet and rubbed at it with his moistened finger. In a way it was too bad you could only wear your uniform on duty. Alec pulled on his gray trousers and sealed the fly seam. Striped blazers were in style in Scattergood now and Alec had two conservative ones. He put on the green blazer and snapped on a bow tie. He walked to the wall mirror and studied himself, smoothing out his crewcut. He always looked shorter in street clothes.

Gil Miley, Alec's partner in Detective Central, came out of the dry room. "That's Lynn, huh?"

"Yeah," said Alec, straddling a straight metal chair.

"Pretty. Nice legs. I prefer blondes, though."

"Lynn's a blonde. Well, auburn I guess is the color."

"I mean blonde like—oh, like those stag show dancers we brought in last month."

"Dyed," said Alec.

Miley shrugged and put on a pair of work denims. "Tough being separated from her for so long."

"Sure was. I told you Lynn was a stewardess for Transpace, didn't I? Well, when the chance came up for a long haul, she took it. Double pay. That was about the time Uncle Jake said he could get me on here if I wanted to earn some money before I went back to Mars Grad for my masters."

Miley took a yellow blazer out of his closet. "So now you've got a pile and'll settle down by a quiet canal?"

"I guess. I sort of like it on Metro though. I mean, here in Scattergood."

"Good Lord," said Miley. "I'd rather get a hardship post on Pluto."

"I enjoy the work is the thing." Alec looked up at the wall clock. "Going toward the Old Scattergood House?"

"No. I got a tip there's a bordello going in the Quaker Quarter. With a live piano player."

"Going to raid it?"

"Eventually."

Alec smiled and went out. The soda fountain next to Detective Central headquarters was full of laughing couples. Old Pop Arnold waved at Alec as he passed.

Alec stopped at the corner to let an ice cream truck clatter by. The scarlet plumes of the horses flickered brightly. Too bad you had to pass through the fringes of the Cropper Quarter to get to the Old Scattergood House. Alec didn't like to go through there out of uniform and with none of his equipment. Off duty you could only carry one small blaster in a shoulder holster.

The swinging doors of the Green Lama, a known hangout of Zen Buddhists, flapped wide and three bearded men tumbled out into the street. One of them swung a buggy whip in his hand. The man on the bottom of the pile crawled to the curb and broke his beer bottle into a jagged weapon.

Alec, a block away from the brawl, slowed his pace slightly. Trouble would delay him. And he always felt a lack of authority in plain clothes. He stopped and looked in the window of a bicycle repair shop, trying not to hear the crack of the whip.

Two more bearded men joined the fight, waving stools and shouting.

Alec took a deep breath. Maybe he would have to stop this. But then out of the twilight came a DC flyer. And two patrolmen flew into the fight.

Smiling, Alec crossed the street and took a shortcut to the hotel. It would be good to be with Lynn again. Even though he would have to tell her he wanted to stay on with Detective Central. Scattergood wasn't a bad place to settle.

Coming down the wooden-railed stairs into the lobby of the Old Scattergood, Lynn Pettiford smiled. She recognized Alec at once this time. His quiet grin, the way he twisted his head to one side as if his collar were too tight. He always did that when waiting in a public place.

She squeezed the hand he held out to help her down the last step. "You look much more yourself now."

Alec nodded. "Lynn, I've got a hansom cab out front. Thought we'd go out to the Weary Traveler's Haven Inn on the outskirts of town."

"That would be appropriate."

The night was warm and clear, still darkening. The long ride to the inn was smooth and soothing. Six months was a long time, and they didn't talk much on the way out, except early in the journey when Alec pointed out DC headquarters and Lynn made an admiring remark.

In the shadowy hansom Alec was much more like the Alec Lynn had fallen in love with in her senior year at Mars Union University. Lynn felt that sighing was something you got out of your system by your second term in your sorority. Still, she allowed herself to sigh twice.

The inn was run by a round bald man known as Pop Bachtold. He greeted them warmly and led them to a secluded, candle lit table near one of the dining room's stained-glass windows. Something was singing beneath the window and Lynn assumed it was a nightingale, although she had never heard one.

"I love to see young people eat soup," said Pop Bachtold, clasping his hands over his aproned stomach and smiling as they began the first course. He chuckled and tiptoed away from them.

Lynn took three courses to tell Alec about the long haul with Transpace. The touch down ports, the blue man who'd made a pass at her during a fireworks display in a Plutonian bazaar. Then over her apple pie she said, "And how's Detective Central? I suppose you'll be glad to get back to Mars. Not that this hasn't been the practical thing to do." She smiled. "I'm proud of us, being able to do the practical things the universe requires. Now we have a nest egg and can settle down on Mars."

Alec coughed and the candle went out. "Excuse me." He got out the lighter Lynn had given him for graduation and re-lit the fat blue candle. "Funny thing, Lynn."

"What?" She set down her fork.

"Well, when I first got out here, I expected to dislike police work.

Even though 97% of the testing machines at VocVac said I had an aptitude. But it turns out I enjoy my job. I actually do." He met her eyes briefly.

"Enjoy it? Oh. And I've been feeling sorry for you. You actually like doing things like that business this afternoon?"

He grinned. "Yes. I do. And we'll get a bonus, besides helping the cause of justice."

"By the way," Lynn said, searching in her purse for cigarettes. "How did you do that this afternoon? I meant to ask. Fly and bust through a stone wall."

"Well, Lynn. The set-up here in Scattergood is different than some." He had his napkin wrapped around his fist now and he started untwisting it. "The settlers in this part of Metro went in for a simple sort of life. A semirural, small town life. Of course, some of the mineral strikes later on let in a rougher element. But through the years Detective Central has been quite successful in keeping Scattergood a simple, fairly honest territory." He shook his head. "You shouldn't smoke here. It's considered improper. The way DC does it is by not allowing development beyond a certain point. That follows the principles of the founding fathers and makes law enforcing a little easier. See, we're the only ones with flying machines or any kind of advanced weapon. What you saw today is a pretty good example of how we work. A lot of it is showmanship. Gil, that's my partner—Gil Miley, a great guy—had a disassembler in that back box and a stun beam under his hat. That's what got the house and dazed the robbers. I had a flying belt on. It's, you know, just applied science. But we make it look like DC guys are pretty much invincible. Fear is the strongest weapon a police force can have. It keeps all but the rowdiest element in line."

"Why did you have makeup on?" Lynn dropped her cigarette absently back into her purse.

"Look, Lynn, most of it is makeup of one sort or another. Trappings, stage effects. The people are sort of simple here. They've been kept that way. They simply go in for a little color. DC likes us to have an outdoorsy look. I never did tan well. You remember that week on the Left Bank."

"Seems like a silly way to run a police force."

"Police work varies from territory to territory, from planet to planet. Detective Central is adaptable. Anyway, the Universe Combine sets DC policy." Alec grinned. "Anyhow, I enjoy the work here. And I'd like to stay on."

"I thought we wanted to settle on Mars. Have our children grow up there. Now you say you want to run around out here and act like some school boy hero."

Alec rolled his napkin into a ball along the table edge. "But in these last few months I really think I've become a more mature person, Lynn. I don't want to give that up."

"Maturity is something you can take with you."

"I'm not sure. It's more a way I feel on duty, Lynn. I'm afraid if I quit DC now, I'll just go back to being the kind of person I was."

"You don't want that?"

"How about some steaming coffee, ground fresh from Earth-grown beans?" asked Pop Bachtold, smiling down at them.

"Fine," said Alec.

Pop chuckled and withdrew, humming to himself.

"You just want to stay here and fly through the air and poke your head through stone walls. It's childish."

"No, Lynn. I feel more confident, more at ease with DC. I'm reluctant to lose that." He looked across at her. "I feel—well—safe in a way."

"My God, didn't you feel safe in college? That is sure as hell a safe place."

"They don't like to hear girls use harsh language in public out here, Lynn," Alec said, lowering his voice. "Sure, I felt secure in college. But with DC I have a little more authority, prestige. I know I was Senior Class Treasurer, but it's not quite the same."

After Pop Bachtold had left the coffee Lynn said, "I don't think I want my coffee. May we go back now?"

Alec stopped his cup halfway to his mouth. "I thought you claimed to understand me?"

"I do," she said, gathering up her purse and gloves and standing. She walked carefully across the dining room, hoping Alec would follow her. He did.

Applying his makeup Alec said, "It's okay now, Gil. Patched up."

Gil Miley pulled on a boot, frowning at the scuffed toe. "So what are you going to do?"

"Well, Lynn's going to try to get based here and we'll both keep on working for possibly another year."

Miley rubbed saliva on his boot toe. "You like this routine that much?"

"Sure." Alec buttoned his blouse and squinted out the window. "Kind of overcast. Think I'll wear my cape."

"I'm only staying in because you can retire at forty. Then I think I'll settle on one of those bordello satellites."

"This is my first real job, of course, but I like it." Alec brushed the scarlet lining of his cape and then flapped it twice in the air.

Miley strapped on his helmet and flipped his cigarette into the floor dispozer. "Well, let's go."

"I've got a new routine worked out for breaking up unlawful rallies, Gil," Alec said, fastening his cape. "Indoor ones. See, you'd come in through the wall and then I'd follow through the ceiling. Or if we're lucky the building might have a skylight. All that shattering glass makes a nice effect."

"Most secret meetings are held in basements," said Miley. He grinned briefly and went out the door to the landing lot.

Old Pop Donner at the livery stable gave Alec and Lynn the best horse and buggy he had. It was, he said, his gesture to young love.

Alec concentrated on controlling the horse until they were out of town and on the straight road that led to Old Lovers' Point. Nobody went there much anymore, but it would be a fine spot for a picnic. "I'm glad things are settled," Alec said after a while.

Lynn twisted her hand over the handle of the basket on the seat between them. "If you think staying with Detective Central another year is such a good thing, well, I guess I can't object. Oh, and I stopped at the Transpace office this morning."

"And?"

"There's a pretty good chance I'll be able to work out of here. Or at least out of Metro."

"Great. After the picnic we can drive by the new development and look around at cottages." He put his hand over Lynn's. "Maybe we could lease one for a year." He slid his hand under hers and took the handle of the picnic basket. He lifted the basket into the back of the buggy and drew Lynn over nearer to him. "Sound okay?"

"Fine." Lynn rested her head on his shoulder, her auburn hair fluttering in the warm breeze. "Much more comfortable without epaulets."

Old Lovers' Point was deserted and the yellow grass high. Alec tethered the horse and he and Lynn wandered downhill. "I've never been out here before," Alec said.

"I'm glad," Lynn said. A sign hung askew on a dead tree. Lynn stopped in front of it and straightened it with her hand. "Old Lovers' Point," she read. "This is the place all right." Paint flakes stuck to her finger as she let go and the sign swung back to its old position.

"People used to come out here often. Place has a big reputation. But I guess things go out of style, even in a controlled society. Gil, that's my partner, comes out here now and then."

Hand in hand they moved down a gradual slope. Lynn spotted another faded sign. "Old Lovers' Bridge. Let's find that."

"I think that's the wood bridge over Old Lovers' Canyon. Not much of a canyon. Only a half mile or so deep."

They climbed over a rise and then were in front of an ancient wooden bridge about a thousand feet long. Beyond the bridge was a cool, shadowy forest. "Let's eat lunch over there," Lynn said. "I bet we can find a clearing and maybe a pool."

"Lunch," said Alec. "Left it in the buggy. Wait now and I'll get it." He touched Lynn's cheek with his fingertips and ran back to the buggy.

He had the basket in his hand when he heard the splintering and Lynn's cry. "My Lord," he said, dropping the basket.

When he got near the edge of the small canyon there was no Lynn. No bridge. He knelt at the rim and stared over.

Lynn was hanging a hundred feet down, her arms locked around a bridge cable that was still secured. "Pull me up, Alec," she shouted. "Pull."

Alec tried to stand and suddenly his legs went numb. His hands turned cold and wet and he almost pitched forward. Finally, he found his voice. "I can't like this," he yelled down. "Hold on till I get my stuff."

By the time he got into his uniform and back out to the edge of the canyon Lynn was gone.

Starships had mysteriously disappeared, and Earth's leaders announced that humans were not alone in the universe—and the neighbors weren't friendly. William Mandella was a draftee in a new kind of war, where soldiers had genius-level IQs, trained with live ammunition—sometimes with fatal results—and rode starships into battle. Losses were heavy, and even if Mandella survived, while mere minutes passed during starship travel, years, even decades, were passing on Earth. And what sort of world would Mandella and the other veterans return to?

Hero

Joe Haldeman

I

"Tonight we're going to show you eight silent ways to kill a man." The guy who said that was a sergeant who didn't look five years older than me. So if he'd ever killed a man in combat, silently or otherwise, he'd done it as an infant.

I already knew eighty ways to kill people, but most of them were pretty noisy. I sat up straight in my chair and assumed a look of polite attention and fell asleep with my eyes open. So did most everybody else. We'd learned that they never scheduled anything important for these after-chop classes.

The projector woke me up and I sat through a short tape showing the "eight silent ways." Some of the actors must have been brainwipes, since they were actually killed.

After the tape a girl in the front row raised her hand. The sergeant nodded at her and she rose to parade rest. Not bad looking, but kind of chunky about the neck and shoulders. Everybody gets that way after carrying a heavy pack around for a couple of months.

"Sir"—we had to call sergeants "sir" until graduation—"Most of those methods, really, they looked . . . kind of silly."

"For instance?"

"Like killing a man with a blow to the kidneys, from an entrenching tool. I mean, when would you *actually* have only an entrenching tool, and no gun or knife? And why not just bash him over the head with it?"

"He might have a helmet on," he said reasonably.

"Besides, Taurans probably don't even *have* kidneys!"

He shrugged. "Probably they don't." This was 1997, and nobody had ever seen a Tauran; hadn't even found any pieces of Taurans bigger than a scorched chromosome. "But their body chemistry is similar to ours, and we have to assume they're similarly complex creatures. They *must* have weaknesses, vulnerable spots. You have to find out where they are.

"That's the important thing." He stabbed a finger at the screen. "Those eight convicts got caulked for your benefit because you've got to find out how to kill Taurans, and be able to do it whether you have a megawatt laser or an emery board."

She sat back down, not looking too convinced.

"Any more questions?" Nobody raised a hand.

"Okay Tench-hut!" We staggered upright and he looked at us expectantly.

"Fuck you, sir," came the familiar tired chorus.

"Louder!"

"FUCK YOU, SIR!" One of the army's less-inspired morale devices.

"That's better. Don't forget, pre-dawn maneuvers tomorrow. Chop at 0330, first formation, 0400. Anybody sacked after 0340 owes one stripe. Dismissed."

I zipped up my coverall and went across the snow to the lounge for a cup of soya and a joint. I'd always been able to get by on five or six hours of sleep, and this was the only time I could be by myself, out of the army for a while. Looked at the newsfax for a few minutes. Another ship got caulked, out by Aldebaran sector. That was four years ago. They were mounting a reprisal fleet, but it'll take four years more for them to get out there. By then, the Taurans would have every portal planet sewed up tight.

Back at the billet, everybody else was sacked and the main lights were out. The whole company'd been dragging ever since we got back from the two-week lunar training. I dumped my clothes in the locker, checked the roster and found out I was in bunk *31.* Goddammit, right under the heater.

I slipped through the curtain as quietly as possible so as not to wake up the person next to me. Couldn't see who it was, but I couldn't have cared less. I slipped under the blanket.

"You're late, Mandella," a voice yawned. It was Rogers.

"Sorry I woke you up," I whispered.

"'Sallright." She snuggled over and clasped me spoon-fashion. She was warm and reasonably soft.

I patted her hip in what I hoped was a brotherly fashion.

"Night, Rogers."

"G'night, Stallion." She returned the gesture more pointedly.

Why do you always get the tired ones when you're ready and the randy ones when you're tired? I bowed to the inevitable.

II

"Awright, let's get some goddamn *back* inta that! Stringer team! Move it up—move your ass up!"

A warm front had come in about midnight and the snow had turned to sleet. The permaplast stringer weighed five hundred pounds and was a bitch to handle, even when it wasn't covered with ice. There were four of us, two at each end, carrying the plastic girder with frozen fingertips. Rogers was my partner.

"Steel!" the guy behind me yelled, meaning that he was losing his hold. It wasn't steel, but it was heavy enough to break your foot. Everybody let go and hopped away. It splashed slush and mud all over us.

"Goddammit, Petrov," Rogers said, "why didn't you go out for the Red Cross or something? This fucken thing's not that fucken heavy." Most of the girls were a little more circumspect in their speech. Rogers was a little butch.

"Awright, get a fucken *move* on, stringers—epoxy team! Dog 'em! Dog 'em!"

Our two epoxy people ran up, swinging their buckets. "Let's go, Mandella. I'm freezin' my balls off."

"Me, too," the girl said with more feeling than logic.

"One—two—heave!" We got the thing up again and staggered toward the bridge. It was about three-quarters completed. Looked as if the second platoon was going to beat us. I wouldn't give a damn, but the platoon that got their bridge built first got to fly home. Four miles of muck for the rest of us, and no rest before chop.

We got the stringer in place, dropped it with a clank, and fitted the static clamps that held it to the rise-beam. The female half of the epoxy team started slopping glue on it before we even had it secured. Her partner was waiting for the stringer on the other side. The floor team was waiting at the foot of the bridge, each one holding a piece of the light, stressed permaplast over his head like an umbrella. They were dry and clean. I wondered aloud what they had done to deserve it, and Rogers suggested a couple of colorful, but unlikely, possibilities.

We were going back to stand by the next stringer when the field first (name of Dougelstein, but we called him "Awright") blew a whistle and bellowed, "Awright, soldier boys and girls, ten minutes. Smoke 'em if you got 'em." He reached into his pocket and turned on the control that heated our coveralls.

Rogers and I sat down on our end of the stringer and I took out my weed box. I had lots of joints, but we were ordered not to smoke them until after night-chop. The only tobacco I had was a cigarro butt about three inches long. I lit it on the side of the box; it wasn't too bad after the first couple of puffs. Rogers took a puff, just to be sociable, but made a face and gave it back.

"Were you in school when you got drafted?" she asked.

"Yeah. Just got a degree in physics. Was going after a teacher's certificate."

She nodded soberly. "I was in biology..."

"Figures." I ducked a handful of slush. "How far?"

"Six years, bachelor's and technical." She slid her boot along the ground, turning up a ridge of mud and slush the consistency of freezing ice milk. "Why the fuck did this have to happen?"

I shrugged. It didn't call for an answer, least of all the answer that the UNEF kept giving us. Intellectual and physical elite of the planet, going out to guard humanity against the Tauran menace. Soyashit. It was all just a big experiment. See whether we could goad the Taurans into ground action.

Awright blew the whistle two minutes early, as expected, but Rogers and I and the other two stringers got to sit for a minute while the epoxy and floor teams finished covering our stringer. It got cold fast, sitting there with our suits turned off, but we remained inactive on principle.

There really wasn't any sense in having us train in the cold. Typical army half-logic. Sure, it was going to be cold where we were going, but not ice-cold or snow-cold. Almost by definition, a portal planet remained within a degree or two of absolute zero all the time—since collapsars don't shine—and the first chill you felt would mean that you were a dead man.

Twelve years before, when I was ten years old, they had discovered the collapsar jump. Just fling an object at a collapsar with sufficient speed, and out it pops in some other part of the galaxy. It didn't take long to figure out the formula that predicted where it would come out: it travels along the same "line" (actually an Einsteinian geodesic) it would have followed if the collapsar hadn't been in the way—until it reaches another collapsar field, whereupon it reappears, repelled with the same speed at which it approached the original collapsar. Travel time between the two collapsars . . . exactly zero.

It made a lot of work for mathematical physicists, who had to redefine simultaneity, then tear down general relativity and build it back up again. And it made the politicians very happy, because now they could send a shipload of colonists to Fomalhaut for less than it had once cost to put a brace of men on the moon. There were a lot of people the politicians would love to see on Fomalhaut, implementing a glorious adventure rather than stirring up trouble at home.

The ships were always accompanied by an automated probe that followed a couple of million miles behind. We knew about the portal planets, little bits of flotsam that whirled around the collapsars: the purpose of the drone was to come back and tell us in the event that a ship had smacked into a portal planet at .999 of the speed of light.

That particular catastrophe never happened, but one day a drone limped back alone. Its data were analyzed, and it turned out that the colonists' ship had been pursued by another vessel and destroyed. This happened near Aldebaran, in the constellation Taurus, but since

"Aldebaranian" is a little hard to handle, they named the enemy "Tauran."

Colonizing vessels thenceforth went out protected by an armed guard. Often the armed guard went out alone, and finally the colonization group got shortened to UNEF, United Nations Exploratory Force. Emphasis on the "force."

Then some bright lad in the General Assembly decided that we ought to field an army of footsoldiers to guard the portal planets of the nearer collapsars. This led to the Elite Conscription Act of 1996 and the most elitely conscripted army in the history of warfare.

So here we were, fifty men and fifty women, with IQs over 150 and bodies of unusual health and strength, slogging elitely through the mud and slush of central Missouri, reflecting on the usefulness of our skill in building bridges on worlds where the only fluid is an occasional standing pool of liquid helium.

III

About a month later, we left for our final training exercise, maneuvers on the planet Charon. Though nearing perihelion, it was still more than twice as far from the sun as Pluto.

The troopship was a converted "cattlewagon" made to carry two hundred colonists and assorted bushes and beasts. Don't think it was roomy, though, just because there were half that many of us. Most of the excess space was taken up with extra reaction mass and ordnance.

The whole trip took three weeks, accelerating at two gees halfway, decelerating the other half. Our top speed, as we roared by the orbit of Pluto, was around one-twentieth of the speed of light—not quite enough for relativity to rear its complicated head.

Three weeks of carrying around twice as much weight as normal... it's no picnic. We did some cautious exercises three times a day and remained horizontal as much as possible. Still, we got several broken bones and serious dislocations. The men had to wear special supporters to keep from littering the floor with loose organs. It was almost impossible to sleep; nightmares of choking and being crushed, rolling over periodically to prevent blood pooling and bedsores. One girl got so fatigued that she almost slept through the experience of having a rib push out into the open air.

I'd been in space several times before, so when we finally stopped decelerating and went into free fall, it was nothing but relief. But some people had never been out, except for our training on the moon, and succumbed to the sudden vertigo and disorientation. The rest of us cleaned up after them, floating through the quarters with sponges and inspirators to suck up the globules of partly digested "Concentrate, High-protein, Low-residue, Beef Flavor (Soya)."

We had a good view of Charon, coming down from orbit. There wasn't much to see, though. It was just a dim, off-white sphere with a few smudges on it. We landed about two hundred meters from the base. A pressurized crawler came out and mated with the ferry, so we didn't have to suit up. We clanked and squeaked up to the main building, a featureless box of grayish plastic.

Inside, the walls were the same drab color. The rest of the company was sitting at desks, chattering away. There was a seat next to Freeland.

"Jeff—feeling better?" He still looked a little pale.

"If the gods had meant for man to survive in free fall, they would have given him a castiron glottis." He sighed heavily. "A little better. Dying for a smoke."

"Yeah."

"*You* seemed to take it all right. Went up in school, didn't you?"

"Senior thesis in vacuum welding, yeah. Three weeks in Earth orbit." I sat back and reached for my weed box for the thousandth time. It still wasn't there. The life-support unit didn't want to handle nicotine and THC.

"Training was bad enough," Jeff groused, "but this shit—"

"Tench-hut!" We stood up in a raggety-ass fashion, by twos and threes. The door opened and a full major came in. I stiffened a little. He was the highest-ranking officer I'd ever seen. He had a row of ribbons stitched into his coveralls, including a purple strip meaning he'd been wounded in combat, fighting in the old American army. Must have been that Indochina thing, but it had fizzled out before I was born. He didn't look that old.

"Sit, sit." He made a patting motion with his hand. Then he put his hands on his hips and scanned the company, a small smile on his face. "Welcome to Charon. You picked a lovely day to land; the temperature outside is a summery eight point one five degrees Absolute. We expect little change for the next two centuries or so." Some of them laughed halfheartedly.

"Best you enjoy the tropical climate here at Miami base; enjoy it while you can. We're on the center of sunside here, and most of your training will be on darkside. Over there, the temperature stays a chilly two point zero eight.

You might as well regard all the training you got on Earth and the moon as just an elementary exercise, designed to give you a fair chance of surviving Charon. You'll have to go through your whole repertory here: tools, weapons, maneuvers. And you'll find that, at these temperatures, tools don't work the way they should; weapons don't want to fire. And people move v-e-r-y cautiously."

He studied the clipboard in his hand. "Right now, you have forty-nine women and forty-eight men. Two deaths on Earth, one psychiatric release. Having read an outline of your training program, I'm frankly surprised that so many of you pulled through.

"But you might as well know that I won't be displeased if as few as fifty of you, half, graduate from this final phase. And the only way not to graduate is to die. Here. The only way anybody gets back to Earth—including me—is after a combat tour.

"You will complete your training in one month. From here you go to Stargate collapsar, half a light away. You will stay at the settlement on Stargate 1, the largest portal planet, until replacements arrive. Hopefully, that will be no more than a month; another group is due here as soon as you leave.

"When you leave Stargate, you will go to some strategically important collapsar, set up a military base there, and fight the enemy, if attacked. Otherwise, you will maintain the base until further orders.

"The last two weeks of your training will consist of constructing exactly that kind of a base, on darkside. There you will be totally isolated from Miami base: no communication, no medical evacuation, no resupply. Sometime before the two weeks are up, your defense facilities will be evaluated in an attack by guided drones. They will be armed."

They had spent all that money on us just to kill us in training?

"All of the permanent personnel here on Charon are combat

veterans. Thus, all of us are forty to fifty years of age. But I think we can keep up with you. Two of us will be with you at all times and will accompany you at least as far as Stargate. They are Captain Sherman Stott, your company commander, and Sergeant Octavio Cortez, your first sergeant. Gentlemen?"

Two men in the front row stood easily and turned to face us. Captain Stott was a little smaller than the major, but cut from the same mold: face hard and smooth as porcelain; cynical half-smile, a precise centimeter of beard framing a large chin, looking thirty at the most. He wore a large, gunpowder-type pistol on his hip.

Sergeant Cortez was another story, a horror story. His head was shaved and the wrong shape, flattened out on one side, where a large piece of skull had obviously been taken out. His face was very dark and seamed with wrinkles and scars. Half his left ear was missing, and his eyes were as expressive as buttons on a machine. He had a moustache-and-beard combination that looked like a skinny white caterpillar taking a lap around his mouth. On anybody else, his schoolboy smile might look pleasant, but he was about the ugliest, meanest-looking creature I'd ever seen. Still, if you didn't look at his head and considered the lower six feet or so, he could have posed as the "after" advertisement for a body-building spa. Neither Stott nor Cortez wore any ribbons. Cortez had a small pocket-laser suspended in a magnetic rig, sideways, under his left armpit. It had wooden grips that were worn smooth.

"Now, before I turn you over to the tender mercies of these two gentlemen, let me caution you again:

"Two months ago there was not a living soul on this planet, just some leftover equipment from an expedition of 1991. A working force of forty-five men struggled for a month to erect this base. Twenty-four of them, more than half, died in the construction of it. This is the most dangerous planet men have ever tried to live on, but the places you'll be going will be this bad and worse. Your cadre will try to keep you alive for the next month. Listen to them . . . and follow their example; all of them have survived here much longer than you'll have to. Captain?" The captain stood up as the major went out the door.

"Tench-*hut!*" The last syllable was like an explosion and we all jerked to our feet.

"Now I'm only gonna say this *once,* so you better listen," he growled.

"We *are* in a combat situation here, and in a combat situation there is only *one* penalty for disobedience or insubordination." He jerked the pistol from his hip and held it by the barrel, like a club. "This is an army model 1911 automatic *pistol*, caliber .45, and it is a primitive but effective weapon. The sergeant and I are authorized to use our weapons to kill to enforce discipline. Don't make us do it, because we will. We *will*." He put the pistol back. The holster snap made a loud crack in the dead quiet.

"Sergeant Cortez and I between us have killed more people than are sitting in this room. Both of us fought in Vietnam on the American side and both of us joined the United Nations International Guard more than ten years ago. I took a break in grade from major for the privilege of commanding this company, and First Sergeant Cortez took a break from sub-major, because we are both *combat* soldiers and this is the first *combat* situation since 1987.

"Keep in mind what I've said while the first sergeant instructs you more specifically in what your duties will be under this command. Take over, Sergeant." He turned on his heel and strode out of the room. The expression on his face hadn't changed one millimeter during the whole harangue.

The first sergeant moved like a heavy machine with lots of ball bearings. When the door hissed shut, he swiveled ponderously to face us and said, "At ease, siddown," in a surprisingly gentle voice. He sat on a table in the front of the room. It creaked, but held.

"Now the captain talks scary and I look scary, but we both mean well. You'll be working pretty closely with me, so you better get used to this thing I've got hanging in front of my brain. You probably won't see the captain much, except on maneuvers."

He touched the flat part of his head. "And speaking of brains, I still have just about all of mine, in spite of Chinese efforts to the contrary. All of us old vets who mustered into UNEF had to pass the same criteria that got you drafted by the Elite Conscription Act. So I suspect all of you are smart and tough—but just keep in mind that the captain and I are smart and tough *and* experienced."

He flipped through the roster without really looking at it. "Now, as the captain said, there'll be only one kind of disciplinary action on maneuvers. Capital punishment. But normally *we* won't have to kill you for disobeying; Charon'll save us the trouble.

"Back in the billeting area, it'll be another story. We don't much care what you do inside. Grab-ass all day and fuck all night, makes no difference.... But once you suit up and go outside, you've gotta have discipline that would shame a Centurian. There will be situations where one stupid act could kill us all.

"Anyhow, the first thing we've gotta do is get you fitted to your fighting suits. The armorer's waiting at your billet; he'll take you one at a time. Let's go."

IV

"Now I know you got lectured back on Earth on what a fighting suit can do." The armorer was a small man, partially bald, with no insignia or rank on his coveralls. Sergeant Cortez had told us to call him "sir," since he was a lieutenant.

"But I'd like to reinforce a couple of points, maybe add some things your instructors Earthside weren't clear about or couldn't know. Your first sergeant was kind enough to consent to being my visual aid. Sergeant?"

Cortez slipped out of his coveralls and came up to the little raised platform where a fighting suit was standing, popped open like a man-shaped clam. He backed into it and slipped his arms into the rigid sleeves. There was a click and the thing swung shut with a sigh. It was bright green with CORTEZ stenciled in white letters on the helmet.

"Camouflage, Sergeant." The green faded to white, then dirty gray.

"This is good camouflage for Charon and most of your portal planets," said Cortez, as if from a deep well. "But there are several other combinations available." The gray dappled and brightened to a combination of greens and browns: "Jungle." Then smoothed out to a hard light ochre: "Desert." Dark brown, darker, to a deep flat black: "Night or space."

"Very good. Sergeant. To my knowledge, this is the only feature of the suit that was perfected after your training. The control is around your left wrist and is admittedly awkward, but once you find the right combination, it's easy to lock in.

"Now, you didn't get much in-suit training Earthside. We didn't want you to get used to using the thing in a friendly environment. The fighting suit is the deadliest personal weapon ever built, and with no weapon is it easier for the user to kill himself through carelessness. Turn around, Sergeant.

"Case in point." He tapped a large square protuberance between the shoulders. "Exhaust fins. As you know, the suit tries to keep you at a comfortable temperature no matter what the weather's like outside. The material of the suit is as near to a perfect insulator as we could get, consistent with mechanical demands. Therefore, these fins get *hot*—especially hot, compared to darkside temperatures—as they bleed off the body's heat.

"All you have to do is lean up against a boulder of frozen gas; there's lots of it around. The gas will sublime off faster than it can escape from the fins; in escaping, it will push against the surrounding 'ice' and fracture it . . . and in about one-hundredth of a second, you have the equivalent of a hand grenade going off right below your neck. You'll never feel a thing.

"Variations on this theme have killed eleven people in the past two months. And they were just building a bunch of huts.

"I assume you know how easily the waldo capabilities can kill you or your companions. Anybody want to shake hands with the sergeant?" He paused, then stepped over and clasped his glove. "He's had lots of practice. Until *you* have, be extremely careful. You might scratch an itch and wind up breaking your back. Remember, semilogarithmic response: two pounds' pressure exerts five pounds' force; three pounds' gives ten; four pounds', twenty-three; five pounds', forty-seven. Most of you can muster up a grip of well over a hundred pounds. Theoretically, you could rip a steel girder in two with that, amplified. Actually, you'd destroy the material of your gloves and, at least on Charon, die very quickly. It'd be a race between decompression and flash-freezing. You'd die no matter which won.

"The leg waldos are also dangerous, even though the amplification is less extreme. Until you're really skilled, don't try to run, or jump. You're likely to trip, and that means you're likely to die.

"Charon's gravity is three-fourths of Earth normal, so it's not too bad. But on a really small world, like Luna, you could take a running jump and not come down for twenty minutes, just keep sailing over the horizon. Maybe bash into a mountain at eighty meters per second. On a small asteroid, it'd be no trick at all to run up to escape velocity and be off on an informal tour of intergalactic space. It's a slow way to travel.

"Tomorrow morning, we'll start teaching you how to stay alive inside this infernal machine. The rest of the afternoon and evening, I'll call you one at a time to be fitted. That's all, Sergeant."

Cortez went to the door and turned the stopcock that let air into the airlock. A bank of infrared lamps went on to keep the air from freezing inside it. When the pressures were equalized, he shut the stopcock, unclamped the door and stepped in, clamping it shut behind him. A pump hummed for about a minute, evacuating the airlock; then he stepped out and sealed the outside door.

It was pretty much like the ones on Luna.

"First I want Private Omar Almizar. The rest of you can go find your bunks. I'll call you over the squawker."

"Alphabetical order, sir?"

"Yep. About ten minutes apiece. If your name begins with Z, you might as well get sacked."

That was Rogers. She probably was thinking about getting sacked.

V

The sun was a hard white point directly overhead. It was a lot brighter than I had expected it to be; since we were eighty AUs out, it was only one-6400th as bright as it is on Earth. Still, it was putting out about as much light as a powerful streetlamp.

"This is considerably more light than you'll have on a portal planet." Captain Stott's voice crackled in our collective ear. "Be glad that you'll be able to watch your step."

We were lined up, single file, on the permaplast sidewalk that connected the billet and the supply hut. We'd practiced walking inside, all morning, and this wasn't any different except for the exotic scenery. Though the light was rather dim, you could see all the way to the horizon quite clearly, with no atmosphere in the way. A black cliff that looked too regular to be natural stretched from one horizon to the other, passing within a kilometer of us. The ground was obsidian-black, mottled with patches of white or bluish ice. Next to the supply hut was a small mountain of snow in a bin marked OXYGEN.

The suit was fairly comfortable, but it gave you the odd feeling of simultaneously being a marionette and a puppeteer. You apply the impulse to move your leg and the suit picks it up and magnifies it and moves your leg *for* you.

"Today we're only going to walk around the company area, and nobody will *leave* the company area." The captain wasn't wearing his .45—unless he carried it as a good luck charm, under his suit—but he had a laser-finger like the rest of us. And his was probably hooked up.

Keeping an interval of at least two meters between each person, we stepped off the permaplast and followed the captain over smooth rock. We walked carefully for about an hour, spiraling out, and finally stopped at the far edge of the perimeter.

"Now everybody pay close attention. I'm going out to that blue slab of ice"—it was a big one, about twenty meters away—"and show you something that you'd better know if you want to stay alive."

He walked out in a dozen confident steps. "First I have to heat up a rock—filters down." I squeezed the stud under my armpit and the filter slid into place over my image converter. The captain pointed his finger at a black rock the size of a basketball, and gave it a short burst. The glare rolled a long shadow of the captain over us and beyond. The rock shattered into a pile of hazy splinters.

"It doesn't take long for these to cool down." He stooped and picked up a piece. "This one is probably twenty or twenty-five degrees. Watch." He tossed the "warm" rock onto the ice slab. It skittered around in a crazy pattern and shot off the side. He tossed another one, and it did the same.

"As you know, you are not quite *perfectly* insulated. These rocks are about the temperature of the soles of your boots. If you try to stand on a slab of hydrogen, the same thing will happen to you. Except that the rock is *already* dead.

"The reason for this behavior is that the rock makes a slick interface with the ice—a little puddle of liquid hydrogen—and rides a few molecules above the liquid on a cushion of hydrogen vapor. This makes the rock or *you* a frictionless bearing as far as the ice is concerned, and you *can't* stand up without any friction under your boots.

"After you have lived in your suit for a month or so you *should* be able to survive falling down, but right *now* you just don't know enough. Watch."

The captain flexed and hopped up onto the slab. His feet shot out from under him and he twisted around in midair, landing on hands and knees. He slipped off and stood on the ground.

"The idea is to keep your exhaust fins from making contact with the frozen gas. Compared to the ice they are as hot as a blast furnace, and contact with any weight behind it will result in an explosion."

After that demonstration, we walked around for another hour or so and returned to the billet. Once through the airlock, we had to mill around for a while, letting the suits get up to something like room temperature. Somebody came up and touched helmets with me.

"William?" She had MCCOY stenciled above her faceplate.

"Hi, Sean. Anything special?"

"I just wondered if you had anyone to sleep with tonight." That's right; I'd forgotten. There wasn't any sleeping roster here. Everybody chose his own partner. "Sure, I mean, uh, no . . . no, I haven't asked anybody. Sure, if you want to . . ."

"Thanks, William. See you later." I watched her walk away and thought that if anybody could make a fighting suit look sexy, it'd be Sean. But even she couldn't.

Cortez decided we were warm enough and led us to the suit room, where we backed the things into place and hooked them up to the charging plates. (Each suit had a little chunk of plutonium that would power it for several years, but we were supposed to run on fuel cells as much as possible.) After a lot of shuffling around, everybody finally got plugged in and we were allowed to unsuit— ninety-seven naked chickens squirming out of bright green eggs. It was *cold*—the air, the floor and especially the suits—and we made a pretty disorderly exit toward the lockers.

I slipped on tunic, trousers and sandals and was still cold. I took my cup and joined the line for soya. Everybody was jumping up and down to keep warm.

"How c-cold, do you think, it is, M-Mandella?" That was McCoy.

"I don't, even want, to think, about it." I stopped jumping and rubbed myself as briskly as possible, while holding a cup in one hand. "At least as cold as Missouri was."

"Ung...wish they'd, get some, fucken, heat in, this place." It always affects the small women more than anybody else. McCoy was the littlest one in the company, a waspwaist doll barely five feet high.

"They've got the airco going. It can't be long now."

"I wish I, was a big, slab of, meat like, you."

I was glad she wasn't.

VI

We had our first casualty on the third day, learning how to dig holes.

With such large amounts of energy stored in a soldier's weapons, it wouldn't be practical for him to hack out a hole in the frozen ground with the conventional pick and shovel. Still, you can launch grenades all day and get nothing but shallow depressions—so the usual method is to bore a hole in the ground with the hand laser, drop a timed charge in after it's cooled down and, ideally, fill the hole with stuff. Of course, there's not much loose rock on Charon, unless you've already blown a hole nearby.

The only difficult thing about the procedure is in getting away. To be safe, we were told, you've got to either be behind something really solid, or be at least a hundred meters away. You've got about three minutes after setting the charge, but you can't just sprint away. Not safely, not on Charon.

The accident happened when we were making a really deep hole, the kind you want for a large underground bunker. For this, we had to blow a hole, then climb down to the bottom of the crater and repeat the procedure again and again until the hole was deep enough. Inside the crater we used charges with a five-minute delay, but it hardly seemed enough time—you really had to go it slow, picking your way up the crater's edge.

Just about everybody had blown a double hole; everybody but me and three others. I guess we were the only ones paying really close attention when Bovanovitch got into trouble. All of us were a good two hundred meters away. With my image converter tuned up to about forty power, I watched her disappear over the rim of the crater. After that, I could only listen in on her conversation with Cortez.

"I'm on the bottom, Sergeant." Normal radio procedure was

suspended for maneuvers like this; nobody but the trainee and Cortez was allowed to broadcast.

"Okay, move to the center and clear out the rubble. Take your time. No rush until you pull the pin."

"Sure, Sergeant." We could hear small echoes of rocks clattering, sound conduction through her boots. She didn't say anything for several minutes.

"Found bottom." She sounded a little out of breath.

"Ice or rock?"

"Oh, it's rock, Sergeant. The greenish stuff."

"Use a low setting, then. One point two, dispersion four."

"God dam it, Sergeant, that'll take forever."

"Yeah, but that stuff's got hydrated crystals in it—heat it up too fast and you might make it fracture. And we'd just have to leave you there, girl. Dead and bloody."

"Okay, one point two dee four." The inside edge of the crater flickered red with reflected laser light.

"When you get about a half a meter deep, squeeze it up to dee two."

"Roger." It took her exactly seventeen minutes, three of them at dispersion two. I could imagine how tired her shooting arm was.

"Now rest for a few minutes. When the bottom of the hole stops glowing, arm the charge and drop it in. Then *walk* out, understand? You'll have plenty of time."

"I understand. Sergeant. Walk out." She sounded nervous. Well, you don't often have to tiptoe away from a twenty-microton tachyon bomb. We listened to her breathing for a few minutes.

"Here goes." Faint slithering sound, the bomb sliding down.

"Slow and easy now. You've got five minutes."

"Y-yeah. Five." Her footsteps started out slow and regular. Then, after she started climbing the side, the sounds were less regular, maybe a little frantic. And with four minutes to go—

"Shit!" A loud scraping noise, then clatters and bumps. "Shit—shit."

"What's wrong, Private?"

"Oh, shit." Silence. "Shit!"

"Private, you don't wanna get shot, you *tell me what's wrong!*"

"I . . . shit, I'm stuck. Fucken rockslide . . . shit. . . . DO SOMETHING! I can't move, shit I can't move, I, I—"

"Shut up! How deep?"

"Can't move my, shit, my fucken legs. HELP ME—"

"Then goddammit use your arms—push! You can move a ton with each hand." Three minutes.

She stopped cussing and started to mumble, in Russian, I guess, a low monotone. She was panting, and you could hear rocks tumbling away.

"I'm free." Two minutes.

"Go as fast as you can." Cortez's voice was flat, emotionless.

At ninety seconds she appeared, crawling over the rim. "Run, girl.... You better run." She ran five or six steps and fell, skidded a few meters and got back up, running; fell again, got up again—

It looked as though she was going pretty fast, but she had only covered about thirty meters when Cortez said, "All right, Bovanovitch, get down on your stomach and lie still." Ten seconds, but she didn't hear or she wanted to get just a little more distance, and she kept running, careless leaping strides, and at the high point of one leap there was a flash and a rumble, and something big hit her below the neck, and her headless body spun off end over end through space, trailing a red-black spiral of flash-frozen blood that settled gracefully to the ground, a path of crystal powder that nobody disturbed while we gathered rocks to cover the juiceless thing at the end of it.

That night Cortez didn't lecture us, didn't even show up for night-chop. We were all very polite to each other and nobody was afraid to talk about it.

I sacked with Rogers—everybody sacked with a good friend—but all she wanted to do was cry, and she cried so long and so hard that she got me doing it, too.

VII

"Fire team *A*—move out!" The twelve of us advanced in a ragged line toward the simulated bunker. It was about a kilometer away, across a carefully prepared obstacle course. We could move pretty fast, since all of the ice had been cleared from the field, but even with ten days' experience we weren't ready to do more than an easy jog.

I carried a grenade launcher loaded with tenth-microton practice grenades. Everybody had their laser-fingers set at point oh eight dee one, not much more than a flashlight. This was a *simulated* attack—the bunker and its robot defender cost too much to use once and be thrown away.

"Team *B*, follow. Team leaders, take over."

We approached a clump of boulders at about the halfway mark, and Potter, my team leader, said, "Stop and cover." We clustered behind the rocks and waited for team *B*.

Barely visible in their blackened suits, the dozen men and women whispered by us. As soon as they were clear, they jogged left, out of our line of sight.

"Fire!" Red circles of light danced a half-klick downrange, where the bunker was just visible. Five hundred meters was the limit for these practice grenades; but I might luck out, so I lined the launcher up on the image of the bunker, held it at a forty-five-degree angle and popped off a salvo of three.

Return fire from the bunker started before my grenades even landed. Its automatic lasers were no more powerful than the ones we were using, but a direct hit would deactivate your image converter, leaving you blind. It was setting down a random field of fire, not even coming close to the boulders we were hiding behind.

Three magnesium-bright flashes blinked simultaneously about thirty meters short of the bunker. "Mandella! I thought you were supposed to be *good* with that thing."

"Damn it, Potter—it only throws half a klick. Once we get closer, I'll lay 'em right on top, every time."

"Sure you will." I didn't say anything. She wouldn't be team leader forever. Besides, she hadn't been such a bad girl before the power went to her head.

Since the grenadier is the assistant team leader, I was slaved into Potter's radio and could hear *B* team talk to her.

"Potter, this is Freeman. Losses?"

"Potter here—no, looks like they were concentrating on you."

"Yeah, we lost three. Right now we're in a depression about eighty, a hundred meters down from you. We can give cover whenever you're ready."

"Okay, start." Soft click: "*A* team, follow me." She slid out from behind the rock and turned on the faint pink beacon beneath her powerpack. I turned on mine and moved out to run alongside of her, and the rest of the team fanned out in a trailing wedge. Nobody fired while *A* team laid down a cover for us.

All I could hear was Potter's breathing and the soft *crunch-crunch* of my boots. Couldn't see much of anything, so I tongued the image converter up to a log-two intensification. That made the image kind of blurry but adequately bright. Looked like the bunker had *B* team pretty well pinned down; they were getting quite a roasting. All of their return fire was laser. They must have lost their grenadier.

"Potter, this is Mandella. Shouldn't we take some of the heat off *B* team?"

"Soon as I can find us good enough cover. Is that all right with you? Private?" She'd been promoted to corporal for the duration of the exercise.

We angled to the right and lay down behind a slab of rock. Most of the others found cover nearby, but a few had to hug the ground.

"Freeman, this is Potter."

"Potter, this is Smithy. Freeman's out; Samuels is out. We only have five men left. Give us some cover so we can get—"

"Roger, Smithy." *Click.* "Open up, *A* team. The *B*'s are really hurtin.'"

I peeked out over the edge of the rock. My rangefinder said that the bunker was about three hundred fifty meters away, still pretty far. I aimed a smidgeon high and popped three, then down a couple of degrees, three more. The first ones overshot by about twenty meters; then the second salvo flared up directly in front of the bunker. I tried to hold on that angle and popped fifteen, the rest of the magazine, in the same direction.

I should have ducked down behind the rock to reload, but I wanted to see where the fifteen would land, so I kept my eyes on the bunker while I reached back to unclip another magazine—

When the laser hit my image converter, there was a red glare so intense it seemed to go right through my eyes and bounce off the back of my skull. It must have been only a few milliseconds before the converter overloaded and went blind, but the bright green afterimage hurt my eyes for several seconds.

Since I was officially "dead," my radio automatically cut off, and I had to remain where I was until the mock battle was over. With no sensory input besides the feel of my own skin (and it ached where the image converter had shone on it) and the ringing in my ears, it seemed like an awfully long time. Finally, a helmet clanked against mine.

"You okay, Mandella?" Potter's voice.

"Sorry, I died of boredom twenty minutes ago."

"Stand up and take my hand." I did so and we shuffled back to the billet. It must have taken over an hour. She didn't say anything more, all the way back—it's a pretty awkward way to communicate— but after we'd cycled through the airlock and warmed up, she helped me undo my suit. I got ready for a mild tongue-lashing, but when the suit popped open, before I could even get my eyes adjusted to the light, she grabbed me around the neck and planted a wet kiss on my mouth.

"Nice shooting, Mandella."

"Huh?"

"Didn't you see? Of course not. . . . The last salvo before you got hit—four direct hits. The bunker decided it was knocked out, and all we had to do was walk the rest of the way."

"Great." I scratched my face under the eyes, and some dry skin flaked off. She giggled.

"You should see yourself. You look like . . ."

"All personnel, report to the assembly area." That was the captain's voice. Bad news, usually.

She handed me a tunic and sandals. "Let's go." The assembly area-chop hall was just down the corridor. There was a row of roll-call buttons at the door: I pressed the one beside my name. Four of the names were covered with black tape. That was good, only four. We hadn't lost anybody during today's maneuvers.

The captain was sitting on the raised dais, which at least meant we didn't have to go through the tench-hut bullshit. The place filled up in less than a minute; a soft chime indicated the roll was complete.

Captain Stott didn't stand up. "You did *fairly* well today. Nobody killed, and I expected some to be. In that respect you exceeded my expectations but in *every* other respect you did a poor job.

"I am glad you're taking good care of yourselves, because each of you represents an investment of over a million dollars and one-fourth of a human life.

"But in this simulated battle against a *very* stupid robot enemy, thirty-seven of you managed to walk into laser fire and be killed in a *sim*ulated way, and since dead people require no food, *you* will require no food, for the next three days. Each person who was a casualty in this battle will be allowed only two liters of water and a vitamin ration each day."

We knew enough not to groan or anything, but there were some pretty disgusted looks, especially on the faces that had singed eyebrows and a pink rectangle of sunburn framing their eyes.

"Mandella."

"Sir?"

"You are far and away the worst-burned casualty. Was your image converter set on normal?"

Oh, shit. "No, sir. Log two."

"I see. Who was your team leader for the exercises?"

"Acting Corporal Potter, sir."

"Private Potter, did you order him to use image intensification?"

"Sir, I ... I don't remember."

"You don't. Well, as a memory exercise you may join the dead people. Is that satisfactory?"

"Yes, sir."

"Good. Dead people get one last meal tonight and go on no rations starting tomorrow. Are there any questions?" He must have been kidding. "All right. Dismissed."

I selected the meal that looked as if it had the most calories and took my tray over to sit by Potter.

"That was a quixotic damn thing to do. But thanks."

"Nothing. I've been wanting to lose a few pounds anyway." I couldn't see where she was carrying any extra.

"I know a good exercise," I said. She smiled without looking up from her tray. "Have anybody for tonight?"

"Kind of thought I'd ask Jeff ..."

"Better hurry, then. He's lusting after Maejima." Well, that was mostly true. Everybody did.

"I don't know. Maybe we ought to save our strength. That third day ..."

"Come on." I scratched the back of her hand lightly with a fingernail. "We haven't sacked since Missouri. Maybe I've learned something new."

"Maybe you have." She tilted her head up at me in a sly way. "Okay."

Actually, she was the one with the new trick. The French corkscrew, she called it. She wouldn't tell me who taught it to her though. I'd like to shake his hand. Once I got my strength back.

VIII

The two weeks' training around Miami base eventually cost us eleven lives. Twelve, if you count Dahlquist. I guess having to spend the rest of your life on Charon with a hand and both legs missing is close enough to dying.

Foster was crushed in a landslide and Freeland had a suit malfunction that froze him solid before we could carry him inside. Most of the other deaders were people I didn't know all that well. But they all hurt. And they seemed to make us more scared rather than more cautious.

Now darkside. A flyer brought us over in groups of twenty and set us down beside a pile of building materials thoughtfully immersed in a pool of helium II.

We used grapples to haul the stuff out of the pool. It's not safe to go wading, since the stuff crawls all over you and it's hard to tell what's underneath; you could walk out onto a slab of hydrogen and be out of luck.

I'd suggested that we try to boil away the pool with our lasers, but ten minutes of concentrated fire didn't drop the helium level appreciably. It didn't boil, either; helium II is a "superfluid," so what evaporation there was had to take place evenly, all over the surface. No hot spots, so no bubbling.

We weren't supposed to use lights, to "avoid detection." There was plenty of starlight with your image converter cranked up to log three or four, but each stage of amplification meant some loss of detail. By log four the landscape looked like a crude monochrome painting, and you couldn't read the names on people's helmets unless they were right in front of you.

The landscape wasn't all that interesting, anyhow. There were half a dozen medium-sized meteor craters (all with exactly the same level of helium II in them) and the suggestion of some puny mountains just over the horizon. The uneven ground was the consistency of frozen spiderwebs; every time you put your foot down, you'd sink half an inch with a squeaking crunch. It could get on your nerves.

It took most of a day to pull all the stuff out of the pool. We took shifts napping, which you could do either standing up, sitting or lying on your stomach. I didn't do well in any of those positions, so I was anxious to get the bunker built and pressurized.

We couldn't build the thing underground—it'd just fill up with helium II—so the first thing to do was to build an insulating platform, a permaplast-vacuum sandwich three layers thick.

I was an acting corporal, with a crew of ten people. We were carrying the permaplast layers to the building site—two people can carry one easily—when one of "my" men slipped and fell on his back.

"Damn it, Singer, watch your step." We'd had a couple of deaders that way.

"Sorry, Corporal. I'm bushed. Just got my feet tangled up."

"Yeah, just watch it." He got back up all right, and he and his partner placed the sheet and went back to get another.

I kept my eye on Singer. In a few minutes he was practically staggering, not easy to do in that suit of cybernetic armor.

"Singer! After you set that plank, I want to see you."

"Okay." He labored through the task and mooched over.

"Let me check your readout." I opened the door on his chest to expose the medical monitor. His temperature was at two degrees high; blood pressure and heart rate both elevated. Not up to the red line, though.

"You sick or something?"

"Hell, Mandella, I feel okay, just tired. Since I fell I been a little dizzy."

I chinned the medic's combination. "Doc, this is Mandella. You wanna come over here for a minute?"

"Sure, where are you?" I waved and he walked over from poolside.

"What's the problem?" I showed him Singer's readout.

He knew what all the other little dials and things meant, so it took him a while. "As far as I can tell, Mandella . . . he's just hot."

"Hell, I coulda told you that," said Singer.

"Maybe you better have the armorer take a look at his suit." We had two people who'd taken a crash course in suit maintenance; they were our "armorers."

I chinned Sanchez and asked him to come over with his tool kit.

"Be a couple of minutes, Corporal. Carryin' a plank."

"Well, put it down and get over here." I was getting an uneasy feeling. Waiting for him, the medic and I looked over Singer's suit.

"Uh-oh," Doc Jones said. "Look at this." I went around to the back and looked where he was pointing. Two of the fins on the heat exchanger were bent out of shape.

"What's wrong?" Singer asked.

"You fell on your heat exchanger, right?"

"Sure, Corporal—that's it. It must not be working right."

"I don't think it's working at *all*," said Doc.

Sanchez came over with his diagnostic kit and we told him what had happened. He looked at the heat exchanger, then plugged a couple of jacks into it and got a digital readout from a little monitor in his kit. I didn't know what it was measuring, but it came out zero to eight decimal places.

Heard a soft click, Sanchez chinning my private frequency.

"Corporal, this guy's a deader."

"What? Can't you fix the goddamn thing?"

"Maybe . . . maybe I could, if I could take it apart. But there's no way—"

"Hey! Sanchez?" Singer was talking on the general freak. "Find out what's wrong?" He was panting.

Click. "Keep your pants on, man, we're working on it." *Click.* "He won't last long enough for us to get the bunker pressurized. And I can't work on the heat exchanger from outside of the suit."

"You've got a spare suit, haven't you?"

"Two of 'em, the fit-anybody kind. But there's no place . . . say . . ."

"Right. Go get one of the suits warmed up." I chinned the general freak. "Listen, Singer, we've gotta get you out of that thing. Sanchez has a spare suit, but to make the switch, we're gonna have to build a house around you. Understand?"

"Huh-uh."

"Look, we'll make a box with you inside, and hook it up to the life-support unit. That way you can breathe while you make the switch."

"Soun's pretty compis . . . compil . . . cated t'me."

"Look, just come along—"

"I'll be all right, man, jus' lemme res'. . . ."

I grabbed his arm and led him to the building site. He was really weaving. Doc took his other arm, and between us, we kept him from falling over.

"Corporal Ho, this is Corporal Mandella." Ho was in charge of the life-support unit.

"Go away, Mandella. I'm busy."

"You're going to be busier." I outlined the problem to her. While her group hurried to adapt the LSU—for this purpose, it need only be an air hose and heater—I got my crew to bring around six slabs of permaplast, so we could build a big box around Singer and the extra suit. It would look like a huge coffin, a meter square and six meters long.

We set the suit down on the slab that would be the floor of the coffin. "Okay, Singer, let's go."

No answer.

"Singer!" He was just standing there. Doc Jones checked his readout.

"He's out, man, unconscious."

My mind raced. There might just be room for another person in the box. "Give me a hand here." I took Singer's shoulders and Doc took his feet, and we carefully laid him out at the feet of the empty suit.

Then I lay down myself, above the suit. "Okay, close 'er up."

"Look, Mandella, if anybody goes in there, it oughta be me."

"Fuck you, Doc. *My* job. My man." That sounded all wrong. William Mandella, boy hero.

They stood a slab up on edge—it had two openings for the LSU input and exhaust—and proceeded to weld it to the bottom plank with a narrow laser beam. On Earth, we'd just use glue, but here the only fluid was helium, which has lots of interesting properties, but is definitely not sticky.

After about ten minutes we were completely walled up. I could feel the LSU humming. I switched on my suit light—the first time since we landed on darkside—and the glare made purple blotches dance in front of my eyes.

"Mandella, this is Ho. Stay in your suit at least two or three minutes. We're putting hot air in, but it's coming back just this side of liquid." I watched the purple fade for a while.

"Okay, it's still cold, but you can make it." I popped my suit. It wouldn't open all the way, but I didn't have too much trouble getting out. The suit was still cold enough to take some skin off my fingers and butt as I wiggled out.

I had to crawl feet-first down the coffin to get to Singer. It got darker fast, moving away from my light. When I popped his suit a rush of hot stink hit me in the face. In the dim light his skin was dark red and splotchy. His breathing was very shallow and I could see his heart palpitating.

First I unhooked the relief tubes—an unpleasant business—then the biosensors; and then I had the problem of getting his arms out of their sleeves.

It's pretty easy to do for yourself. You twist this way and turn that way and the arm pops out. Doing it from the outside is a different matter: I had to twist his arm and then reach under and move the suit's arm to match—it takes muscle to move a suit around from the outside.

Once I had one arm out it was pretty easy; I just crawled forward, putting my feet on the suit's shoulders, and pulled on his free arm. He slid out of the suit like an oyster slipping out of its shell.

I popped the spare suit and, after a lot of pulling and pushing, managed to get his legs in. Hooked up the biosensors and the front relief tube. He'd have to do the other one himself; it's too complicated. For the nth time I was glad not to have been born female; they have to have two of those damned plumber's friends, instead of just one and a simple hose.

I left his arms out of the sleeves. The suit would be useless for any kind of work, anyhow; waldos have to be tailored to the individual.

His eyelids fluttered. "Man ... della. Where ... the fuck.

I explained, slowly, and he seemed to get most of it. "Now I'm gonna close you up and go get into my suit. I'll have the crew cut the end off this thing and I'll haul you out. Got it?"

He nodded. Strange to see that—when you nod or shrug inside a suit, it doesn't communicate anything.

I crawled into my suit, hooked up the attachments and chinned the general freak. "Doc, I think he's gonna be okay. Get us out of here now."

"Will do." Ho's voice. The LSU hum was replaced by a chatter, then a throb. Evacuating the box to prevent an explosion.

One corner of the seam grew red, then white, and a bright crimson beam lanced through, not a foot away from my head. I scrunched back as far as I could. The beam slid up the seam and around three corners, back to where it started. The end of the box fell away slowly, trailing filaments of melted 'plast.

"Wait for the stuff to harden, Mandella."

"Sanchez, I'm not that stupid."

"Here you go." Somebody tossed a line to me. That *would* be smarter than dragging him out by myself. I threaded a long bit under his arms and tied it behind his neck. Then I scrambled out to help them pull, which was silly—they had a dozen people already lined up to haul.

Singer got out all right and was actually sitting up while Doc Jones checked his readout. People were asking me about it and congratulating me, when suddenly Ho said, "Look!" and pointed toward the horizon.

It was a black ship, coming in fast. I just had time to think it wasn't fair, they weren't supposed to attack until the last few days, and then the ship was right on top of us.

IX

We all flopped to the ground instinctively, but the ship didn't attack. It blasted braking rockets and dropped to land on skids. Then it skied around to come to a rest beside the building site.

Everybody had it figured out and was standing around sheepishly when the two suited figures stepped out of the ship.

A familiar voice crackled over the general freak. "Every *one* of you saw us coming in and not *one* of you responded with laser fire. It wouldn't have done any good but it would have indicated a certain amount of fighting spirit. You have a week or less before the real thing and since the sergeant and *I* will be here *I* will insist that you show a little more will to live. Acting Sergeant Potter."

"Here, sir."

"Get me a detail of twelve people to unload cargo. We brought a hundred small robot drones for *target* practice so that you might have at least a fighting chance when a live target comes over.

"Move *now*. We only have thirty minutes before the ship returns to Miami."

I checked, and it was actually more like forty minutes.

Having the captain and sergeant there didn't really make much difference. We were still on our own; they were just observing.

Once we got the floor down, it only took one day to complete the bunker. It was a gray oblong, featureless except for the airlock blister and four windows. On top was a swivel-mounted bevawatt* laser. The operator—you couldn't call him a "gunner"—sat in a chair holding dead-man switches in both hands. The laser wouldn't fire as long as he was holding one of those switches. If he let go, it would automatically aim for any moving aerial object and fire at will. Primary detection and aiming was by means of a kilometer-high antenna mounted beside the bunker.

It was the only arrangement that could really be expected to work, with the horizon so close and human reflexes so slow. You couldn't have the thing fully automatic, because in theory, friendly ships might also approach.

The aiming computer could choose among up to twelve targets appearing simultaneously (firing at the largest ones first). And it would get all twelve in the space of half a second.

The installation was partly protected from enemy fire by an efficient ablative layer that covered everything except the human operator. But then, they *were* dead-man switches. One man above guarding eighty inside. The army's good at that kind of arithmetic.

---

* The editors decided to keep this term intact, but for the curious, Haldeman wrote the following in the afterword to his 1978 collection, *Infinite Dreams*: "Nobody can be an expert on everything from ablation physics to zymurgy, so you have to work from a principle of exclusion: know the limits of your knowledge and never expose your ignorance by attempting to write with authority when you don't really know what's going on. This advice is easier to give than to take. I've been caught in basic mistakes in genetics, laser technology, and even metric nomenclature—in the first printing of *The Forever War* I referred time and again to a unit of power called the 'beva-watt.' What I meant was 'gigawatt'; the only thing 'bev' means is billion-electron-volt, a unit of energy, not power. I got letters. Boy, did I get letters."

Once the bunker was finished, half of us stayed inside at all times—feeling very much like targets—taking turns operating the laser, while the other half went on maneuvers.

About four klicks from the base was a large "lake" of frozen hydrogen; one of our most important maneuvers was to learn how to get around on the treacherous stuff.

It wasn't too difficult. You couldn't stand up on it, so you had to belly down and sled.

If you had somebody to push you from the edge, getting started was no problem. Otherwise, you had to scrabble with your hands and feet, pushing down as hard as was practical, until you started moving, in a series of little jumps. Once started, you'd keep going until you ran out of ice. You could steer a little bit by digging in, hand and foot, on the appropriate side, but you couldn't slow to a stop that way. So it was a good idea not to go too fast and wind up positioned in such a way that your helmet didn't absorb the shock of stopping.

We went through all the things we'd done on the Miami side: weapons practice, demolition, attack patterns. We also launched drones at irregular intervals, toward the bunker. Thus, ten or fifteen times a day, the operators got to demonstrate their skill in letting go of the handles as soon as the proximity light went on.

I had four hours of that, like everybody else. I was nervous until the first "attack," when I saw how little there was to it. The light went on, I let go, the gun aimed, and when the drone peeped over the horizon—*zzt!* Nice touch of color, the molten metal spraying through space. Otherwise not too exciting.

So none of us were worried about the upcoming "graduation exercise," thinking it would be just more of the same.

Miami base attacked on the thirteenth day with two simultaneous missiles streaking over opposite sides of the horizon at some forty kilometers per second. The laser vaporized the first one with no trouble, but the second got within eight klicks of the bunker before it was hit.

We were coming back from maneuvers, about a klick away from the bunker. I wouldn't have seen it happen if I hadn't been looking directly at the bunker the moment of the attack.

The second missile sent a shower of molten debris straight toward the bunker. Eleven pieces hit, and, as we later reconstructed it, this is what happened:

The first casualty was Maejima, so well-loved Maejima, inside the bunker, who was hit in the back and the head and died instantly. With the drop in pressure, the LSU went into high gear. Friedman was standing in front of the main airco outlet and was blown into the opposite wall hard enough to knock him unconscious; he died of decompression before the others could get him to his suit.

Everybody else managed to stagger through the gale and get into their suits, but Garcia's suit had been holed and didn't do him any good.

By the time we got there, they had turned off the LSU and were welding up the holes in the wall. One man was trying to scrape up the recognizable mess that had been Maejima. I could hear him sobbing and retching. They had already taken Garcia and Friedman outside for burial. The captain took over the repair detail from Potter. Sergeant Cortez led the sobbing man over to a corner and came back to work on cleaning up Maejima's remains, alone. He didn't order anybody to help and nobody volunteered.

X

As a graduation exercise, we were unceremoniously stuffed into a ship—*Earth's Hope,* the same one we rode to Charon—and bundled off to Stargate at a little more than one gee.

The trip seemed endless, about six months subjective time, and boring, but not as hard on the carcass as going to Charon had been. Captain Stott made us review our training orally, day by day, and we did exercises every day until we were worn to a collective frazzle.

Stargate 1 was like Charon's darkside, only more so. The base on Stargate 1 was smaller than Miami base—only a little bigger than the one we constructed on darkside—and we were due to lay over a week to help expand the facilities. The crew there was very glad to see us, especially the two females, who looked a little worn around the edges.

We all crowded into the small dining hall, where Submajor Williamson, the man in charge of Stargate 1, gave us some disconcerting news:

"Everybody get comfortable. Get off the tables, though, there's plenty of floor.

"I have some idea of what you just went through, training on Charon. I won't say it's all been wasted. But where you're headed, things will be quite different. Warmer."

He paused to let that soak in.

"Aleph Aurigae, the first collapsar ever detected, revolves around the normal star Epsilon Aurigae in a twenty-seven-year orbit. The enemy has a base of operations, not on a regular portal planet of Aleph, but on a planet in orbit around Epsilon. We don't know much about the planet, just that it goes around Epsilon once every 745 days, is about three-fourths the size of Earth, and has an albedo of 0.8, meaning it's probably covered with clouds. We can't say precisely how hot it will be, but judging from its distance from Epsilon, it's probably rather hotter than Earth. Of course, we don't know whether you'll be working ... fighting on lightside or darkside, equator or poles. It's highly unlikely that the atmosphere will be breathable—at any rate, you'll stay inside your suits.

"Now you know exactly as much about where you're going as I do. Questions?"

"Sir," Stein drawled, "now we know where we're goin' ... anybody know what we're goin' to do when we get there?"

Williamson shrugged. "That's up to your captain—and your sergeant, and the captain of *Earth's Hope,* and *Hope's* logistic computer. We just don't have enough data yet to project a course of action for you. It may be a long and bloody battle; it may be just a case of walking in to pick up the pieces. Conceivably, the Taurans might want to make a peace offer"—Cortez snorted—"in which case you would simply be part of our muscle, our bargaining power." He looked at Cortez mildly. "No one can say for sure."

The orgy that night was amusing, but it was like trying to sleep in the middle of a raucous beach party. The only area big enough to sleep all of us was the dining hall; they draped a few bedsheets here and there for privacy, then unleashed Stargate's eighteen sex-starved men on our women, compliant and promiscuous by military custom (and law), but desiring nothing so much as sleep on solid ground.

The eighteen men acted as if they were compelled to try as many permutations as possible, and their performance was impressive (in a strictly quantitative sense, that is). Those of us who were keeping count led a cheering section for some of the more gifted members. I think that's the right word.

The next morning—and every other morning we were on Stargate 1—we staggered out of bed and into our suits, to go outside and work on the "new wing." Eventually, Stargate would be tactical and logistic headquarters for the war, with thousands of permanent personnel, guarded by half a dozen heavy cruisers in *Hope*'s class. When we started, it was two shacks and twenty people; when we left, it was four shacks and twenty people. The work was hardly work at all, compared to darkside, since we had plenty of light and got sixteen hours inside for every eight hours' work. And no drone attack for a final exam.

When we shuttled back up to the *Hope,* nobody was too happy about leaving (though some of the more popular females declared it'd be good to get some rest). Stargate was the last easy, safe assignment we'd have before taking up arms against the Taurans. And as Williamson had pointed out the first day, there was no way of predicting what *that* would be like.

Most of us didn't feel too enthusiastic about making a collapsar jump, either. We'd been assured that we wouldn't even feel it happen, just free fall all the way.

I wasn't convinced. As a physics student, I'd had the usual courses in general relativity and theories of gravitation. We only had a little direct data at that time—Stargate was discovered when I was in grade school—but the mathematical model seemed clear enough.

The collapsar Stargate was a perfect sphere about three kilometers in radius. It was suspended forever in a state of gravitational collapse that should have meant its surface was dropping toward its center at nearly the speed of light. Relativity propped it up, at least gave it the illusion of being there... the way all reality becomes illusory and observer-oriented when you study general relativity. Or Buddhism. Or get drafted.

At any rate, there would be a theoretical point in space-time when one end of our ship was just above the surface of the collapsar, and the other end was a kilometer away (in our frame of reference). In any sane universe, this would set up tidal stresses and tear the ship apart, and we would be just another million kilograms of degenerate matter on a theoretical surface, rushing headlong to nowhere for the rest of eternity or dropping to the center in the next trillionth of a second. You pays your money and you takes your frame of reference.

But they were right. We blasted away from Stargate 1, made a few course corrections and then just dropped, for about an hour.

Then a bell rang and we sank into our cushions under a steady two gravities of deceleration. We were in enemy territory.

XI

We'd been decelerating at two gravities for almost nine days when the battle began. Lying on our couches being miserable, all we felt were two soft bumps, missiles being released. Some eight hours later, the squawkbox crackled: "Attention, all crew. This is the captain." Quinsana, the pilot, was only a lieutenant, but was allowed to call himself captain aboard the vessel, where he outranked all of us, even Captain Stott. "You grunts in the cargo hold can listen, too.

"We just engaged the enemy with two fifty-bevaton tachyon missiles and have destroyed both the enemy vessel and another object which it had launched approximately three microseconds before.

"The enemy has been trying to overtake us for the past 179 hours, ship time. At the time of the engagement, the enemy was moving at a little over half the speed of light, relative to Aleph, and was only about thirty AUs from *Earth's Hope*. It was moving at .47c relative to us, and thus we would have been coincident in space-time"— rammed!—"in a little more than nine hours. The missiles were launched at 0719 ship's time, and destroyed the enemy at 1540, both tachyon bombs detonating within a thousand klicks of the enemy objects."

The two missiles were a type whose propulsion system was itself only a barely controlled tachyon bomb. They accelerated at a constant rate of one hundred gees, and were traveling at a relativistic speed by the time the nearby mass of the enemy ship detonated them.

"We expect no further interference from enemy vessels. Our velocity with respect to Aleph will be zero in another five hours; we will then begin to journey back. The return will take twenty-seven days." General moans and dejected cussing. Everybody knew all that already, of course; but we didn't care to be reminded of it.

So after another month of logy calisthenics and drill, at a constant two gravities, we got our first look at the planet we were going to attack. Invaders from outer space, yes sir.

It was a blinding white crescent waiting for us two AUs out from Epsilon. The captain had pinned down the location of the enemy base from fifty AUs out, and we had jockeyed in on a wide arc, keeping the bulk of the planet between them and us. That didn't mean we were sneaking up on them—quite the contrary; they launched three abortive attacks—but it put us in a stronger defensive position. Until we had to go to the surface, that is. Then only the ship and its Star Fleet crew would be reasonably safe.

Since the planet rotated rather slowly—once every ten and one-half days—a "stationary" orbit for the ship had to be 150,000 klicks out. This made the people in the ship feel quite secure, with 6,000 miles of rock and 90,000 miles of space between them and the enemy. But it meant a whole second's time lag in communication between us on the ground and the ship's battle computer. A person could get awful dead while that neutrino pulse crawled up and back.

Our vague orders were to attack the base and gain control, while damaging a minimum of enemy equipment. We were to take at least one enemy alive. We were under no circumstances to allow ourselves to be taken alive, however. And the decision wasn't up to us; one special pulse from the battle computer, and that speck of plutonium in your power plant would fiss with all of .01% efficiency, and you'd be nothing but rapidly expanding, very hot plasma.

They strapped us into six scoutships—one platoon of twelve people in each—and we blasted away from *Earth's Hope* at eight gees. Each scoutship was supposed to follow its own carefully random path to our rendezvous point, 108 klicks from the base. Fourteen drone ships were launched at the same time, to confound the enemy's antispacecraft system.

The landing went off almost perfectly. One ship suffered minor damage, a near miss boiling away some of the ablative material on one side of the hull, but it'd still be able to make it and return, keeping its speed down while in the atmosphere.

We zigged and zagged and wound up first ship at the rendezvous point. There was only one trouble. It was under four kilometers of water.

I could almost hear that machine, 90,000 miles away, grinding its mental gears, adding this new bit of data. We proceeded just as if we were landing on solid ground: braking rockets, falling, skids out, hit the water, skip, hit the water, skip, hit the water, sink.

It would have made sense to go ahead and land on the bottom— we were streamlined, after all, and water is just another fluid—but the hull wasn't strong enough to hold up a four-kilometer column of water. Sergeant Cortez was in the scoutship with us.

"Sarge, tell that computer to *do* something! We're gonna get—"

"Oh, shut up, Mandella. Trust in th' lord." "Lord" was definitely lower-case when Cortez said it.

There was a loud bubbly sigh, then another, and a slight increase in pressure on my back that meant the ship was rising. "Flotation bags?" Cortez didn't deign to answer, or didn't know.

That was it. We rose to within ten or fifteen meters of the surface and stopped, suspended there. Through the port I could see the surface above, shimmering like a mirror of hammered silver. I wondered what it would be like to be a fish and have a definite roof over your world.

I watched another ship splash in. It made a great cloud of bubbles and turbulence, then fell—slightly tail-first—for a short distance before large bags popped out under each delta wing. Then it bobbed up to about our level and stayed.

"This is Captain Stott. Now listen carefully. There is a beach some twenty-eight klicks from your present position, in the direction of the enemy. You will be proceeding to this beach by scoutship and from there will mount your assault on the Tauran position." That was *some* improvement; we'd only have to walk eighty klicks.

We deflated the bags, blasted to the surface and flew in a slow, spread-out formation to the beach. It took several minutes. As the ship scraped to a halt, I could hear pumps humming, making the cabin pressure equal to the air pressure outside. Before it had quite stopped moving, the escape slot beside my couch slid open. 1 rolled out onto the wing of the craft and jumped to the ground. Ten seconds to find cover—I sprinted across loose gravel to the "treeline," a twisty bramble of tall sparse bluish-green shrubs. I dove into the briar patch and turned to watch the ships leave. The drones that were left rose slowly to about a hundred meters, then took off in all directions with a bone-jarring roar. The real scoutships slid slowly back into the water. Maybe that was a good idea.

It wasn't a terribly attractive world but certainly would be easier to get around in than the cryogenic nightmare we were trained for. The sky was a uniform dull silver brightness that merged with the mist over the ocean so completely it was impossible to tell where water ended and air began. Small wavelets licked at the black gravel shore, much too slow and graceful in the three-quarters Earth-normal gravity. Even from fifty meters away, the rattle of billions of pebbles rolling with the tide was loud in my ears.

The air temperature was 79 degrees Centigrade, not quite hot enough for the sea to boil, even though the air pressure was low compared to Earth's. Wisps of steam drifted quickly upward from the line where water met land. I wondered how long a man would survive exposed here without a suit. Would the heat or the low oxygen (partial pressure one-eighth Earth normal) kill him first? Or was there some deadly microorganism that would beat them both? ...

"This is Cortez. Everybody come over and assemble on me." He was standing on the beach a little to the left of me, waving his hand in a circle over his head. I walked toward him through the shrubs. They were brittle, unsubstantial, seemed paradoxically dried-out in the steamy air. They wouldn't offer much in the way of cover.

"We'll be advancing on a heading .05 radians east of north. I want Platoon One to take point. Two and Three follow about twenty meters behind, to the left and right. Seven, command platoon, is in the middle, twenty meters behind Two and Three. Five and Six, bring up the rear, in a semicircular closed flank. Everybody straight?" Sure, we could do that "arrowhead" maneuver in our sleep. "Okay, let's move out."

I was in Platoon Seven, the "command group." Captain Stott put me there not because I was expected to give any commands, but because of my training in physics.

The command group was supposedly the safest place, buffered by six platoons: people were assigned to it because there was some tactical reason for them to survive at least a little longer than the rest.

Cortez was there to give orders. Chavez was there to correct suit malfunctions. The senior medic, Doc Wilson (the only medic who actually had an M.D.), was there, and so was Theodopolis, the radio engineer, our link with the captain, who had elected to stay in orbit.

The rest of us were assigned to the command group by dint of special training or aptitude that wouldn't normally be considered of a "tactical" nature. Facing a totally unknown enemy, there was no way of telling what might prove important. Thus I was there because I was the closest the company had to a physicist. Rogers was biology. Tate was chemistry. Ho could crank out a perfect score on the Rhine extrasensory perception test, every time. Bohrs was a polyglot, able to speak twenty-one languages fluently, idiomatically. Petrov's talent was that he had tested out to have not one molecule of xenophobia in his psyche. Keating was a skilled acrobat. Debby Hollister—"Lucky" Hollister—showed a remarkable aptitude for making money, and also had a consistently high Rhine potential.

XII

When we first set out, we were using the "jungle" camouflage combination on our suits. But what passed for jungle in these anemic tropics was too sparse; we looked like a band of conspicuous harlequins trooping through the woods. Cortez had us switch to black, but that was just as bad, as the light of Epsilon came evenly from all parts of the sky, and there were no shadows except ours. We finally settled on the dun-colored desert camouflage.

The nature of the countryside changed slowly as we walked north, away from the sea. The thorned stalks—I guess you could call them trees—came in fewer numbers but were bigger around and less brittle; at the base of each was a tangled mass of vine with the same blue-green color, which spread out in a flattened cone some ten meters in diameter. There was a delicate green flower the size of a man's head near the top of each tree.

Grass began to appear some five klicks from the sea. It seemed to respect the trees' "property rights," leaving a strip of bare earth around each cone of vine. At the edge of such a clearing, it would grow as timid blue-green stubble, then, moving away from the tree, would get thicker and taller until it reached shoulder high in some places, where the separation between two trees was unusually large. The grass was a lighter, greener shade than the trees and vines. We changed the color of our suits to the bright green we had used for maximum visibility on Charon. Keeping to the thickest part of the grass, we were fairly inconspicuous.

We covered over twenty klicks each day, buoyant after months under two gees. Until the second day, the only form of animal life we saw was a kind of black worm, finger-sized, with hundreds of cilium legs like the bristles of a brush. Rogers said that there obviously had to be some larger creature around, or there would be no reason for the trees to have thorns. So we were doubly on guard, expecting trouble both from the Taurans and the unidentified "large creature."

Potter's second platoon was on point; the general freak was reserved for her, since her platoon would likely be the first to spot any trouble.

"Sarge, this is Potter," we all heard. "Movement ahead."

"Get down, then!"

"We are. Don't think they see us."

"First platoon, go up to the right of point. Keep down. Fourth, get up to the left. Tell me when you get in position. Sixth platoon, stay back and guard the rear. Fifth and third, close with the command group."

Two dozen people whispered out of the grass to join us. Cortez must have heard from the fourth platoon.

"Good. How about you, first? . . . Okay, fine. How many are there?"

"Eight we can see." Potter's voice.

"Good. When I give the word, open fire. Shoot to kill."

"Sarge . . . they're just animals."

"Potter—if you've known all this time what a Tauran looks like, you should've told us. Shoot to kill."

"But we need . . ."

"We need a prisoner, but we don't need to escort him forty klicks to his home base and keep an eye on him while we fight. Clear?"

"Yes. Sergeant."

"Okay. Seventh, all you brains and weirds, we're going up and watch. Fifth and third, come along to guard."

We crawled through the meter-high grass to where the second platoon had stretched out in a firing line.

"I don't see anything," Cortez said.

"Ahead and just to the left. Dark green."

They were only a shade darker than the grass. But after you saw the first one, you could see them all, moving slowly around some thirty meters ahead.

"Fire!" Cortez fired first; then twelve streaks of crimson leaped out and the grass wilted black, disappeared, and the creatures convulsed and died trying to scatter.

"Hold fire, hold it!" Cortez stood up. "We want to have something left—second platoon, follow me." He strode out toward the smoldering corpses, laser-finger pointed out front, obscene divining rod pulling him toward the carnage.... I felt my gorge rising and knew that all the lurid training tapes, all the horrible deaths in training accidents, hadn't prepared me for this sudden reality...that I had a magic wand that I could point at a life and make it a smoking piece of half-raw meat; I wasn't a soldier nor ever wanted to be one nor ever would want—

"Okay, seventh, come on up." While we were walking toward them, one of the creatures moved, a tiny shudder, and Cortez flicked the beam of his laser over it with an almost negligent gesture. It made a hand-deep gash across the creature's middle. It died, like the others, without emitting a sound.

They were not quite as tall as humans, but wider in girth. They were covered with dark green, almost black, fur—white curls where the laser had singed. They appeared to have three legs and an arm. The only ornament to their shaggy heads was a mouth, a wet black orifice filled with flat black teeth. They were thoroughly repulsive, but their worst feature was not a difference from human beings, but a similarity.... Whenever the laser had opened a body cavity, milk-white glistening veined globes and coils of organs spilled out, and their blood was dark clotting red.

"Rogers, take a look. Taurans or not?"

Rogers knelt by one of the disemboweled creatures and opened a flat plastic box, filled with glittering dissecting tools. She selected a scalpel. "One way we might be able to find out." Doc Wilson watched over her shoulder as she methodically slit the membrane covering several organs.

"Here," She held up a blackish fibrous mass between two fingers, a parody of daintiness through all that armor.

"So?"

"It's grass, Sergeant. If the Taurans can eat the grass and breathe the air, they certainly found a planet remarkably like their home." She tossed it away. "They're animals, Sergeant, just fucken animals."

"I don't know," Doc Wilson said. "Just because they walk around on all fours, threes maybe, and eat grass..."

"Well, let's check out the brain." She found one that had been hit in the head and scraped the superficial black char from the wound. "Look at that."

It was almost solid bone. She tugged and ruffled the hair all over the head of another one. "What the hell does it use for sensory organs? No eyes, or ears, or..." She stood up.

"Nothing in that fucken head but a mouth and ten centimeters of skull. To protect nothing, not a fucken thing."

"If I could shrug, I'd shrug," the doctor said. "It doesn't prove anything—a brain doesn't have to look like a mushy walnut and it doesn't have to be in the head. Maybe that skull isn't bone, maybe *that's* the brain, some crystal lattice..."

"Yeah, but the fucken stomach's in the right place, and if those aren't intestines I'll eat—"

"Look," Cortez said, "this is real interesting, but all we need to know is whether that thing's dangerous, then we've gotta move on; we don't have all—"

"They aren't dangerous," Rogers began. "They don't—"

"Medic! DOC!" Somebody back at the firing line was waving his arms. Doc sprinted back to him, the rest of us following.

"What's wrong?" He had reached back and unclipped his medical kit on the run.

"It's Ho. She's out."

Doc swung open the door on Ho's biomedical monitor. He didn't have to look far. "She's dead."

"Dead?" Cortez said. "What the hell—"

"Just a minute." Doc plugged a jack into the monitor and fiddled with some dials on his kit. "Everybody's biomed readout is stored for twelve hours. I'm running it backwards, should be able to—there!"

"What?"

"Four and a half minutes ago—must have been when you opened fire—Jesus!"

"Well?"

"Massive cerebral hemorrhage. No ..." He watched the dials. "No ... warning, no indications of anything out of the ordinary; blood pressure up, pulse up, but normal under the circumstances ... nothing to ... indicate—" He reached down and popped her suit. Her fine oriental features were distorted in a horrible grimace, both gums showing. Sticky fluid ran from under her collapsed eyelids, and a trickle of blood still dripped from each ear. Doc Wilson closed the suit back up.

"I've never seen anything like it. It's as if a bomb went off in her skull."

"Oh fuck," Rogers said, "she was Rhine-sensitive, wasn't she?"

"That's right." Cortez sounded thoughtful. "All right, everybody listen up. Platoon leaders, check your platoons and see if anybody's missing, or hurt. Anybody else in seventh?"

"I ... I've got a splitting headache, Sarge," Lucky said.

Four others had bad headaches. One of them affirmed that he was slightly Rhine-sensitive. The others didn't know.

"Cortez, I think it's obvious," Doc Wilson said, "that we should give these ... monsters wide berth, especially shouldn't harm any more of them. Not with five people susceptible to whatever apparently killed Ho."

"Of course, God damn it. I don't need anybody to tell me that. We'd better get moving. I just filled the captain in on what happened; he agrees that we'd better get as far away from here as we can before we stop for the night.

"Let's get back in formation and continue on the same bearing. Fifth platoon, take over point; second, come back to the rear. Everybody else, same as before."

"What about Ho?" Lucky asked.

"She'll be taken care of. From the ship."

After we'd gone half a klick, there was a flash and rolling thunder.

Where Ho had been came a wispy luminous mushroom cloud boiling up to disappear against the gray sky.

XIII

We stopped for the "night"—actually, the sun wouldn't set for another seventy hours—atop a slight rise some ten klicks from where we had killed the aliens. But they weren't aliens, I had to remind myself—*we* were.

Two platoons deployed in a ring around the rest of us, and we flopped down exhausted. Everybody was allowed four hours' sleep and had two hours' guard duty.

Potter came over and sat next to me. I chinned her frequency.

"Hi, Marygay."

"Oh, William," her voice over the radio was hoarse and cracking. "God, it's so horrible."

"It's over now—"

"I killed one of them, the first instant, I shot it right in the, in the…"

I put my hand on her knee. The contact made a plastic click and I jerked it back, visions of machines embracing, copulating. "Don't feel singled out, Marygay; whatever guilt there is, is … belongs evenly to all of us … but a triple portion for Cor—"

"You privates quit jawin' and get some sleep. You both pull guard in two hours."

"Okay, Sarge." Her voice was so sad and tired I couldn't bear it. I felt if I could only touch her, I could drain off the sadness like ground wire draining current, but we were each trapped in our own plastic world—

"G'night, William."

"Night." It's almost impossible to get sexually excited inside a suit, with the relief tube and all the silver chloride sensors poking you, but somehow this was my body's response to the emotional impotence, maybe remembering more pleasant sleeps with Marygay, maybe feeling that in the midst of all this death, personal death could be soon, cranking up the procreative derrick for one last try … lovely thoughts like this. I fell asleep and dreamed that I was a machine, mimicking the functions of life, creaking and clanking my clumsy way through the world, people too polite to say anything but giggling behind my back, and the little man who sat inside my head pulling the levers and clutches and watching the dials, he was hopelessly mad and was storing up hurts for the day—

"Mandella—wake up, goddammit, your shift!"

I shuffled over to my place on the perimeter to watch for God knows what . . . but I was so weary I couldn't keep my eyes open. Finally I tongued a stimtab, knowing I'd pay for it later.

For over an hour I sat there, scanning my sector left, right, near, far, the scene never changing, not even a breath of wind to stir the grass.

Then suddenly the grass parted and one of the three-legged creatures was right in front of me. I raised my finger but didn't squeeze.

"Movement!"

"Movement!"

"Jesus Chri—there's one right—"

"HOLD YOUR FIRE! F'shit's sake don't shoot!"

"Movement."

"Movement." I looked left and right, and as far as I could see, every perimeter guard had one of the blind, dumb creatures standing right in front of him.

Maybe the drug I'd taken to stay awake made me more sensitive to whatever they did. My scalp crawled and I felt a formless *thing* in my mind, the feeling you get when somebody has said something and you didn't quite hear it, want to respond, but the opportunity to ask him to repeat it is gone.

The creature sat back on its haunches, leaning forward on the one front leg. Big green bear with a withered arm. Its power threaded through my mind, spiderwebs, echo of night terrors, trying to communicate, trying to destroy me, I couldn't know.

"All right, everybody on the perimeter, fall back, slow. Don't make any quick gestures. . . . Anybody got a headache or anything?"

"Sergeant, this is Hollister." Lucky.

"They're trying to say something . . . I can almost . . . no, just . . ."

"All I can get is that they think we're, think we're . . . well, *funny.* They're not afraid."

"You mean the one in front of you isn't—"

"No, the feeling comes from all of them, they're all thinking the same thing. Don't ask me how I know, I just do."

"Maybe they thought it was funny, what they did to Ho."

"Maybe. I don't feel they're dangerous. Just curious about us."

"Sergeant, this is Bohrs."

"Yeah."

"The Taurans've been here at least a year—maybe they've learned how to communicate with these . . . overgrown teddybears. They might be spying on us, might be sending back—"

"I don't think they'd show themselves if that were the case," Lucky said. "They can obviously hide from us pretty well when they want to."

"Anyhow," Cortez said, "if they're spies, the damage has been done. Don't think it'd be smart to take any action against them. I know you'd all like to see 'em dead for what they did to Ho, so would I, but we'd better be careful."

I didn't want to see them dead, but I'd just as soon not have seen them in any condition. I was walking backwards slowly, toward the middle of camp. The creature didn't seem disposed to follow. Maybe he just knew we were surrounded. He was pulling up grass with his arm and munching.

"Okay, all of you platoon leaders, wake everybody up, get a roll count. Let me know if anybody's been hurt. Tell your people we're moving out in one minute."

I don't know what Cortez had expected, but of course the creatures followed right along. They didn't keep us surrounded; just had twenty or thirty following us all the time. Not the same ones, either. Individuals would saunter away, new ones would join the parade. It was pretty obvious *they* weren't going to tire out.

We were each allowed one stimtab. Without it, no one could have marched an hour. A second pill would have been welcome after the edge started to wear off, but the mathematics of the situation forbade it; we were still thirty klicks from the enemy base, fifteen hours' marching at the least. And though you could stay awake and energetic for a hundred hours on the tabs, aberrations of judgment and perception snowballed after the second one, until *in extremis* the most bizarre hallucinations would be taken at face value, and a person could fidget for hours deciding whether to have breakfast.

Under artificial stimulation, the company traveled with great energy for the first six hours, was slowing by the seventh, and ground to an exhausted halt after nine hours and nineteen kilometers. The teddybears had never lost sight of us and, according to Lucky, had never stopped "broadcasting." Cortez's decision was that we would stop for seven hours, each platoon taking one hour of perimeter guard. I was never so glad to have been in the seventh platoon, as we stood guard the last shift and thus were able to get six hours of uninterrupted sleep.

In the few moments I lay awake after finally lying down, the thought came to me that the next time I closed my eyes could well be the last. And partly because of the drug hangover, mostly because of the past day's horrors, I found that I really didn't give a shit.

XIV

Our first contact with the Taurans came during my shift.

The teddybears were still there when I woke up and replaced Doc Jones on guard. They'd gone back to their original formation, one in front of each guard position. The one who was waiting for me seemed a little larger than normal, but otherwise looked just like all the others. All the grass had been cropped where he was sitting, so he occasionally made forays to the left or right. But he always returned to sit right in front of me, you would say *staring* if he had had anything to stare with.

We had been facing each other for about fifteen minutes when Cortez's voice rumbled:

"Awright everybody, wake up and get hid!"

I followed instinct and flopped to the ground and rolled into a tall stand of grass.

"Enemy vessel overhead." His voice was almost laconic.

Strictly speaking, it wasn't really overhead, but rather passing somewhat east of us. It was moving slowly, maybe a hundred klicks per hour, and looked like a broomstick surrounded by a dirty soap bubble. The creature riding it was a little more human-looking than the teddybears, but still no prize. I cranked my image amplifier up to forty log two for a closer look.

He had two arms and two legs, but his waist was so small you could encompass it with both hands. Under the tiny waist was a large horseshoe-shaped pelvic structure nearly a meter wide, from which dangled two long skinny legs with no apparent knee joint. Above that waist his body swelled out again, to a chest no smaller than the huge pelvis. His arms looked surprisingly human, except that they were too long and undermuscled. There were too many fingers on his hands. Shoulderless, neckless. His head was a nightmarish growth that swelled like a goiter from his massive chest. Two eyes that looked like clusters of fish eggs, a bundle of tassles instead of a nose, and a rigidly open hole that might have been a mouth sitting low down where his Adam's apple should have been. Evidently the soap bubble contained an amenable environment, as he was wearing absolutely nothing except his ridged hide, that looked like skin submerged too long in hot water, then dyed a pale orange. "He" had no external genitalia, but nothing that might hint of mammary glands. So we opted for the male pronoun by default.

Obviously, he either didn't see us or thought we were part of the herd of teddybears. He never looked back at us, but just continued in the same direction we were headed, .05 rad east of north.

"Might as well go back to sleep now, if you can sleep after looking at *that* thing. We move out at 0435." Forty minutes.

Because of the planet's opaque cloud cover, there had been no way to tell, from space, what the enemy base looked like or how big it was. We only knew its position, the same way we knew the position the scoutships were supposed to land on. So it too could easily have been underwater, or underground.

But some of the drones were reconnaissance ships as well as decoys: and in their mock attacks on the base, one managed to get close enough to take a picture. Captain Stott beamed down a diagram of the place to Cortez—the only one with a visor in his suit—when we were five klicks from the base's radio position. We stopped and he called all the platoon leaders in with the seventh platoon to confer. Two teddybears loped in, too. We tried to ignore them.

"Okay, the captain sent down some pictures of our objective. I'm going to draw a map; you platoon leaders copy." They took pads and styli out of their leg pockets, while Cortez unrolled a large plastic mat. He gave it a shake to randomize any residual charge, and turned on his stylus.

"Now, we're coming from this direction." He put an arrow at the bottom of the sheet. "First thing we'll hit is this row of huts, probably billets or bunkers, but who the hell knows. . . . Our initial objective is to destroy these buildings—the whole base is on a flat plain; there's no way we could really sneak by them."

"Potter here. Why can't we jump over them?"

"Yeah, we could do that, and wind up completely surrounded, cut to ribbons. We take the buildings.

"After we do that . . . all I can say is that we'll have to think on our feet. From the aerial reconnaissance, we can figure out the function of only a couple of buildings—and that stinks. We might wind up wasting a lot of time demolishing the equivalent of an enlisted-men's bar, ignoring a huge logistic computer because it looks like . . . a garbage dump or something."

"Mandella here," I said. "Isn't there a spaceport of some kind— seems to me we ought to . . ."

"I'll *get* to that, damn it. There's a ring of these huts all around the camp, so we've got to break through somewhere. This place'll be closest, less chance of giving away our position before we attack.

"There's nothing in the whole place that actually looks like a weapon. That doesn't mean anything, though; you could hide a bevawatt laser in each of those huts.

"Now, about five hundred meters from the huts, in the middle of the base, we'll come to this big flower-shaped structure." Cortez drew a large symmetrical shape that looked like the outline of a flower with seven petals. "What the hell this is, your guess is as good as mine. There's only one of them, though, so we don't damage it any more than we have to. Which means . . . we blast it to splinters if I think it's dangerous.

"Now, as far as your spaceport, Mandella, is concerned—there just isn't one. Nothing.

"That cruiser the *Hope* caulked had probably been left in orbit, like ours has to be. If they have any equivalent of a scoutship, or drone missiles, they're either not kept here or they're well hidden."

"Bohrs here. Then what did they attack with, while we were coming down from orbit?"

"I wish we knew, Private.

"Obviously, we don't have any way of estimating their numbers, not directly. Recon pictures failed to show a single Tauran on the grounds of the base. Meaning nothing, because it *is* an alien environment. Indirectly, though . . . we count the number of broomsticks, those flying things.

"There are fifty-one huts, and each has at most one broomstick. Four don't have any parked outside, but we located three at various other parts of the base. Maybe this indicates that there are fifty-one Taurans, one of whom was outside the base when the picture was taken."

"Keating here. Or fifty-one officers."

"That's right—maybe fifty thousand infantrymen stacked in one of these buildings. No way to tell. Maybe ten Taurans, each with five broomsticks, to use according to his mood.

"We've got one thing in our favor, and that's communications. They evidently use a frequency modulation of megahertz electromagnetic radiation."

"Radio!"

"That's right, whoever you are. Identify yourself when you speak. So it's quite possible that they can't detect our phased-neutrino communications. Also, just prior to the attack, the *Hope* is going to deliver a nice dirty fission bomb; detonate it in the upper atmosphere right over the base. That'll restrict them to line-of-sight communications for some time; even those will be full of static."

"Why don't . . . Tate here . . . why don't they just drop the bomb right in their laps? Save us a lot of—"

"That doesn't even deserve an answer, Private. But the answer is, they might. And you better hope they don't. If they caulk the base, it'll be for the safety of the *Hope*. *After* we've attacked, and probably before we're far enough away for it to make much difference.

"We keep that from happening by doing a good job. We have to reduce the base to where it can no longer function; at the same time, leave as much intact as possible. And take one prisoner."

"Potter here. You mean, at least one prisoner."

"I mean what I say. One only. Potter . . . you're relieved of your platoon. Send Chavez up."

"All right, Sergeant." The relief in her voice was unmistakable.

Cortez continued with his map and instructions. There was one other building whose function was pretty obvious; it had a large steerable dish antenna on top. We were to destroy it as soon as the grenadiers got in range.

The attack plan was very loose. Our signal to begin would be the flash of the fission bomb. At the same time, several drones would converge on the base, so we could see what their antispacecraft defenses were. We would try to reduce the effectiveness of those defenses without destroying them completely.

Immediately after the bomb and the drones, the grenadiers would vaporize a line of seven huts. Everybody would break through the hole into the base... and what would happen after that was anybody's guess.

Ideally, we'd sweep from that end of the base to the other, destroying certain targets, caulking all but one Tauran. But that was unlikely to happen, as it depended on the Taurans' offering very little resistance.

On the other hand, if the Taurans showed obvious superiority from the beginning, Cortez would give the order to scatter. Everybody had a different compass bearing for retreat—we'd blossom out in all directions, the survivors to rendezvous in a valley some forty klicks east of the base. Then we'd see about a return engagement, after the *Hope* softened the base up a bit.

"One last thing," Cortez rasped. "Maybe some of you feel the way Potter evidently does, maybe some of your men feel that way... that we ought to go easy, not make this so much of a bloodbath. Mercy is a luxury, a weakness we can't afford to indulge in at this stage of the war. *All* we know about the enemy is that they have killed seven hundred and ninety-eight humans. They haven't shown any restraint in attacking our cruisers, and it'd be foolish to expect any this time, this first ground action.

"*They* are responsible for the lives of all of your comrades who died in training, and for Ho, and for all the others who are surely going to die today. I can't *understand* anybody who wants to spare them. But that doesn't make any difference. You have your orders and, what the hell, you might as well know, all of you have a post-hypnotic suggestion that I will trigger by a phrase, just before the battle. It will make your job easier."

"Sergeant..."

"Shut up. We're short on time; get back to your platoons and brief them. We move out in five minutes."

The platoon leaders returned to their men, leaving Cortez and ten of us—plus three teddybears, milling around, getting in the way.

XV

We took the last five klicks very carefully, sticking to the highest grass, running across occasional clearings. When we were five hundred meters from where the base was supposed to be, Cortez took the third platoon forward to scout, while the rest of us laid low.

Cortez's voice came over the general freak: "Looks pretty much like we expected. Advance in a file, crawling. When you get to the third platoon, follow your squad leader to the left or right."

We did that and wound up with a string of eighty-three people in a line roughly perpendicular to the direction of attack. We were pretty well hidden, except for the dozen or so teddybears that mooched along the line munching grass.

There was no sign of life inside the base. All of the buildings were windowless and a uniform shiny white. The huts that were our first objective were large featureless half-buried eggs some sixty meters apart. Cortez assigned one to each grenadier.

We were broken into three fire teams: team *A* consisted of Platoons Two, Four, and Six; team *B* was One, Three, and Five; the command platoon was team *C*.

"Less than a minute now—filters down!—when I say 'fire,' grenadiers, take out your targets. God help you if you miss."

There was a sound like a giant's belch, and a stream of five or six iridescent bubbles floated up from the flower-shaped building. They rose with increasing speed until they were almost out of sight, then shot off to the south, over our heads. The ground was suddenly bright, and for the first time in a long time, I saw my shadow, a long one pointed north. The bomb had gone off prematurely. I just had time to think that it didn't make too much difference; it'd still make alphabet soup out of their communications—

"Drones!" A ship came screaming in just above tree level, and a bubble was in the air to meet it. When they contacted, the bubble popped and the drone exploded into a million tiny fragments. Another one came from the opposite side and suffered the same fate.

"FIRE!" Seven bright glares of 500-microton grenades and a sustained concussion that surely would have killed an unprotected man.

"Filters up." Gray haze of smoke and dust. Clods of dirt falling with a sound like heavy raindrops.

"Listen up:

> *Scots, wha hae wi' Wallace bled;*
> *Scots, wham Bruce has often led,*
> *Welcome to your gory bed,*
> *Or to victory!"*

I hardly heard him for trying to keep track of what was going on in my skull. I knew it was just post-hypnotic suggestion, even remembered the session in Missouri when they'd implanted it, but that didn't make it any less compelling. My mind reeled under the strong pseudo-memories: shaggy hulks that were Taurans (not at all what we now knew they looked like) boarding a colonists' vessel, eating babies while mothers watched in screaming terror (the colonists never took babies; they wouldn't stand the acceleration), then raping the women to death with huge veined purple members (ridiculous that they would feel desire for humans), holding the men down while they plucked flesh from their living bodies and gobbled it (as if they could assimilate the alien protein) . . . a hundred grisly details as sharply remembered as the events of a minute ago, ridiculously overdone and logically absurd. But while my conscious mind was rejecting the silliness, somewhere much deeper, down in that sleeping animal where we keep our real motives and morals, something was thirsting for alien blood, secure in the conviction that the noblest thing a man could do would be to die killing one of those horrible monsters. . . .

I knew it was all purest soyashit, and I hated the men who had taken such obscene liberties with my mind, but I could even *hear* my teeth grinding, feel my cheeks frozen in a spastic grin, bloodlust . . . A teddybear walked in front of me, looking dazed. I started to raise my laser-finger, but somebody beat me to it and the creature's head exploded in a cloud of gray splinters and blood.

Lucky groaned, half-whining, "Dirty . . . filthy fucken bastards." Lasers flared and crisscrossed, and all of the teddybears fell dead.

"*Watch* it, goddammit," Cortez screamed. "*Aim* those fucken things—they aren't toys!

"Team *A*, move out—into the craters to cover *B*."

Somebody was laughing and sobbing. "What the fuck is wrong with *you,* Petrov?" Strange to hear Cortez cussing.

I twisted around and saw Petrov, behind and to my left, lying in a shallow hole, digging frantically with both hands, crying and gurgling.

"Fuck," Cortez said. "Team *B!* Ten meters past the craters, get down in a line. Team *C*—into the craters with *A*."

I scrambled up and covered the hundred meters in twelve amplified strides. The craters were practically large enough to hide a scoutship, some ten meters in diameter. I jumped to the opposite side of the hole and landed next to a fellow named Chin. He didn't even look around when I landed, just kept scanning the base for signs of life.

"Team *A*—ten meters, past team *B*, down in line." Just as he finished, the building in front of us burped, and a salvo of the bubbles fanned out toward our lines. Most people saw it coming and got down, but Chin was just getting up to make his rush and stepped right into one.

It grazed the top of his helmet and disappeared with a faint pop. He took one step backwards and toppled over the edge of the crater, trailing an arc of blood and brains. Lifeless, spreadeagled, he slid halfway to the bottom, shoveling dirt into the perfectly symmetrical hole where the bubble had chewed indiscriminately through plastic, hair, skin, bone and brain.

"Everybody hold it. Platoon leaders, casualty report...check... check, check...check, check, check...check. We have three deaders. Wouldn't be *any* if you'd have kept low. So everybody grab dirt when you hear that thing go off. Team *A*, complete the rush."

They completed the maneuver without incident. "Okay. Team *C*, rush to where *B*...hold it! Down!"

Everybody was already hugging the ground. The bubbles slid by in a smooth arc about two meters off the ground. They went serenely over our heads and, except for one that made toothpicks out of a tree, disappeared in the distance.

"*B*, rush past *A* ten meters. *C*, take over *B*'s place. You *B* grenadiers, see if you can reach the Flower."

Two grenades tore up the ground thirty or forty meters from the structure. In a good imitation of panic, it started belching out a continuous stream of bubbles—still, none coming lower than two meters off the ground. We kept hunched down and continued to advance.

Suddenly, a seam appeared in the building and widened to the size of a large door. Taurans came swarming out.

"Grenadiers, hold your fire. *B* team, laser fire to the left and right—keep'm bunched up. *A* and *C*, rush down the center."

One Tauran died trying to run through a laser beam. The others stayed where they were.

In a suit, it's pretty awkward to run and keep your head down at the same time. You have to go from side to side, like a skater getting started; otherwise you'll be airborne. At least one person, somebody in *A* team, bounced too high and suffered the same fate as Chin.

I was feeling pretty fenced-in and trapped, with a wall of laser fire on each side and a low ceiling that meant death to touch. But in spite of myself, I felt happy, euphoric, finally getting the chance to kill some of those villainous baby-eaters. Knowing it was soyashit.

They weren't fighting back, except for the rather ineffective bubbles (obviously not designed as an antipersonnel weapon), and they didn't retreat back into the building, either. They milled around, about a hundred of them, and watched us get closer. A couple of grenades would caulk them all, but I guess Cortez was thinking about the prisoner.

"Okay, when I say 'go,' we're going to flank 'em. *B* team will hold fire. . . . Second and fourth platoons to the right, sixth and seventh to the left. *B* team will move forward in line to box them in.

"Go!" We peeled off to the left. As soon as the lasers stopped, the Taurans bolted, running in a group on a collision course with our flank.

"*A* team, down and fire! Don't shoot until you're sure of your aim—if you miss you might hit a friendly. And fer Chris' sake save me one!"

It was a horrifying sight, that herd of monsters bearing down on us. They were running in great leaps—the bubbles avoiding them— and they all looked like the one we saw earlier, riding the broomstick; naked except for an almost transparent sphere around their whole bodies, that moved along with them. The right flank started firing, picking off individuals in the rear of the pack.

Suddenly a laser flared through the Taurans from the other side, somebody missing his mark. There was a horrible scream, and I looked down the line to see someone—I think it was Perry—writhing on the ground, right hand over the smoldering stump of his left arm, seared off just below the elbow. Blood sprayed through his fingers, and the suit, its camouflage circuits scrambled, flickered black-white-jungle-desert-green-gray. I don't know how long I stared—long enough for the medic to run over and start giving aid—but when I looked up the Taurans were almost on top of me.

My first shot was wild and high, but it grazed the top of the leading Tauran's protective bubble. The bubble disappeared and the monster stumbled and fell to the ground, jerking spasmodically. Foam gushed out of his mouth-hole, first white, then streaked red. With one last jerk he became rigid and twisted backwards, almost to the shape of a horseshoe. His long scream, a high-pitched whistle, stopped just as his comrades trampled over him. I hated myself for smiling.

It was slaughter, even though our flank was outnumbered five to one. They kept coming without faltering, even when they had to climb over the drift of bodies and parts of bodies that piled up high, parallel to our flank. The ground between us was slick red with Tauran blood—all God's children got hemoglobin—and like the teddybears, their guts looked pretty much like guts to my untrained eye. My helmet reverberated with hysterical laughter while we slashed them to gory chunks, and I almost didn't hear Cortez:

"Hold your fire—I said HOLD IT, goddammit! *Catch* a couple of the bastards; they won't hurt you."

I stopped shooting and eventually so did everybody else. When the next Tauran jumped over the smoking pile of meat in front of me, I dove to try to tackle him around those spindly legs.

It was like hugging a big, slippery balloon. When I tried to drag him down, he popped out of my arms and kept running.

We managed to stop one of them by the simple expedient of piling half a dozen people on top of him. By that time the others had run through our line and were headed for the row of large cylindrical tanks that Cortez had said were probably for storage. A little door had opened in the base of each one.

"We've *got* our prisoner," Cortez shouted. *"Kill!"*

They were fifty meters away and running hard, difficult targets. Lasers slashed around them, bobbing high and low. One fell, sliced in two, but the others, about ten of them, kept going and were almost to the doors when the grenadiers started firing.

They were still loaded with 500-mike bombs, but a near miss wasn't enough—the concussion would just send them flying, unhurt in their bubbles.

"The buildings! Get the fucken buildings!" The grenadiers raised their aim and let fly, but the bombs only seemed to scorch the white outside of the structures until, by chance, one landed in a door. That split the building just as if it had a seam; the two halves popped away and a cloud of machinery flew into the air, accompanied by a huge pale flame that rolled up and disappeared in an instant. Then the others all concentrated on the doors, except for potshots at some of the Taurans, not so much to get them as to blow them away before they could get inside. They seemed awfully eager.

All this time, we were trying to get the Taurans with laser fire, while they weaved and bounced around trying to get into the structures. We moved in as close to them as we could without putting ourselves in danger from the grenade blasts, yet too far away for good aim.

Still, we were getting them one by one and managed to destroy four of the seven buildings. Then, when there were only two aliens left, a nearby grenade blast flung one of them to within a few meters of a door. He dove in and several grenadiers fired salvos after him, but they all fell short or detonated harmlessly on the side. Bombs were falling all around, making an awful racket, but the sound was suddenly drowned out by a great sigh, like a giant's intake of breath, and where the building had been was a thick cylindrical cloud of smoke, solid-looking, dwindling away into the stratosphere, straight as if laid down by a ruler. The other Tauran had been right at the base of the cylinder; I could see pieces of him flying. A second later, a shock wave hit us and I rolled helplessly, pinwheeling, to smash into the pile of Tauran bodies and roll beyond.

I picked myself up and panicked for a second when I saw there was blood all over my suit—when I realized it was only alien blood, I relaxed but felt unclean.

"*Catch* the bastard! Catch him!" In the confusion, the Tauran had gotten free and was running for the grass. One platoon was chasing after him, losing ground, but then all of *B* team ran over and cut him off. I jogged over to join in the fun.

There were four people on top of him, and a ring around them of about fifty people, watching the struggle.

"Spread out, dammit! There might be a thousand more of them waiting to get us in one place." We dispersed, grumbling. By unspoken agreement we were all sure that there were no more live Taurans on the face of the planet.

Cortez was walking toward the prisoner while I backed away. Suddenly the four men collapsed in a pile on top of the creature.... Even from my distance I could see the foam spouting from his mouth-hole. His bubble had popped. Suicide.

"Damn!" Cortez was right there. "Get off that bastard." The four men got off and Cortez used his laser to slice the monster into a dozen quivering chunks. Heartwarming sight.

"That's all right, though, we'll find another one—everybody! Back in the arrowhead formation. Combat assault, on the Flower."

Well, we assaulted the Flower, which had evidently run out of ammunition (it was still belching, but no bubbles), and it was empty. We scurried up ramps and through corridors, fingers at the ready, like kids playing soldier. There was nobody home.

The same lack of response at the antenna installation, the "Salami," and twenty other major buildings, as well as the forty-four perimeter huts still intact. So we had "captured" dozens of buildings, mostly of incomprehensible purpose, but failed in our main mission, capturing a Tauran for the xenologists to experiment with. Oh well, they could have all the bits and pieces they'd ever want. That was something.

After we'd combed every last square centimeter of the base, a scoutship came in with the real exploration crew, the scientists. Cortez said, "All right, snap out of it," and the hypnotic compulsion fell away.

At first it was pretty grim. A lot of the people, like Lucky and Marygay, almost went crazy with the memories of bloody murder multiplied a hundred times. Cortez ordered everybody to take a sed-tab, two for the ones most upset. I took two without being specifically ordered to do so.

Because it *was* murder, unadorned butchery—once we had the antispacecraft weapon doped out, we hadn't been in any danger. The Taurans hadn't seemed to have any conception of person-to-person fighting. We had just herded them up and slaughtered them, the first encounter between mankind and another intelligent species. Maybe it was the second encounter, counting the teddybears. What might have happened if we had sat down and tried to communicate? But they got the same treatment.

I spent a long time after that telling myself over and over that it hadn't been *me* who so gleefully carved up those frightened, stampeding creatures. Back in the twentieth century, they had established to everybody's satisfaction that "I was just following orders" was an inadequate excuse for inhuman conduct . . . but what can you do when the orders come from deep down in that puppet master of the unconscious?

Worst of all was the feeling that perhaps my actions weren't all that inhuman. Ancestors only a few generations back would have done the same thing, even to their fellow men, without any hypnotic conditioning.

I was disgusted with the human race, disgusted with the army and horrified at the prospect of living with myself for another century or so. . . . Well, there was always brainwipe.

A ship with a lone Tauran survivor had escaped and had gotten away clean, the bulk of the planet shielding it from *Earth's Hope* while it dropped into Aleph's collapsar field. Escaped home, I guessed, wherever that was, to report what twenty men with hand-weapons could do to a hundred fleeing on foot, unarmed.

I suspected that the next time humans met Taurans in ground combat, we would be more evenly matched. And I was right.

About the Authors

National best-selling author **Quincy J. Allen**, one of the four founders of The Eldros Legacy, is a cross-genre author with a growing number of published novels under his belt. He has published *Seeds of Dominion* in the Eldros Legacy and will be releasing its sequel, *Demons of Veynkal*, in the spring of 2023.

His media tie-in novel *Colt the Outlander: Shadow of Ruin* was a Scribe Award finalist in 2019, and his noir novel *Chemical Burn* was a Colorado Gold Award finalist in 2010. He is the author of The Blood War Chronicles fantasy steampunk series. His numerous short story publications include "Sons of the Father" in Larry Correia's *Monster Hunter Files* from Baen Books, as well as several novelettes in Chris Kennedy Publishing's military science fiction anthologies, appearing in and out of the Four Horseman universe. He works out of his home in Charlotte, North Carolina, and hopes one day to be a *New York Times* best-selling author. You can follow him on Facebook and at quincyallen.com.

Best-selling author **Jason Cordova** has had his novels published in multiple languages around the world. He was both a John W. Campbell Award and Dragon Award finalist (though not in the same year). Editor of the anthology *Chicks in Tank Tops* (Baen Books), author of the forthcoming Black Tide Rising novel *Mountain of Fire,* and coauthor of *Monster Hunter Memoirs: Fever,* with Larry Correia, he currently resides in North Carolina with his muse and a plethora of animals.

Ron Goulart (1932–2022) was noted for writing wacky science fiction short stories, often with technology going wrong, abetted by bumbling human incompetence. His first publication in an SF magazine was a parody of a pulp magazine letter column, which *The Magazine of Fantasy & Science Fiction* reprinted from a college humor magazine. When he began writing SF novels, the wackiness continued, although his 1979 novel, *After Things Fell Apart,* about a future United States fragmented into several disputatious enclaves, is more restrained in its humor, for a more believable, though hardly desirable, future. He also wrote books under a large collection of pseudonyms, including romance novels under a female pseudonym, novels featuring the pulp hero The Avenger, and comic strip heroes The Phantom and Flash Gordon. He wrote many mystery stories and was twice nominated for the Edgar Award of the Mystery Writers of America. In nonfiction, he often wrote authoritative articles about pop culture, and at greater length in the book, *Cheap Thrills,* subtitled "An Informal History of the Pulp Magazines." My (Hank's) favorite Goulart remains his series of short stories about Max Kearney, which slyly parody such classic investigators of the supernatural as John Silence and Jules de Grandin. Of particularly fond memory is the time Kearney had to deal with a haunting by the ghosts of a big band of the swing era and its conductor. I'll bet the music was great!

Joe Haldeman (b. 1943) is a Vietnam veteran whose classic novels *The Forever War* and *Forever Peace* have the rare distinction of having won both the Hugo and Nebula Awards for best novel of the year. He has served twice as president of the Science Fiction & Fantasy Writers of America. That organization also made him a Grand Master of the Field. He was an adjunct professor teaching writing at the Massachusetts Institute of Technology until his recent retirement. Stephen King has said, "Haldeman writes with wit, grace, and ease. If there was a Fort Knox for the science fiction writers who really matter, we'd have to lock Haldeman up there." His most recent science fiction work is the Marsbound trilogy comprising *Marsbound, Starbound,* and *Earthbound.* More recently, he has published a suspense novel, *Work Done for Hire.*

Harry Harrison (1925–2012) was known for his popular fast-paced adventure novels, often enlivened by an undercurrent of humor and satire, notably *Deathworld* and *The Stainless Steel Rat,* both of which were followed by popular sequels. Another such was his *Bill, the Galactic Hero,* which was strongly influenced by Joseph Heller's *Catch-22.* Later in his career, he wrote more serious novels, such as the "Eden" series, and the despairing novel of overpopulation, *Make*

Room, Make Room, which was the loose basis for the movie, *Soylent Green.* Harrison was a prolific short story writer, with over a hundred stories published in SF magazines of the fifties through the nineties. He was named to the Science Fiction Hall of Fame in 2004, and the Science Fiction and Fantasy Writers of America made him a Grand Master in 2008.

Karin Lowachee was born in South America, grew up in Canada, and worked in the Arctic. She has been a creative writing instructor, adult education teacher, and volunteer in a maximum security prison. Her novels have been translated into French, Hebrew, and Japanese, and her short stories have been published in numerous anthologies, best-of collections, and magazines.

Christopher Ruocchio (b. 1996) is the internationally award-winning author of the Sun Eater series, which blends elements of both science fiction and fantasy, as well as more than twenty works of short fiction. A graduate of North Carolina State University, he sold his first novel, *Empire of Silence,* at twenty-two, and his books have appeared in seven languages. He curated several short story anthologies for Baen Books, including *Sword & Planet, Time Troopers,* and *Worlds Long Lost.* His work has also appeared in Marvel Comics. Christopher lives in Raleigh, North Carolina, with his family.

Brandon Sanderson (b. 1975) has published seven solo novels with Tor Books and Gollancz—*Elantris,* the Mistborn series, *Warbreaker,* and *The Way of Kings*—as well as four books in the middle-grade Alcatraz Versus the Evil Librarians series from Scholastic. He was chosen to complete Robert Jordan's Wheel of Time series, writing *The Gathering Storm* (2009), *Towers of Midnight* (2010), and the final book in the series, *A Memory of Light* (2012). In addition to his writing, Brandon continues to teach aspiring authors.

Ethan Skarstedt is a Sergeant First Class in the Utah National Guard and has deployed to Kuwait, Iraq, Afghanistan, and Senegal. He has written a military SF novel as well as many short stories in several genres, and he occasionally blogs about things at ethanskar.com. He is author of *Vetus Bellator* and *Among the Apple Trees,* available from Amazon Kindle.

George Henry Smith (1922–1996) was a prolific author of over a hundred novels, most of which weren't science fiction, some with such intriguing titles as *Brutal Ecstasy* and *Lesbian Triangle*. When not supporting the sexual revolution, Smith was a frequent contributor to science fiction magazines under his own name during the fifties, sixties, and seventies. He also wrote such novels as *Doomsday Wing, The Forgotten Planet,* and *The Four-Day Weekend,* and notably, the trilogy set on a world parallel to Earth comprising *Kar Kaballa, The Second War of the Worlds,* and *The Island Snatchers,* with invasions by parallel Mongols and Martians, a Lovecraftian *thing* which wants to eat the world, and Gallic gods interfering with mortal affairs. This George H. Smith should not be confused with another George H. Smith who is a prominent libertarian writer.

Allen Steele (b. 1958), after working as a journalist, began writing SF in 1988, and has garnered an impressive number of awards, beginning with his novel, *Orbital Decay,* which received a *Locus* Award. His short stories, "The Death of Captain Future," "Where Angels Fear to Tread," and "The Emperor of Mars" have all received Hugo Awards. He serves on the Boards of Advisors for the Space Frontier Foundation and the Science Fiction and Fantasy Writers of America. His Coyote series of novels, described by one critic as "blue-collar space opera," has been very popular, and his most recent work includes his Captain Future series, consisting of the novel, *Avengers of the Moon,* and four novellas with the overall title of *The Return of Ul Quorn.*

Larry S. Todd (b. 1948) has had a long and notable career as a cartoonist and illustrator, with work appearing in publications ranging from science fiction magazines, such as *Galaxy* and *Fantastic* to slick men's magazines, to a long list of underground comics and magazines, such as *Last Gasp*. His notable creations include *Dr. Atomic* and *Miami Mice*. Another notable project by Todd was illustrating Harlan Ellison's *Chocolate Alphabet* for *Last Gasp*. Todd studied art at Syracuse University, where he met Vaughn Bodē which led to him and Bodē doing many collaborations until Bodē's untimely death. Later Vaughn Bodē's son, Mark, also a talented artist, collaborated with Todd, reviving Vaughn Bodē *Cobalt 60* series.

John C. Wright has been an attorney, a newspaperman, a technical writer, and most important (of course), a notable science fiction and fantasy writer. His first novel, *The Golden Age,* was praised by *Publishers Weekly,* whose reviewer wrote that Wright "may be this fledgling century's most important new SF talent." The novel was followed by *The Phoenix Exultant* and *The Golden Transcendence,* to make up the major space opera trilogy The Golden Oecumene, which reads like a collaboration between A.E. Van Vogt and Jack Vance. Speaking of Van Vogt, Wright wrote a powerful continuation (and possible culmination) of the classic Null-A novels, the *Null-A Continuum,* as well as a companion book to another classic, William Hope Hodgson's *The Night Land,* titled *Awake in the Night Land.* His fantasy novel *Orphans of Chaos* was a Nebula Award finalist, and his novel *Somewhither* won the Dragon Award for the best novel of 2016. In 2015, he was nominated for six Hugo Awards in both fiction and nonfiction: one short story, one novelette, three novellas, and one nonfiction related work, setting a historical record for the most Hugo Award nominations in a single year. His short fiction has appeared in *The Magazine of Fantasy & Science Fiction, Asimov's SF Magazine, Absolute Magnitude,* and other publications. For more details on his work, visit his website, scifiwright.com. He lives in Virginia with his wife, fellow writer L. Jagi Lamplighter, and their four children.